DIVINE KING

A.B. COHEN & JP RINDFLEISCH IX

This is a work of fiction. Names, characters, businesses, places, events, locales, and incidents are either the products of the author's imagination or used in a fictitious manner. Any resemblance to actual persons, living or dead, or actual events is purely coincidental.

Copyright © 2026 by A.B. Cohen & JP Rindfleisch IX

All rights reserved.

No part of this book may be reproduced in any form or by any electronic or mechanical means, including information storage and retrieval systems, without written permission from the author, except for the use of brief quotations in a book review.

Cover design by Getcovers.com

To our dear readers,
thank you for staying with us to the end.

Tree of Life

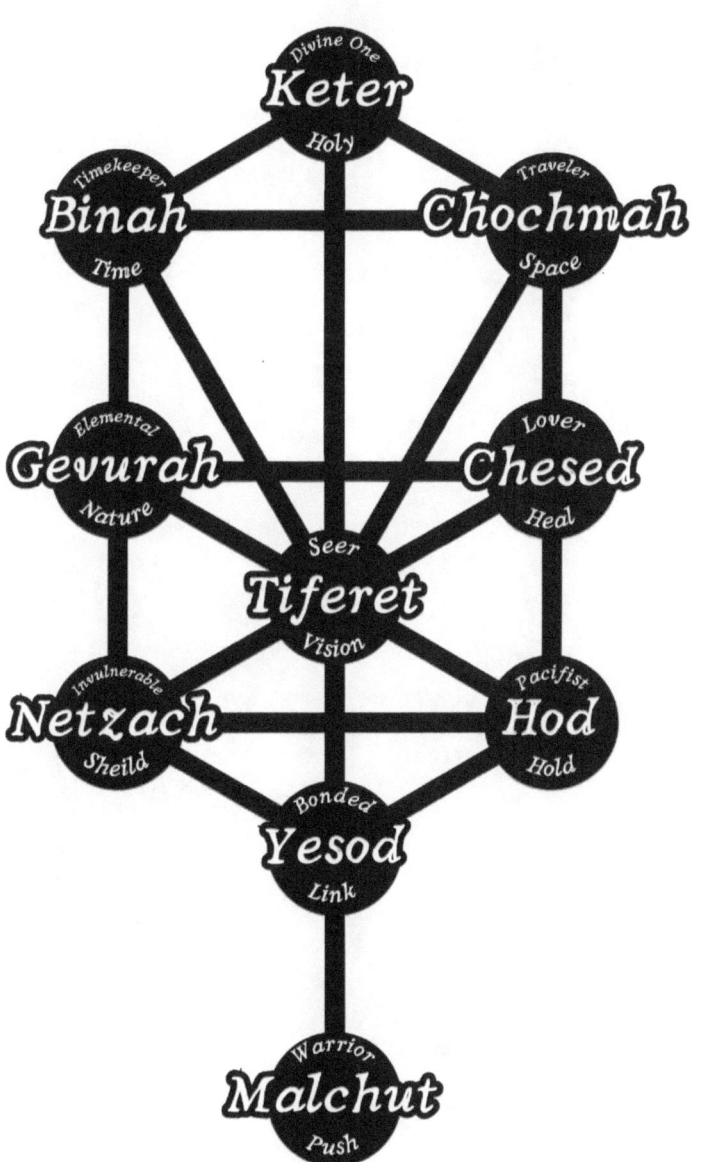

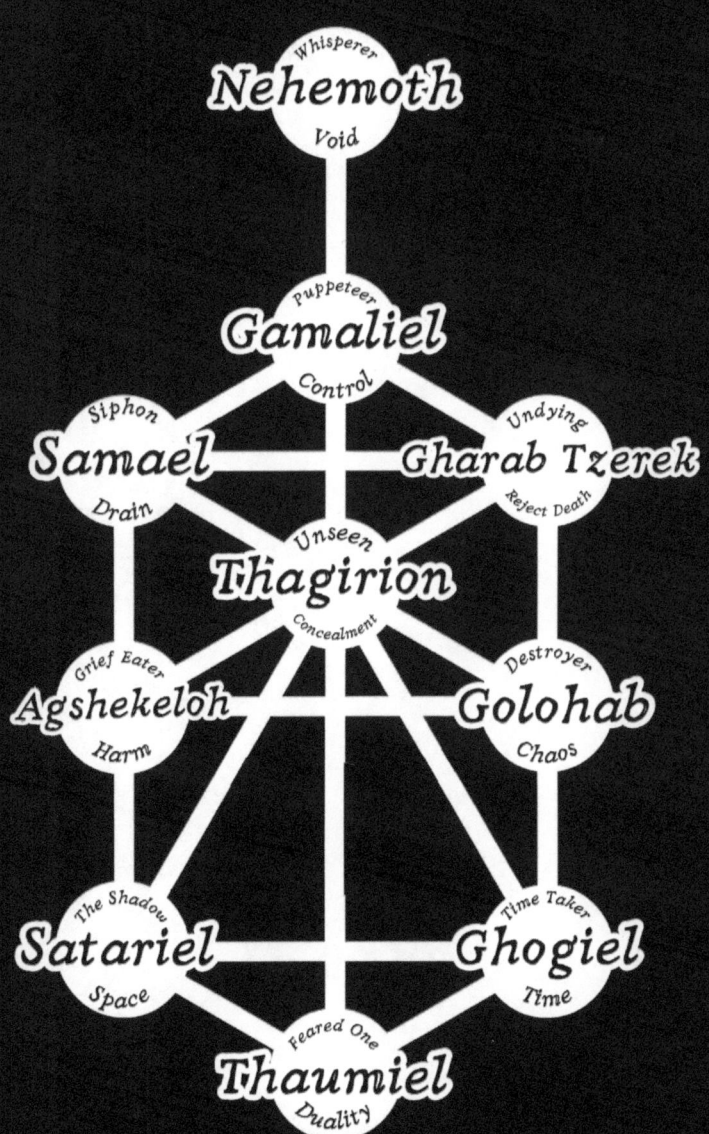

Tree of Death

The Infinity Board

 King

 White Queen

 Black Queen

 White Rook / Sage

 Black Rook

 White Bishop

 White Knight

 Black Bishop

 Black Knight

 White Pawn

 Black Pawn

 Square

CHAPTER 1
THE FAMILY

The lights flashed blue and violet as the rave peaked, and white smoke billowed, showering the sweaty dancers. The heavy bass of the EDM song beat on Leah's eardrums as she walked past them, her eyes on a raised platform overlooking the dancefloor.

A man with short gray hair in a full white suit sipped from his scotch, his back against Leah, while a woman wearing nothing but black lingerie and a bunny mask danced for him. Leah's fist tightened around the bloody bag she was carrying, and she dreaded every step she took towards the metal stairs leading up to the platform. Two large bouncers stood by, their predatory eyes locked on Leah.

Leah rolled hers as she reached them and yelled over the music, "Are we going to do this every time? Don't you werewolves have a super sharp nose? Should know my scent by now!"

They exchanged expressionless looks before the taller and bigger one turned and unclipped the velvet rope stanchions to let her through. Leah went up the curved stairs, pulling her hood forward. Black hair fell past her shoulders, dyed to hide who she used to be. She was Ashley Ryan now, and this girl didn't have brown hair or the reputation of a Black Knight. Ashley Ryan was nobody, just another Mystic mercenary desperate for money.

She'd been working for the Family for six months now. Six months of delivering blood and hunting rogue demons while Sarah and Isaac remained trapped in the Library. She pushed the anger and frustration down. Getting to the Ancient One was the only way forward. He was the oldest vampire on the continent, old enough to know what she needed.

She reached the top of the platform and saw the man transfixed by the woman, his gaze fixed on her as she moved sensually for him, like a predator salivating over its prey. The bite marks on her neck confirmed Leah's suspicions and made her stomach turn. Leah threw the bloodied bag onto the low round table, scattering the scotch glasses to the floor. The shattering sounds made him turn to Leah with murderous intent, his black pupils barely visible in his pale blue eyes, before coming back to his senses. He snapped his fingers once, and the dancer blinked, confused, before she quickly picked up her clothes and rushed past Leah.

"That was an expensive drink." The man didn't raise his voice, but Leah heard him clearly over the pounding music.

Leah's fist tightened around the bag. "And what I brought will cost you even more."

His lips curled. He reached for the bag, breathed deep over it. "This Oni should have thought it through before stepping into our territory." He pulled out viscous liquid with two fingers, licked them, spat. "Oni blood is definitely not a delicacy. Akira has terrible taste."

"Can I get my payment now?"

His nostrils flared, and he pursed his lips. His eyes darted to Leah's shoulder and nodded once.

A pale arm extended around her as a whisper spoke in her ear. "Here you go, cutie."

Leah spun, ripping herself free from the touch and putting three feet between them in an instant. Her hand went to her side, where a knife should have been, but the Family didn't allow weapons in the club.

A vampire stood where she'd been, one hand extended with a roll of cash, the other raised in mock surrender. Brown eyes instead of Edmond's pale blue. Long curly hair that was too perfect. Defined jawline with calculated scruff.

He was a young vampire. Dangerous in a different way than the old ones.

He smiled, fangs visible even in the colored lighting. "Easy there."

Leah snatched the rolled dollars from his hand and shoved them in her pocket without taking her eyes off him. "And you are?"

"He is your new superior," the man in the suit said with a satisfied expression as he leaned back, his arms spread.

Leah clenched her jaw. "You know what I'm looking for. Working for one of your dogs isn't it. When can I see him?"

"When I say you can see him."

"I've been doing your dirty work—"

"And I've paid you your fair share for it." He scratched his chin and added, "Do this work with Marcel, and we'll take it to the back room."

They exchanged looks for a couple of seconds. Leah could feel her *Malchut* energy flowing in and out of her fists, begging to be released and break that cocky face. But there were bigger stakes at play here. Sarah and Isaac depended on her.

A cold hand landed on her shoulder. "Come, let's go to

the front, cutie. You don't want to keep bothering Edmond."

Leah shrugged off the touch and gave the vampire a scornful look as he turned and went down the stairs. She followed, keeping a distance between them.

They walked past the dance floor and the crowded bar, opened a door that led to a dimly lit hallway, and climbed a long set of stairs. The sounds of the rave slowly died with each step. Leah eyed Marcel as he walked with both hands in his pockets, seemingly without a care in the world. His tight white shirt matched his pristine white shoes but contrasted with his ripped black jeans. The two reached the second set of stairs, and Marcel opened the heavy metal door, which seemed to be wrapped in acoustic material. As the door closed behind them, the loud music died altogether, and they walked through a small vestibule where another bouncer stood. Marcel nodded, and the bouncer opened yet another door for them. The smell of fried food reached Leah's nostrils as they stepped into the small kitchen where a short man with a mustache was flipping burgers while another took fries out of the fryer.

"Want anything to drink?" Marcel asked as they stepped out of the kitchen and into a crowded dive bar.

"I'm okay."

Marcel reached the bar and raised a hand. One of the bartenders sprang to attend to him, ignoring a customer mid-sentence.

"Scotch. Black Label. Neat."

Meanwhile, Leah let *Tiferet* warm her vision and scanned the bar. Colors sharpened. The energy signatures of humans pulsed differently from the supernatural. She found a hooded figure playing at a pool table in the back, but that one was too far. She needed someone she could make eye contact with.

"Guess I should properly introduce myself if we're working together. Name's Marcel Hernandez."

Leah looked back and shook Marcel's cold hand. "Ashley Ryan."

Even after months of using it, the fake name felt odd. Taking over her best friend's name from her old life felt strange. Ashley, who thought Leah had moved away to some boarding school. Ashley, who was safe and normal and had no idea her name was being used to negotiate with vampires in Chicago.

The bartender brought the scotch, and Marcel took a sip before turning to Leah with a smile. "What is a Mystic doing working for the Family?"

"Can you just tell me the job? I want to get going."

Marcel remained silent, his predatory eyes scanning her.

"What?" Leah asked, annoyed.

"I asked you a question."

"Yes, but I don't need to answer it."

"Oh, but I think you do." His voice distorted ever so slightly and sounded clear in Leah's ears over the crowded sounds of the bar.

Leah felt his power try to weasel its way into her mind. To compel her. She took in a breath and smiled. "Incredible how you vampires are all the same." She was glad to see surprise in Marcel's eyes. "You need to be older and stronger if you want that to work on me. You're clearly a young one."

Marcel bit his lower lip and shook his head, letting out a small chuckle. Leah took the opportunity to scan for another hooded figure closer by. One sat a couple of tables away, watching her. Leah nodded to the door ever so slightly, and the hooded figure stood and moved toward the pool tables.

"You have balls, I give you that."

"Ovaries, but I appreciate the sentiment. Now, are you going to tell me what the job is, or should I go back and ask Edmond myself?" Leah asked, feeling her *Malchut* coiling within her, itching to come out.

"Must be hard to contain yourself. Your lust for violence smells so sweet. But as you probably already know, the Family does not fuck around. Touch one of us, and you mess with all of us."

Leah remained silent to hide her annoyance at the vampire's ability to read her. Marcel squinted his eyes ever so slightly while he placed his tongue on his fang.

"There have been reports of a Shifter who has crossed into our territory."

Leah frowned, hearing something interesting for the first time that night. "A Shifter in Chicago? I thought they were nearly dead down in Venezuela." This would be useful information for later.

"The Mystic is well informed." He took another sip of his scotch before carrying on. "Yes, we believe this is a deserter or a scout. Seeing if they can flee somewhere else. Why they think it'll be a good idea to come to Chicago is anyone's guess. Our job is to capture him and bring him here alive."

Leah shivered slightly, remembering the creature that attacked her Squares back at camp. She wondered how they were now, but quickly snapped out of it. "Any idea where it might be? Chicago is a pretty big place."

"There have been reports of animals disappearing at the Lincoln Park Zoo close by." He checked his watch and added, "It's almost dawn, so we can aim to meet tomorrow evening at the zoo parking lot at around 8:00 PM."

"Sounds good to me." Leah turned to leave, but felt a hand wrapping around her arm.

She looked back and saw Marcel's predator eyes once again, his pupils small and fixated on her neck.

"You still haven't answered my question. What is a Mystic doing working for the Family?"

Leah's annoyance turned to anger. "Get your hand off me."

Marcel's grip tightened as his lips curled into a smile. "Or what?"

Her anger boiled within. There was nothing she wanted more than to *Malchut* punch this cocky bastard into a pulp. So much contained anger that craved release, craved vengeance.

Marcel pulled her in forcefully, their faces inches from one another, and Leah could smell the metallic scent of copper from his breath.

Leah clenched her jaw and spoke through gritted teeth. "Let go." Her cursed speech tightened her throat, sending jolts of pain.

Marcel's face twisted into a shocked expression, and he released her arm before the black threads came out. Leah turned and left him there, dumbfounded.

CHAPTER 2
SHADOW CLONES

The dimly lit alleyway drowned out the city noise, a perfect disguise for the rave inside. On the outside, the only clue was the heavy metal doors and a well-dressed bouncer.

The cool spring night washed over Leah as she stepped out, pulling up her hoodie. She swallowed, her throat still raw, and knew Asmodeus would be pissed. She scanned her surroundings with *Tiferet* to make sure no one was following before taking a left. Working with vampires had made her wary of dark places. They had a disturbing ability to hide in shadows without being detected.

Leah stepped out of the alleyway, crossed another block, and took a right toward a small parking lot. The back door of an old gray Dodge van cracked open. A hooded figure waved her in.

Leah paused a couple of feet away, scanning her surroundings one more time before stepping inside.

The hooded figure closed the van door behind her. "Took you long enough."

Leah exhaled, annoyed. "Sorry, got delayed by my new 'partner.'" She made air quotes with her fingers.

"New partner?" The figure at the wheel turned slightly.

Leah dropped onto one of the seats. "Edmond put us together. His name is Marcel, and he's a relatively new vampire who'll be with us on a mission tomorrow. One of our youngest turned. We're meeting him at dusk near the Zoo. Apparently, there's a shifter close by that we need to track down."

The figure in the passenger seat spun around, her hood falling off.

Leah blinked. Six months of creating shadow clones, and the uncanny feeling of talking to someone who looked and sounded exactly like her never got old. But seeing herself with elbow-length black hair? That still caught her off guard every time. She'd let it grow out and dyed it to stay under the radar, but seeing the change reflected back at her made it real. Made everything that had happened since she'd returned feel real.

"Wait, that can't be right." The clone's brow furrowed. "I've heard the Bishops discussing how the shifters were on the brink of defeat down in Venezuela."

Leah crossed her arms and rested her chin on her fingers. "We've been hearing that for months." She paused. "Could this be a sign it's true?"

The clone sitting next to her tapped the driver's shoulder. "We should get moving. You three need to merge back."

The driver nodded, turned on the engine, and began to drive. She glanced at Leah in the rearview mirror. "Did you get the money? We're due at the motel."

"Yeah, I..." Leah winced, her throat scratching. *Shit, that hurts.*

The clone in the passenger seat pursed her lips. "Did you use *Gamaliel* again?"

Leah rolled her eyes and cleared her throat. "Dude, let me be."

The clone's nostrils flared. When she spoke, the cadence shifted. Formal. Strategic. Asmodeus. "How many times are we going to go through this? You are far more vulnerable when you're split. You have a quarter of your strength to be exact."

Still getting used to him just taking over like that.

"Just stop, Asmodeus. I was in an awkward situation with a vampire and needed to get out."

"Then why did you send us away?" The anguish in her own voice made Leah's chest tighten.

"Yeah, because we could have merged back right in front of everyone."

"We could have caused some sort of distraction, Leah. There is no need for you to do that."

"Easy for you to say," said the clone in the passenger seat.

"Sometimes we don't have an easy way out." The driver's eyes met Leah's in the mirror.

Leah leaned back. "And the situation happened after I sent you back."

"Okay, enough!" Asmodeus rubbed her face. "It is already difficult enough to deal with one Leah. When three of you gang up on me, you become impossible! All I am saying is that we need to be careful. The Family takes their motto very seriously: 'Touch our blood...'"

"'...spill your own,'" said the three Leahs in unison.

The driver added, "They all repeat their stupid motto every chance they get. We know."

Silence filled the van. The engine hummed beneath them. Outside, streetlights blurred past.

The clone driving broke the quiet. "I did hear something interesting near a table full of rootworkers. Apparently, Jan Xie is stepping down as Black Queen. Similar to the rumor we heard last week from that drunk Black Knight."

"Could this be a reaction to Helen's self-proclamation as King?" Asmodeus asked.

Leah's jaw clenched. Her chest tightened. Just hearing her name made her blood boil. "Those two never got along. It wouldn't surprise me if Helen kicked Jan Xie out to promote Mystics loyal to her."

"There have been murmurs of a break within the Infinity Board." The clone in the passenger seat shifted.

Asmodeus shook his clone's head. "Doubtful. Helen has been rebuilding the Infinity Board for the past two and a half years. And recently, they have taken new ground against the shifters and the warlocks in Haiti. She has been restoring order, and the Infinity Board emanates strength. Plus, she herself seems stronger than ever. A break seems unlikely."

Leah took a deep breath, trying to control the volatile mix of emotions. Every time she thought of Helen, the betrayal followed immediately after. How Helen had manipulated her in so many ways to get the Core. She ground her teeth and clenched her fist, thinking of the many lives lost, of Sarah and Isaac locked in that Library.

Then her mind circled back to her conversation with the vampire. Her Squares. The last time she'd seen them, they'd been unconscious in beds at Sekrè Fami. Their skin was ashen, sweat-covered, and IVs dripped into their arms. Callum's forehead had been cold to the touch.

"Has anyone confirmed the rumors about the sick Squares? Is it true that Helen healed them?"

No one answered. The engine hummed. Outside, streetlights continued to blur past.

Callum. Ashley. Zoe. Ricky. Jenna. What happened to them was a mystery that still haunted her. The fact that she'd come back over a year and a half later meant everything was different, including them. She knew they were no longer at Sekrè Fami. One of her shadows had heard an obscure rumor about a group of Squares who'd survived a rootworker attack. Helen had healed them somehow, and because of their bravery, they'd been promoted to White Pawns. A classic Infinity Board move that Leah herself had experienced before. But she'd lost all track of her Squares. With her limited time and resources, locating them was impossible.

Besides, if the rumor was true, they might be Knights and Bishops by now. Their loyalty probably belonged to the King who'd saved their lives.

Leah's hands closed into tight fists. The conflicting emotions clashed and combined into a frustrating resentment.

A squeeze on her shoulder brought her back. She looked up to see Asmodeus with an understanding expression. "We're here. Better get on with it, or the twin story will become far less believable with quadruplets."

Leah blinked a couple of times, realizing they were parked at the motel. The two clones were watching her.

Right. Let's get this over with.

She extended her arms and wrapped her hands around her clones' hands. Eyes closed, she pictured two green flames floating in a void. The flames shrank as she squeezed.

Her body jerked. High-pitched ringing pierced her ears. Images crashed into her mind. The sharp crack of pool balls. Tequila burning her tongue. Rootworkers laughing. Everything her clones had experienced in the last hour flooded her mind at once, an overload of smells, tastes, sounds, and sensations.

From one second to the next, she was back in the van, breathing heavily, mouth slack, and a string of drool rolling out of her mouth. A cloud of green smoke dissipated in the air. Asmodeus held her steady.

The remaining clone wrinkled her nose. "Gross. You got drool everywhere."

"Prolonged shadows do not get any easier to absorb, do they?" Asmodeus said lightly.

Leah pulled herself upright in her seat, eyes closed, trying to reconnect with her own reality. "It fucking sucks. I preferred when they just puffed away."

Asmodeus chuckled. "And yet, we need those memories. It is a lot for your mind to handle, so accept the drool for now." He opened the door, letting in cold air that felt like heaven against Leah's flushed skin. "Come. We have some leftover pizza. Tomorrow we will pay for next month's rent."

Leah followed Asmodeus up the stairs, blinking hard as her eyes readjusted to the cheap, cold fluorescent light in the motel's exterior hallway. Asmodeus took out a key and opened room 4H, turning on the table lamp beside the small round table. On it rested a set of old tomes, the top one reading Death and its Power. Leah eyed the large book, thinking of the small but valuable knowledge it contained. After all, *Satariel* was one of the top three obscure wells of the Tree of Death.

The room had an old-school, questionable vibe—more dated than vintage. Green carpet. Red bedsheets. The once-white walls had yellowed with time, but the most characteristic features were the broken furniture and the cracked mirror on the vanity. Even the bathroom door had a crack and was missing a corner piece.

That and the smell. A combination of musty and stale air made her jaw clench. This scent always pissed her off. It was a stench that reminded her she was stuck, unable to do anything while her friends were trapped.

Asmodeus took the pizza out of the mini fridge and threw it in the microwave. "Okay, we still have half a pizza."

Leah looked up, saw her clone turning on the microwave, and realized she'd been staring at the green carpet, her shoes glued to the entrance.

She took a couple of steps and dropped onto the squeaky bed.

The images wouldn't stop coming. Her mom's body on that couch. Eric stepping between her and Legion to stop the chain. Gabe's glassy eyes as he lay dead on the ground. The look of despair in Sarah and Isaac's eyes as Leah disappeared from the Library. All the memories made her chest tighter, her anger growing by the second. They all saw it. Desmond, Zafira, Mica, and the others. They all saw what Helen did. And yet they remain on the Infinity Board, still working for her.

The microwave dinged. Her clone opened it to take out the pizza, the smell of cheese mingling with the room's peculiar scent, not making it any better.

She raised her right arm and saw the scars that coiled around it, seared into her skin by Helen's chains. A reminder of Helen's betrayal. She moved it around and saw the blue eye open in her palm, staring back at her.

The anger surged, uncoiling in her chest. She smacked her hand on the nightstand next to her, cracking it.

"Shit, Leah! What's wrong with you!" Asmodeus yelled with her voice, the pizza in his hands, the plate empty beside him.

Leah looked at her clone, an annoyed expression on his face. Her anger boiled. How was he able to be so calm? So emotionless? And what was worse, that wasn't his face. It was hers. Something about seeing her face so relaxed, so centered on their mission, compared to Leah's own, which was ever tainted by an anger, a rage so profound it burned in her chest from the moment she woke up to the moment she finally found sleep. And even then, the nightmares that followed only made things worse.

She sat up on the bed and tilted her head slightly. "What's wrong with me? Are you fucking kidding me? I'm sick and tired of working for fucking vampires!"

Her clone rubbed his eyes with one hand. "We have been over this."

Leah stood, her face now inches from Asmodeus's clone. Her face was hot. Her hands curled into tight fists. "Yeah? Well, I'm sick of hearing how Helen is fixing everything! How the Infinity Board is 'back to its former glory' and how she's about to defeat the shifters! The fucking bitch who manipulated us, who used us, is now praised as a hero by other Mystics. Even those who saw her take the Core don't seem to mind or do anything about it! All this while some ultra-dimensional monster stole my friends!" Her voice rose. "Do you even care?"

Her words were sharp. She wanted nothing more than to jump and punch her clone, make her bleed for all the mistakes she'd made. For playing that Ouija Board. For trusting Helen. For making that stupid deal with the Librarian.

"Of course I do! They are my friends, too."

"Then act like it! You're standing there heating pizza like nothing is wrong."

Her clone's face flushed with anger. "What else do you want me to do? Destroy the whole room like you have?"

"It's been over six months since we've been back, Asmodeus. Two and a half years since the fight against Legion." She waved her hands desperately. "Time works differently in that Library. For all we know, they could be eighty or..." Leah choked, unable to say her biggest fear yet. As if speaking it aloud could make it happen.

She took a step back, feeling lightheaded. Her chest tightened. She could hear her heart racing in her ears. Cold sweat formed on her forehead. She had trouble breathing.

Asmodeus wrapped an arm around her and spoke softly. "Leah, listen to me. Time moves slower in the Library than it does here. Maybe by the time we rescue them, it might just feel like five minutes?"

Leah pushed her clone's arm away and took a step back. "First time we were there for a couple of hours, and it translated to a couple of days here. The second time I was there for a couple of seconds, which turned out to be over two years here! Nothing is guaranteed. But by all means, order another pizza. Let's go on another mission for those vicious monsters. You know the type of work we've had to do for them. It's disgusting. Only a matter of time before they send us to capture humans or kill someone."

"For the love of God, Leah, how many times do I need to explain to you that we are not strong enough to face Helen. The only way I can think of getting there is to meet with the Ancient One. And guess what... you cannot just schedule a meeting with the oldest vampire on this continent. We need to be strategic and patient if we—"

"Just shut up! It's so easy for you to say that."

"What is that supposed to mean?"

"Well, you're a demon, aren't you? For you, all this misery and despair is normal." Leah moved closer to him. "Were you this strategic and calm when you murdered my mother? Because I remember you then. I remember you in my dad's body, festering in your anger in that cabin."

Leah felt a small satisfaction to see her own dumbfounded face staring back. Her clone stood there, mouth slightly open. Asmodeus seemed at a loss for words.

"Leah, this is not you talking. I know you are angry, but—"

"Angry? I'm fucking livid! And I'm done talking!"

She reached her clone's arm and held it tightly, extinguishing the last green flame in her mind in an instant. She kept her eyes open, fighting through the seizure, just to see Asmodeus's shocked expression before the clone disappeared.

Leah stood there breathing hard for a couple of minutes, cold sweat dripping down her forehead. She crouched, picked up the pizza hastily, and threw it in the trash before heading out, slamming the door behind her.

CHAPTER 3
THE SHIFTER

A violet mist swirled in thick spirals, forming a wall that stretched endlessly in both directions. Behind it, far in the distance, Leah could see the silhouettes of a male and a female. Their voices reached her, distorted and hard to understand.

"...coordinates..." The woman's voice.

"...survival..." the man said.

This dream, unlike the nightmares, gave her some peace. Some purpose. They were always too far away, and every time she tried to call to them, her words echoed without response.

Leah stepped forward. The mist curled around her feet, cool but not wet. She reached out.

The mist wrapped around her hand. Her wrist. Her arm.

She pushed forward, trying to cross through.

The mist tightened, pulling her under.

Leah opened her eyes and sighed in frustration. She dragged herself out of bed and opened the blinds. The afternoon sun was already closing in on the horizon. As she stared at the purple sky and the almost full moon, Leah thought of the voices. Part of her liked to believe they were Sarah and Isaac, keeping strong, talking about survival.

But she knew that was wishful thinking. There was no way to know.

The nightmares had cycled through the rest of the night. Asmodeus's grotesque smile on her father's body. Legion's ambush on the Academy. Helen's betrayal. They were a constant, pulling her in and out of sleep, never letting her rest.

Asmodeus hadn't said a single word since their fight last night. Part of Leah knew she had gone too far. At the end of the day, the fight had only distracted her anger for a few hours, but it hadn't reduced it in the slightest.

She reached for the presence in her mind.

Are you going to talk to me?

The silence sat heavy, deliberate. Like a door slammed shut.

Leah's chest tightened. "Fine."

The shower water scalded. Leah cranked it hotter, letting the steam fill the cramped bathroom. She watched the water trace down her scars, the raised tissue on her arm and torso. Souvenirs from every fight that had brought her here.

Sarah's scream echoed in her memory.

Isaac's face as the portal closed.

Her chest heaved. The sob caught her by surprise, then

another, then she couldn't stop. Leah slid down the tile wall and pulled her knees to her chest in the corner of the tub. Water beat against her back and shoulders, scalding hot.

They're gone because of you. Not strong enough. Not fast enough.

She dug her fingernails into her knees, leaving marks. The physical pain helped; it gave her something to focus on.

The water turned cold.

Leah gasped as the icy spray hit her. Her hands unclenched. The cold shocked her system, clearing the fog just enough.

She stood slowly, legs shaking. Turned off the water and stood there dripping for far too long before grabbing a towel.

After eating a microwaved breakfast sandwich, she put on some jeans, a plain white shirt, and a jacket, then headed to the lobby.

The receptionist, a man with a round belly, thick gray hair, and a mustache, stared at a small TV behind a tall wooden stand. It took him a couple of seconds to notice Leah, and a couple more to turn away from the game.

"Was wondering when you were going to show up. Another month?" he asked.

"Yes." Leah unwrapped one thousand dollars from the tight pack she'd gotten from Marcel.

The man counted the money quickly. "I'll have clean towels later today. Can drop them by then."

Leah bit her cheek, thinking of the broken things in the room. The lamp. The mirror. The hole in the wall. She shook her head. "I'll be out the rest of today and tonight. Do you mind if I pick them up tomorrow?"

The man frowned, then shrugged. "Sure." He turned back and continued watching the football game.

Leah stepped out of the lobby into a nice late afternoon,

with a clear gradient sky from deep blue to purple, the sun almost down. She got in the van and drove out into the city. It took her about an hour to get there, given Chicago's heavy traffic.

She pulled into the parking lot, stepped out into the cool evening, and began walking to the East entrance.

Mid-step, something made her stop. She turned.

Marcel stood right next to her van, wearing a blazer. His eyes were fixed on her neck.

Leah raised an eyebrow. "It would be nice if you'd stop staring at me like that."

The vampire's lips curled. "Why? Does it make you uncomfortable?"

Leah rolled her eyes moved back from him. "As a matter of fact, it does. You look like a creeper. Mind walking me through the plan instead?"

Marcel's dark eyes darted up to hers, his smirk widening. "I can check the north, and you can check the south. Remember, we are here to capture it alive. Father and Mother want to speak with it and..."

His gaze shifted quickly. Leah looked in that direction and noticed a guard walking inside the park.

Leah slapped Marcel's cold chest. "Don't even think about it."

The vampire grunted and turned. "Just don't get in my way."

He took off with supernatural speed and light feet, almost as if he was running on mute. He jumped over a brick building, and Leah lost sight of him.

"I hate working with vampires," she muttered.

Leah reached for the Tree of Death, specifically *Thagirion*. The invisibility well should have wrapped around her like a shadow, but instead, the well resisted.

Are you going to help or not? she asked Asmodeus.

He didn't reply.

"Fine." She said it louder through gritted teeth.

Leah rushed inside the zoo.

She pulled on *Tiferet*, and the seeing well opened easily. Her vision flooded with glowing silhouettes. Animals sleeping in their cages, their forms pulsing with soft light. A few workers in the distance.

She scanned the area and stopped when she noticed the Kovler Lion House.

A flashback made her knees weak. It was her favorite part of the zoo when she was little. Too scared to enter the first time they came, so her dad held her as they walked through the building. He'd made jokes and waved at the lions and lionesses inside, making Leah giggle. After that, it became their spot.

Leah found herself walking toward the building, drawn by memory. Her hand reached for the door handle.

Locked.

The cold metal brought her back. She took a deep breath and rubbed her eyes with her shirt before carrying on.

She checked the animal cages. The trees. Even the sewers. The only time she'd interacted with a shifter was a young teenager in the form of a raven. She spent time observing the animals, noting any odd behaviors. Most of them were sleeping, their glowing figures calm in their resting places.

Then she saw the guard's glowing silhouette approaching. He stopped, looked around, and turned toward the Kovler Lion House. He looked around once more before unlocking the door.

Leah frowned and rushed back, pulling on *Malchut* to enhance her steps. Pressure built in her chest as kinetic energy coiled tight. Her feet barely touched the ground as she closed the distance.

The guard had already locked the door behind him.

Through *Tiferet*, Leah tracked his silhouette inside. He opened a second door next to the lion's den and walked through.

The silhouette disappeared.

Leah took a couple of steps back and pulled hard on *Malchut*. The pressure exploded from her chest, launching her upward. She landed on the roof, looking down.

Through *Tiferet*, she searched for the guard's glow.

Nothing.

Instinct took over. Leah drew on *Netzach*, the well of invulnerability. Protection surged through her body like armor settling into place, a shell between her skin and the world. She checked on the lions, concerned the shifter might want to absorb one, but they seemed unharmed.

Something massive slammed into her back.

The roof crumbled beneath her.

Leah crashed through, hitting the floor hard. Air exploded from her lungs.

A large snout wrapped around her throat. Sharp teeth pressed against her neck, trying to pierce.

Netzach held. The invulnerability pulsed, protecting Leah's spine. But the pressure was crushing.

Leah twisted. She planted both palms against fur and muscle. Drew on *Malchut*.

The pressure coiled tight until it felt like her ribs might crack.

She released it.

The kinetic force exploded outward. The thick glass of the lion cages shattered. The creature flew back, slamming into the far wall.

Leah rolled to her feet. Her back screamed, but adrenaline dulled the worst of it.

In front of her, a giant grizzly bear roared and charged forward. It closed in quickly and struck with a claw the size of a large pan.

Netzach held when the blow connected, but the power sent her flying backward. She crashed through the door and fell off the stairs, her body tumbling.

Before she could recover, the bear was on her again.

Leah pulled on *Malchut* and released focused bursts. Kinetic bullets tore through the air and pierced the bear square in the chest.

Viscous black liquid leaked out of the fresh wounds.

Leah did a *Malchut* jump and moved back, creating distance. She remembered Jaime's tales of the shifter as well as her own encounter with a young one back at the camp. How contagious their thick black blood was. If it entered the body, no amount of *Netzach* could protect you. That's why they were so dangerous and difficult to deal with. How that was the thing Jaime held in his neck, slowly consuming him. A single drop of that liquid could be enough to transform her into a shifter.

The bear roared and charged again.

Leah planted her feet. Drew on *Malchut*, pulling harder than before. The pressure built in her chest until it felt like her sternum might crack.

She released it.

The push lifted the creature off its feet and crashed it into the brick wall of the lion's den building. The wall cracked on impact.

Leah turned *Tiferet* back on, searching for the creature among the rubble.

The large bear was gone.

Instead, something bright, no bigger than a baseball, shot straight toward her.

Leah ducked just in time.

Her *Tiferet* eyes caught some of the black liquid spilling from the projectile. Drops arcing toward her.

Instinct kicked in. Leah released a *Malchut* pulse in all directions. The kinetic force radiated outward like a shockwave, deflecting the liquid.

She turned and saw a barn owl making a U-turn, coming back straight for her.

Instead of dodging, she waited.

Let it close the distance.

Twenty feet.

Ten.

Five.

Leah reached for *Gevurah*, the elemental power. Heat built in her palms until her skin felt like it might combust.

She released flames straight at the bird.

It tried to dodge, but Leah followed, continuing to burn it as it crashed to the ground and rolled past her.

By the time it stopped rolling, the creature had taken a more humanoid form, though it reminded Leah of the Chimeras she had seen back at the Maimonides Academy. Seven feet tall, with uneven, thick fur covering arbitrary parts of its body. Much of it was burned away, exposing bright red muscle, with black blood dripping out.

Black liquid still dripped from the wounds in its chest, and its bear-like ears were flattened against its head.

But Leah could see the brown eyes reflecting fear on its more human face.

"It's over." Her voice came out steady. "You're coming with me."

CHAPTER 4
WANING GIBBOUS

The shifter's head snapped side to side. "I'm not going back." His voice came out low, almost a growl. "I'm not—"

"I wasn't asking." Leah retook her fighting stance.

Slow claps caught her attention. Marcel stood beside her, his eyes on the shifter.

Damn vampires.

Leah's heart had barely settled from the fight when Marcel appeared. Half a year working with them, and she still couldn't get used to it.

"Perfect little Ashley." Marcel's smile showed off his fangs. "I understand now why you are Edmond's favorite dog."

Leah cocked her head. "You were watching this whole time? Could've helped."

"You seemed to be doing a fine job on your—"

Heavy footfalls made them both turn.

The shifter charged, his hand already morphing mid-stride. Bone cracked and reformed. Fur sprouted. His fingers extended into massive bear claws.

Leah raised her arms. The claw came down.

Netzach absorbed most of the impact, but momentum sent her flying backwards. She crashed through an outdoor bench. Planks splintered beneath her back.

Pain shot up her spine.

Leah pushed herself up with *Malchut*, but the shifter was already on her. He slammed her back down, pinning her to the broken wood. His weight pressed the air from her lungs.

"You'll be one of us now." Black liquid dripped from his wounds onto her shirt. "You'll see then what real pain is. What your King did to us!" His voice cracked, and she saw the desperation in his eyes.

Leah watched with growing horror as the Shifter stabbed his own hand. Thick black blood welled up between his fingers.

Moving toward her face.

No. One drop. That's all it takes.

"No!" Leah released a *Malchut* wave.

The force rippled outward, but the shifter was ready this time. He dug his claws into the ground, holding on.

"That won't save you again." His grin was too wide. Too many teeth.

The blood slid down his hand.

Leah's chest tightened. Her breath came short and sharp. She tried to twist away, but his weight had her pinned.

Three inches.

Two.

Marcel's fist connected with the shifter's jaw. The crack echoed across the empty zoo.

The creature's grip loosened. Leah rolled out from under him, scrambling to her feet. Her fingers found the hem of her jacket. She ripped it off, threw it aside.

Did any land on me? Did it get through?

Her skin was clean. Dry.

Marcel turned and landed a back kick to the shifter's neck. The creature went down hard.

But it wasn't knocked out.

It pushed itself up, shaking its head. Black blood dripped from its mouth.

Marcel retrieved a bundle of rope from his blazer. "Better finish this, Ashley. I want to see what you're made of." He glanced at her, one eyebrow raised. "Let's find out why Edmond thinks you're so special."

The shifter's form rippled. Fur receded. Bones cracked and reformed. It was shrinking.

In a second, the massive bear-man became something smaller.

A raven burst upward, wings beating hard.

It's running.

"Marcel—"

"Your fight." Marcel crossed his arms, watching.

The raven banked hard, aiming for the tree line beyond the enclosures.

Leah drew on *Malchut*. The familiar pressure built in her chest. She released focused bursts.

The kinetic bullets tore through the air.

One. Two. Three.

The first missed. The second clipped a wing. The third hit the center mass.

The raven tumbled from the sky, but mid-fall its body convulsed. Feathers melted away. The form expanded. A wolf hit the ground running, favoring one leg.

It was fast.

Leah sprinted after it, pulling harder on *Malchut*. The pressure in her chest grew until her ribs ached. She planted her feet and released.

The kinetic push lifted the wolf off its paws. It slammed

into the brick wall of the lion enclosure. The impact left cracks in the stone.

Leah waited, breathing heavily. Sweat dripped down her back despite the cold.

The wolf twitched.

Leah invoked *Tiferet*, sharpening her vision. As she did, the wolf melted, and something small leapt into the air.

A barn owl.

Black liquid poured from its wounds as the bird arced toward her.

Instinct kicked in. Leah released a *Malchut* pulse in all directions. The shockwave deflected the drops. They splattered against the concrete.

The owl banked hard, coming back for another pass.

Leah waited. Let it close the distance.

Heat built in her palms. *Gevurah* uncoiled in her core, rising through her chest. Her hands burned.

Five feet.

Leah released the flames.

Fire engulfed the owl. It shrieked, a sound too human, and crashed behind her. The creature rolled across the concrete, wings beating uselessly at the flames consuming them.

When it stopped rolling, its form had changed again. It was nearly seven feet tall and human-like. Thick fur covered random patches of its body. Burnt flesh exposed red muscle beneath. Black blood leaked from at least a dozen wounds.

The shifter's chest heaved, and its too-human eyes fixed on Leah.

She pulled on *Malchut* again. The pressure was getting harder to build. She'd been drawing on it too much.

The shifter lunged.

Leah released everything she had left.

The kinetic force caught it mid-leap. Sent it flying backward into a wall. This time, when it hit, it stayed down.

Leah walked forward slowly. Her legs shook. Her hands trembled.

The shifter didn't move.

She stopped three feet away, ready to invoke *Gevurah* again if needed.

Marcel appeared beside her. "Not bad. Edmond was right about you."

"Thanks," Leah said between breaths.

"Don't mention it." Marcel knelt by the shifter, rope already in hand. "Help me tie this thing up before it wakes. I don't want any more of its blood spilling around."

Leah hesitated, eyeing the black liquid pooling beneath the creature.

"You would know if it infected you," Marcel said, wrapping the Shifter's arms. "Open wounds only. You're fine."

After a moment, she joined him. Her fingers fumbled with the rope around the shifter's legs. The thick fur made it difficult to get a secure hold.

"Now cauterize the wounds," Marcel said. "All of them."

Heat built in Leah's palms again. She traced *Gevurah*'s flames along the shifter's chest wounds, then its hand. The flesh sizzled, and the shifter whined, but didn't wake. The smell made Leah's stomach turn.

When she finished, Marcel hoisted the creature onto his shoulder with a grunt. "Heavy bastard."

They started back toward the entrance.

"Thank you," Leah said, rubbing her left side where the claw had struck. "For that."

Marcel glanced at her. "Don't mention it. You are lucky the full moon isn't up yet. The waning gibbous still gives us some strength." He gestured at her discarded shirt and jacket on the ground. "You should burn those. Their blood stays contagious for a day outside the host. In fact, we should check for any blood trails you left."

Leah stopped and looked back at her shirt. The jet-black blood was still fresh, glistening in the moonlight.

She invoked *Gevurah*. Fire consumed the fabric in seconds.

They walked together, Leah burning every trail of blood she found along the way. On the concrete. In the dirt. Splattered on the bench she'd crashed through. By the time she finished, cold had seeped into her bones.

Gevurah's price.

She rubbed her arms, but the chill came from within. The spring air cut through her sports bra, making it worse.

As they reached the zoo entrance, Marcel looked back. After a quick scan, he said, "That should be all." He looked her up and down.

Leah crossed her arms tighter. "What?"

Marcel set the shifter down. He removed his blazer and held it out to her, looking away.

Leah raised an eyebrow.

"You are cold. Just take it." Marcel kept his eyes on the tree line. "We don't have all night."

Leah frowned. She'd never met a vampire who would do something nice for another being.

Still, a monster was a monster.

"I'm good." Leah started toward the parking lot. "I have a change of clothes in my car."

CHAPTER 5
A SOMBER TALE

Marcel placed the unconscious shifter in the back seat of Leah's van while she pulled on a fresh white shirt and black hoodie. The extra layers trapped warmth against her skin. The shivering finally stopped.

She climbed into the back, positioning herself across from the creature. Marcel slid behind the wheel without a word and started the engine.

You'll see then what real pain is. What your King did to us!

The shifter's words looped in Leah's head. She watched its chest rise and fall, ready for the slightest twitch. But her focus kept slipping back to that voice at the zoo. Not the words themselves—the way it had spoken them.

Fear. Raw, desperate fear.

The shifters had been winning when she disappeared. Two years later, she'd heard the rumors of their defeats, territories lost, bodies burned. But how? What tilted the war they'd been dominating?

"So." Marcel's eyes tilted up toward the rearview mirror. The reflection showed an empty front seat. "Want to tell me about that energy you invoked at the bar?"

"I don't know what you're talking about."

"We vampires have a close connection to the Tree of Death for obvious reasons. Specifically, *Gamaliel*, which gives us our speech." He paused. "You can imagine my surprise when I sensed you tapping into that well. After all, *Gamaliel* is quite dangerous, especially for a Mystic. And yet, you seemed unharmed."

Leah wanted to punch herself. She'd let her emotions get the best of her and exposed herself too easily. She held her tongue and stayed quiet.

The car reached a red light. Marcel turned. "What is more interesting is how you did not use the Tree of Death at all today. Not even when your life was in danger. One command with *Gamaliel* and that shifter would have been off your face." He squinted. "That means your access to the Tree of Death is limited. But why?"

Leah's nostrils flared. She nodded toward the windshield. "It's green."

Marcel's lips curled. He looked back at the road. "You are a curious creature. I do wonder if Edmond knows about it."

Leah bit her cheek harder. Marcel was more clever than he looked. "You could have helped me a little sooner, instead of watching."

"You seemed to handle yourself well. For the most part."

Leah leaned forward. "Or maybe you were concerned your strength might not have been enough. After all, it is a waning gibbous. We're almost at a full moon. You vampires struggle with that, don't you?" She snapped her fingers. "Maybe that's why Edmond asked me to come with you."

Marcel stayed silent. Leah was pleased with herself. It felt good to put these smug creatures in their place.

The shifter shuffled in its seat. Its head tilted, neck

cracking. It blinked several times, inspecting its surroundings. It glared. Its body began to contort, growing in size as it pressed against the ropes around its chest.

Leah clasped her hands together, invoking *Hod*. The creature froze in place.

"Don't even think about it."

Its eyes darted from the front of the van to Leah. They looked more human now, though patches of hair covered random spots across its body.

Marcel's voice distorted slightly, becoming clearer and more seductive, almost muting the sound of the engine and the street noises around them. "I suggest you relax. We have no problem knocking you out again. Do not make us hurt you."

Vampire speech. Leah recognized it immediately and saw the shifter's shoulders drop. She released *Hod*, and its body returned to a more human form, but it remained skittish.

"Are you with the Infinity Board?" its voice trembled.

"We will be the ones asking the questions," Marcel said.

Leah frowned. Something felt off. "No, we're not."

"But you are a Mystic."

"I am."

It looked over its shoulder. "Where are you taking us?"

"You are in vampire territory. Big mistake," Marcel said.

The shifter made a sound halfway between a laugh and a grunt. "You think we fear you after what we've faced?"

"You should—"

"What did you face?" Leah interrupted Marcel.

The shifter pursed its dark lips, meeting Leah's eyes. "Death."

"You will face death tonight. It is your fate for crossing into our territory."

"You've fought King Helen, haven't you?" Leah's gaze sharpened.

The shifter's jaw clenched. It blinked like it hadn't heard right. But it stayed silent.

"Please. I need to know everything about Helen." Leah leaned forward.

"Why do you care?" the shifter snapped.

"I..." Leah eyed Marcel, but this was precious information she wouldn't get later. "I'm going to kill her."

She could feel Marcel's eyes on her even though there was no reflection in the mirror above him.

The shifter sat up straight, looking down at Leah. "Why?"

Leah bit her lip. Marcel was listening. But this was the first time she'd had an opportunity to hear from someone who'd faced King Helen directly. "It's complicated. Let's just say that because of her, the people who matter most to me are out of reach. And to rescue them, I have to kill her. It would seem we have a common enemy. Anything you could tell me would help."

The shifter's face twisted. Its mouth opened, then closed. "We've fought the King with everything we had." Its voice dropped to almost a whisper. "She is unstoppable."

"How? What did she do?"

The shifter looked away, shaking its head. Its eyes tracked something past Leah's shoulder—something that wasn't there. "We've been building unity. Everyone equal, everyone connected. All living as one—"

"By infecting people and taking over their bodies?" Marcel snorted. "That is not harmony. It's slavery."

The shifter's head snapped toward him. For a moment, its face contorted—too many expressions fighting for control. When it spoke again, dozens of voices seemed to overlap in its throat. "The Infinity Board tried to stop us. Of course they did. But killing us?" Its lips pulled back in something between a smile and a snarl. "We're hard to kill. Especially on our ground."

The van hit a pothole. The shifter's body jerked, but it didn't blink.

"We held them off. Months. Years. We even expanded through the government, the police, and the courts. We thought we were winning. We thought..."

It stopped. Went rigid. Eyes glazing over.

"What?" Leah leaned forward. "What happened?"

The shifter's breathing quickened. "Silence. The attacks stopped. No more Mystics came. We consolidated our power, spread through the population." It paused, and a tremor ran through its body. "But one day everything changed."

Leah tried to swallow, but her throat was dry.

"A self-proclaimed King came with a small force of Mystics. We'd heard of Queen Helen, of course. We knew she was formidable." The shifter's hands started to shake. "But this was on a whole different level."

"What did she do?" Leah asked.

"She tried to control us first. Or at least that's what she said." The shifter's pupils dilated. "We just remember her pinning us down with a determined look. But that look quickly changed from determination to realization." Its voice cracked. "She then said, 'If you can't be directed, you'll be exterminated.' We'll never forget those words."

The shifter closed its eyes. The shaking spread to its whole body.

"Her look changed to one of chill indifference. That's when she began to exterminate us. No negotiation. No mercy." It gasped. "It was like fighting an army of Mystics compressed into one person."

Jaime's stories flashed through Leah's mind. Shifters

tearing through trained Mystics. His son, dead in hours. Jaime himself barely escaped. And she'd barely survived one with Marcel's help.

Helen killed them by the dozens. Alone.

Sweat slicked Leah's palms. "How is that even possible?"

"Unlimited power." The shifter's voice broke. "We thought we understood what that meant. We didn't." Its hands wouldn't stop shaking. "She'd appear. Strike. Gone. Appear somewhere else. Strike. Gone. Over and over, faster and faster. We'd try to scatter—ground, air, didn't matter. Those eyes found us. Always found us."

"She did that on her own?" Leah struggled to keep her voice steady.

The shifter stared at nothing. "Dozens dead in minutes. But it wasn't just—" A wet sound escaped its throat. "We didn't just see them die. We felt it. Every single one. Their fear flooding into us, their pain, their..."

Its head tilted back. Mouth open. Silent.

Leah's chest felt tight. "What?"

"Another one." The shifter's eyes rolled back. "She's taking another one of us right now."

The words dropped like stones into water. Leah's stomach twisted.

"You feel it?" Her voice came out too quiet. "When she kills you?"

"We feel everything." The shifter's eyes refocused on Leah. "We went defensive. Gave some of us autonomy, told them to run, scatter, spread. Hid the first one. We thought maybe she'd give up. Maybe she'd go back." A laugh bubbled up from its throat. "We were so stupid."

"What do you mean?" Leah asked.

"We're still dying. Right now. Today. Yesterday. Tomorrow." The shifter met her eyes. "She's closing in on the first one. Once she kills it..." Its voice dropped to a whisper. "We'll all die at once. Everybody. Every one of us."

The van came to a halt as they reached the alley leading to the club's back door. But neither Marcel nor Leah had moved to leave the car.

"There must be a way," Leah said quietly.

The shifter looked at her with resignation. "There isn't. We can see her coming. It does not matter how far away this body goes, or how many others we bring in." It closed its eyes. "We're living on borrowed time. Once she gets to the first one, it will all be over."

CHAPTER 6
THE HEAD OF THE FAMILY

"We're here," Marcel said after a long silence. Two bouncers approached the car and opened the back door. They sniffed the air. Both expressions twisted, sharp teeth on display.

"There better not be a problem." The first one's words came out like a growl.

"Relax. It won't try anything stupid." Leah looked at the shifter. "Right?"

It met her eyes briefly and nodded once.

The shifter stood and joined them, head hanging and its shoulders drooping. Leah bit her cheek and stepped out, wincing as she held her side. The bear clash had pushed through her *Netzach* enough to leave bruising. She pressed her ribs gently. Still intact, at least.

"You okay?" Marcel asked, closing the driver's side.

Leah nodded and tried to stretch. "Just some bruises."

Marcel's brown eyes caught hers, and his lips curved into a quick smile. He tossed her the car keys.

Leah caught them and opened her mouth to protest.

"Come. You and I are going to the back room." Marcel gestured to the parking area. "Leave the van there."

They followed the bouncers who flanked the shifter through the side door. Heat and noise washed over them, filled with voices, laughter, and loud thumping music. They moved through a dark corridor that ended at a metal door. Leah knew the kitchen and the rave entrance were on the other side. Part of her wondered if they'd parade the shifter through the crowd. The Family wasn't known for subtlety.

They stopped halfway down the corridor. One bouncer knocked on the wall.

A few seconds passed before a section of the wall opened, revealing a secret door.

The bouncers dragged the shifter through. Marcel followed, hands in his pockets. Leah trailed them past another bouncer who sealed the door behind them. A small elevator sat next to a narrow staircase. The shifter was too big for the elevator, so they took the stairs down. The muffled thump of the rave grew louder as they descended.

At one of the turns, Leah glanced at the shifter, noting its naked body, fur covering parts, but not enough. Looking felt like a violation. She turned her gaze away and focused on the steps.

She was about to meet the higher-ups. This could be it. The breakthrough she'd been hunting for months. Edmond was mid-level. Marcel was young. Asmodeus had explained all this to her. Vampires followed a strict hierarchy. Age meant status. The Ancient One was the oldest, strongest vampire on the continent. Retired long ago, but impossible to reach without going through The Family first.

"We need to find him," Asmodeus had told her. "At the height of my power in the last war, I faced him, looking for an alliance. I knew almost immediately that I had made a terrible miscalculation. Next to Legion, he is one of the strongest foes I have ever faced. His mastery of the Tree of Death is something else. Powers I have never seen in other vampires. That is why we need to find him. We need to convince him to train us in the Dark Arts to reach Helen's level and kill her."

That was the explanation Asmodeus had used to convince her six months ago.

But now, after hearing the shifter's story, Leah wondered if she'd made her own terrible miscalculation. How could she defeat Helen? How could she kill the King?

She looked down at her palm. The slit formed, opening a blue eye staring back at her.

Her jaw clenched. She closed her fist tight.

No other choice. She had to do this. She had to rescue them.

The shifter stopped suddenly. The whole group paused.

The bouncers tried to drag it down the last set of stairs. It refused, eyes darting around frantically.

"Keep moving." The bouncer's words came through gritted teeth.

"We hear her. She is close." The shifter's voice shook.

Ice pooled in Leah's gut. She met Marcel's eyes. For the first time, the vampire looked rattled.

The bouncers weren't fazed. They both yanked hard.

"Don't play games with us."

They managed to drag it down the remaining steps and through another door. But the Shifter's calm was gone. It returned to the skittish behavior from the car, head swiveling, muscles tense.

A pleasant scent hit her. Leather, earthy and rich.

The room opened up to a massive space. Two stories at least. Bouncers moved into position the second they crossed the threshold, spreading around the perimeter. A dozen, maybe more. At the far end, a bar stretched the length of the wall. Two bartenders polished glasses like this was just another night. One had long blond hair. The other sported a silver mohawk.

But the marble table dominating the center pulled Leah's attention. Twice as wide as any normal table. At its far end, two people sat, and the whole room bent toward them.

Eight people sat in leather chairs on either side of the table. Sixteen total, plus the two at the head. Edmond sat closest to them in a crisp white suit and shirt, farthest from the power at the table's end. All eyes turned in their direction as they entered.

The woman was striking. Long wavy brown hair, red lips, matching her red dress. She sat leaning to one side, a glass in her left hand. But her brown eyes killed any beauty pageant comparison. They matched the hunter eyes of the bouncers scattered around the club. Predator's eyes.

To her left sat a man who looked like he'd walked out of a cologne ad. Slender build, crisp blue suit, pristine white shirt, matching his white hair. His short gray beard framed a jawline that could cut glass. They seemed like opposites in every way except for the eyes. His blue ones held the same lethal intensity as her brown ones. A hunger radiated from them both like heat from a furnace.

The bouncers dragged the shifter to the opposite end of the table and held it in place with large hands on its shoulders. The creature kept looking back at Leah and Marcel, but its gaze remained fixed on a point behind them.

Leah's stomach twisted. Something was wrong here.

"Do you know why you're here?" the woman asked.

Her heavy Spanish accent, combined with her looks, reminded Leah of the Miss Universe contestants from Latin America. She and her mom used to watch those when Leah was younger. Her mom would have red wine, while Leah sipped grape juice from a wine glass. They'd drink and talk about the gorgeous women, their dresses, their bikinis. The memory felt like it belonged to someone else's life.

One of the bouncers yanked the shifter's arm. "Answer the question."

The shifter blinked and looked around like it was seeing the room for the first time. It cleared its throat. "We are in your territory."

"And what is a shifter doing in wolf-vampire territory?"

"We are trying to escape."

The woman's frown was subtle, but she leaned forward with a hungry smile. "We know what you did in Venezuela. The werewolf communities you slaughtered. The absolute control you imposed." She slowly swirled the amber liquid in her glass. "Now you come here, claiming you're escaping?" Her eyes narrowed. "I don't buy it. King Helen or not, you're here to expand."

The shifter let out a laugh that sounded more like a grunt. "We don't care. It'll all be over soon."

The woman studied the glass in her hand. "I can usually smell fear on people. Acrid. Bitter." She lifted her gaze to the shifter. "But not on you." Her lips curved, showing teeth. "Abominations don't fear. Now I'm going to ask one more time—"

"She found us! It's over!" The shifter's voice boomed through the room.

Its head tilted back. Arms went stiff. Its head began to twitch, then the torso, then the whole body convulsed like it was having a seizure.

Leah and Marcel exchanged looks. Before either could react, the shifter's arms transformed and broke free. Both bouncers went flying backward.

Leah moved, energy coiling in her chest. She invoked *Hod* and felt the familiar pressure build, but something was wrong. The well felt thin. She clapped her hands together.

The shifter froze mid-lunge.

Wait. That shouldn't have worked. Not this easily.

It wasn't trying to escape. It crouched, large hairy hands hovering over its head. Its eyes darted back and forth, tracking things that weren't there.

The room fell silent. All eyes on the shifter.

Leah tightened her grip on *Hod*, but the energy kept slipping. The shifter moved anyway, fighting against it, lifting its head slowly, staring at the empty space.

Her *Hod* had failed completely. But the shifter was still frozen.

Someone else was holding it.

Her chest tightened. Another Mystic. Here. In this room.

She forced herself to stay still, to keep her eyes on the shifter. Looking around now would give away that she'd noticed. The Family had a Mystic, and they'd kept it hidden. That couldn't be good. Better to play ignorant. Better to let them think she hadn't figured it out.

But her mind raced. Who? Where? How strong were they?

"The new King, here for revenge." The shifter's voice sounded different. Weaker and older. "You can kill us all. But you can't control us."

The shifter's expression twisted into horror. It leaned back, straining against the invisible restraints, fighting harder now. Whatever was holding it was far stronger than Leah's failed attempt.

Its head snapped back. It moved slowly, trembling, observing every person in the room. When its gaze landed on Leah, its look shifted. Eyes narrowed. Mouth hung open in shock.

"Leah. You're alive."

The shifter took a final exhale. Its body went limp.

How did it know her name? Why was it shocked she was alive? Unless...

Leah blinked several times, trying to process what just happened. Her hands fell to her sides.

The body stayed frozen in place.

The woman at the head of the table broke the silence.

"You can drop your *Hod*, Paige. That thing is dead."

CHAPTER 7
AN OLD ACQUAINTANCE

Leah's heart skipped a beat. Movement behind the bar caught her eye—a woman stepping through the service entrance, her hands unclasping. The invisible pressure holding the shifter released, and the creature's body slumped to the floor.

Paige.

The wolf-like features were gone. Paige looked human again—blond hair pulled back in a tight ponytail, dressed in all-black tactical gear like the other bouncers. No fur. No claws. Just Paige Jones, standing there like the past four years hadn't happened. But when their eyes met, Leah saw it. Those same blue eyes that had stared at her with terror in that warehouse, now sharp and guarded.

Cold.

Leah's breath caught in her throat.

"You seem to know each other," the woman at the table said, glancing between them.

"We did once." Paige's voice carried an edge. "Leah is an old acquaintance from my time in the Infinity Board."

The room turned back to Leah, who replied, "Yeah. Old acquaintances."

Be careful. Asmodeus's voice cut through her shock. *This changes everything.*

"Interesting," the man at the end of the table said, his voice deep, smooth, and naturally persuasive. He aimed two fingers at the shifter's corpse, now dissolving into thick black liquid, and two bouncers carried it toward a back door.

"Edmond, you never mentioned she was a former Infinity Board member. Were you aware of this?"

Leah glanced at the man as the room quieted. The others had called him Father, but after some sleuthing, she learned his name was Thomas. Some kind of leader, clearly. An old vampire, judging by the white hair and the way everyone deferred to him.

"I..." Edmond said, and Leah felt some satisfaction seeing him so uncomfortable. "No, Father, she lied."

The vampire leader placed an elbow on the table and rested his chin on his fingers. "Incompetent child. You get distracted too easily. Women. Alcohol. Drugs. They've clouded your judgment."

Edmond waved both hands, panic creeping into his voice. "Father, please, I was just using her—"

"Do not interrupt me if you want to keep your tongue, Edmond." The man's tone was serene, yet his words carried real danger. "You could have brought in a spy, for all we know."

Leah's mind raced. All these months of keeping her identity hidden, and a dying shifter had blown it all to hell.

And Paige. Paige was here, alive, working for these people.

"I..." Edmond looked at Leah with anguish, then pointed at her with anger. "She tricked me. She said her name was Ashley, and that she was just looking for work as a bounty hunter. She—"

Marcel stepped forward and bowed. "Father, if I may."

The vampire leader's cold, light-blue eyes fell on Marcel. He nodded once.

"Edmond had good intuition. Leah is no spy. She used *Gamaliel* on me back at the bar yesterday, with seemingly no consequences. Plus..." Marcel's eyes shifted to Leah. Her heart hammered against her ribs. "She wants to kill King Helen."

The man raised his white eyebrow. "Look at that, Edmond. Even your subordinate knows more about our guest than you do. I've heard enough. Please, empty your chair."

Edmond looked back at him, dumbfounded. "Father, please, I—"

"Don't make me repeat it."

The words hung in the air. The bouncers straightened. Even the vampires at the table shifted in their seats. Edmond stood slowly, his face pale, and gave Leah a murderous stare before walking past her and slamming the door behind him.

The woman sitting beside the vampire leader snapped her fingers, and the bartender rushed in with a glass of dark red wine. He held it and took a long sip before putting it down. Leah caught a glimpse of Paige near the wall. For a fraction of a second, their gazes locked. Paige's expression stayed carefully neutral, but her head moved. The slightest shake.

A warning.

Four years wondering if Paige had survived. If the transformation had consumed her. And here she was, human again, telling Leah to stay quiet.

"Leah Ackerman. Care to tell us what your intentions are?"

Leah hesitated. So many things happening at once. She couldn't breathe. Was that really a sign from Paige? How much could she trust a room full of vampires and werewolves? How had the shifter recognized her before its death? Could that have been Helen somehow? The frustration burned in her chest. Six months under the radar, and her cover was gone.

Leah cleared her throat and spoke calmly. "Yes, my real name is Leah Ackerman. Paige and I were acquaintances back at the Infinity Board before she left. I was part of the special forces who faced Legion. You might have heard of him."

"We have. Queen Helen sought our support to fight him a couple of years ago. Go on."

Leah put her clammy hands behind her back. "Right. Well, after the battle where we defeated him, I left the Infinity Board due to a personal quarrel with Queen Helen. Two years later, I discovered The Family, and I've been working as a bounty hunter ever since. I intend to meet the Ancient One and learn as much as I can from him to kill Helen."

The room burst into laughter. Even the leader and the woman beside him were smiling and exchanging looks.

The leader then leaned forward in his seat, placing his arms on the table. "Silence."

His command pierced the room. It fell silent in an instant. His eyes locked on Leah, and cold fear slid down her spine.

"And how are you able to use *Gamaliel* from the Tree of Death? Other wells are more forgiving, but cursed speech drives the user mad very quickly. Your vocal cords should be shattered by now, too."

Leah's heart pounded in her ears. "I've studied and discovered a way to mitigate the effects. It'll eventually bite me in the ass, but for now, all I care about is killing King Helen."

"There are spells and potions I've seen Mystics use before, but they all end up consumed by the Tree in the end." He sniffed something in the air, and his lips curled into a cruel smile. "That would explain your peculiar smell. You are already rotting."

He leaned back toward the woman beside him, and they exchanged a few words, more like lip-reading than speaking. He reached for his glass of dark wine and took a long drink.

She could tell he wanted to do something to her. *Gamaliel*, if he could get away with it.

Leah held her breath. If the vampire used cursed speech, she wasn't sure she could fight it back. That meant spilling everything. Asmodeus, the scroll, her real plans. She doubted these vampires would react well to learning they had a demon-bonded Mystic in their midst.

Finally, he put the glass down and intertwined his fingers. "You'll continue to work for us, Leah Ackerman." His eyes darted toward Marcel. "As for you, Marcel. Edmond's seat is now open. Keep an eye on this one, and the seat might be yours."

Marcel bowed. "Yes, Father."

The man turned his head toward an Asian woman sitting to his left. She was as pale as he was, though her hair still had streaks of blond combined with white. She took out a stack of cash, counted the hundred-dollar bills, placed them in an envelope, and handed it to a bouncer, who brought it to Leah.

As she grabbed the thick envelope and placed it in her back pocket, Father said, "For your services tonight. We'll send word with Marcel for your next bounty. You are both dismissed."

Leah blinked and took a step forward. "Wait, what about the Ancient One?"

A half smile crossed his face, and he chuckled. The rest of the room did the same, though more subdued.

"No one meets the Ancient One. He's retired."

Leah's nostrils flared. "That's not what Edmond said."

"Edmond lied then."

Leah shook her head. "You think King Helen is stopping at the shifters? She's rebuilt the Infinity Board from the rubble for the past two and a half years, ever since the defeat of Legion. Now she's expanding her power, re-establishing the Infinity Board's authority around the world. Some talk of a new world order. Do you really think vampires and werewolves have a place in that world?"

The woman spoke with fiery passion. "We've had a treaty with the Infinity Board since the 1920s. She wouldn't be stupid enough to break that. The Family's reach is quite long."

"The shifters had full control of Venezuela. They were defeating the Infinity Board until the self-proclaimed King came into the picture. Helen is dangerous, and I'm afraid she might be unstoppable at this point. Meeting the Ancient One and training with him might be the only way to defeat her. And even then—"

"Enough." The vampire leader's calm voice cut through her words. "Out of respect for your services tonight, I've let you talk after your dismissal. But we've heard enough. Marcel, please escort Miss Ackerman out."

Marcel wrapped his cold hand around Leah's arm, but she snapped it away. Immediately, all the bouncers in the room stepped forward. A couple of the seated vampires and werewolves stood, baring their fangs. Even Paige's hands moved, ready to clasp together.

Leah clenched her jaw. There was nothing she could do,

especially with Asmodeus being stubborn. Her words came through gritted teeth. "She will come for you all. Don't say I didn't warn you."

Leah gave Paige one last glance. Their eyes met again, and for a heartbeat, Leah thought she saw something beneath the surface. Pain, maybe. Exhaustion. Then Paige's expression shuttered closed, and she turned away.

Leah walked out, Marcel following close behind her.

CHAPTER 8
RESET

Leah's ribs ached where the shifter had pinned her. Her throat burned from invoking *Gamaliel*. The fluorescent lights buzzed overhead as she headed toward the bar's exit, too bright after hours in the Family's underground lair.

Paige was alive.

The shifters were dead.

Helen had seen her.

And Asmodeus—nothing. Not even a whisper when the shifter had her by the throat. Not a warning when everything went to shit.

Morning light hit her face as she pushed through the exit door. She squinted, fumbling for her keys in her jacket pocket.

Empty.

"Looking for this?"

Marcel leaned against her van, dangling her keys from one finger. That goddamn smirk.

"That was quite the scene downstairs."

Leah rubbed her eyes. Her whole body felt like it weighed twice as much as it should. "Give me my keys."

"Direct as always."

"Marcel."

"I'm merely—"

"Give me my fucking keys, or I'll drag you into the sunlight and pick them up from the ashes." The words came out flat. She didn't have the energy for his games.

Marcel's smirk widened. He tossed the keys, and she caught them. The metal bit into her palm.

"Aggressive this morning."

"I know where to find you," he said. "I'll contact you with the next bounty soon."

Leah climbed into the van and slammed the door. The engine turned over on the third try, and she pulled onto the street without checking her mirrors.

The city blurred past. Early commuters. Delivery trucks. A homeless man pushing a shopping cart. Normal people living everyday lives. No magic. No demons. No dead friends haunting every thought. And all Leah could think of was Helen.

How could she kill her?

Even at Queen level, Helen had been stronger. Now she was a King. Now she had the Core. Now she consumed her enemies like Legion had, feeding that thing inside her.

Sarah and Isaac were trapped in the Library of Alexandria because she'd been stupid. Because she hadn't understood what a Three-Fold deal meant. The Librarian's terms had seemed so simple: retrieve the information, return it, leave one member behind until the task was complete. She should have bargained for more time. Should have explained. Should have asked for another way.

You could not have known, a small voice whispered in the back of her mind. Her own inner voice, not Asmodeus'. *There was no way to know what it meant.*

A tear slid down her cheek.

Then another.

She rubbed them away, but more came, blurring her vision. Breathing didn't help. The pressure in her chest kept building.

Months of being alone.

Months of talking only to Asmodeus. Of pretending to be someone else at the Family's bar. Of shadows for company while Sarah and Isaac sat trapped in the Library.

"I'm sorry," she said out loud.

The highway stretched ahead, and her vision glazed over.

Memories came to her in a flood. Her dad's laugh echoed in her mind as he held a plank. Her mom, humming while she braided Leah's hair before bed. Alma's stern nod when Leah finally got *Malchut* right. Constance's patient voice explaining magic theory that seemed impossible. Sid making everyone groan with another bad joke. Grace sitting beside her outside the Academy, comfortable in the quiet.

Eli approaching barefoot across the Astral plane, those curious eyes when he realized how easily she navigated his realm.

Gabe's arms around her after training, the smell of sweat and soap. His lips finding hers between the library stacks.

Eric's leather jacket smelling like scotch as he drove her away from everything she'd ever known. The way he'd thrown himself between her and Legion's final strike.

So much loss. So much pain.

That was the cost of Helen's games. Her gamble for power. Her plan to use everyone else to clean up the mess she'd made when she and Leah's mom brought Legion into their world.

Part of Leah wanted to be angry at her mother. For

going along with Helen's plan. For not stopping it sooner. But hadn't Leah done the same? Followed Helen with absolute loyalty until the very end? Until it was too late?

She wiped her eyes again.

Even with everything Helen had done, Leah couldn't ignore the truth stewing in her gut. The Infinity Board had been rebuilt. Expanded. The demons loyal to Legion were dead. Word on the street said crime was at an all-time low. There was order and safety in the world again.

King Helen had brought a new world order.

For everyone she wanted.

A loud noise pulled Leah out of her thoughts.

The horn of a vehicle.

Eyes wide, Leah slammed on the brakes and swerved into the other lane, barely missing the truck in front of her. She'd missed her exit. By a lot.

"Holy shit," she said, catching her breath.

Calming herself, she moved right, checking for the next exit. A familiar yellow sign caught her eye. Bright yellow. A donut with wings.

Flyby Donuts.

Her hands tightened on the wheel.

She took the exit and pulled into the parking lot, staring at the sign through the windshield.

The last time she'd been to a Flyby Donuts, Eric had brought her. Right after her parents died. She'd been wearing that dirty dress, still in shock, and he'd told her to eat even though food made her sick. She'd picked apart a blueberry-glazed donut piece by piece while he drank his third coffee and pretended everything would be okay.

Four years ago. Right before the Academy. Before she lost him, too. Before everything changed.

Leah counted the bills in the envelope the Family had paid her, pulled out a twenty, and got out of the van.

The door chimed when she walked in. The smell hit her immediately. Sweet glaze. Warm dough. Coffee brewing behind the counter.

"What can I get you?"

"Half a dozen blueberry glazed." Her voice came out rough. "And two small decaf coffees."

She paid, took the warm box, and headed back to the van.

The first bite of the donut tasted exactly like she remembered. Blueberry glaze coating her tongue. Warmth spreading through her chest that had nothing to do with temperature.

She wasn't going to eat all these alone.

Leah closed her eyes, and the shift came fast. That familiar tug behind her sternum. The world tilting sideways. When she opened her eyes, she stood in their shared mental space.

The room looked the same as always. Gray walls that seemed to absorb light. A simple wooden table with two chairs. No windows. No doors. Just the space they'd carved out between his consciousness and hers.

Asmodeus sat at the table, arms resting on the surface, fingers interlaced. Those starry eyes closed.

Leah cleared her throat.

Nothing. No response.

"Asmodeus." Her voice echoed through the gray space. "We need to talk."

Silence stretched. Then, without opening his eyes, "You have already said everything that needs to be said. Now, if you do not mind, I would prefer to continue my rest. I will be ready for the next time you require my power."

Leah crossed the space between them and pulled out the chair across from him. The scrape of wood on the floor echoed too loudly.

"Why are you being dramatic? It was just a fight."

His eyes opened. Stars swirled in those black depths, more agitated than usual. "Just a fight?"

The temperature in the room dropped.

"I get it. I said harsh things. I was stressed and scared, and I lashed out." Leah leaned forward. "But you can't shut me out like that. The shifter almost killed me. If Marcel hadn't shown up—"

"I did not sense it because I was resting." Asmodeus' voice stayed level, but something dangerous lurked beneath. "When I enter deep rest, I see nothing. Feel nothing. I simply recharge what essence remains after you use me."

Leah frowned. "But I've used the Tree of Death before without you being active."

"I leave deep rest to match your sleep schedule. We remain aligned that way."

"Then what happened this time?"

His nostrils flared. "I did not feel like waking."

"But if you do that and I get killed, then you die, too."

Asmodeus raised an eyebrow. Stars pulsed in his eyes. "So? I am a demon, remember? All this misery and despair is normal to me, isn't it? If I die, then your parents' killer will be dead as well. That is what you want, correct?"

Heat rushed to Leah's face and neck. "I'm sorry. That was fucked up to say."

"You need to stop using me as a tool." He shifted in his chair. Tension radiated from his rigid posture. "It's difficult enough to having my essence trapped here. Sharing your body. Being *inside* your body."

"But *Samael* is helping with that, right? You get your own body now. More autonomy."

Asmodeus pursed his lips. His head tilted, slow and deliberate. Was that redness around his pale cheeks?

"That is the thing." His fingers drummed once against the table. "Our essences keep merging. I don't feel like a demon anymore. The old me wouldn't have cared about your comments. Wouldn't have cared if you died." He stared at his hands. Long fingers. Pale skin. "I'd hoped the shadow power would restore some independence. Some sense of my old self. But it did the opposite."

The drumming stopped.

"It reminded me what it's like to have my own body. To taste. To feel temperature. To experience sensation beyond your filtered perception." He looked up. Those starry eyes met hers. "And then you called the shadow back. The illusion dissipated. I no longer feel like myself anymore."

Leah's throat tightened. She reached across the table and wrapped her hands around his. Cold skin, but solid. Real.

"I think this is a huge improvement over your old self."

The corner of his mouth twitched.

"I mean it." She squeezed his hands. "I'm sorry for what I said. It won't happen again." She paused. "For what it's worth, I've changed too. I don't know if it's because of you or because of everything else. Doesn't matter anymore, does it? We're here. We're who we are. We're facing this together."

Asmodeus' lips curled into a genuine smile. "Thank you."

They sat like that for a moment, hands clasped across the table. Two beings sharing one body, trying to figure out how to be more than the sum of their damaged parts.

"Do not thank me yet." Leah released his hands and leaned back. "Make a shadow. I have a surprise for you."

Green flames erupted around her. That familiar sensation of splitting in two. Heat and cold at the same time. Her essence dividing, reforming, existing in two places at once.

She opened her eyes and found herself sitting in the van, staring at an exact copy of herself.

Up close, she could see just how tired she looked. Dark bags under her eyes. Skin too pale. Hair needing a wash. When was the last time she'd actually taken care of herself?

Her shadow's eyes locked onto the donut box, mouth falling open slightly.

"You got blueberry donuts." The words came out reverent. "Those are delicious."

Leah smiled and handed over the box. "Peace offering. Figured it's the least I could do."

Her shadow took out a donut and bit off half at once. Glaze stuck to her fingers. Crumbs fell on her jacket.

"Easy there. You're only half of me, so technically half the calories."

"I cannot—" Her clone spoke around a mouthful of donut. "These are too good."

Leah laughed. She scooped up a donut for herself and picked it apart, savoring each bite.

Her shadow gulped down the last of the first donut, took a sip of decaf coffee, and reached for a second one without hesitation.

"So." Her clone settled back against the passenger seat. "Want to bring me up to speed?"

Leah told him everything. The shifter's death. The way it had frozen mid-attack. How it had looked at her with shock and recognition, using her name. The voice that didn't sound like the shifter, saying she was alive.

Her shadow listened while eating, maintaining that patient focus Leah always struggled with. Another way they were different.

"That is some ominous last word from the shifter." Her clone rested her chin on interlaced fingers. Coffee sat forgotten in the cupholder. "My guess is that Helen consumed it and saw you through its eyes."

Leah's stomach twisted. Legion's final form flashed through her mind—that massive snout, those teeth, the way he'd consumed Asmodeus piece by piece.

"Can she do that?"

"The Core needs energy to sustain itself. It would not surprise me if that is how it works." Her shadow's eyes unfocused, thinking. "As she consumed the first shifter, she could momentarily access the hive mind. See through its eyes. Control it, perhaps. Before the essence disintegrated into pure energy to feed the Core."

Leah's eyes widened. "The shifter said Helen told them, 'If you can't be directed, you'll be exterminated.' Those were her exact words. Maybe she can control people like a demon would?"

Her clone shook her head and took another sip of coffee. "A Mystic's essence cannot possess another body the way a demon can. And she said, directed, not controlled or possessed. Semantics matter here."

"So, what does it mean?"

"I am not certain." Her shadow finished the second donut and licked the glaze from her fingers. "What concerns me most is that we have spent months staying under the radar. How will she act now that she knows? Assuming it was her talking through the shifter."

Leah bit her lip. Her clone mirrored the gesture a split second later.

"There is a strong possibility Helen was talking," her shadow continued. "Our cover is blown. But there is nothing we can do about it now except stay alert and keep moving forward."

"Yeah, about that." Leah rubbed her face. Exhaustion

pressed down on her shoulders. "What do we do about the Family? They're not letting me meet the Ancient One."

Her clone thought for a moment, fingers tapping against the coffee cup. "The plan has a setback, yes. But we made contact with the higher-ups. If we keep proving ourselves, we will gain access eventually."

"When?"

"Soon, I believe. We must be patient."

He knows I'm frustrated. Leah's jaw clenched. She wanted to argue, wanted to demand a better timeline. But pushing would just start another fight, and they'd barely finished making peace from the last one.

"We have discussed this in the past," her shadow said. "But are you certain the Immortal Witches are gone? We could try collecting more intel on that front."

"Cora tried to contact Frank. Nothing." Leah shook her head. "Even if he's still alive—and that's a big if—he's doing a great job staying hidden. You already tried to contact him through the Astral Realm. No success. I think we should keep an eye out, but chasing them might be a waste of time."

Leah glanced down at her arm. The chain marks from the Librarian seared into her skin, coiling up from her wrist. Permanent reminder of her failure.

"Crazy to think Paige just showed up out of nowhere."

"I was wondering about her." Her shadow tilted her head. "How long has it been?"

Leah took another bite. The tartness of the blueberries cut through the exhaustion. She swallowed. "Last time we saw each other was at the academy. Four years ago. She seemed okay. Barely acknowledged my existence, but I figured she didn't want the Family linking us together. Sarah and Isaac would have freaked out."

Her stomach dropped. Sarah and Isaac. Trapped because of her.

"Sarah would have made a scene in front of everyone." Her shadow's voice went soft. "And Isaac would have been behind her, nervously asking her to chill. Then you would have jumped in. Channeled Sarah's emotions. Eased Isaac's anxiety."

Tears pricked at Leah's eyes again. She blinked them back.

A hand landed on her shoulder. She turned. Her shadow gave her an understanding look that reflected her own grief back at her.

"I know." Her clone squeezed once. "I miss them, too. We do not have a bounty yet. Maybe tomorrow we can try to find Paige. Let you two catch up in private."

Leah rubbed her eyes and nodded. "Yeah. That sounds good."

Her shadow finished the last donut, drained the coffee, and leaned back with a satisfied exhale.

"We will figure this out," her clone said. "We always do."

Leah wanted to believe that. Wanted to feel the confidence her words suggested. But sitting in this parking lot, exhausted and alone except for the demon sharing her body, she mostly just felt tired.

"We should get home," she said. "Get some sleep."

Her shadow nodded. Green flames erupted again, that pulling sensation as the essence recombined. When Leah opened her eyes, she sat alone in the van.

The empty donut box sat on the passenger seat. Two empty coffee cups in the holders. Morning sun streaming through the windshield.

She started the engine and pulled back onto the road. This time, she didn't miss her exit.

CHAPTER 9
FULL MOON

After an uncomfortable day of sleep, Leah stepped out of her motel room, stretching and testing her rib cage. She was glad to realize that although there was a dull pain, it was mostly healed at this point. She went to the front desk, picked up the fresh towels that smelled like cheap detergent, and dropped them off in her room before heading out.

Leah walked through the parking lot, lit in part by the dim silver light of the full moon, hopped in the van, and drove away.

Should we create a shadow clone? Asmodeus asked.

"No, I want to keep our energy in one place. Werewolves might be a bit too excited tonight with the full moon, so I don't want to risk anything."

Fair enough.

Leah found parking on a quieter street a couple of blocks away from the bar, stepped out, and walked there. The night was somewhat chilly, even though spring was almost over, so she pulled her black hoodie up and placed her hands in the leather jacket pockets she wore over it. The bouncer gave her a quick nod and opened the door for her.

He looked the same as always, which contradicted a lot of the fantastical lore Leah had heard in popular culture. She couldn't help but think of all the movies she used to watch with her mom when she was younger.

Real werewolves were so different. Most were docile, stoic, serene, and obedient, though she knew they could turn deadly at the flip of a switch. Funnily enough, the one they called Mother seemed to be the most passionate she-wolf Leah had met.

Leah stepped inside and quickly scanned the space for signs of Paige. There were a few people sitting around the bar, and two tables with a couple of people drinking beers. Leah frowned when she noticed the billiards tables were empty, but walked up to the bar and waited for the bartender to finish helping a big, bald guy with a long beard who seemed to come right out of a biker gang.

"Weird to see you around here when there is no bounty," Marcel's soft voice whispered behind her, giving Leah goosebumps.

"A girl can't get a beer around here?" Leah kept her eyes on the bartender, who looked at her and raised a finger, pleading to give him a minute.

"Is the girl old enough to drink?"

Leah's nostrils flared, and she finally looked at Marcel, who smirked back at her. He leaned his back against the bar, resting his elbows on the counter. His dark eyes held hunger.

"Is the vampire stupid enough to ask?"

Marcel chuckled and raised his hand. The bartender, an attractive guy in his early twenties with a thick black beard, came almost immediately.

"Scotch for me, please. And you want...?"

"A Corona. Put it on his tab," Leah said, and the bartender got to it.

If she was going to deal with Marcel for a bit, he might as well pay for her drink. The bartender was back in less than a minute with a scotch glass and a Corona with a lime on the top. Leah pushed it inside and took a couple of gulps, the carbonated cold drink calming her thirst and her thoughts. She noticed Marcel inspecting the seared marks on her arm, but the vampire didn't make any comments. Instead, he took the scotch glass and swirled it in his hand before taking a sip.

"Let me guess. You are here to find Paige."

Leah rolled her eyes, annoyed at how easily vampires were able to read her. Instead of answering, she fired back, "Shouldn't you be hiding tonight? Given the full moon? If there is one night to take you on, tonight seems ideal. Especially after you rat out my plan to the whole Family. Ballsy to come here and tease me in that state."

Marcel smirked, enjoying the chase. "Touch our blood, spill your own, Leah. That's why this partnership with the wolves has lasted so long. They protect us at our weakest, and we protect them at their weakest, during the new moon." He took another sip, watching her over the rim. "Besides, I am your boss now, so threatening me is not in your best interest."

Marcel said it playfully, but something in his tone made Leah pause. She'd almost forgotten about Edmond's demotion and Marcel's promotion. The vampire seemed to be enjoying his new position a bit too much.

"Careful. That power is already getting into your head," Leah said, holding back a smile, before taking another gulp of her beer.

Marcel moved close, his face inches from Leah, his expression hardening. "On a more serious note, this is my opportunity to sit at the table, so do not fuck this up."

She stood her ground, staring back at his big brown

eyes. His cologne, combined with the scotch, hid the scent of metallic copper, though Leah could still smell it.

"Tell you what... I'll work extra hard to get you that seat, if you help me meet the Ancient One."

"You really think the Ancient One will help you kill Helen?"

"Yes," Leah said, without hesitation.

"But you have not been able to convince the Family to take you to him. If you cannot persuade an old vampire, what makes you think you can persuade the oldest one of them all?"

Leah thought of Sarah and Isaac, and swallowed, feeling her throat tightening. "Because I have no other choice."

After a few seconds of silently staring at one another, Marcel's expression softened and his lip curled into a half-smirk. He raised his scotch glass. "You have yourself a deal, Leah Ackerman."

Leah raised her beer glass and clinked his cup, then both drank.

Marcel leaned back against the bar, his expression shifting to something more calculating. "Are you going to tell me about your relationship with Paige?"

Leah looked into his dark brown eyes. "Why do you want to know?"

"Unlike Edmond, I like to know the people who work for me." He swirled his scotch. "Besides, your interaction yesterday was quite dramatic. I was front row and close enough to hear your heartbeat rising the moment you saw her."

She looked down at her cup and said, "There's nothing to it, really. We're just old acquaintances from years ago. Nothing more."

Marcel raised an eyebrow. "Are you sure you're not former lovers?"

Leah shook her head and chuckled. "No, not my type. She was my former bully when we first met. But then she got a bit better. Then she was gone. Kidnapped."

Leah wondered why she'd even considered telling him that. Maybe it was the beer. Maybe it was the loneliness. Maybe it was just the relief of talking about someone from before all this shit happened.

"Well, that is a relief, and matches my story, so I am glad you are being honest with me."

A relief? Because Leah was honest or because she wasn't Paige's former lover? Leah pushed the thought away and instead focused on Paige.

"Well, care to share?"

They exchanged looks for a moment before he gestured to a high top nearby.

Marcel took a seat and leaned forward slightly. "Since you were honest, I will return the favor. But understand something first." His voice dropped lower. "Edmond has been asking about you. Wanted to know where you would be tonight."

Leah's grip tightened on her beer. "And?"

"And I told him you were lying low at the motel." Marcel's smile widened slightly. "I bought you some time, but he is persistent. Unstable, even. I thought you should know what you are walking into with Paige. She is connected to some dangerous dynamics in the Family."

Why is he warning me? Leah studied his face. She hadn't known Marcel long, but it seemed he never did anything without an angle.

"Information is not free in the Family," she said carefully.

"No, it is not." He took another sip of his scotch. "But

consider it an investment. You help me get that seat at the table with the Ancient One, and I will help you navigate the Family's complexities."

Leah nodded once. It was transactional, which made sense for Marcel. At least she knew where she stood.

"Your friend Paige is a bit unstable."

Leah tilted her head. "How so?"

"It is known that she was kidnapped and forced to become a Chimera, though I know that you need some level of desire in your heart to become one." He swirled his scotch again. "Still, both Legion and the Infinity Board hunt the Chimeras down hard. Cannot blame them. Those things are abominations, just like the shifters."

Leah's jaw clenched at the casual way he said it.

"In any case, Maria, our mother, rescued her from a warehouse. Apparently, Legion was holding Chimeras at the ready to be sacrificed in rituals, or that is what Paige said." He took another sip. "She was lucky Maria took pity on her. Her wolfish Chimera form made her more... how would you say the word?" He paused, eyes on the ceiling. "Familiar?"

"Familiar how?"

"The other werewolves did not want to bring her in, but Maria is the boss. I think she saw in Paige a bit of a daughter figure. She did lose her daughter a couple of years ago, so I am assuming that is what happened."

"Her daughter died?" Leah asked.

Marcel shook his head. "No, she just left the pack and The Family altogether. Not sure why, but I think she joined a rival pack or something." He shrugged and added, "Wolf drama."

"So, Paige joined them but is still a Chimera?" Leah leaned closer, lowering her voice to make sure no one could hear them.

"That is the oddity. Apparently, Maria turned her. So her Chimera features seem to be gone, as you saw yesterday. But then again, she is also a Mystic, so others are quite wary of her. Think of her as unstable. Some even say Maria turned her into a Mystic under the Family. Just like you." He finished with a smile.

Leah sat on the information for a minute. If what Marcel said was true, Paige had been through hell, and even now she seemed to be ostracized by her peers. An unstable but strong weapon. It reminded Leah of her time as a war hero. Someone strong but different.

One thing was clear. She needed to talk to Paige.

She downed the rest of her beer and put her glass on the counter. "Thank you for the chat and for telling me this."

"Of course. And thank you for being honest. I will see you around." Marcel winked at her.

Leah nodded and left the bar, heading to the secret back door in the kitchen that led to the rave below. She walked past a group of tall women chatting and recognized their voodoo-doll necklaces. Leah lowered her head as she walked past the Rootworkers and went down to the rave. She was a long way from Sekrè Fami, and there were other Rootworker communities around the US. Still, she was always extra careful around them, given her time in that town had been eventful, to say the least.

A bouncer opened the door for her, and the loud music wrapped around her, beating in her chest and eardrums.

Ugh, I really hate this place. Asmodeus said.

"That makes two of us."

Leah checked the raised platform that oversaw the dancefloor out of habit. For the first time since she began working for The Family, the table was empty. Her lips curled ever so slightly, and she moved around the crowded club, walking by the periphery, between big round private tables and the dancefloor where people were going at it, the flashes of colored light matching the hard beats of the techno music.

Leah scanned the area, keeping a close eye on the bouncers, hoping to find Paige. However, after two laps and barely able to avoid a sloppy guy who tried to hit on her, she was losing hope. Leah could swear she saw Paige shake her head ever so slightly towards her during the encounter last night. But now, doubt began to creep in.

Maybe Leah had imagined it, or maybe Paige did it so Leah wouldn't speak to her in front of everyone. Still, the other place she could be at was the back room she was in yesterday, but without an active member of the Family escorting her, she had little hope of making it through. Even if she found Paige, there was no way she could see her alone.

She stopped in her tracks, crestfallen, as her reasoning finally seemed to take over her emotions. Seeing Paige after all this time had given her some hope of rekindling her past. To relatively simpler times. Times when she wasn't so lonely.

Maybe I imagined it. Leah stood near the edge of the dance floor, watching bodies move under the strobing lights. Six months of working for the Family, and this was the closest she'd come to feeling like she might reconnect with her old life. With someone who knew her before all of this.

A hand wrapped around her arm, startling her.

She turned with a glimmer of hope that Paige had found her, but it was extinguished when she found Edmond holding her. He wore the same white suit he had last night, though there were a couple of fresh red and brown stains in both his shirt and jacket. However, his cold blue eyes seemed sharp, his pupils pinpricks.

"This is all your fault," he said, and Leah sniffed a strong metallic scent combined with booze.

Leah pulled her arm back and said, "I didn't do shit."

He is drunk, just ignore him and get out. He is still part of The Family, so do not pick a fight with him, Asmodeus said.

"You'll pay for that," Edmond said, dragging his words, but his eyes spelled danger.

Leah felt a serpent of energy uncoiling within but kept it together. She had better things to worry about, so she simply turned back and walked away.

"Don't Move!"

Leah stopped in her tracks and looked back. "Haven't I told you already? Your vampire speech is useless against me. Now, fuck off."

Edmond's glare burned into her back as she stepped out on a side exit that led to a long, tight staircase, and out into the rainy alleyway. It was dim, thanks to a blinking floodlight above the door and the silver light of the moon. Rats scurried along the opposite side of the alleyway, and Leah shivered slightly. She pulled her hood up to cover herself from the cold drops and headed back to the parking spot.

I am sorry we could not find her. Asmodeus said.

"It is what it is. I probably imagined Paige's gesture."

What are we going to do now? Asmodeus wondered.

"Head back and lay low like they asked us to. Maybe we can do some more research on *Satariel*. It's been a minute since—"

Someone is following us.

Leah immediately activated *Tiferet* and turned. The dark alleyway was now bright, though the blinking floodlight made it almost a bit too bright to follow. Still, she was able to see a figure on the other side.

"Edmond..." Leah whispered, letting her energy flow,

and calling on *Netzach* to harden herself, and had *Malchut* ready.

The vampire attacked head-on, taking long strides. He leaped the last few feet, and Leah saw bloodlust in his eyes and fangs that grew four times their size. But her *Tiferet* was sharp, and she dodged him with ease. He landed behind her and immediately swung his arm at her, his elongated, sharp fingers inches from Leah, who dodged again.

She aimed at the ground and unleashed a *Malchut* push that sent her flying back, allowing her to put some space between them. She landed hard in an alleyway across the street, splattering water back.

"Edmond, stop!" she yelled, but the vampire had leaped forward again and was on her, releasing one frenzied attack after another.

Leah slipped past the first swipe. Ducked the second. The third came too fast. She threw up her arm, *Netzach* absorbing the hard blow. Even with the full moon, Leah could tell that one blow like that without her protection could easily fracture her arm.

She used an even stronger push to jump back and put more space between them. But this time, as she landed, she clasped her hands together, invoking *Hod*, stopping Edmond in his tracks. He tried to push against his invisible constraints to no avail.

"There's no use! You need to stop, now!" Leah said.

Edmond stopped struggling and looked at her with pure hatred. "You are going to pay for what you did!"

"Don't force me to hurt you! It won't end well for you!"

Edmond's cackle was bitter. "I'm still part of the Family, you bitch. Touch our blood, spill your own."

"Yeah, but I'm not going to let you just kill me."

"You can't keep me trapped forever."

"No, but I can keep you here until morning. Want to see how that ends for you?"

The vampire's hate faltered, realizing the predicament he was in. His eyes darted to Leah's right, and he yelled, "Bite!"

Leah frowned, confused, and that's when she felt pressure on her leg. She looked down and saw five rats trying to bite her leg. Disgust and panic took over, and she broke form, using *Malchut* to push them away. She stepped back, and as she did so, she saw Edmond's threatening face, inches from her own.

The vampire tackled her to the ground, and she hit the back of her head hard against the pavement. Stars filled her vision. Edmond went for the neck, and Leah forced herself to focus. She pulled on her anger until it finally uncoiled into a *Malchut* punch that landed square in Edmond's jaw. It sent the vampire rolling to the side, and Leah swayed back and forth as she got on her feet, wincing as she touched the back of her head.

For a moment, the vampire lay still, and she thought the worst. But then it grunted, seemingly choking on something. He slowly got up and turned towards her. Leah looked with horror at how Edmond's whole face was drenched in a thick dark liquid, his jaw broken, and hanging on its left side. But his eyes spelled something different: triumph.

Fuck, Leah, we need to... Asmodeus' speech was cut off mid-way by something big that tackled Leah with such force that it sent her flying several feet into the air.

Leah landed on her side, the air getting pushed out of her lungs. She gasped for air, looking back at the massive thing that had hit her. It looked like a giant wolf, except it stood on its hind legs. It was at least eight feet tall, covered in white fur, with long, thick arms that ended in large paws, though they seemed to have longer fingers, and looked more like hands. It dwarfed the shifter bear she fought before.

Its elongated snout displayed sharp teeth, and it growled, its beady eyes on her. Still, there was a recognizable air around the werewolf. The white fur intermixed with blond streaks, and there seemed to be hesitation in the creature's eyes.

"Paige?"

CHAPTER 10
THE ATTACK

Edmond stood beside the wolf, the open wound on his jaw healing as sinew and muscle stitched back together.

"That'll leave a mark," he said, wiping a dark liquid that wasn't quite blood from his face.

"Paige, he attacked me first!" Leah scrambled to her feet.

Edmond laughed. "You think that matters?" He stepped forward, fangs extended. "Touch our blood, spill your own. That's the rule, Mystic. I have to admit that I got a little nervous when you managed to jump past the block. I wasn't sure if one of us would detect your attacks anymore. But I guess the little wolf saw us." He patted the creature's flank. "Good dog. Now, kill her."

Paige, in her full wolf form, rose taller on two legs, and Leah caught something in her posture that made her stomach drop. A hesitation. Something almost human in the tilt of her massive head.

Edmond frowned, looking between them. "What are you waiting for, you half-breed idiot? Kill her!"

The creature's arm rose. Leah's *Netzach* flared, but she was too slow. The massive paw came down fast.

But instead of hitting Leah, the blow caught Edmond square in the head, and Leah heard bone crack. His head tumbled backward in a spray of dark liquid. The body stood for one impossible moment before it collapsed to its knees and toppled sideways. The head landed a few feet back, rolling to a stop.

No splash of blood. No arteries pumping. Just dark liquid oozing from the neck, diluted by rain.

Leah's breath caught in her throat. Paige stood over the body, chest heaving, rain streaming down her fur.

"Thank you..." The words came out strangled.

"Why are you here?" Paige snapped back.

Leah frowned. "I need to kill Helen. To do that, I need to find the Ancient One."

"You said that already." Paige's eyes were fixed on her. "Why are you looking for me?"

Leah took a step forward. Rain plastered her hair to her face. "Because you're my friend."

Paige lurched toward her, and Leah's arms came up. But instead of attacking, she wrapped massive arms around her, pulling her close. The fur was wet and matted, smelling of rain and something wild underneath.

Leah stood frozen. When was the last time someone had touched her like this?

The form against her rippled. Bones cracked and shifted. Leah felt the fur recede, replaced by smooth skin that was too cold. Human arms replaced paws, and when Leah opened her eyes, Paige stood there. The way she remembered her, but older.

Blond hair, drenched and hanging past her shoulders. Blue eyes that seemed sharper than Leah remembered. Pale skin that held an unnatural smoothness, like marble.

But it was her. Paige Jones.

Paige pulled back quickly, her cheeks flushing. "Sorry, I just..." She looked away. "Seeing a familiar face after all this time, I don't know. I wasn't thinking."

"It's okay." Leah's throat tightened.

Paige grabbed Leah's hands, her grip strong. "It's good to see you."

"Likewise." Leah glanced at the body behind them. "Aren't you going to be in trouble for killing Edmond?"

"Oh!" Paige looked back, her expression shifting to something casual. Too casual. "Don't worry about it. Even though The Family defends one another, fighting within The Family happens. In this case, he disrespected me, so I decapitated him."

Something in Leah's stomach twisted. The way Paige said it, so matter-of-fact, like discussing the weather.

Your friend Paige is a bit unstable.

Marcel's warning echoed in her head. Something must have crossed her face. Paige waved a hand.

"Don't worry about it. Maria tasked me with keeping an eye on him. Edmond's derangement has caused a lot of trouble for the Family. Besides, he's not dead."

Leah raised an eyebrow. "He's not?"

"Well, not dead *yet* at least. His head will regenerate, though it'll take a long time. *Arab Zarak* keeps them immortal." She pointed at Edmond's head. "See?"

Leah looked. The head had turned black and flaky, like charred paper. At the neck, something red was forming on the body. A small ball.

Her stomach lurched. She turned away.

"If you were keeping an eye on him, why did you attack me when I was defending myself?"

Paige scratched the back of her head. "Family rules. I had orders to watch him, so when you punched him..." She shrugged. "Had to defend him. But as soon as he called me a half-breed idiot and disrespected me, he was fair game."

Leah cocked her head. "What would have happened if he hadn't disrespected you?"

Paige waved a hand. "You know Edmond. He always insults me eventually. I would have just played with his patience, dragged it out until he lost it. Given my background, insults are common."

"I see..." Leah studied Paige's face, trying to reconcile this cold calculation with the girl she'd known at the academy. "You've changed."

Paige squinted. "So have you."

Silence stretched between them.

"Where's Sarah?" Paige's voice came out quieter. "Is she..."

Leah's chest tightened. "She's alive."

"And Isaac?"

"Alive too." The words hurt to say, pain welling up inside her. "But they're lost. Until I get Helen."

Paige's eyes flashed, pupils contracting. "Helen has them?"

"No. It's a long story. But stopping Helen will get them back."

"That's why you're here." It wasn't a question.

"That's why I need the Ancient One." Leah's hands curled into fists. "He's my only shot at killing Helen."

Paige's lips curved into something that wasn't quite a smile. "Yeah. I figured." She tilted her head. "Would you like to go somewhere to catch up? Somewhere dry? I'll call someone to clean this mess."

Leah nodded. "Sure."

They walked toward the alley's overhang, but Paige suddenly stopped. Her ears elongated and shifted back slightly.

"Someone's coming." She sniffed the air. "Two people. And they're not friendly."

She moved fast, grabbing Leah's arm and pulling her behind a dumpster. Before Leah could protest, a flashlight cut through the alley, landing on Edmond's body. Two figures approached.

One took a knee nearby.

"This is F8X, here with C2X. We just found a vampire body, over."

"What's your location, over?" The radio crackled.

"Alley between Dwight and King Street, over."

"Scan the area. We'll send more units to back you up, over."

Leah heard a low growl from Paige and quickly covered her mouth. She felt cold water wash over them, saw the lights shift to a sickly yellow as *Thagirion* wrapped around her. Leah mouthed, *It's the Infinity Board,* to Paige.

The flashlights went dark. The two Mystics in black cloaks approached slowly, their steps barely audible through the rain. They walked past the dumpster, looking directly where Leah and Paige hid, their eyes glowing faintly. They held their breath until the Mystics looked away and continued down the alley.

This is not good. Two uniformed, armed Mystics means only one thing, Asmodeus said. *Helen ordered them to attack.*

Paige tried to shove free, protesting quietly. "What the fuck was that?"

Leah tightened her grip. "I'm using *Thagirion*, a Tree of Death well that makes us invisible." She nodded toward Paige's confused expression. "It's a long story, but you can't let go of me, or you'll become visible. Now listen. They were setting up a perimeter and calling for backup. That means..." Leah looked over the dumpster, then back at Paige. "We need to go back now. They're going to attack."

Leah pulled Paige from behind the dumpster, and they ran, holding hands. The fight with Edmond had pushed them more than two blocks away. The closer they got, the more Mystics they saw securing the perimeter.

Do you think Helen is here? Leah asked.

I do not see why she would attack The Family. They had a treaty of no aggression. The only explanation is that she saw you through that shifter.

"Leah. You are alive." Those words still made her sick. Leah's jaw clenched, and she picked up her pace, practically dragging Paige now. Helen. The shifter had seen her, recognized her, and now the Infinity Board was attacking because of her.

Do not do anything stupid, Leah. We are not ready to face Helen.

Asmodeus's warning only fed her frustration.

They stopped a few feet from the side door. Three figures stood guard, two in black cloaks flanking one in white.

Gunshots erupted from the front of the building. Screams followed. A crowd scattered down the street as Mystics detained people.

Paige eyed the guards. "What are you doing? We can attack while we're invisible and take them out."

Leah shook her head. "I'm not killing them, Paige. Besides, that'll only draw attention. We're here to rescue, not fight."

Paige looked taken aback. "Don't insult me. I'm going to tear them apart. Them and all the other Mystics who dared attack my pack." Her eyes flashed yellow, fangs forming in her mouth.

Leah grabbed Paige with both hands and shook her. "Paige, listen to me! We need to focus on rescuing the leaders. If the Infinity Board attacked, they sent enough

Mystics to outnumber you. Plus, the vampires are at their weakest."

Paige ignored her and began to transform, so Leah grabbed her face. "Listen!" She pulled her car keys from her pants. "Take my keys and find my car. I parked at the old lot nearby. It's an old gray Dodge van. You get the car ready without attacking anyone, while I sneak in and rescue the vampire and werewolf leaders."

Paige looked away, her transformation complete, eyeing the Mystics with predator focus.

"Paige! It's the only way to rescue Maria."

The wolf turned to Leah, growling. Leah pushed back the fear radiating from Paige and jingled the keys near her chest.

"Trust me. It's the only way to sneak them out stealthily. Take the keys and get to the car. Make sure to avoid drawing attention; otherwise, the escape will be compromised."

Paige finally took the keys with her giant paws. She flashed her fangs at Leah but nodded, then squatted and jumped. She reached the bar's roof easily.

Three sickly yellow flashlights aimed at Leah, then traced upward, trying to track Paige. For them, a giant figure had just appeared mid-flight.

Leah saw the leader raising an arm to touch his earpiece. She moved forward, her stride enhanced with *Malchut*, and aimed a punch at the head of the one with the white cloak. The figure lifted several feet in the air before landing hard on their back. Asmodeus activated *Nehemoth*, both hands aiming at the two black-cloaked Mystics that flanked her. A void pulled both their heads together, crashing them into each other. They dropped instantly.

Leah moved to check they were breathing, but a familiar voice stopped her.

"Leah Ackerman. It's been a while."

Leah turned. The Mystic in white stood, pushing back her hood. Dark hair. Sharp features. Eyes that seemed to see straight through *Thagirion*.

Zafirah Nasser. The Sage of *Gevurah*.

Leah's stomach dropped.

CHAPTER 11
BETRAYAL

Water droplets hung suspended in the air, surrounding Zafirah, who stood fifteen feet away, her arms extended in either direction.

"You can drop your *Thagirion*. I can clearly see you through the water drops anyway."

Leah's options collapsed into nothing. Running meant a Sage chasing her down. Fighting meant hurting Zafirah, maybe worse. The thought twisted something in her gut. She needed to get Thomas and Maria out before Helen arrived.

Let me go get them. Asmodeus said. *You stay here and deal with Zafirah while I go grab Thomas and Maria.*

Splitting would expose Asmodeus the moment he peeled away from her. She needed Zafirah focused on her, distracted. Her *Thagirion* was making her stomach churn anyway, the Tree of Death pulling at her insides. She let the well drop.

The water shifted and fell to the ground in a splash as Zafirah moved forward, arms opening.

"Leah! Where have you been? We've been looking everywhere for you."

Leah stepped back and dropped into a ready stance, pulling *Malchut* into her fists. Pressure built in her chest as the well responded.

Zafirah stopped. Her arms lowered slowly, confusion crossing her face. "What are you doing?"

"You work for her." The words came out flat.

"Work for *who*?" Zafirah's eyebrows pulled together. She took another step forward.

Leah shifted her weight, keeping the distance between them. "Helen."

"The King?" Zafirah shook her head and spread her hands wide. "Leah, we all work for the King. You did too, before you disappeared for two and a half years." Her voice softened. "We thought you were dead, or had been captured. Sarah and Isaac, too." She took another step. "What happened to you?"

Rain soaked through Leah's jacket. Gunshots echoed from inside the bar, muffled but getting louder. The Infinity Board was pushing deeper into the building.

"Have you been looking for Sarah and Isaac?" Leah asked.

"Of course we have!" Zafirah threw her hands up. "We figured you three escaped together somehow, but we never understood why. Eyewitnesses said they disappeared under a blue haze, just like you did." She stepped closer. "Some Rooks wanted to name you deserters, but the King refused. She defended you. All of you."

Leah's jaw tightened. "She took the Core, Zafirah."

"She saved us." Zafirah's voice rose, passion bleeding through. "If it weren't for you freeing the King from Legion's control, he would still possess the Core. You saw what he did to her, how he twisted her. Helen did what she needed to do to protect humanity."

"By stealing Legion's power for herself?"

Zafirah moved closer, and Leah could see her mentor's eyes now. Brown and intense, exactly how she remembered from training sessions where Zafirah pushed her past her limits. "The Infinity Board had a treaty with The Family for over a century." Zafirah gestured toward the bar. "You know what they do in there? What they have been doing since this country was founded?"

Images of Edmond manipulating the dancers flashed through Leah's mind. His hands on them, feeding. The bite marks on their necks. Her stomach turned.

"They slip up sometimes," Leah said. "Make mistakes. That doesn't justify genocide."

Zafirah's nostrils flared. "Mistakes? You think manipulation and feeding on human lives is a mistake?" She took another step forward, and the rain around them intensified. "They harm so many people in their wake. You must know that. You're not naive."

"And Helen?" Leah's voice cracked. "How long until the Core corrupts her the same way it corrupted Legion? How long until she becomes exactly what we fought against?"

Zafirah squared her shoulders, and her voice boomed with the authority Leah remembered from lessons years ago. "The King knows how to control the Core. She has the training, the discipline, the strength to wield it without falling to the hunger." She lifted her fists into a ready position. "Where were you while humanity's enemies fell one by one? While we fought and bled to keep people safe?"

Leah looked down. Her fists were shaking. Two and a half years trapped in the Library, working to get her friends out, to find a way to stop Helen. And Zafirah stood here defending the woman who betrayed them all.

Asmodeus, get ready. On my signal, split and immediately turn Thagirion on to avoid detection. Go in and out, and do not *kill anyone.*

Asmodeus grunted in her mind, and she felt his acknowledgment.

"You disappeared," Zafirah continued, her voice softening. "You attacked me while trying to sneak into this bar to help The Family." She stepped closer, and Leah could smell the rain on her, mixed with the familiar scent of the lotion she always used for her dry skin. "What happened to you, Leah? Talk to me."

For a moment, Leah saw her mentor again. The woman who pushed her to be stronger, who called her 'little Pawn' with something almost like pride. Who taught her that Sages push their limits and pay the price for power.

But that woman served Helen now. Defended her. Believed in her.

"Betrayal," Leah said.

Zafirah's expression hardened. She shook her head slowly, disappointment etched in every line of her face. "You're coming with me, Leah. Whether you like it or not."

Asmodeus, now!

Leah pulled from *Netzach*, and invulnerability washed through her flesh like armor coating her from the inside out. She pushed herself forward with *Malchut*, pressure releasing from her chest as the well propelled her toward Zafirah. Mid-flight, half her power tore away. Asmodeus splitting off, peeling away from her shadow.

She crashed into Zafirah and wrapped her arms around her mentor's shoulders. Exactly the way she'd been taught to grapple.

Zafirah reacted on instinct. Her body twisted, weight shifting as she turned into the momentum. The world spun. Leah's back slammed into the pavement, knocking the air from her lungs. Rain pounded her face as Zafirah's knee pressed into her spine, pinning her down. Strong hands locked around Leah's wrists.

But Zafirah faced away from the bar entrance now, and she couldn't see Asmodeus slipping inside the bar.

Leah released the breath she'd been holding, rain mixing with the water already soaking her clothes. The plan had worked. Now she just had to deal with one of the strongest Sages in the Infinity Board with half her power gone.

Zafirah's grip tightened on her arms.

CHAPTER 12
LEAH'S SHADOW

Zafirah's knee pressing harder into Leah's spine. Rain hammered the pavement around them.

"What are you playing at?" Zafirah's breath was hot against Leah's ear.

Leah twisted, pulled from *Malchut*, and the pressure building in her sternum exploded outward. The push broke Zafirah's hold, sending her stumbling back several steps. Leah rolled, got her feet under her, and stood. Rain soaked through her jacket, plastering hair to her face.

The plan had worked. Asmodeus was inside the bar now, invisible, getting Thomas and Maria out. She just had to keep Zafirah busy. Half her power was gone, split away with her shadow, but Asmodeus still had his connection to the Tree of Death. She could feel it thrumming under her ribs like a second heartbeat.

Leah held up her fists.

"You want to fight?" Zafirah cracked her knuckles and grinned. "Be my guest."

The Sage stepped forward. Leah raised her hands, but Zafirah was already moving. The first punch came fast. Leah slipped it, barely, and felt the air displacement against her cheek. She tried to create distance, but Zafirah closed the gap like she always did during training. Relentless. Every strike carried a little more *Malchut* than the last, building pressure behind each blow.

Netzach held. The invulnerability coating on Leah's skin absorbed most of the impact, but the strategy was obvious. Wear her down. Force her to burn energy maintaining the well while Zafirah barely pulled from anything.

Leah ducked under a hook and drove her fist into Zafirah's jaw. *Malchut* flared in her knuckles. The Sage's head snapped to the side, but she turned with the momentum and brought her knee up hard into Leah's ribs. No pain, but the air left Leah's lungs anyway. A second punch caught her across the face and dropped her to one knee.

The third punch came for her temple. Leah pulled from *Nehemoth*, felt the cold void open in her gut. The punch curved mid-flight, redirected by the pull, and slammed into Zafirah's own palm instead. Leah grabbed the Sage's wrist, used the momentum to turn, and flipped Zafirah over her shoulder. The Sage hit the ground hard, water splashing up around her.

Zafirah rolled and sent a slide kick at Leah's legs. Leah jumped back. Her boots hit a puddle, and she nearly slipped but caught herself against the brick wall. Rain ran down the rough surface, pooling in the mortar gaps.

Zafirah was already up, hands extended, fingers spread wide. She lifted them, and roots burst from the cracks in the pavement. They coiled around Leah's ankles, wrists, and torso, pinning her against the wall.

"If you use your tricks, I'll use mine."

Heat built in Leah's palms. She drew on *Gevurah*, and fire flared brightly between the roots binding her hands. The wood crackled, split, and fell away in smoking pieces.

She sent *Malchut* waves cutting through the restraints at her feet and waist. The roots fell slack.

Something hit her in the head. Hard as concrete. Leah's vision blurred. The ground rushed up to meet her, and she landed on her back. The world spun above her, rain falling sideways, then straight down, then sideways again. More roots pushed up through the pavement, reaching for her legs.

Leah shoved herself up with *Malchut*, launched into the air, and put distance between herself and the Sage. She landed in a crouch twenty feet away. Blood ran into her left eye. She wiped it away with the back of her hand and blinked hard.

Zafirah watched her, arms crossed. Not even breathing hard.

"What's your end goal, Leah?" Zafirah tilted her head. "Why are you holding back? I'm clearly stronger, so if you don't go all out, it's over for you." She dropped her arms. "I'm going to give you one last chance. Either you come with me, or I take you in. You decide."

Leah's nails dug into her palms. Her mentor was right. Without her full power, everything was limited. Attacks, defense, and even pulling from the Trees took longer and required more focus. She needed more time to stall, but she wouldn't get it standing still.

"How did you end up following Helen?" Leah circled left, kept moving. "Even though she took the Core?"

Zafirah pivoted, tracked her movement. "The King has scripture in her body. Gives her the ability to control the Core, to use it to defend humanity." She took a step forward. "That ritual was first created with your mother, actually."

The words landed like a punch. Leah stopped moving.

She knew her mother had helped, but hearing it still cut deep.

"She hid it from everyone." Leah's voice came out sharper than she intended. She ducked under a root that sprouted from the wall behind her and kept talking. "Helen worked with Legion for years. He took Reginald Platt's identity. The vote, the attack on HQ?" She dodged right as Zafirah closed in. "All designed to destabilize the Board. To get her into position."

"That's not—"

"Even in the warehouse, only a handful of us fought Legion." Leah cut her off, backing toward the alley's mouth. "Because Helen wanted as few witnesses as possible. She knew what she was doing was wrong. She sacrificed lives to get where she is."

Zafirah's face changed. Softened. Her mouth opened like she was going to speak, and for a heartbeat, her eyes cleared. The fierce brown Leah remembered from training, when Zafirah would argue with Desmond or challenge the Queens. Then her pupils dilated. Her eyes went empty, flat, like someone had reached in and scraped out everything that made her Zafirah. Her expression hardened into a blank mask.

She took a fighting stance. "The King did not work with Legion." The words came out monotone. "She used the ritual prepared with your mother and did what was necessary to protect us."

Leah's jaw dropped. Zafirah didn't talk like that. Never had. The Elemental was fire and passion and rebellion wrapped in a human body. But the woman standing in front of her spoke as if she were reading from a script.

"Don't you understand?" Leah slammed her fist against the brick wall behind her. A small hole opened in the mortar. "How do you think Legion got here? That ritual invoked an Ethereal to Earth. That's why my mother left the Board!" Her voice cracked. "What's wrong with you? It's like talking to a wall! You've never been the type to blindly follow orders."

"Things have changed." Still flat. Still empty.

The voice reminded her of Eli, the Sage of *Yesod* who'd been murdered right in front of her. Sandeep had gutted him while he was trying to help. Zafirah and Eli had been close. If anything could break through whatever was wrong with her mentor, it would be that.

"Eli died in that fight." Leah pushed off the wall and moved closer. "The one Helen orchestrated. The one she designed so she could take the Core."

Zafirah looked down. Blinked. "Eli..." she whispered. Her hand came up to her temple, fingers pressing hard, rubbing in circles. Her face twisted like she was fighting something inside her skull. A sound escaped her throat, something between a gasp and a cry.

"Zafirah..." Leah reached out.

The Sage's head jerked up. She screamed, "Enough!" The word tore out of her, too loud, like it was forced through her vocal cords. "It's thanks to the King we're where we're today. King Helen put herself on the line for us, killing countless threats to protect humanity. Those are facts, Leah." Her voice shook on the last sentence, broke on Leah's name. "No matter how you spin it. Why are you so insistent on fighting?"

Something in Leah's stomach dropped. This was wrong. Every time Zafirah got close to the truth, something seemed to pull her back.

Leah had thought she was fighting her former mentor. But the person in front of her wasn't really Zafirah. Not anymore.

"I have no choice." The words came out quietly. Leah

met Zafirah's eyes anyway, trying to find her friend underneath. "Unlike you, I'll fight for the people I love until the end. Lies and betrayal don't get moral justification. Not when they cost this many lives."

Zafirah's arms dropped to her sides. Her expression changed. Disappointment, maybe. Or grief. Hard to tell which.

"Then there's nothing else to talk about."

She raised one hand, palm tight, toward Leah. The rain around them stopped falling mid-air. Every drop hung suspended. Then they moved. All at once. Toward Leah. Like iron shavings pulled to a magnet.

The water hit her face, her arms, her legs. Clung there. More drops joined, then more, building on themselves, a film spreading across her skin. She tried to shake it off, sending *Malchut* pushes in every direction. If she'd been stronger or had more energy, she'd be able to fight it. The water bounced back, returned, grew thicker with each attempt.

Her hands were covered now. Her feet as well, the film crawling up her legs and arms like living things. It felt like being dragged underwater, pressure building everywhere at once. More water climbed her neck.

"No, no, no, n—"

The film sealed over her mouth, her nose, the rest of her face. She tried to scream, but nothing came out. The water wrapped tighter, thicker, forming a sphere around her completely. She was inside a bubble, suspended, unable to move. Her *Malchut* push did nothing against the constant inward pressure.

She searched for another well. Any well. *Gevurah* sparked in her palm and immediately went out, suffocated. *Hod* wouldn't help, couldn't slow the water. *Chesed* might heal her, but she'd still be trapped. *Gamaliel*? No, draining energy wouldn't break the sphere. *Nehemoth*? She pulled from the void, but the water just flowed back into place, shapeless, impossible to grab.

Air left her lungs. Her body screamed for breath. She fought it, knew better, but her throat opened anyway, and water poured in. She couldn't die. Not now. Not with Sarah and Isaac still trapped.

Water burned her lungs. Her vision shrank into a tunnel, and the only point of light was Zafirah staring back at her.

Then everything went black.

CHAPTER 13
ASMODEUS' SHADOW

Asmodeus slipped through the door and pulled it shut. Gunshots echoed down the hall. The metallic door at the end of the corridor was dented and warped.

The secret entrance hung open.

Edgar lay sprawled on the floor, the werewolf guard who had let them through before. Dead. A pool of dark blood spread beneath him.

Asmodeus descended the stairs, hearing Leah's voice whisper through their shared consciousness. She'd let him take total control of this clone, but even then, a piece of her was always there.

Don't kill them, she said.

Yelling erupted from below, along with the distinct crack of bones breaking.

When Asmodeus reached the bottom landing, two Black Knights blocked the entrance. Their heads turned as they scanned the space. If it weren't for *Thagirion*, they would have spotted Leah running straight toward them.

Asmodeus ground his teeth. He pulled from *Gamaliel*.

Energy coiled in his throat, constricting. Each syllable would cut his vocal cords, but he had no choice. He spoke softly in cursed speech. "They need reinforcements in the rave area. You should go now."

Pain lanced through his throat with every word. The Black Knights exchanged confused looks, then nodded and walked past Leah, heading up the stairs.

Asmodeus stepped through the entrance and stopped.

Bodies everywhere. Mystics, werewolves, vampires, all torn apart. Blood slicked the concrete floor. The destruction made it difficult to distinguish battle damage from the warped reality of the Astral Realm they occupied while using *Thagirion*. The walls seemed to ripple and breathe. Shadows moved where nothing stood.

In the center of the carnage, a massive werewolf traded blows with a Mystic in white. The Mystic's cloak hung in tatters, exposing a scarred, muscular chest. The werewolf lunged. The Mystic caught its giant claw with his bare forearm. Energy surged around him. He thrust forward with a *Malchut* push, launching the creature across the room. It crashed into the far wall, cement cracking.

The Mystic turned. Asmodeus recognized the bald head, the gray mustache, and the deep, scarred face immediately.

Desmond Hawthorne. The Invulnerable.

Oh no, Leah said in his mind.

Asmodeus scanned the room, calculating. Thomas lay near the werewolf, a wooden stake protruding from his stomach. Dark liquid pooled beneath him, but his chest rose and fell. Still breathing. The werewolf next to him had brown fur matted with blood, yet her eyes burned with defiance. Maria—the mother of the pack.

If Desmond killed Maria, Thomas would bleed out

before they could move him. If Maria killed Desmond, the Infinity Board would hunt them all down. Either outcome destroyed their chance to reach the Ancient One.

The werewolf pushed to its feet, growling. Desmond ripped away the remains of his cloak and tossed it aside, revealing burn scars that covered his torso and arms.

Asmodeus took a step forward when movement caught his eye.

A body near Desmond. White clothing, soaked red.

"Yuki!" Leah shouted, her mind feebly attempting to push forward.

Asmodeus rushed forward and dropped to his knees beside her. Three deep gashes ran from her torso up through her chest and face. He pressed his fingers to her neck. Soft pulse. Faint. Her breathing came shallow and wet.

That explained Desmond's fury.

Asmodeus looked back at Maria and Desmond, who stood locked in their stare down. Then back to Yuki.

We need to heal her, Leah said.

Those two are about to tear each other apart, Asmodeus responded. *And my bet is with the Invulnerable. If we do not stop them, Thomas and Maria will die. With them, our chance to reach the Ancient One.*

Save Yuki or save The Family. Save Leah's former mentor and friend but risk the entire plan. Or let Yuki die and preserve their path forward.

Leah's anguish surfaced. Asmodeus felt her desperation mixing with his own frustration.

Perhaps there was a third option.

Asmodeus dropped *Thagirion*. The astral layer vanished. He cradled Yuki and invoked *Chesed*. Warmth emanated from his fingers. He let Leah channel as much of the Tree of Life as she could muster. Heat spread and pulsed around

Yuki's broken body. Asmodeus guided the energy through Leah's arms, pouring it over the wounds.

Nothing happened. The gashes remained open, bleeding.

Fuck! Leah's voice echoed sharply in his mind.

Chesed had always been more difficult for them.

Desperation clawed at them both. Asmodeus raised his voice. "Desmond! Yuki is dying. We need to heal her."

Both the Sage and the werewolf turned toward Leah.

Desmond's mouth fell open. Shock washed over his scarred features. "Leah." His voice came out hoarse. "You really are alive."

His eyes narrowed. He studied the way she stood, the way she held her hands. His jaw tightened.

"Asmodeus." The name came out flat, not a question.

"Yes." Asmodeus kept his hands on Yuki, feeling her pulse weaken. "And Yuki is as well. But she will not be for long if we do not help her." He turned to face Maria. "Let the Sage assist me, and I will escort you both out."

"Yuki is dead." Desmond's voice went colder.

Asmodeus frowned. "What are you talking about? She is breathing. I can feel her pulse."

"Werewolf wounds." Desmond turned back to Maria. "The corruption in their claws runs too deep for the Tree of Life to cleanse. She has lost too much blood." His hands clenched into fists. "Her fate was sealed the moment this bitch tore her open."

Before Asmodeus could respond, Desmond launched forward with a *Malchut* push. Maria did the same. The two figures collided mid-flight in a brutal clash. Desmond dodged Maria's strikes, but his own punches missed as Maria displayed incredible speed and agility. They separated, circled one another, then crashed together again.

The plan had failed. Now the two combatants

exchanged vicious blows that would kill one or both of them. Asmodeus knew Desmond had the advantage. His *Netzach* affinity made him nearly indestructible. Maria's strength meant nothing if she couldn't land a killing blow, and Desmond would simply outlast her.

Yuki coughed. Blood spilled from her mouth, bubbling and thick.

Something snapped in Leah. Asmodeus felt it fracture through their shared consciousness. She would not lose another mentor. Not another friend. Not after Alma. Not after everyone else Helen had taken.

Nehemoth activated in her chest. The well responded, drawing energy inward from the surrounding space. The temperature plummeted. Frost spread across the floor. Asmodeus saw his breath mist in the frigid air.

"You are not dying today!"

The words erupted from both of them, fury and desperation braided together. Asmodeus held Leah's hands over Yuki's torn body.

Chesed flowed through them again, stronger this time. Warmer. Faster. The well pulsed and surged. But Yuki's wounds did not budge. They were losing her. The warmth dissipated into a dark void as Asmodeus pushed harder. Sweat beaded on his brow despite the cold. He shut his eyes, pouring everything they had into this. His hands grew hot. Then searing.

Leah and Asmodeus refused to let someone else die. They had endured enough of Helen's game. All of this was her fault. Anger fueled them now. Leah's hands burned white-hot above Yuki's chest.

Something massive crashed into them from the side, slamming Asmodeus to the ground. He opened his eyes and found Thomas's pale face inches from his own. The vampire's eyes were wide.

"Stop." Thomas's voice came out quiet. Dangerous. "Or you will kill Maria."

Asmodeus looked past him. Both Desmond and Maria lay slumped on the concrete. He tried to stand, but the vampire had him pinned, fangs inches from Leah's throat.

"What are you?" Thomas asked. "No Mystic can wield both Trees like that. The corruption alone should have killed you."

"Get off me if you and Maria want to live."

Nehemoth still churned within her. Frost continued spreading across the floor around them. Thomas hesitated, then shifted aside. Asmodeus pushed to his feet and rushed back to Yuki.

A thin layer of new skin covered the deep gashes. Pink and raw, but sealed. He pressed his fingers to her neck. A pulse, stronger than before. Stable.

Relief washed through him, followed immediately by horror.

Asmodeus moved to Desmond. The Sage lay unconscious, his breathing shallow but steady. Then to Maria. She had shifted back to human form, her clothes torn and bloodstained. Weak pulse, but alive.

If Thomas had not stopped him, there was a strong possibility both would be dead now. The realization settled like ice in his gut. He had lost control. Nearly killed them. Let Leah's desperation override his own thinking. Stupid. This was not his body. Not his energy to command without consequence. He had pushed too far, drawn too deep from Leah's wells.

He looked down at the shadow clone's hands. They still trembled.

"*Agshekeloh.*" Thomas's voice came from behind him. "How did you invoke the Tree of Death like that? You should be dead."

Asmodeus turned. The vampire stood upright now, the wound in his stomach apparently healed. Dark veins still showed beneath his pale skin, but the stake was gone.

"You healed quickly," Asmodeus said.

"You brought enough Tree of Death energy for me to borrow some for myself." Thomas tilted his head, studying Leah's face. "We are not creatures of the living. We thrive on corruption." His ancient eyes searched hers. "You aren't her. Not entirely." He paused. "You are something else. Something inside her."

Asmodeus said nothing.

A loud explosion shook the room. Dust rained from the ceiling.

Asmodeus thrust a hand forward, using *Malchut* to push falling debris from hitting them. "I would love to discuss this further, but we have no time. Grab Maria. Drag Desmond. We are leaving."

"You chose to heal one of them and endangered Mother's life."

Asmodeus met Thomas's eyes. "Do not start with me. Your entire Family is dead. More Mystics are coming. In fact, you would both be dead had I not arrived. Paige is outside with a vehicle." Another explosion, closer this time. "So, are we leaving, or are we waiting here to die?"

The vampire moved with inhuman speed, appearing directly in front of Asmodeus. They locked eyes for several seconds. Thomas's gaze was unreadable, ancient, calculating. A third explosion rattled the walls.

Thomas looked up at the ceiling, then back at Leah. "This is not over." He walked to Maria and lifted her gently in his arms.

Asmodeus checked on Desmond, feeling a flicker of guilt. But this was the best outcome they could achieve. The Sage would survive. So would Yuki. He grabbed Desmond under the arms and dragged him toward Yuki, who had regained some color in her cheeks.

"What are you doing?" Thomas asked from the doorway.

"Nothing." Asmodeus looked back at Thomas. "Let's go."

CHAPTER 14
NOT AS PLANNED

Gunshots echoed from above.
"Take my hand," Asmodeus said.
They stood at the bottom of the stairs. The vampire eyed the offered hand with disdain, then repositioned Maria on his shoulder and grabbed hold.

Asmodeus pulled from *Thagirion* once more, letting it wash over the three of them. The sounds of fighting at the rave dulled. The fluorescent white light from the stairs turned sickly yellow. They rushed up.

When they stepped back into the hallway, Asmodeus stopped.

Two Knights. On the ground. The ones he had sent away.

Deep gashes covered one. The other's throat was torn out, and blood pooled beneath him.

No... Leah whispered in their shared consciousness.

No time for mourning.

They rushed down the hall and threw open the door. Outside, Zafirah carried Leah's wet body over her shoulder, walking toward the street with a phone to her ear.

Asmodeus's and Leah's vision tunneled. Their world shrank as they saw their body, limp Zafirah's arms.

Could Zafirah have done it? Killed Leah just like that?

There's no way! Leah said. *She wouldn't do that.*

What would happen if one of the shadows died? That was one question that the book, *Death and Its Power*, had not answered. But the mere thought of Zafirah betraying them sparked something primal. Anger bled into rage. Their hands shook with it.

They leaped forward, letting go of Thomas's hand, letting go of everything except that fury. Their steps, enhanced by *Malchut*, allowed them to catch Zafirah in seconds.

Asmodeus pulled from *Nehemoth*, gripping Zafirah's head with invisible force. Coldness spread through their shared body. Simultaneously, Leah drove *Malchut* forward, pressure building in their chest and releasing through their fist.

The Sage reacted instinctively, dropping Leah and raising her hands. But it is difficult to stop a punch you cannot see. It landed square on her head and sent her flying across the street. She crashed hard into the opposite wall, concrete spiderwebbing around the impact.

"You will pay for what you did," Leah and Asmodeus said in unison, letting go of *Thagirion*.

Coldness spread around them as *Nehemoth* pulled energy and refilled their collective wells. Sparks began to blow from their left arm. Leah could feel the call of *Golohab*, the well of chaotic fire. One of the most potent and dangerous wells in existence. Its black flames pressed against their mind, dulling their senses.

That would be appropriate. An eye for an eye.

You killed me, so I get to kill you.

Something grabbed them by the leg. They looked down,

ready to strike, when they found Leah, who had crawled toward them.

"You are alive!" Asmodeus exclaimed and kneeled quickly.

"Leave her." Leah's voice came out hoarse, water still dripping from her hair. "She just drowned me and then revived me so I would stop fighting. We need to go."

Asmodeus looked back at Zafirah, who struggled to get up. She was disoriented, her *Netzach* clearly wearing off. Leah pulled her shadow's face back.

"Hey! Look at me. We need to go. We can merge back in the car."

Asmodeus nodded. "Let me carry you."

He lifted Leah gently and realized Thomas stood next to them. Another reminder of vampires' uncanny ability of stealth.

"There is a lot you need to answer, but there is no time. More Mystics are coming. We need to go."

"Hold my arm and do not let go," Asmodeus said.

The vampire did as he was told, holding just a bit tighter than needed. *Thagirion* washed over them once more, and they rushed away.

They easily passed the rings of Mystics that covered the perimeter, most of which had been knocked out or killed, and finally reached the parking lot. Paige was waiting for them with the engine running, though she looked restless. Next to her—much to Asmodeus's surprise—was Marcel. Asmodeus dropped *Thagirion*.

Both Marcel and Paige jumped as two Leahs materialized in front of them, one cradling the other.

"Jesus! It's about time!" Paige's eyes darted between them. Her mouth opened slightly, then closed. "What the hell? There are two of you."

Marcel got out of the car and stared. "How is there..." He looked from one Leah to the other. "Leah, what is this?"

"It is complicated," Asmodeus said.

"No shit it's complicated!" Paige's voice rose. "You never mentioned having a twin."

"Because I don't," Asmodeus said.

Thomas pushed past them, carrying Maria. "Explanations later. We need to leave. Now."

Marcel approached Thomas, probably intending to help, but Thomas shook him off and carried Maria into the van himself. Marcel turned back to Asmodeus, who still held the weakened Leah. His confusion had shifted to something else. Wariness.

"Get in," Thomas snapped from inside the van.

Asmodeus climbed into the back, positioning himself against the door with Leah across his lap. Behind them, Thomas settled into the rear bench seat with Maria cradled in his arms. Marcel took the front passenger seat. Paige slid behind the wheel.

"Go!" Asmodeus said while closing the door.

Paige pressed the gas, and they sped out of the parking lot. For the first few minutes, no one spoke. Paige kept checking her rearview mirror. Marcel twisted in his seat to look out the back window.

"We clear?" Paige asked.

"For now," Marcel said. "But they will track the vehicle. We need to switch cars."

"Not until we are far enough away," Asmodeus said. "Keep driving."

Paige took a left and hopped on the highway. She exhaled and finally broke the silence.

"What the hell happened?"

Asmodeus looked up. The words caught in his throat.

The blue eye of the Librarian materialized in the back of

the front seat, looking down on them. Asmodeus turned Leah's head away from it.

"The Infinity Board is going to pay for this," Thomas said from the back. Then his eyes darted to Marcel. "Where were you? You know that in an imminent attack, the members at the table come back to defend the family." Every word he said was sharp and made the hair on the back of Asmodeus's neck stand up.

Marcel looked back with an uncharacteristic coldness. "I stepped outside to try and locate Edmond. I knew he had been drinking, and when I spotted Leah, I knew he might try to go for it. I found him decapitated in an alley, and that is when the attack began. My intention was to go back when I found Paige, seemingly out of nowhere, leaving the area. I caught up to her, and she explained the plan, so we worked together to clear an exit path for you all and get the car ready."

After a few seconds of silence, Thomas said, "Sounds like a convenient truth."

"He did help me, Father," Paige said.

"No one asked for your opinion," Thomas said, eying Paige with disgust. Though he knew better than to insult her further.

"Apologies..." Paige mumbled, then added, "Where are we heading?"

"Minnesota. There is a safehouse there," Thomas said.

Marcel nodded. "We'll make stops along the way to hide from the sun. Rest up, Father. We've got this."

"No," Asmodeus said. "We are going to meet the Ancient One."

"That's not part of the plan. Who do you think you are?" Thomas said, displaying fangs that were longer than usual.

The temperature around them began to drop as

Asmodeus spoke softly. "I am the one who just saved your ass."

Thomas's eyes turned white. Black veins formed around his eyes and neck. "Be very careful with your next words, Mystic."

Asmodeus felt the energy within begin to uncoil, slithering toward his throat and starting to constrict it.

Wait. Leah's presence pushed against his consciousness. *This is wrong.*

We need to reach the Ancient One, Asmodeus responded internally. *Thomas will not take us.*

Because we're forcing him with cursed speech? After he saved us? After Maria nearly died?

After he used us for months, Asmodeus countered. *We are a tool to him. Nothing more.*

That doesn't make this right.

The energy coiled tighter. Asmodeus could feel Leah fighting it, trying to pull back from *Gamaliel*.

Leah. Zafirah saw two of you. If word reaches Helen about your shadow ability...

I know! Her frustration bled through. *I know we're out of options. But that doesn't mean I have to like it.*

No, Asmodeus agreed. *It does not. But let me do this.*

Leah stopped resisting, and power flooded their throat.

Asmodeus spoke with authority. "I have done your dirty work long enough. Time you vampires come through on your promise."

"Your cursed speech won't work on me," Thomas said threateningly, his own cursed words.

"I saved yours and Maria's life. You owe me this much."

"The Ancient One sees no one. Period."

Ice formed around the windows. Thomas's breath as well as Asmodeus's was clearly visible.

"You do not know what I am capable of. Don't tempt me, vampire. I will kill you."

The two stared at one another while Marcel spoke, his voice somewhat shaky.

"Leah, you should..."

"Silence," Asmodeus said, still eyeing Thomas.

Marcel's words stopped.

Finally, Thomas's eyes grew wide. "Demon."

Asmodeus cocked his head, his lips curling into a smile. "Took you long enough. Though we're something more complicated than that."

Thomas's eyes darted to Leah, who still lay on Asmodeus's shadow lap.

"You will take us to the Ancient One," Asmodeus commanded with force, releasing *Gamaliel*.

Energy coiled in his throat, constricting. Each syllable cut his vocal cords. He tasted blood.

"No," Thomas responded.

The car suddenly filled with dark threads, coming from both Asmodeus and Thomas. The commands collided, ripping at one another like snakes. They continued to stare at one another while the cursed speeches fought. The car temperature dropped even lower. Asmodeus felt knives stabbing his throat, but he pushed harder.

Marcel pressed himself back against the passenger door. Paige's knuckles were white on the steering wheel.

Finally, Asmodeus's threads pierced through Thomas's defense and wrapped around the vampire's throat. Thomas's eyes returned to normal, and his black threads dissipated. His eyes lost focus.

"Paige, stop the car," Thomas said. "We'll exchange seats, and you can look after Maria while I drive us to see the Ancient One. That's an order."

CHAPTER 15
UNINVITED GUEST

Leah stood in front of a thick violet mist that swirled into a wall. Surrounding her was a void, and the only light came from behind the fog. It curled around itself and dissipated as it fell away from the wall. She moved closer, slowly, trying to get as near to the mist as possible. Behind it, two silhouettes shifted, and muffled speech reached her ears, though the words were hard to distinguish. Leah took another step. Some of the mist that flowed down began to swirl around her feet.

"That was a really lucky roll. But it's dangerous to leave Leo there!" A male voice with a Scottish accent—familiar, somehow.

"What options do we have? I'm sure he's after the coordinates. We can't risk it." The woman sounded distressed.

"You realize that if the Phovias don't finish him off, Leo will finish us off next time we follow the coordinates. We won't be able to initiate another witch."

"That's a chance we'll have to take. Otherwise, how do you suggest killing him?"

Silence.

Leah stepped forward, arm raised. Her fingers grazed

the cool vapor, and it swirled around them softly at first. Then the mist began to spiral faster, more aggressively. Before Leah could react, the fog engulfed her.

Everything went dark.

Leah's eyes snapped open. Her head rested against the car window, vibrations from the gravel road rattling through the glass. Through the windshield, a massive white house grew larger in the moonlight. Columns lined the front porch. Multiple chimneys jutted from the roof.

They'd been on the road for hours, stopping somewhere in the middle of Minnesota at a rundown motel to hide the vampires from the light. That's when she remerged with Asmodeus, reliving his memories and feeling his exhaustion. Yuki and Desmond were alive. That knowledge settled something inside her.

Leah sat forward and studied the mansion. It was bigger than the main Maimonides Academy building, but older. The Academy had felt institutional despite its age, with its courtyards and dormitory wings. This place was different. Personal. The home of someone who'd lived for centuries.

The car stopped at a circular drive.

Maria had recovered unnaturally fast from her injuries, though she'd been quiet the entire ride. She sat in the front passenger seat while Thomas drove. Neither spoke to Leah, their disdain clear in every glance. But Leah didn't care. They all knew they wouldn't be in this car if it weren't for her. Now they just needed to deal with their pride and get over it.

Marcel and Paige sat in the back seats with Leah, but

they'd been quiet too, obviously mimicking their superiors. Paige had smiled at her before they got in the car, and Marcel had winked while passing to sit in the row behind her.

The group stepped out and approached large wooden double doors. Thomas knocked loudly. A few seconds later, the door swung open to reveal a man in his early forties dressed in a crisp suit. Black hair, thick jet-black beard. A scar split his left eyebrow in half and continued down his cheek. The strong appearance contrasted with the formal attire.

"Lord Ragon was not expecting you, Thomas." His tone stayed polite.

Thomas waved a hand. "These are extraordinary circumstances."

"If this is because of the attack, Lord Ragon expects you to deal with it."

Thomas glanced at Leah with cold eyes, then looked back. "This has nothing to do with the attack."

"Then why are you—"

"For fuck's sake, Bedivere, you know I wouldn't be here if it wasn't important. Just let us in and send word to Father that we've arrived."

The butler's face grew stern, but he bowed and let them in.

Leah stepped inside and stopped. The ceiling stretched up at least two stories, a glass chandelier the size of a small car hanging above marble stairs. Paintings covered every wall—some showed wars from centuries past, others were more abstract. Red was the predominant color. Subtle compared to the rest of the space, which used more muted tones, but there. Deep burgundy leather couches lined both sides. Midway up the central stairs, a large sword with a plain silver shield hung in front of it.

Bedivere gestured for them to sit before walking through a side door.

Thomas sat next to Maria, who seemed to have regained her strength, though her attitude remained subdued. Marcel and Paige sat on either side of Leah. Marcel sat firmly, keeping a stoic expression. Paige looked around with wide eyes at the decorations.

Leah's pulse hammered in her throat. Months of planning, of doing The Family's bidding, of hiding—all for this moment. She had to convince the Ancient One to train her in the dark arts of the Tree of Death. Mastering that power could be the only thing to give her an edge over Helen. She'd hoped the Infinity Board attack would help persuade him. The butler's attitude now casts doubt on that.

Our angle should be that Helen will eventually come for him as well. We can eliminate her on his behalf.

You're awake!

We have been working hard to get here. I am still exhausted, but I was not going to miss this crucial encounter.

Knowing Asmodeus was up and aware gave Leah some comfort. Before they could continue their discussion, Bedivere returned.

"Lord Ragon is not interested. He asks that you kindly escort yourselves out."

Cold dread washed down Leah's spine. Thomas and Marcel stood in unison and turned to leave, closely followed by Maria. Paige stood idle, looking between the group and Leah, who jumped to her feet.

"I'm not leaving until I speak with him." Leah kept her voice firm.

The butler cocked his head, taken aback. "Apologies, Miss, but that is not possible. Lord Ragon was clear. He is not accepting any visitors."

"Enough, Leah. It's time to go." Marcel approached her, voice low.

"No." Leah pulled back before the vampire could grab her. "None of you understand. Helen's attack on the bar is only the beginning. She'll hunt down and kill all of you." She turned and yelled toward the back, "And that includes you as well, Lord Ragon. Your life is at stake here!"

"Leah, please... stop this." Marcel's voice trembled. For the first time, Leah detected something odd in his tone. Fear.

We cannot leave. We must get him to train us.

Leah looked down at the scar that coiled around her left arm and saw a blue glimpse. The Librarian's eye had appeared on the carpet and stared back at her.

"I'm sorry, but leaving is not an option for me. I need to speak to Lord Ragon. Now." Leah walked past Bedivere toward the door he'd gone through.

"Leah, don't..." Marcel's voice followed her, but she carried on.

This was wild, but Leah was desperate. Her friends' lives were on the line, and she wasn't going to give up until she rescued them. Helen had to pay for everything she'd done.

The butler made no attempt to stop her as she opened the door and stepped inside a warm living room, dimly lit by a fireplace. Leather furniture filled the space, and a large rug covered the floor. Unlike the lobby, this room had only one painting on the wall—a tall man who seemed about fifty years old with long, straight white hair, his arms behind his back. He wore a smug expression and looked back at Leah with his protruding chin and high cheekbones slightly tilted upward. He wore an old military uniform.

"Excuse me, Lord Ragon? I need to speak to you!" she called loudly into the dark living room.

A growl made her freeze. She turned and saw a small dog staring back with beady eyes. Its ears bent backward, and it bared his teeth. Despite its attempts to be intimidating, the dog looked more like a plush toy than a guard dog. Still, it barked a couple of times, its barking much deeper and louder than one would expect from a small, cute dog. Leah took a step back, calling on energy. She didn't expect to find a dog here. It looked seconds from attacking when its ears perked up, and it sat on his hind legs.

Leah frowned. Then something rattled behind her.

She turned, calling on *Tiferet*. Pressure built behind her eyes. The light in the room became intense, almost blinding, but whatever moved was too quick. A wisp of air rushed behind her. She spun again. Two flashes of red light stared back at her, and sharp, stabbing pain fired through her chest.

Leah looked down, stunned, as her vision went back to normal. In the dim light, she could see a wrist protruding from her chest. But that was impossible. Where was the hand?

Her hands began to shake as warm liquid spread around her shirt, sliding down her chest. Leah looked back up at the shadow in front of her. Except it was no longer a shadow but the man from the painting, staring back at her with a flat expression. He pulled back his hand with one swift motion, and pain seared through her as blood sprayed free from her. Her legs gave out, a cold took over her, and she fell to the floor, landing on the blood-stained rug.

Lord Ragon took out a handkerchief and began to wipe the blood from his hand.

"Bedivere, please come clean this up." His voice remained calm.

Leah gasped, her mouth failing to work as blood poured from the wound. Nausea boiled up her throat. Her pulse beat rapidly in her ears, matching the waves of blood pouring out from her. Footsteps rushed in. A door opened behind her.

This cannot be it. This cannot... Asmodeus whispered in her mind.

"Apologies, my Lord. I tried to tell her off."

"So I heard. No matter. I do hate losing a good rug, though. That one was a gift from Nicholas II. Try to be careful when cleaning it; it's a relic."

"Of course, my Lord. What about the girl?"

"You can dispose of her. I don't want Zeus feasting on the body. Her blood smells...off."

Leah's mind drifted in and out as cold sweat slid down her forehead. An eyelid formed and opened in the soaked rug next to her. The blue eye stared back at her. No expression. No words. Only silent judgment. And behind that eye, Leah knew her friend's kidnapper watched. Sarah and Isaac, alone in that Library, forever. All because she pushed her luck. All because she entered a house uninvited. All because she made a deal that comprised them. All because of her.

Something within her began to burn. As it pulsed, cold spread across her skin and the pain faded to nothing. At first, it covered her body. Then it started to shrink and focus on the wound in her chest.

We are not done. Asmodeus took over.

"I'm... not done... yet..." Leah managed to whisper between ragged breaths.

"Huh? What did the girl say?" Lord Ragon sounded annoyed.

Leah's body twitched and contorted as the room's temperature dropped. The fire was reduced to embers, throwing the room into more darkness. Her arms were pulled upward, raising her to her feet like a rag doll on puppet strings. Strength flowed back quickly. The hole inside of her shifted, bones cracking and reshaping. She screamed as the stab wound wound in her chest sealed beneath a layer of obsidian skin. Marbled black veins spread across her chest like cracks in ice, pulsing once, twice—then receding, leaving only a small black scar where Lord Ragon's hand had pierced through. Finally, her breathing stabilized. The invisible strings that dragged her up were cut, and Leah landed on her feet. The dog hid behind one of the couches.

"I said I'm not done."

Lord Ragon cocked his head in amusement, and his lips curled into a smile. "*Gharab Tzerek*. Death rejection. That explains the spoiled scent. A Mystic that fiddles with the Tree of Death."

"Lord Ragon, we need to talk. It's urgent." Leah's voice came out steady. Energy surged through her, and with it, confidence.

The vampire eyed her up and down with predatory red eyes, which remained focused briefly on the blue eye that had appeared on the rug. His smile widened, and he limped toward Leah. Every other step he took made a thumping hollow sound on the wooden floor, until he stepped particularly hard on the blue eye.

"No corruption left either..." He grabbed Leah's chin with cold fingers and raised her head up, inspecting her with seemingly X-ray vision she'd only seen Helen perform before. What was the vampire looking for? "Oh, I see. There is a lot more than meets the eye with you." He snapped his fingers. "Bedivere, get the dining room ready. We're having guests." He glanced at Leah's bloodied shirt with the hole over her chest. "And find this young lady something clean to wear. That won't do for dinner."

CHAPTER 16
LORD RAGON

The scar on Leah's chest ached with every breath. Lord Ragon had stabbed her through the heart only ten minutes ago. Now, she sat at his dinner table, wearing borrowed clothes that smelled faintly of lavender and old wood.

Thomas and Maria sat across from her. Marcel and Paige flanked her on either side. Everyone kept glancing at her, but nobody spoke. Her leg bounced under the table. She forced herself to look around the room instead of meeting their stares.

The dining hall looked like a museum. Crossed swords hung on one wall, their blades etched with symbols Leah didn't recognize. Above them, a family crest showed a bat with spread wings and a knight's helmet perched on its head. Everything was deep crimson. On the opposite wall, an axe with gems embedded in the handle caught the light from the chandelier overhead. Even the silverware had the family crest stamped into each piece.

What threw her off most was the dog. It sat next to her chair, panting and staring up at her with bright eyes. Black and white curly fur. A tail that curled like a pom-pom. The dark patches around its ears and eyes made it look like a raccoon. Getting stabbed by the oldest vampire in the world, then sitting at dinner next to his fluffy dog ten minutes later. Yeah, that hadn't been on Leah's bingo card for today.

They all stood when Lord Ragon entered wearing a crisp black suit, white shirt, and blood red tie.

He stopped at the head of the table opposite them. "Sit."

Leah dropped back into her chair. The dog trotted past her and settled near Lord Ragon's feet. A server appeared immediately and began filling their wine glasses.

"Maria and Thomas." Lord Ragon's voice was quiet but carried weight. "Who are these three you have brought me?"

"My name is Marcel Hernandez, my Lord." Marcel bowed his head slightly. "It is an honor."

Paige raised her hand in a casual wave. "I'm Paige Jones. Werewolf."

Lord Ragon's eyes narrowed just slightly. "You smell like a Chimera."

Paige froze. "What?"

"You are a Chimera, not a werewolf, yes? The one Maria took in. Own the name. Do not let others weaponize your heritage against you."

Paige's mouth opened, then closed. She nodded once, something shifting in her expression.

"Leah Ackerman," Leah said.

"Welcome to Ragon Manor." Lord Ragon gestured to the table.

Leah tried to follow Thomas and Maria's lead with the formalities and bow, but the black scar tissue under her borrowed shirt pulled tight. She wondered what would have happened if he had aimed for her head instead of her chest. The thought made her skin prickle. But something else stirred inside her. Some instinct that said Lord Ragon was testing her. That he respected strength, not cowering.

She opened her mouth to speak.

House staff entered carrying silver trays. The smell of roasted meat hit her first and her stomach twisted hard. A thick cut of ribeye appeared in front of her, the surface caramelized and glistening, steam rising off the plate. Mashed potatoes whipped smooth with butter. Rice pilaf with bright green herbs. Two whole roasted chickens sat in the center of the table, skin golden and crispy.

Holy shit, even my mouth is watering. And I do not technically have one. Asmodeus said. *We have not eaten like this in months. Finally, something other than those microwave meals.*

Leah felt saliva pool under her tongue. She couldn't remember the last time she had seen food like this.

Everyone sat still until Lord Ragon spoke.

"What are you waiting for?" He gestured with one hand. "Eat."

Leah and Asmodeus moved together, reaching for the steak. The first bite melted on her tongue. Rich. Savory. Perfect. She barely stopped herself from moaning. Across the table, Maria and Paige tore into the roasted chicken. Thomas and Marcel drank from tall goblets filled with what had to be blood.

Lord Ragon's plate held something different. A cut of dark meat, nearly purple where the blood pooled thickest. Steam rose from it like it had been killed minutes ago, the flesh still raw. He slowly cut small pieces, picking them up with his fork and chewing with deliberate patience.

He caught Leah staring and set his silverware down. "I suppose you are wondering how I can enjoy this while those two drink blood, yes?"

"No." Leah swallowed her bite. "I'm more surprised by how you eat. It's so... formal."

Lord Ragon's lips curved slightly. "I enjoy every bit of my meal. Centuries of hunger while watching humans waste world-class meals set before them teaches one to appreciate the art of eating."

"Yeah." Leah took another bite. "And you can justify that sort of manner along with killing people without giving them a chance to speak?"

"Leah!" Thomas half-rose from his seat.

Maybe it was *Gharab Tzerek* still running through her system. Maybe it was the steak. But something in her had shifted. Lord Ragon was powerful. But he didn't stop her from reviving herself. That meant something.

She felt Asmodeus's approval ripple through their connection.

"Leah!" Thomas half-rose from his seat.

Lord Ragon raised one hand at Thomas without looking away from Leah. His reddish eyes held hers. "Is breaking into someone's home uninvited also a habit of yours?"

"If what I need to discuss is life or death? Yes." Leah met his stare. "And that includes your life, Lord Ragon." She ignored the blue eye that formed on the wall behind Maria. The Librarian watched but didn't interfere.

Maria leaned forward. "You insolent child."

Lord Ragon raised his hand again. This time Maria went silent. He studied Leah for a long moment. "The mania from *Gharab Tzerek* still affects you."

Before Leah could respond, he turned to Thomas. "Care to explain why you brought this girl into my home?"

"Yes, my Lord. She helped us escape the attack."

"Helped you?" Leah's voice rose. "I saved you. I warned you it was coming and I fought to get you out."

"Silence."

The word burrowed into her ear like a worm. Her throat locked. Magic wrapped around her vocal cords and squeezed tight. When she tried to speak, not even air would pass.

Panic spiked through her. Her jaw worked uselessly. She slammed her palm flat on the table, but no sound escaped. The wells in her chest surged in response. *Malchut* pressed against her ribs. *Gamaliel* burned in her throat where the magic held her silent.

She couldn't even scream.

Lord Ragon gestured for Thomas to continue. Thomas pressed his lips together, clearly struggling with something internal.

"My Lord, if I may." Marcel placed a hand on his chest and bowed. Lord Ragon nodded. "The attack was not coincidence. It was planned. Methodical. They would have succeeded if not for Leah and Paige."

Leah forced herself to breathe through her nose. In. Out. Her hands trembled on the table.

Marcel leaned forward. "The Infinity Board knew exactly where to strike. They brought the Warrior, the Elemental, and the Invulnerable. Full force. Their goal was clear: wipe us out completely."

"Who would betray the Family?" Maria's voice had an edge.

"I believe it was Edmond." Marcel kept his tone measured. "Recently demoted. Outside the bar when the attack began, fighting Leah and Paige."

Leah tried to speak. To argue. Edmond had been many things, but a betrayer seemed wrong. Her throat wouldn't budge. She grabbed the edge of the table until her knuckles went white.

"I caught him attacking Leah," Paige said quietly. "He insulted me. I decapitated him. The Infinity Board found his body after."

"Why would he do such a thing?" Lord Ragon asked.

Marcel's explanation continued but Leah barely heard it. Sweat beaded on her forehead. Her heart hammered too fast. The magic wouldn't let go. She tried pulling on *Gamaliel*, worked to force the command away, but it held firm.

Maria grabbed a piece of chicken and gestured with it. "Why are we blaming Edmond when she is the Mystic? She was part of the Infinity Board. She could have planned this whole thing."

Leah's vision swam. She wanted to scream at them. To defend herself. Her fist hit the table again.

"She does not have access to our defensive positions," Marcel said. "Only someone in the Family's inner circle would know those details. Someone who sat at this table for years. Also, she has been clear about her objective. She wants to kill King Helen."

Thomas raised an eyebrow. "That could be a lie. I think this was her plan from the beginning. She told us two nights ago that she wanted to meet the Ancient One, learn from him, then kill King Helen. After we refused, she betrayed us. Used the attack to force her way here."

This is not good.

The wells churned inside Leah. Begging. Pleading. She shoved back from the table slightly, her chair scraping against the floor. Her whole body felt like a live wire.

"And why is she here, Thomas?" Lord Ragon's voice held no emotion. Something about his tone made Leah's instincts scream danger. Even through her panic, she felt the wells recoil slightly.

"I..." Thomas looked at Maria. Fear showed in both their eyes for the first time.

"Do I need to command you?" Lord Ragon picked up his silver knife casually.

Thomas bowed his head and pressed his hands together. "Forgive me, my Lord. She commanded me to bring her here. Using *Gamaliel*."

Lord Ragon grinned. "Ah. So, her cursed speech overpowered yours." He looked at Leah and a smile crossed his face. "You are full of surprises, Leah Ackerman."

He threw the knife in one swift motion without breaking eye contact with Leah. The blade cut through several strands of Maria's hair before embedding in the wall. Everyone jumped.

Thomas stood, his body tensing like he was preparing for a fight he knew he would lose.

Lord Ragon glared at him. Thomas sat back down.

"Do not be embarrassed, Thomas. This one is unusual. That demon of hers amplifies her connection to the Tree of Death. No Mystic can do that alone."

Cold washed through Leah. How could he see Asmodeus? Not even Thomas had managed that.

Lord Ragon turned his full attention on her. "You may speak again if you tell me the truth. Did you plan the attack?"

The pressure on her throat eased just enough. The words came out on their own. "No. I did not."

"And why do you want to kill Helen Nielsen?"

"Because she betrayed me." The words scraped past her teeth.

Lord Ragon looked at Thomas with satisfaction. "You and Maria will leave now. Gather the survivors. The treaty is broken. You are at war." He chuckled softly. "Your Family is at war, I should say. These two"—he pointed at Marcel and Paige—"will stay here with us. I need sparring partners for this one. Between the two of you, we can cover the full moon cycle."

Leah stared at him. Her mouth fell open slightly. She had done it. Months of planning. Months of hiding what she was. Months of working for Thomas and Maria. All of it had led here.

He had agreed.

Thomas spoke with more force than before. "My Lord, I must express serious concern about this decision."

"Thomas." Lord Ragon's voice was patient. "You are loyal. Respectful. But sometimes, emotion clouds judgment. Leah here offers to kill the one who commanded the raid on your bar. My training her is the best help you will receive in this war. Moreover, there are forces in this universe that even you cannot understand." He waved one hand respectfully. "You are excused. I wish you good fortune in the days ahead." The dismissal in his tone was absolute.

Thomas clenched his jaw but stood. Maria followed. They both glared at Leah before leaving the dining room.

Lord Ragon rose to his feet. "Leah, you are not in the best state of mind. The mania from *Gharab Tzerek* still runs through you. Rest tonight. Let it pass. We begin training tomorrow at dusk. Meet me in the courtyard." He looked at Marcel and Paige. "Please, enjoy dessert."

Marcel stood and bowed. Paige and Leah followed his lead.

"Thank you," Leah managed to say.

Lord Ragon paused. He looked at her with those ancient eyes. "You may speak freely now."

Her throat opened. Air rushed in. The magic released its grip all at once and she gasped. The relief was so sudden she almost collapsed back into her chair.

"You are welcome." Lord Ragon's expression was

unreadable. The small dog followed him as he left the dining room.

Leah sat down hard and rubbed her throat. Her hands were still shaking.

She watched Lord Ragon disappear through the doorway. Then her eyes caught on something. The knife he had thrown at Maria had embedded in the wall where the Librarian's blue eye had been watching.

Exactly where the eye had been.

CHAPTER 17
HURTFUL TRUTHS

After pecan pie, Bedivere came to escort them to their chambers. Leah followed Paige and Marcel through the living room. The bloodied rug was gone, replaced with something cream-colored and pristine. No stains on the hardwood either. Like the fight never happened.

They climbed a circular staircase in a second living room lined with more eccentric pieces. A large devil mask caught Leah's eye—bright colors, huge bulging eyes, features that looked almost alive. Something about it made her skin prickle. She hurried up the stairs to catch up.

"We prepared visitors' chambers for you and got you some fresh clothes in the dressers," Bedivere said, glancing at Paige's torn shirt and jeans.

Paige crossed her arms. "Sorry, I didn't have time to grab my yoga pants before I shifted."

"We think we got your measurements right, but if something is too tight or too loose, please let us know." Bedivere bowed once, turned, and left.

They exchanged glances before each stood in front of their own door. Leah walked in and stopped. The room was easily twice the size of her motel room. A king-size bed with thick pillows. A massive dresser against one wall. A door on the side swung open.

Paige appeared in the doorway. "Looks like we're sharing a bathroom. Check out the marble."

Leah peered inside. Black and white marble covered the floor and walls. Double sinks with brass fixtures. A clawfoot tub in the corner that looked deep enough to drown in.

"Better than the bathrooms at the academy," Leah said.

Paige scoffed and grinned. "By a long shot."

Leah sat on the edge of the bed. The mattress sank under her weight, softer than anything she'd felt in months. They'd done it. Months of planning, months of running, months of working for The Family while hiding what she was. And it worked. Lord Ragon agreed to train her.

He stabbed you through the heart, Asmodeus whispered.

Leah snorted and fell back, arms spread. She closed her eyes.

The round table appeared. Asmodeus sat across from her, steam rising from a teacup in his hands. Another cup waited for Leah. She sat and took a sip. Ginger burned down her throat.

"That was close," Leah said. "I really thought that was it."

"What you did was risky. Bordering on reckless."

"We didn't have another option."

Asmodeus took a slow sip. "No, we did not. If we left empty-handed, I am not certain where we would have gone next."

Leah touched her chest where the black scar was. Through the borrowed shirt, she could feel the raised skin. "I didn't know you could use *Gharab Tzerek*. I mean, I figured it was possible, but something about it feels wrong."

"It was our last resort." Asmodeus set his cup down. "After that encounter with the Elemental at headquarters, when we nearly burned the place down with *Golohab*, I realized some wells are more difficult to control than others."

Leah remembered waking up in the hospital wing. Zafirah sitting beside her bed, two IVs in each arm.

"That conversation changed how I approached the Tree of Death," Asmodeus continued. "The corruption does not affect me, but that is not the only consequence of using those wells."

"Zafirah banned *Golohab* and *Gamaliel*," Leah said. "She never mentioned *Gharab Tzerek*."

"Because she assumed it would be used as a last resort. If the alternative is death, I do not believe the Infinity Board would prefer that outcome, considering how powerful we have become. That said, I still remember William at the academy. He reeked of corruption after using it. His mind was all but gone by the end of that fight. I have been hesitant to use it again."

"I still feel the mania," Leah admitted. "It's like everything's buzzing under my skin."

"That will fade." Asmodeus picked up his cup again. "Lord Ragon knows much about the Tree of Death. We should learn what we can."

They drank in silence. The tea warmed Leah from the inside, grounding her. She'd done it. She was here. She had a real chance now.

"We really ignored her warning about *Gamaliel*, huh"? Leah said.

Asmodeus raised an eyebrow. "You enjoy cursed speech far too much."

"It makes things easier."

"Until you lose your voice entirely. There is only so much your body can withstand."

"I know, but—"

"Someone is approaching," Asmodeus said, cutting her off.

Leah pulled herself out of the mental space and opened her eyes. Two large orbs stared back at her in the dim light. She jerked upright, energy flooding her arms.

"Whoa!" Paige waved both hands. "I didn't mean to scare you."

Leah let the energy drain away. "Shit. Sorry. I'm a little on edge."

"I figured." Paige tilted her head, studying Leah's face. Then her nose wrinkled. "You smell like blood, and your shirt is different."

Leah looked down. The borrowed shirt was clean, but there were flecks of dried blood on her arms. "Yeah. Lord Ragon tried to kill me."

"What?" Paige sat on the edge of the bed, close enough that Leah could smell earth and sweat on her. "Before dinner?"

Leah nodded. "He put his hand through my chest."

"And you're alive!?"

"*Gharab Tzerek*." Leah rubbed her sternum where the scar was. "Death rejection."

Paige whistled low. "That's the same well Dean White used at the academy. He looked pretty mangled when he did it."

"Yeah. Asmodeus helps keep the corruption away."

Paige went still. Her eyes widened. "Asmodeus?"

Shit, Asmodeus thought.

The name hung in the air. *Shit*. She'd said it without

thinking, the exhaustion and leftover mania making her careless.

"Asmodeus," Paige repeated. Her voice went flat. "The same Asmodeus from the Outpost? The one that possessed your father? The demon that killed Alma?"

Leah opened her mouth, but nothing came out. Her hands started shaking.

Paige stood, backing toward the bathroom door. Her movements had changed. More animal than human. "It's him. The one that nearly killed all of us. The one you said died."

"Paige, wait. Let me explain."

"Explain what?" Paige's voice cracked. "That you're walking around with the demon that murdered our teacher? That killed how many people at the Outpost? That you've been lying this whole time?"

"The Infinity Board knows about him!" Leah stood. "He's changed. We've done good things together. If you'd just listen—"

"Listen?" Paige's lip curled, baring elongated teeth. "I watched that demon tear through the Outpost like we were nothing."

"That was Legion forcing him. That wasn't—"

"I don't care." Paige turned and walked toward the window. Her shoulders were hunched, her breathing too fast. Fur grew heavy on her arms. "If I'd known, I would've let Edmond finish you off at the bar. Can't believe I actually thought..." She shook her head. "Doesn't matter."

Leah followed her to the window. "Paige, please. Just talk to me."

"About what?" Paige yanked the window open. Cool air rushed in. "About how you're possessed by the thing that killed people I knew? You think we can be friends with that thing inside you? He's a demon."

"I'm not possessed. It's not like that."

"Sure looks like it from where I'm standing." Paige braced her hands on the windowsill. The moonlight washed over her skin. "Maria's waiting for me anyway. Full moon. I need to run."

"You don't have to go. We can—"

"Yeah, I do." Paige's voice went quiet. "Maria took me in when the others wouldn't. I'd do anything for my pack. And that means being the werewolf she believes I am, "She looked back at Leah. "At least with them, I know where I stand. With you? I don't know what's real and what's the demon talking."

Leah's throat closed. "Paige—"

But Paige was already changing. Her spine curved, bones shifting under skin. Fur sprouted along her arms. Her face elongated, jaw cracking as it reformed. In seconds, the massive wolf stood in her place. White fur with blond streaks catching the moonlight. Yellow eyes that looked nothing like Paige's.

The wolf stared at Leah for one long moment. Then it jumped.

Leah rushed to the window and watched Paige sprint across the moonlit field toward the tree line. Toward Maria, probably.

Leah stood at the window until Paige disappeared into the darkness. The field stretched out empty under the moon. Somewhere in the distance, a wolf howled.

She closed the window and turned back to the room. Her hands wouldn't stop shaking. The bed looked too big now. Too empty.

She will come around, Asmodeus said.

"Will she?"

Give her time.

Leah walked to the dresser and pulled out pajamas

from the bottom drawer. Blue cotton pants and a matching shirt. She changed in the bathroom with the door shut, then climbed into bed.

The mania was wearing off. She could feel it draining away, leaving exhaustion in its place. Her body hurt. The black scar on her chest throbbed with each heartbeat.

She'd gotten what she wanted. Lord Ragon agreed to train her. She was finally learning the Tree of Death properly. She had a real shot at Helen now.

But Gabe's face kept surfacing in her mind. The way he'd looked at her when he found out about Asmodeus. The way he'd stepped back like she was something dangerous. Something wrong.

And now Paige.

CHAPTER 18
THE DARK ART OF DEATH

Sleep didn't come easily. Every time Leah closed her eyes, she saw Paige's face. The way she'd looked at her through the window before jumping. Like Leah was something dangerous.

Leah rolled over and pulled the pillow over her head. Hours passed. Finally, exhaustion won.

The violet fog was just forming when someone knocked.

Leah groaned and cracked one eye open. Sunlight streamed through the curtains, and she glanced at a clock on the nightstand. She'd barely slept two hours.

The knock came again, sharper.

"Yes?" Her voice sounded rough.

"Miss?" Bedivere's voice filtered through the door. "Lord Ragon has summoned you."

Leah pushed herself upright and rubbed her face. Why would he call for her while the sun was still up? "Give me five minutes."

"Of course."

She dragged herself out of bed and pulled on jeans and the plain white T-shirt Bedivere had left in the dresser. Her stomach growled, but the thought of food made her feel sick. Too much had happened. Paige's words kept looping through her head.

At least with them, I know where I stand.

Leah splashed water on her face in the bathroom and stared at her reflection. The black dye job was growing out, and now roots of auburn showed at her scalp. She looked tired. Felt tired.

We should focus, Asmodeus said. *Lord Ragon would not summon us without purpose.*

Leah dried her face and headed for the door.

Bedivere stood in the hallway, patient as ever. He gestured down the corridor. "This way, please."

They walked through rooms Leah hadn't seen yet. More weird decorations covered the walls. Wooden sculptures that looked hand carved. Stone carvings of figures she didn't recognize. A globe sat on a side table, gold hinges gleaming. Everything in this place screamed money and age.

A door stood half-open ahead. Something small and white shot out and rushed straight for Leah.

The dog.

He sniffed her shoes, then backed up, ears flattening.

Leah knelt and held out her hand. "Hey, little one."

Zeus crept forward and sniffed her fingers. After a moment, he licked them, and his tail started wagging. Within seconds, he was all over her, circling and jumping for pets.

At least someone here didn't hate her.

Someone cleared their throat.

Leah looked up. Lord Ragon stood at the end of the corridor, wearing another black suit. His red eyes watched her with that same unreadable expression.

She got to her feet quickly. "Sorry."

Lord Ragon tilted his head slightly and turned. The dog started to follow, but Lord Ragon spoke without looking back. "Zeus, stay. You know your limits."

Zeus's ears lowered. He sat and watched as Leah followed the Ancient One.

They reached a small door and Lord Ragon opened it, revealing a dimly lit staircase leading down. He was already descending before Leah pulled from *Tiferet*. Light bloomed around her, pushing back the darkness. The well hummed through her veins, warm and familiar.

"Close the door," Lord Ragon called up. "This will be dangerous. I do not want him sneaking in."

Leah glanced back at Zeus sitting in the hallway. She reached down and petted him one more time before closing the door.

The stairs were steep. At the bottom, Leah found a cramped basement full of objects wrapped in blankets or covered in plastic. Some kind of storage area. Everything had a place, but the space felt crowded.

"You can drop your *Tiferet*," Lord Ragon said from somewhere ahead. "We will not be using the Tree of Life here."

Leah hesitated, but then let the well fade. Her vision struggled to adjust. Lord Ragon's red eyes glowed in the darkness, two points of light near the back wall.

He moved, and something clicked. Part of the wall swung inward.

"Follow me."

Leah hurried forward and stubbed her toe on something metal. Pain shot through her foot. She bit back a curse and hopped on one leg toward the opening, pulling the hidden door shut behind her.

The tunnel was narrow. Leah could hear Lord Ragon's prosthetic leg, the hollow thump every other step. She remembered her conversation with Paige about vampire regeneration after she'd killed Edmond. Why hadn't Lord Ragon's leg grown back? Was it because he was the first vampire? She'd have to ask Marcel later.

Her stomach twisted. Why was she trusting him? Lord Ragon was still a vampire. A killer. The man was calculating. Dangerous.

And yet here she was, following him into a hidden tunnel beneath his house.

You are having doubts, Asmodeus observed.

Shouldn't I?

Perhaps. But we are here now. And we need what he can teach us.

I know.

Then stop overthinking.

The tunnel ended at a set of doors. Lord Ragon opened the one straight ahead and stepped through. Leah followed and found herself in a large dungeon. Metal cells lined both sides. Bare bulbs hung from the ceiling, throwing weak yellow light across stone floors. They descended a few steps into the space. The air felt cool and damp.

A clever way to move around during the day without facing sunlight.

Lord Ragon walked to the far end of the dungeon, maybe twenty-five yards away. He turned to face her.

"I want you to show me each well of the Tree of Death you can control. Don't hold back."

Are you ready? Leah asked Asmodeus.

Ready.

Leah drew a breath and pulled from *Nehemoth*. Cold swept through her. Her breath misted white in front of her mouth. The temperature in the dungeon dropped fast. Energy built slowly, like water filling a basin. She raised her arm and focused on the void between them.

Lord Ragon shot forward. The pull yanked him across

the space. Metal cell doors flung open and slammed against their frames. He planted his foot hard and stopped himself a few feet from her.

"Good." His voice stayed calm. "Stop now."

Leah tried to release the well. It took several seconds before *Nehemoth* finally let go. The pull faded.

Lord Ragon raised an eyebrow. "Your start is strong, but stopping is difficult for you. I assume the longer you use *Nehemoth*, the harder it becomes to release."

Leah nodded and flexed her fingers. "Usually, I switch it to *Malchut*. Pushing instead of pulling. That makes it easier."

"Makes sense. Sister wells. Two sides of the same coin." Lord Ragon clasped his hands behind his back. "However, you need to sharpen your control of *Nehemoth* itself. When you invoke the well, you must command it. Not the other way around. Make it submit through your emotions. That way, you can stop cleanly without relying on *Malchut*."

"Understood."

"Good. You seem to have the most basic well handled." He cleared his throat. "Show me *Gamaliel*—your cursed speech."

Leah frowned. "What should I order you to do?"

"It doesn't matter. You will not be able to overcome mine." Lord Ragon raised his chin slightly.

Leah pulled from *Gamaliel* and said, "Bow."

"Bow." Lord Ragon mimicked.

Energy coiled around her throat immediately, tightening like a fist. Black threads shot from her mouth, but in the next instant, she found herself staring at the stone floor. She didn't remember moving. Didn't remember dropping to her knees. The position hurt. She tried to push herself back up, but her body refused to obey.

Lord Ragon's hand squeezed her shoulder. Suddenly,

she could move again. She stood quickly and rubbed her throat.

"Your cursed speech is quite strong. Most people cannot even produce the threads against mine." His expression softened slightly. Something that might have been pride. Then it vanished. "But you struggle with the aftermath, yes? Your throat."

"If I use it too much, I can't talk for days."

"Understandable." Lord Ragon began pacing. "But there are levels to cursed speech. You think only in commands. If you use it more suggestively, the intensity reduces, as do the consequences. But if you scream a command, it's stronger and damages your throat worse. The best users manipulate rather than command. Do you understand?"

Leah nodded.

"Good. Now show me your chest."

Leah took a step back. "What?"

"Your scar. I need to see how much corruption remains." His tone stayed clinical.

"Oh. Right." Leah pulled down the collar of her T-shirt and looked down at the black mark. Deep purple at the center where Lord Ragon had stabbed her. Black veins spider-webbed outward.

Lord Ragon stepped closer and studied the wound from different angles. His red eyes narrowed.

Leah's cheeks blushed, having a man this close to her, eyeing her chest. She looked up at the ceiling.

"A scar like that, straight through the heart, should be far darker," Lord Ragon said. "These veins should cover half your chest by now." He straightened. "I doubt your life expectancy is considerably reduced. Your demon is containing the corruption. However, this remains a last resort. Two or three more scars like this will drive you mad or kill you. Possibly both, the madness leading to your inevitable death."

William's face flashed through Leah's mind. His manic laughter. The black veins covering his skin. The madness in his eyes before she'd killed him.

"How many times can I use *Gharab Tzerek* before that happens?" Her voice came out quieter than she wanted.

Lord Ragon shook his head. "I can't say for certain. Treat it as your final option."

"But *Gharab Tzerek* only activates in life-or-death situations. How am I supposed to know when I've crossed the line?"

"Have someone keep watch. Your demon could do it." Lord Ragon tilted his head. "You two have developed a symbiotic relationship that is quite unique. Use that."

Warmth crept up Leah's neck. "Yeah. I guess."

"We will discuss this further another time. For now, let us focus on the remaining wells. *Thagirion* is tricky. Can you pull it off?"

Leah pulled from *Thagirion*. A familiar chill settled over her like a blanket. Sounds muffled. The lights turned sickly yellow. There was rubble on the left side of the dungeon now. One of the metal cells lay on the ground, door hanging off its hinges.

But Lord Ragon held her attention. He looked taller. More imposing. All his limbs were intact in this place. But instead of radiating light like humans did, he seemed made of darkness itself. Two red orbs burned where his eyes should be, cutting through the gloom. Watching her.

A shiver ran down Leah's spine.

Keep it together, Asmodeus said. *What did you expect of the oldest vampire alive?*

"Good. Very good." Lord Ragon's voice sounded distant, muffled. "Drop it now."

Leah released the well. The dungeon snapped back to normal. Lord Ragon stood in front of her, whole and present. She swallowed hard.

He showed no reaction to her discomfort. "Now show me your control of *Samael*."

Leah looked around for a target.

"On me, you silly girl." Impatience edged into his voice.

"Oh. Yes. Sorry."

Leah stood firm and let Asmodeus guide her hands. He pressed her knuckles together, one set of fingers pointing at her chest, the other at Lord Ragon's. She closed her eyes.

Samael requires rage, Asmodeus said. *Focus on Helen.*

Helen's face surfaced immediately. That smile when she'd ordered the raid on the bar. The way she sat on her throne while everyone praised her. While she was the reason Sarah and Isaac were held captive. While she pretended to be a savior.

Heat built in Leah's chest. Not the warm pressure of *Malchut*. This felt hungry.

More.

Helen had stolen everything. The crown. The power. She'd turned Leah into a fugitive. Made her friends see her as dangerous. And she got to sit there and play King while the world worshipped her.

The rage cracked through Leah like lightning.

Asmodeus breathed in sharply. The well activated, reaching for Lord Ragon, ready to drain his life force.

Nothing.

Leah gasped and tried to pull harder. Still nothing. Like trying to breathe in a vacuum. Her lungs burned. She took a deeper breath. Her chest ached.

"Very good." Lord Ragon sounded impressed. "You can drop it now. There is nothing for you to consume here."

Leah and Asmodeus released the well. Her body went

weak. Her hands dropped to her sides. She fell to one knee, gasping. Cold sweat covered her face.

"What the hell?" Leah managed.

"*Samael* consumes life energy. Vampires are undead creatures, kept in perpetual stasis by the Tree of Death. There was nothing for you to drain from me."

Leah wiped sweat from her forehead. "Then why did you make me try?"

"Even though I do not have that type of energy, I still felt the pull." Lord Ragon clasped his hands behind his back. "Keep in mind you do not always need deep breaths. Sometimes, quick, short breaths are enough to take energy from your target. This will allow you better control. Does that make sense?"

"It does." Leah pushed herself back to her feet. Her ribs hurt. Nausea rolled through her stomach.

"Good. Let us move on." Lord Ragon watched her with those red eyes. "Are you tired already?"

Leah ground her teeth together and stood straighter, ignoring the pain.

"*Agshekeloh* is difficult to evaluate in a dungeon with no life around us, so we will leave that one for later. How do you feel about *Golohab*?"

"I can't control it very well," Leah remembered training with Zafirah. How the Sage had to engulf her in a sphere of water to put out the chaotic fire.

"Good. You know your limitations." Lord Ragon nodded once. "Just like *Samael*, *Golohab* feeds off Tree of Life energy. If you were to use it in a space like this, especially without supervision, it would burn you alive."

"So how am I supposed to wield it?"

"*Golohab* is destruction in its purest form. It has a mind of its own. A monster that hungers for every living being, every bit of Tree of Life energy around it." Lord Ragon's expression darkened. "Because you have a demon within you, I am not entirely certain how it will react. We can examine that later. Once that monster is unleashed, even I might have trouble controlling it."

Silence fell between them. Leah's skin prickled.

Lord Ragon cleared his throat. "Now tell me what you know about the upper three wells."

Leah thought back to the black book she'd been studying. She'd left it at the motel with the rest of her things. Hopefully, there were more complete books here. "I don't know much about *Thaumiel* or *Ghogiel*, but I can wield *Satariel*."

Lord Ragon's eyes widened. He didn't hide his surprise this time. "*Satariel*? It has been centuries since I've seen someone use that. How many shadows are you able to conjure? When did you first gain access to that power?"

"Three." Pride crept into Leah's voice. "It happened when I got jumped by Rootworkers. We were trapped in a Voodoo circle that cut off our connection to the Trees. That's when Asmodeus saw two flames—one green and black, the other blue and turquoise. He chose the green and black. First time we used that well. It helped us escape."

"When you conjured the shadows, did they evaporate shortly after?"

The question caught Leah off guard. "Yes. But lately, whenever I create new ones, they don't just disappear. I have to reabsorb them, and it's uncomfortable."

Lord Ragon's lips curved into something resembling a smile. He nodded slowly. "Impressive. Short shadows can be conjured for a few seconds and will evaporate on their own. They are not as strong as corporeal shadows, and they consume more *Satariel* energy. However, they are usually safer to use than full shadows."

Leah frowned. "Why is that?"

"*Satariel* is tricky. The longer a shadow exists, the greater the risks involved." Lord Ragon started to say more, then stopped. His head tilted slightly, listening to something Leah couldn't hear. He pulled his phone from his pocket.

"We will go into more details later. You should eat something." He gestured toward the tunnel. "Head back. I will meet you there."

Leah wanted to ask more. About the shadows. About the risks. About why he'd agreed to train her in the first place. But something in his posture told her the conversation was over.

"Thank you. For this. For teaching me."

Lord Ragon chuckled. A dry, humorless sound. "I have not taught you much yet, child. But this gives me an idea of where to focus our training."

Leah bowed slightly and turned toward the exit. She made it a few steps before something made her stop.

"Yes?" Lord Ragon was walking toward one of the cells.

"Could I ask you something?"

"You want to know why I agreed to train you."

Warmth flooded Leah's face. Was it that obvious? She nodded.

"When you live as long as I have, you begin to think you have seen everything." Lord Ragon's voice carried through the dungeon. "When I saw the Librarian observing you and smelled the odd scent in your blood, I knew there was more to you than dyed black hair and honeycomb eyes. Add to that your intention of murdering King Helen for a presumed betrayal, and you had my attention."

Leah's pulse quickened. Her suspicions were correct. Somehow, Lord Ragon could see the Librarian. Up until now, she hadn't met anyone else who could see that blue eye stalking her. Not even the occasional druid who stopped by the bar.

She remembered part of his conversation with Thomas at dinner last night.

Moreover, there are forces and things in this universe that you cannot even understand.

"How can you see the Librarian?" Leah asked.

"That is a conversation for another day. Dinner should be ready soon. I will meet you there." Lord Ragon waved her off, ending the conversation.

Leah made her way back through the tunnel, up the stairs, and into the basement. Zeus was waiting at the top, tail wagging. He followed her through the hallways until she found her way back to the guest wing.

CHAPTER 19
TWENTY-SEVEN CHICKENS

The smell of rotisserie chicken and garlic potatoes hit Leah before she even opened the dining room door. Her stomach growled. Inside, Marcel and Paige sat across from each other at the long table, picking at their food in silence. Leah paused in the doorway. Paige was there. She hadn't been sure Paige would stick around after everything. Paige's eyes found her first, then immediately dropped to her plate. Marcel gave Leah a half smile.

"Good evening. Did you sleep okay?" Marcel asked.

"Yeah, all right. All things considered." Leah took the seat next to him. "What about you two?"

"Lovely sleep if I do say so myself," Marcel said.

Both Leah and Marcel looked at Paige, who rolled her eyes. "Good. Now leave me alone."

Leah bit back a smile despite herself. Even pissed off, Paige sounded exactly like she had back at the Outpost. Some things didn't change.

Marcel leaned forward slightly, lowering his voice. "Did something happen between you two? The tension is rather thick."

Paige's fork scraped against her plate.

"It's complicated," Leah said.

"I see." Marcel sat back.

Paige shoved a piece of chicken into her mouth and chewed aggressively.

Leah glanced between them, her jaw tight. She wanted to say something, anything to cut through whatever wall Paige had built. But before she could find the words, the door opened.

Lord Ragon entered, Zeus, trotting at his heels. The dog's curly, black-and-white fur bounced with each step. Immediately, Paige and Marcel stood. Leah pushed back her chair and followed their lead.

"Evening, everyone. Let's eat." Lord Ragon took his seat at the head of the table.

Everyone else sat back down, and Leah reached for the chicken. Marcel picked up his goblet, drinking slowly. His eyebrows shot up after the first sip. Lord Ragon cut into a thick, rare steak, blood pooling on his plate. Leah watched him for a moment, then glanced at Marcel's goblet.

"Does it taste good?" Leah asked.

Marcel paused, swirling the dark liquid in his goblet like someone examining wine. "This? This is extraordinary." He took another sip, savoring it. "Back in Chicago, blood tastes acrid. Bitter. Probably because we take people no one will miss. People full of fear and desperation."

He held up his goblet to the light. "But this? This has depth. Complexity. Like a vintage wine aged to perfection."

Leah wrinkled her nose. "You can taste a difference?"

"Blood carries the Tree of Life energy within it," Lord Ragon said, cutting another piece of steak. "We are creatures of the Tree of Death. When we consume blood, we consume that opposing energy. It sustains us in ways normal food cannot." He gestured with his knife. "The quality varies greatly. Health, emotional state, and even the person's connection to the Tree itself. All of it affects the taste."

Marcel nodded enthusiastically. "I have never tasted anything like this. What is it?"

"A willing donor," Lord Ragon said simply. "Someone healthy. Content. No fear, no desperation. I also maintain a collection of preserved blood from various sources accumulated over the centuries. Some from nobility. Some from Mystics with powerful connections to the Tree. Tonight, you are drinking from a former Queen, actually."

Marcel stared at his goblet with newfound reverence. "A Queen?"

Lord Ragon inclined his head. "I do not waste good blood on guests I do not respect."

Leah turned her attention to Paige, who had been silently tearing into her chicken throughout the entire exchange.

Asmodeus had called her unstable. Leah could see it now. Paige shifted between moods like someone flipping a switch. Laughing about decapitating vampires one moment, then cold and withdrawn the next. And that rage when she'd learned about Asmodeus—that had been something else entirely.

Leah pushed a potato around her plate. If she could just get Paige to sit down and talk, maybe they could work through this.

When everyone finished eating, Lord Ragon stood. "Follow me to the backyard."

Zeus started to follow, but Lord Ragon pointed at the door. "Stay."

The dog sat, ears drooping.

They stepped out onto the porch. Moonlight washed over the fields, stretching out farther than Leah could see. Lord Ragon led them down the steps and across the grass, past a metal fence. The air smelled like earth and dried hay. In the distance, a chicken coop sat near a cluster of trees. Soft clucking drifted on the breeze as the birds settled in for the night.

Lord Ragon stopped about twenty feet from the coop. He turned to face them. "Leah, you and Paige will be sparring tonight. We will take advantage of the full moon. I want to see how you hold your own against a Chimera with werewolf traits during a full moon. However, you are only allowed to use the Tree of Death wells. Steer away from *Golohab*. I do not want my field to burn away, but everything else is fair game."

Leah frowned. Everything else? That included *Samael*. She could drain Paige of all her energy and kill her.

Paige didn't seem worried. She pulled off her sweater and dropped it on the ground, then stretched her arms over her head. When she looked at Leah, her eyes had already started to change.

Paige's body trembled. Her head jerked to the side with a sharp crack. Fangs pushed through her gums. Bones shifted under her skin, lengthening and thickening. Within seconds, the creature from the alleyway stood a few feet away. White fur with blond streaks shone in the moonlight. Those beady yellow eyes locked onto Leah. Paige growled, low and threatening, her lips pulling back to show rows of sharp teeth. Her ears flattened against her skull.

She will not hold back, Leah. We have to go at it with everything we have. Asmodeus said, his voice tight.

Leah squared her shoulders. Her stomach twisted. She didn't want to hurt Paige. Not like this. Not when everything between them was already so broken.

"Begin!" Lord Ragon's voice cut through the night.

Paige lunged. Leah barely had time to register the movement before massive claws swept toward her face.

Instinct kicked in. She pulled from *Netzach*, feeling the well bloom in her chest.

The claws connected. The force launched Leah into the air and sent her tumbling across the grass. She hit the ground hard, rolled, and came up on one knee. Her shirt hung in tatters where Paige's claws had torn through.

Behind her, the chickens erupted in nervous cackling.

"I said no Tree of Life, Leah. Drop your *Netzach*. Do not make me command you." Lord Ragon's voice carried a warning she couldn't ignore.

She'd activated it on instinct. The well had responded to the threat without her even thinking about it. Leah let the energy dissipate. Her chest felt exposed without it.

Paige charged again, running on all fours. Her claws dug into the earth with each stride.

You want to play? Let's play.

Leah switched wells, pulling from *Gamaliel*. Energy coiled in her throat, lighter than usual. She tried what Lord Ragon had taught her. Suggestive first.

"Paige, you don't want to do this."

The words barely hurt as she said them, trailing black smoke from her to Paige. Paige's ears flicked, but she didn't slow.

Fine. Direct command then.

Leah pulled harder from the well. The pressure built until it felt like her vocal cords might tear. She forced the cursed speech out.

"Stop."

The word scraped against her throat. Pain lanced through her neck.

Paige's ears twitched. Her fur stood on end like a cornered cat's. She shook her head, but she didn't stop. Paige closed the distance and brought her massive paw down.

Leah rolled. Claws stabbed into the ground where she'd been a second ago, sending dirt flying. Paige struck again. Leah rolled in the opposite direction. Again. The ground erupted with each missed blow.

On the fourth roll, everything changed. Leah tumbled into what felt like a dense bubble. Sounds became muffled. Cold wrapped around her like a blanket. Asmodeus had activated *Thagirion* just in time.

Leah pushed to her feet and tried to put some distance between herself and Paige. But Paige's ears immediately swiveled in her direction. She held her breath. The Chimera could hear her even through *Thagirion*. If she could only use Tree of Life wells, this would be over. But Lord Ragon wanted her to strengthen her connection to the Tree of Death, to get better at using it. Fine. She'd give him what he wanted.

Leah aimed both hands at the ground around Paige. She pulled from *Nehemoth*. The well responded instantly. The earth around Paige detonated, a void pulling up grass and dirt. Paige stumbled, momentarily disoriented.

Leah clasped her hands together and pulled from *Samael*. The energy decay well opened in her chest. She felt it start to drain outward.

Don't hurt her, Leah warned.

She is the one trying to hurt us! Asmodeus shot back.

Before Leah could take her first breath with *Samael*, Paige turned and leaped. The impact felt like getting hit by a car. One second, Leah was standing; the next, she was on her back with a massive Chimera crushing her chest. The bubble of *Thagirion* shattered. Sounds rushed back in. The chickens were going wild in their coop, squawking and flapping against the wire.

Paige growled, her muzzle inches from Leah's face. Saliva dripped onto Leah's neck. Leah tried to breathe but couldn't. The pain radiated from the scar from Lord Ragon's stab wound. The corruption flared hot, radiating through her chest. Her ribs creaked. Panic flooded her system.

She clawed at Paige's fur, trying to push her off, but it was like trying to move a boulder. Her vision started to gray at the edges. Why weren't they stopping this? She was clearly losing.

Golohab stirred somewhere deep inside, that chaotic fire responding to her desperation. It wanted out. It wanted to burn everything, including Paige. But Leah shoved it down. She wouldn't. Not to Paige. No matter how angry she was, no matter how much Paige hated her right now, she wouldn't burn her alive.

The world tilted. Colors drained away. Her head felt like it was going to explode.

Asmodeus took over. He pulled from *Satariel*. Leah's vision split in a way that made her stomach lurch. She saw herself still pinned under Paige, and she saw herself standing behind Paige. Her shadow-self clasped her hands together and took a shallow breath with *Samael*, careful not to pull too hard. Just enough.

Paige froze. The pressure on Leah's chest lessened slightly. The shadow breathed in again. Energy flowed from Paige into the shadow, and from the shadow into Leah. Air filled her lungs. Her ribs expanded.

Paige spun and slashed. Her claws caught the shadow square in the stomach. Blood sprayed. The shadow doubled over.

Leah, still on the ground, seized the opportunity. She pulled from *Nehemoth* with everything she had left and aimed at the back of Paige's head.

The void pulled Paige backward. Her body snapped like a whip. The back of her skull slammed into the ground.

CRACK!

The sound echoed across the field. Paige's body went limp. Her fur started to recede immediately, bones shifting back to human proportions.

"No." Leah scrambled forward on her hands and knees. She reached Paige just as the transformation finished. Paige stared up at the sky, tears streaming down her face.

"I can't feel my legs," Paige whispered.

Panic surged through Leah's chest. "No, no, no."

"I can't feel anything."

Leah hovered her hand over Paige's neck. She could fix this. *Chesed*. She pulled from the well, trying to focus on good memories. Her hand started to warm.

"No Tree of Life." Lord Ragon's voice was flat. Emotionless.

Leah spun to look at him. "What the fuck are you talking about? She's hurt!"

She turned back to Paige and closed her eyes, pulling harder from *Chesed*. The well responded. Warmth spread through her palm.

"Use it, and you leave. Tonight." Lord Ragon said. "And your plans of taking down King Helen are gone."

Leah opened her eyes and met Paige's gaze. Paige stared back at her with that same hopeless expression. Leah's jaw clenched. Asmodeus' frustration mixed with her own.

"Fine!" The word came out as a snarl.

She let the anger take over. Let it fill every part of her. The warmth in her hand shifted, growing hotter. Searing. She stopped trying to think of happy memories. Instead, she focused on grief. On frustration. On the rage that had been building inside her for months.

"Keep pushing!" Asmodeus' voice came through her throat, demonic and harsh, layering over her own.

The heat intensified. Her hand felt like it was on fire. Behind her, the nervous cackling of the chickens cut off abruptly. Her hand grew hotter as she pushed harder. The pain in her palm was excruciating, but she didn't care. She wouldn't let Paige stay paralyzed. She refused to add her to the list of people she'd failed.

Cold hands wrapped around her burning one, cooling it. Leah opened her eyes. Paige's hand rested on hers. Leah released the well. The burning sensation faded.

Paige sat up on her own, pulling her hand away. She stood, wobbly at first, then steadier. For a second, their eyes met. Then Paige turned and walked toward the field.

"Paige, I'm sorry, I didn't mean—"

Paige's body rippled. Bones cracked. Fur sprouted. Within seconds, she was a wolf, disappearing into the darkness.

A retching sound made Leah turn. Her shadow was on its side, blood pouring from its mouth. The wound in its stomach was worse than she'd thought.

"No." Leah crawled to where the clone lay. She placed a hand on its shoulder. She extinguished the green flame in her mind, and the shadow dissolved into green smoke.

Pain bloomed in her stomach. Leah felt her skin tearing open and blood in her throat. She pressed her hand against her stomach. No blood. But the pain was real.

Lord Ragon limped as he approached. "Pull yourself together, and we will meet you back at the house. There is a lot to discuss." He started to turn, then paused. "You also owe me twenty-seven chickens."

Leah frowned and turned toward the coop. The silence pressed against her ears. There was no clucking, just a silent coop.

CHAPTER 20
VIOLET MIST

Leah stayed where she'd fallen, knees pulled to her chest. The night air bit at her exposed skin, doing nothing for the stabbing pain in her stomach. She stared at the tree line where Paige had disappeared.

Marcel stepped past her, hands in his pockets and his gaze following the same direction. "We should head back. I doubt she will return until tomorrow."

Leah exhaled slowly and pressed a hand to her stomach, half-expecting to find blood. Nothing. The wound was on her shadow, not her actual body. But the pain was real—worse than any corruption she'd felt before. It intensified with each passing second, like something inside her tearing apart.

She'd never lost a shadow before.

She pushed to her feet, and the earth lurched sideways. Her vision blurred at the edges, and the pain spiked past bearable. She wobbled, started to fall—

Marcel caught her before she hit the ground.

"Take it easy—"

Her stomach turned over. Leah doubled forward and vomited her dinner onto the grass next to them. The retching made everything worse. Her body felt...wrong. Half-empty. Like part of her strength had just vanished into nothing.

Is this what happens when a shadow gets killed? She reached for Asmodeus, tried to picture the room in her mind.

The demon was lying on the floor. His chair had tipped to its side.

"No..." The word barely left her lips before her knees buckled. Marcel's face blurred. Then nothing.

Leah stood in front of the violet mist. It rose before her, thick and swirling, forming that familiar wall she'd seen so many times now. Voices drifted through it—that same cadence, that same rhythm. Words just out of reach, sounds she almost recognized but couldn't quite grasp.

She approached slowly, knowing any sudden movement could make everything vanish. She'd been here before. Multiple times. But never this close.

Leah extended her arm forward. The mist swirled around her hand, cool against her skin but not wet. It crept up her arm, around her neck, and onto her chest.

"We need to find more and convince them to join us. Currently, we are very exposed. With the coordinates, we can initiate them." The male voice spoke with that accent she'd heard before.

The female silhouette turned abruptly toward Leah.

Leah tried to pull back her arm, but the mist held her in place and swirled faster.

"What? What's wrong?" the man asked.

Two violet orbs formed in the woman's eyes. Leah froze.

The mist began to pull back, retreating around the silhouette and revealing features Leah had never seen before.

The woman had dark skin, a toned body, and blond shoulder-length locs. She was beautiful in a way that seemed almost unreal. But it was her eyes—those shining violet eyes—that reminded Leah of Cora.

Could this be them?

Leah looked past her, but the mist still hid the second silhouette.

"Who are you?" The woman's voice echoed around them.

"I'm Leah. Who are you?"

"Name is Mo." The woman's violet eyes narrowed. "Why am I able to see you?"

"Oy! Who are you talking to?" The guy's accent got slightly thicker.

"I'm...not sure." Mo frowned and tilted her head.

"Leah." A voice cut through the dream, and someone shook her shoulder lightly.

Leah opened her eyes and blinked several times. The image of Mo burned in her retina. Marcel stood next to her bed, and she bit down hard on the inside of her cheek.

So close. She'd finally broken through that mist—made contact with someone—and Marcel had woken her up.

"Sorry for waking you, but Lord Ragon expects you. Bedivere requested I retrieve you."

Leah swallowed her frustration and sat up, wincing at the stabbing pain in her stomach. Still there, but more bearable than before. She rubbed her face and wiped cold sweat from her forehead.

"How long have I been asleep?"

"A bit over twenty-four hours. You passed out, and the Ancient One said to put you to bed."

"Is Paige back?"

"Yes, she came back in the morning, but she has been avoiding me. I am quite bored, to be honest." Marcel placed his hands on his hips.

"No cunning plan to get more power to keep you busy?" Leah raised an eyebrow, though her lips curled.

Marcel snorted. "Not at the moment, no. Lord Ragon does not seem too interested in interacting with me."

"Why?"

Marcel shrugged. "I was turned into a vampire about fifty years ago. He probably considers me an infant. Still, I will see if he needs my help on something."

Leah thought about that for a moment. Fifty years was nothing to Lord Ragon, who'd lived for over fifteen centuries. Marcel was barely out of infancy by vampire standards, especially if he was one of the youngest vampires of the family.

"I mean, you are an infant, I guess," Leah said.

He snorted and turned toward the door. "And still old enough to be your grandfather. Get ready. He is waiting."

Marcel left her bedroom and closed the door behind him. Leah took a deep breath and dragged herself out of bed, then shuffled to the bathroom to assess the damage. What she saw made her wince. Her skin had a greenish tint, dark bags carved hollows under her eyes, and her auburn roots were showing through the black dye in her short hair.

She splashed cold water on her face to shake off the grogginess, then got in the shower. The hot water felt good against her sore muscles, but her mind kept drifting back to that woman.

Could that be an Immortal Witch? That seemed impossible. Legion had wiped them all out. Cora said so herself...

"Not all of them." Leah's eyes widened.

"The only one he didn't get was Frank. That lucky witch's

gift of his let him slip through the cracks. But the rest of us are gone."

Those were Cora's exact words. The High Priestess had tried contacting Frank when they were in the camp on the outskirts of the Voodoo town. In fact, Cora had been looking for Frank, but Leah was the one who responded by pure coincidence.

Leah had tried to find information on the Immortal Witches when she first got back from the Library. Every story aligned—they were attacked, and there were no survivors. No one seemed concerned, though. To the outside world, or at least to the secret layers where these parallel societies existed, the Immortal Witches were a fringe, isolated group with odd rituals. They rarely interacted or got involved in public affairs.

Most of Leah's energy back then had been focused on Helen. The hatred and resentment were combined with guilt over everything that happened. She'd gotten matching information from different groups her shadows had been eavesdropping on at the bar. Frank never responded to Cora's call back at the camp, so Leah had assumed he was dead.

But now things were different. If what she saw was right, then Frank was with at least one more Immortal Witch—that blond woman she'd just seen.

The hot water ran over her stomach, and a sharp pain made her jerk away. She bit her lip and looked down, but there was no wound. Slowly, she let the water flow through again until her skin adjusted to the ghostly pain.

Could her Immortal Witch potential be telling her something? Should she try to find them?

Leah shook her head, water flying from her hair. There was no time for that. After six months of searching, she'd finally found the Ancient One and convinced him to train her. Leaving now wasn't an option. Helen and the Infinity Board were closing in—more spies, more tracked locations, more days Sarah and Isaac stayed trapped. She knew there was only so much time she could spend hiding.

But then why was she having these dreams? In the past, they'd always shown her something meaningful. The problem was that they never provided clear explanations. She stretched under the water, her sore muscles loosening some of the tension.

Leah ran her fingers through her short, wet hair and closed her eyes to check on Asmodeus. The demon was still passed out on the floor. This time, she was able to go into the room and help him back to his chair. He didn't wake up; he just sat there with his head tilted slightly to one side. From that angle, he looked like an average man sleeping on the subway during his commute to work.

Leah opened her eyes and wondered how long Asmodeus would be resting. He'd been doing it more lately, especially after extended Tree of Death use. She shivered as she remembered the loud cracking sound from the fight. How Paige had been paralyzed until Leah healed her.

It horrified her to think this could bury any remaining hope of recovering her friendship with Paige.

She looked down at her scratched hands. This training was brutal. But would it be enough to beat Helen?

CHAPTER 21
OLD LEGEND

Leah went down the stairs and found Bedivere waiting for her at the bottom.

"Miss." He bowed slightly. "I hope you are feeling better. Lord Ragon is waiting for you at his studio. Please, follow me."

Leah followed the butler through a maze of hallways. The house stretched impossibly large inside, way bigger than the exterior suggested.

Bedivere stopped at tall double doors carved with intricate patterns. The same doors Zeus had burst through the other day. He opened them and stepped aside.

Leah's breath caught.

Books. Floor to ceiling, wrapping around three stories of open space. A spiral staircase twisted upward through the center, connecting each level. The wooden columns looked like tree trunks, natural and gnarled. Above, a massive glass chandelier cast light across a ceiling mosaic of deep blues swirling like ocean waves.

The scent of burning wood and old paper hit her nose. Her grandfather's library had smelled like this. Before everything went to hell.

To her left, a fireplace crackled. Leather chairs surrounded it. Above the mantel hung a large painting of a young girl. Blond curls, light brown eyes, navy blue dress. On her lap sat a small dog with black patches around its eyes and ears, white everywhere else. Its mouth hung open, tongue out. It was almost like it was smiling.

Lord Ragon sat in one of the leather chairs, book in hand. Zeus leaped from his lap and rushed toward Leah.

"Hey, little guy." Leah crouched down, and Zeus immediately flipped over for belly rubs.

"That's a nice smile. I do not believe I've seen you smile since you arrived."

Leah looked up at Lord Ragon's red eyes. No matter how civilized the vampire looked, that stare always made her uneasy. "Well, you did stab me, so I didn't have much of a chance."

The vampire chuckled and gestured to the leather chair next to him. "Sit."

Leah did as she was told. Zeus returned to Lord Ragon's lap. Bedivere walked in carrying a bowl of stew. The pleasant scent made her stomach growl.

"Chicken stew with sage. It should help you recover your strength." Lord Ragon aimed his book at a small circular table. "Besides, we have a lot of chicken to eat now."

Leah eyed the bowl.

"A dead chicken through *Agshekeloh* is still a dead chicken. It won't poison you. Eat."

Leah took a spoonful. The hot liquid stung her mouth but soothed her throat.

"That was quite the sparring session. It's not every day I see a possessed Mystic use the Tree of Death to snap the spine of a werewolf during a full moon."

Leah shivered. The sound of Paige's spine snapping echoed in her head.

"I'm not possessed." She took another bite.

"No? Then what are you?"

"I don't know."

Lord Ragon set his book on the table and stroked Zeus's fur. "But you do know your objective. What you want to do?"

Leah nodded.

"So, you do not know who or what you are, but you do know what you want. Most people I've encountered usually have the opposite problem."

"I'm not like most people." Leah heard her friends' desperate screams in the echoes of her memories.

"No, you are not. You have a demon within you who is not possessing you, at least according to you. And you have all the requirements to be an Immortal Witch. You are peculiar, Leah Ackerman."

Leah frowned. "How did you know?"

Lord Ragon leaned forward. "Your dream had a very specific scent like a field of lavender. It's a magic older than even myself, but one I'm familiar with. I've known many Immortal Witches. Cora and I go way back. I was sad to hear of her passing."

The thought of the High Priestess made a knot form in Leah's throat. Her sacrifice to take down Legion still fresh in her memory.

Leah took another spoonful. The stew helped relax her throat. "Cora offered to make me a witch once. Years ago."

Lord Ragon raised an eyebrow. "And you refused."

"She said the initiation would purify me. That it would burn away any bonds or connections." Leah's hand moved to her arm, where Asmodeus had marked her. "That Asmodeus wouldn't survive it."

Lord Ragon was quiet for a moment, stroking Zeus's fur. "She told you that?"

"Yes. So I chose not to. I'd saved him from Legion. I couldn't—" Leah's throat tightened. "I need him. To fight Helen, I need every advantage I can get."

"And now you think that door is closed to you."

Leah nodded.

Lord Ragon stood and walked to the fireplace, hands clasped behind his back. "Cora and I disagreed on many things. The Well was one of them." He turned to face her. "She saw it as absolute. Black and white. But I drank from that Well, Leah. I know what it does."

"It rejected you," Leah said. "Because of your corruption."

"The Tree of Life rejected me, but I am still here. Still alive." He returned to his chair and sat. "But here's what Cora never understood. The Well doesn't care about good and evil. It cares about essence. About what you are at your core."

Leah leaned forward. "I don't understand."

"You and Asmodeus are bonded to the Trees. What you two have isn't a possession. Not anymore. You've walked the Tree's spiral path before, and the Trees accepted you."

So we could drink from the Well, Asmodeus said in her mind.

"Cora said our souls were blending," Leah said quietly. "That he was becoming more human, and I was becoming something else."

"Then perhaps the Well would see you as one essence, not two." Lord Ragon took a sip of his scotch. "When the initiation purifies you, it burns away foreign elements. But if Asmodeus is part of your essence now, part of who you are, the Well might not see anything to burn away."

"Might," Leah emphasized.

"Yes. Might." He didn't look away. "I cannot promise you anything."

"And you think I can be a witch because you can see my dreams?"

Lord Ragon shook his head. "No, just smell them. They are charged with that magic, so it's hard to miss."

"Is that how you detect the Librarian? By sniffing it?" She'd been meaning to ask but hadn't found the right time until now.

Lord Ragon's expression turned stiff. He laid his head back in his chair. "Yes. Though that creature's smell is more distasteful." He paused for several seconds before continuing. "Among other things."

They remained silent for a while, staring at the fireplace. Leah found the burning wood mesmerizing. The embers glowed, and flames danced. Combined with the stew, she could feel some of her strength coming back.

Zeus's tail started wagging the second her eyes met his. This drew the vampire's attention.

"Zeus seems to have grown fond of you."

Leah smiled and stretched in her chair. Her aching muscles sent jolts of pain through her body.

"He is very lovable." Leah looked up at the painting and frowned.

"If you are wondering, no, they are not the same dog. Though I know the resemblance can be perceived as uncanny."

"Who is she?"

Lord Ragon pursed his lips.

Leah waved her hands. "I'm sorry, you don't have to tell me."

"It's all right. That's my daughter. Ursulet. She was murdered back when I was still human." His eyes stayed on the painting.

"I'm sorry to hear that." Leah's voice dropped. "It's not the same, but I've lost loved ones, too. My parents, my uncle, and my boyfriend. It's isolating."

Lord Ragon's eyes met hers. Pain flickered in those red irises. A flash of the vampire's lost humanity.

"I'm sorry to hear that."

The room fell silent as they both stared at the fire.

"Does it get better?" Leah finally asked. "With time, I mean?"

Lord Ragon put Zeus down on the floor and stood. He walked to a small bar in the back and returned with a glass bottle of amber liquid and two cups. He set them on coasters on the table.

"You are still recovering, so I shouldn't. But if we are going to talk about this, might as well do it with a strong spirit. You like scotch?"

Leah shrugged. "I'm not much of a drinker."

"A little bit, then." The vampire poured her a small amount, then took out another coaster for her stew and handed Leah the glass. "This table is old, so please use the coaster."

Leah did as she was told and placed the bowl on the coaster. Lord Ragon poured himself a cup as well. Leah took a small sip. The dense liquid went smoothly down her throat. Surprisingly tasty, though she had to be careful about how much to drink on an empty stomach.

Lord Ragon sat back in his leather chair. "Does time heal grief? No, the pain of losing my daughter still haunts me. The intensity decreases. With time comes understanding. Slowly, your mind begins to focus more on the good memories than the bad ones, the mistakes, the regrets." He took a long gulp. "The problem with immortality is that there is no real end date. I've felt this loss for hundreds of years, and I'm going to continue feeling it for many hundreds more."

The idea of endless grief was daunting. "What happened to her?" Leah asked.

Lord Ragon looked back at Leah with bitter eyes. "I was too late." He took another drink and stared at the fire for a moment. "My mentor was the high priest of the Immortal Witches back then. He found me when I was nobody. Saw my potential. Made me what I became—a warrior who never bled." His voice turned sharp. "But when Ursulet fell ill, there was nothing that seemed to heal her. I'd united all of Britain, killed countless enemies of all shapes, sizes, and forms. Yet I couldn't save an eight-year-old girl from fever."

Lord Ragon poured himself another scotch. His face stayed stern, but his composure held.

"Back in those times, there were rumors of the Holy Grail—a golden chalice that would grant immortality to the one who drank from it. I knew my mentor had to know about this, but he refused to tell me. Said there were things mortals couldn't understand. That my daughter would stay eight years old her whole life." He laughed bitterly. "But I didn't listen. How dare you question your king? Those were my exact words. In my head, it was obvious to have an eight year old live forever rather than have her die. I was so blinded by grief that I was sure I was right. I was a king after all. Kings need to trust their gut and judgment. Who was he to question me?"

Leah frowned. Something about his tale nagged at her. "Who was your mentor?"

Lord Ragon smirked. "The stories all call him Merlin."

"Merlin?"

Lord Ragon nodded. "That was the first time I used *Gamaliel*."

Leah's hand moved to her own throat. She knew what that felt like. The pressure, the corruption spreading.

"It nearly left me mute, but I was able to compel the Immortal Witch to take me to the Holy Grail and help me bring it back to my daughter. And we did. We embarked on a quest, just the two of us, to find it."

He paused and took another sip. The fire crackled. Zeus shifted near Lord Ragon's feet.

"We went through black desert, darkness with creatures that would make your skin crawl, and deep jungles with poisonous mushrooms that released dangerous spores. But in the end, we made it. A peaceful forest with a large moon and floating stones. That's where the other Immortal Witches were waiting for us."

"Did you fight them?" Leah asked.

"Between Merlin and me, we defeated them. After all, he was the high priest, the strongest one of them all." Lord Ragon's jaw tightened. "I remember following him up the floating stones, feeling the vertigo grow with each step. But I was determined. Merlin was under my cursed speech, so he was emotionless, compelled to just follow my command. The journey was quite lonely. With every step, I felt more dread. But I'd taken risks before. You don't unite Britain without taking risks."

He stood and walked to the window. His prosthetic leg creaked with each step. Outside, twilight had faded into full dark.

"We finally reached the moon and saw a crater with a small cave entrance. It was sealed, but Merlin conjured melodies, and the entrance opened. It felt like walking through a cold waterfall. Suddenly, my armor, my sword, and my undergarments were all gone. We were naked in this sacred space. Cold and unwelcoming. I saw marbled steps leading up to a platform and followed Merlin up them. We reached the top and found a circular well in the middle of the platform."

Lord Ragon turned back toward her. His red eyes caught firelight. "The crystalline water was motionless except for two spiral vortexes that turned in opposite directions. It was as if there were two drains next to each other, and the water flowed, forming two identical spirals. Merlin conjured another melody, and a crystal-clear chalice formed in his hand. He dipped it in the water, turned, and handed it to me."

Leah leaned forward slightly.

"I held the chalice. The water in it formed two small identical spirals, mimicking the spirals of the well in front of us. That's when it hit me. How could Ursulet be left immortal for the rest of her life by herself? She would be an eight year old on her own. But if I took the immortality with her, we could be together forever. I could protect her."

Lord Ragon chuckled bitterly. His eyes shifted to the fire. The flames reflected in his pupils. "I could be the Immortal King. After all, it was I who unified Britain, it was I who brought peace and prosperity to my people. And there was so much crystalline water. I didn't see why I couldn't be immortal, too. So, I drank it."

He pursed his lips and poured himself another scotch. Took a small sip. Leah sat frozen, watching him.

"I don't remember what it tasted like, but I remember the vision." He paused. "When you drink from the Holy Grail, you see your demise. Or so I was told, but I don't believe it." His eyes narrowed. "I wanted to believe what I saw. The vision was more real than this moment. More solid than any prophecy I've encountered."

Lord Ragon took a deep breath. "The moment the water touched my tongue, I knew I'd made a mistake. The visions came first, confusing and impossible. Then pain. My body tore itself apart from the inside. The Tree of Life rejected me. All that cursed speech, all that death I'd channeled getting there—it had marked me. Corrupted me beyond redemption."

He looked down at his scotch. "But the Tree of Death doesn't let go so easily. It caught my spirit before it could shatter completely. Remade me into something else. Something that feeds on life instead of creating it."

The fire crackled. Leah's mind spun.

"I just remember waking up in my daughter's chambers. The chalice lay next to me. I was disoriented. The lights and scents were too much. But I stumbled to my feet and approached Ursulet's bed. Her dog lay close, guarding her, and it growled at me. But when I reached for her, she was cold and stiff to the touch. I tried to feed her the water, but it just spilled onto her chin and the red blanket covering her. My daughter was dead."

His voice stayed level, but his bitterness was palpable. "I screamed and called the physician and guards, who seemed puzzled to find me there, considering they were stationed outside my daughter's chambers all night. And that's when I heard it for the first time—their pulse. That was the first time I tasted human blood. And the beginning of the fall of my kingdom."

Leah stared at the vampire. His face remained turned toward the fire. So much pain locked behind those red eyes.

"King Arthur Pendragon."

"In the flesh." He raised his scotch and took a drink.

Leah drank some of her own, hoping the strong spirit would help her process all this information. Her empty stomach protested.

"I'm sorry," she finally said.

"It's a sad story. But it was many moons ago, and since then, I've learned to live with my sins. After all, I don't have much of a choice. A king must be able to live with the decisions he made, both good and bad," he said, but his bitterness was still palpable.

"What about Merlin? What happened to him?"

Lord Ragon shook his head. "I never saw him again."

"But how were you able to compel him with Cursed Speech? You weren't a vampire then."

He cleared his throat and sat a little straighter in his chair. "The same way I was never injured in a battle. I was a Mystic."

CHAPTER 22
NEW STORY

Lord Ragon refilled both glasses. The amber liquid caught the firelight as he poured, and Leah watched the flames dance in the scotch.

A Mystic.

King Arthur had been a Mystic before he became a vampire.

The implications of that were still settling in her mind when her gaze dropped to his prosthetic leg. Metal and wood where flesh should be.

Vampires regenerated. She'd seen it happen. Watched vampires heal from wounds that should have killed them. So why...

"You are wondering about my leg." His voice stayed level. "After all, vampires can regenerate limbs, right?"

Leah forced herself to meet his red eyes. They looked more alive than she'd seen them before, flames dancing in his pupils. Or maybe his own story stirred something inside him.

"I went on an uncontrolled rampage after my daughter died." Lord Ragon took another sip of scotch. "I was stricken with grief and a hunger I had never experienced before. One so deep it forms a pit in your stomach that sucks in all the warmth of your body. The only thing that can give you some of that back is human blood. Metallic, gross, but so filling and warm. I would have killed everyone in Camelot if it were not for Sir Bedivere."

Leah tilted her head.

"Yes, the same Bedivere who serves as a butler. My most loyal knight and companion. A man so loyal to his vows, he was willing to sacrifice his humanity to be with his king."

Lord Ragon paused to refill both glasses. Just a finger of scotch in each. He settled back before continuing. "He used my legendary sword, Excalibur, and stabbed me in the leg. It knocked me out of my blood lust, but the leg... I had to cut it off. You see, Excalibur is an exceptional sword, capable of killing any form of corruption. So even a stabbing wound on my leg would have spread and killed me. Hence why I cannot regrow the limb." He glanced down at the prosthetic. "I like it this way, honestly."

"Why?"

"It is a reminder. A consequence of the mistakes I made. My personal way of payment for all the wrong I did that day. As I said before, that was the beginning of the end." He paused, submerged in thought. Then his eyes shifted to Zeus, who lay next to his chair on the ground. His lips curled slightly. "But surprisingly, when others abandoned me, Ursulet's dog stayed. I am not sure why. Usually, the living steer away from vampires. But the dog stayed with me until his last breath. And ever since, I have rescued new dogs and tried to give them the best life possible. I have had hundreds at this point, but I think Ursulet would have liked that."

He reached down and caressed Zeus's white and black fur. The dog's tail thumped twice against the rug.

Silence settled over the studio. The fire crackled and

popped. Leah watched the flames twist and reshape themselves, thinking about choices and consequences. About the people she loved getting hurt because of the decisions she made. Kidnapped. Killed. The weight of it pressed down on her shoulders.

She understood Lord Ragon in a way few others could.

"How do you do it?" The question came out quieter than she'd intended. "How do you live with the guilt?"

Lord Ragon looked up. Pain flickered in his ancient red eyes. Not just the reflection of firelight, but something deeper. Recognition, maybe. Or old grief surfacing.

"For a while, it ate me up. But I pressed on. I was still a king, and kings cannot spend their whole life dwelling on past mistakes. One must push onward." He swirled his scotch. "But immortality is a long time. At one point, I had to face it head-on and come to terms with it. I could be the stubborn king who turned into a vampire by coercing the strongest wizard alive and killing half of my castle. Or I could be the desperate father who was trying to do anything in his power to save his child."

"Which one are you?"

"I guess both." He stared into his glass. "That is what is so interesting about human nature; no one is ever the evil one in their own story. I do take responsibility for what I have done. I do have regrets. But I also try to be kind to myself. It is hard, but with practice and time, it is possible. And time is something I can spare."

Leah sat with those words. She'd been tearing herself apart ever since the Librarian kidnapped Sarah and Isaac. The place in her palm where the blue eye often formed pulsed once, as if listening. Every time she remembered what happened, she connected more dots, found more questions. Got angrier. If she had just stopped to question Helen...

Her hands curled into fists.

"Mind if I ask, what is the source of your guilt?" Lord Ragon broke the silence.

The idea of retelling her story made her stomach turn. Truth was, Leah had not spoken about it with anyone other than Asmodeus. And yet, after hearing Lord Ragon's story, she felt like she could finally talk to someone who might understand.

"I see you are still hesitant." He turned and grabbed the book he'd been reading when Leah first entered the room. The vampire placed it on the coffee table between them. "I can make it more enticing."

Leah leaned forward, studying the green leather book with no title on the cover and a very old binding.

"You will not be able to spar for the next couple of days. You can spend those resting in your bedroom, or you can spend them here in my studio." He tapped the book twice with his index finger. "I have a rather exclusive set of tomes that will help you in your quest for revenge. Although you are already quite skillful with the Tree of Death, there are blunders you make. Like creating that shadow as a distraction. Shadows created by *Satariel* carry a part of your essence, and if they get hurt, you get hurt too. You were smart to absorb it when you did. If that shadow died, part of your essence would have been dead forever."

Leah blinked. She hadn't known that. The risks she'd taken...

Lord Ragon continued. "Everything you need to know about the Tree of Death, including the upper three wells, is in this book. But for you to get that, you will have to tell me your story. Why do you want to kill King Helen? Why is the Librarian keeping an eye on you?"

Leah stared at the green leather tome. If Lord Ragon was right, the key to defeating Helen could be in there.

She'd been using wells that seemed less dangerous, but she didn't know all the risks. The death of her shadow and its effect on her essence was proof of that.

But telling her story to a vampire who'd tried to murder her a few days ago? Even if he was being honest now, even if he seemed to be helping...

She picked up her empty glass and extended her arm. "I am going to need another one."

Lord Ragon's lips curled into a half smile as he refilled her glass. He did the same with his own and sat back. "I am assuming I will also hear the story of that scar coiling around your arm."

"Well then, buckle up."

Leah took a long sip. The scotch burned going down, but she welcomed it. Then she started talking.

"My mom was a thief." Her voice came out steadier than expected. "Stole information from the Library of Alexandria. The Librarian wanted payback."

Lord Ragon said nothing. Just listened, his red eyes fixed on hers.

The words kept coming. Once she started, it was hard to stop. She told him about the scroll Helen and her mother used to summon Legion. About the threefold deal she'd made to escape the Library. The Librarian's terms had seemed so simple at first, but she hadn't understood what threefold meant. Not really.

"Sarah and Isaac." Her throat tightened around their names. "The Librarian took them because I failed to get the scroll back in time. They're trapped there. Have been for six months."

She told him about her parents. About Eric, her uncle who'd saved her from the Academy raid and later threw himself between her and Legion. Her voice cracked when she got to Gabe. To watching him die in her arms.

Lord Ragon never interrupted. Just refilled her glass when it emptied. Never more than a finger of scotch.

Leah told him about Asmodeus, still resting in her subconscious after their fight. About Helen's betrayal. About every choice she'd made that led to someone getting hurt.

"Every decision..." She stared at her hands. "Everyone I try to protect ends up dead or kidnapped or worse."

By the time she finished, the fire had burned lower. Her throat felt raw. The room seemed warmer than before, or maybe that was just the scotch.

"That is a sad tale." Lord Ragon's voice held no judgment.

Leah swallowed, but her throat stayed dry and bitter. Every time she remembered what happened, the anger built. Helen had been playing them all from the start.

"Well, it is apparent to me that King Helen has been on a quest for power since the beginning. A Mystic with such ambition is a force to be reckoned with." He paused. "But why are you carrying such guilt?"

"I just told you. Every decision I make—"

"You made choices with the information you had." Lord Ragon leaned forward. "We have that in common, you and I."

For a moment, Leah could see humanity in his red eyes. It could have been the firelight reflecting, but she could almost see it. Empathy.

"Can I give you a piece of advice?"

Leah set her glass down and nodded.

"Think about the threefold deal. The one that took your friends." His gaze stayed steady on hers. "I want you to think about a hypothetical scenario. If Sarah had made that deal instead. If she had been the one to escape while you and Isaac remained trapped." He let that sit for a moment.

"If she were in your position now, torturing herself about what happened, what would you say?"

Leah closed her eyes. Tried to picture it. Sarah crying, drowning in regret and guilt. Her best friend tearing herself apart the way Leah had been doing for months.

The image made something twist in her gut.

"That it's not her fault." The words came out quietly. "That she didn't know what she was getting herself into. That she didn't have a choice. It was either that or be locked up in the Library forever."

"And yet, you are not able to tell that to yourself?"

Silence. The fire crackled. Zeus shifted in his sleep.

Fuck. He's right.

"Give your friends some credit. And stop judging yourself so harshly. You did the best you could with the information that you were given. Accept that, and your pain and regret will become more bearable. Ignore it, and your emotions will consume you." Lord Ragon's voice softened. "Trust me. I have been there."

Leah sat with his words. They felt foreign and familiar at the same time. Rationally, the logic made sense. She could see it clearly. But emotionally...

Lord Ragon got to his feet. Zeus stood as well, immediately alert and ready to follow.

"Thank you for the conversation, Leah. I appreciate you sharing."

"Likewise." She hesitated, then decided to ask the question that had been nagging at the back of her mind. "Lord Ragon, may I ask you one more thing?"

"Go ahead."

"You said that when you drank the water from the Holy Grail, it gave you both immortality and also a vision of how you would die. What did you see?"

Lord Ragon took a deep breath. His gaze moved to the

painting of Ursulet on the wall, and his expression shifted. Pain, maybe. Or longing. Leah wasn't sure.

"I saw her. Smiling and hugging me."

Leah frowned. "So you think you'll meet again? In the afterlife or something?"

Lord Ragon shook his head slowly. "No. The Holy Grail punished me. It gave me immortality, but it also turned me into a monster. It was supposed to show me how I died." He turned back to face her. "But I suppose it chose to feed off my grief and leave me with a pain that cannot mend. My daughter is long dead. The vision is impossible, and it has sat heavily on my mind ever since it was given to me, driving me mad."

The cruelty of it landed heavily in the room. To experience that kind of suffering, especially as a father who was just trying to save his daughter...

"I'm sorry." Leah struggled to find the right words. "I can't even imagine how painful that must be."

Lord Ragon smiled sadly at her. "I appreciate your kindness. Now, finish the rest of your stew. I will ask Bedivere to bring some more. We will resume our training once you have fully recovered, so better eat up and rest." He gestured to the green leather book on the table. "Enjoy the book."

Leah stood as well. "Thank you. For everything."

Lord Ragon nodded once. He walked to the door, Zeus padding beside him, then paused with his hand on the handle.

"If I may give you one more piece of advice, it is this: Everyone thinks they are on the side of good. That is what is so deceitful about human nature. King Helen believes she is doing the right thing. You think you are doing the right thing. I thought I was doing the right thing. After all, a father trying to save his sick child? How could that be evil?" He held her gaze. "Everyone thinks they are on the side of good. But in the end, only the consequences of those actions will be the ones defining what we really are." He turned the doorknob. "Happy reading."

The door closed behind him with a soft click.

Leah sat alone in the studio, surrounded by shelves of ancient books. The fire cast dancing shadows on the spines. She picked up the green leather tome and ran her fingers over the cover. The binding cracked slightly when she opened it to the first page.

CHAPTER 23
THE COST OF SHADOWS

The fireplace glowed dimly by the time Leah finished rereading the entry on *Satariel* for the fifth time. She'd been in Lord Ragon's studio for three days now, looking over the same book.

Zeus shifted on her lap and kicked his back leg, lost in a dream. The green leather tome sat open on the mahogany desk, its pages yellowed and brittle under the lamplight. Outside the tall windows, dusk had fallen again. Another day she hadn't left this room.

Another day she hadn't faced Paige.

Leah ran her finger along the text, the words blurring together. She knew them by heart now. Had memorized every clause, every warning, every consequence the author, Lord Shadow, had documented about the upper wells of the Tree of Death.

Warning: If a shadow gets killed, it is safe to assume that part of the conjurer's essence dies too. This will shorten the user's lifespan and could potentially have long-lasting consequences. Full rest and nutrition are critical in the following days to allow the essence to heal as much as possible, but the damage is permanent.

The word sat heavily in her stomach. If Paige's claws had cut deeper. If that shadow hadn't just bled but died. If...

Leah closed her eyes and saw it again. The white fur was streaked with blond. Those yellow eyes locked on her shadow self. Claws slicing through fabric and flesh. Blood spraying across Lord Ragon's field while chickens screamed in their coop.

She'd been so focused on winning, on proving she could handle a full moon Chimera, that she hadn't understood what was at stake. Hadn't realized that creating a shadow meant splitting her essence in two. That losing one meant losing part of herself forever.

How much shorter would her life be? The book didn't say. Years? Decades? Would she even have felt it happen, or would she just wake up one day and realize she was dying faster than she should?

Leah pressed her palms against her eyes until spots danced in her vision.

She could have killed me. And I could have killed her.

The thought had been circling for three days, growing sharper each time it passed through. Paige had gone for the kill. Maybe not consciously. Maybe her Chimera blood and werewolf mentality had made her more aggressive under the full moon. But those claws had been aiming for vital spots. The places that would make a shadow die fast.

Did Paige even know? Did she understand what she'd almost done?

Or had her hatred for Asmodeus finally pushed her over the edge?

Leah's throat tightened. She swallowed hard and looked back at the book, trying to focus on anything else. Any other piece of information she could use. Anything that would let her stop thinking about how she'd paralyzed Paige and the shadow she'd almost lost.

Her eyes found the next section. She'd read this one several times, too.

Golohab: The well of chaotic fire. Summoning such a well can result in the death of the user, consumed by the black flames he conjured. The black flames have been the source of some of the greatest city fires in history. Not even I know how to control them.

Leah thought about the night she'd almost used it on Zafirah. How the sparks had started blowing from her arm. How the well had pressed against her mind, dulling her senses, begging to burn everything. She'd thought Zafirah had killed her shadow-self. Had been ready to burn her alive for it.

Asmodeus had wanted to. She'd felt his rage bleeding through their shared consciousness, urging her on. An eye for an eye.

If she'd let go. If she'd summoned those black flames.

Leah would be dead.

And Zafirah. And probably half the block.

The book made it sound like *Golohab* didn't discriminate. Once unleashed, it consumed everything. The caster. The target. Anyone caught in its path. A monster that hunted Tree of Life energy until nothing was left.

She turned the page, but her mind kept circling back. To shadows that could die. To the flames. To all the ways the Tree of Death could destroy her.

Each well of the Tree of Life had its costs. Leah knew that. Push *Netzach* too hard, and you become reckless, convinced of your own invulnerability. Overuse *Chesed*, and you burn out your capacity for empathy, leaving you unable to feel anything at all. The Sages all bore their scars. Zafirah's dry skin. Nona's blindness. Nick's depression.

But those were manageable. Survivable.

The Tree of Death didn't work that way. It didn't just

take. It consumed. Used you up and left you emptier than before. And if you weren't careful, it killed you in the process.

Leah flipped ahead to the final section of the Appendix. The upper three wells. *Satariel*, she knew now, intimately and terribly. *Ghogiel* had a sparse entry, something about dueling essences and one person dying while the other carried on. She'd save that nightmare for another day.

That left *Thaumiel*.

She scanned the page, but there wasn't much on it. Just three lines about Divine Duality and no recorded history of anyone ever wielding it. Even at the Infinity Board, *Keter* had been equally mysterious. The upper wells of both Trees remained obscure, probably because they were so dangerous that no one survived trying to master them.

Leah was about to close the book when something caught her eye. A faint mark in the margin, barely visible in the lamplight. She angled the page toward the light.

Someone had written there. The ink had faded to a pale brown, but the handwriting was still legible. Tight, cramped letters pressed into the paper.

True Manipulation, the note read.

Leah frowned and reread the *Thaumiel* entry. Divine Duality. No recorded history. Nothing about manipulation. She looked back at the margin note. *Gamaliel* was the well of cursed speech, of forcing people to obey commands. Was the note saying *Thaumiel* did something similar, or something worse?

"You are going to ruin your eyes reading in this light."

Leah jerked back, nearly knocking Zeus off her lap. The dog yelped and jumped down, padding over to greet Lord Ragon as he stepped into the room.

"I didn't hear you come in."

"Of course not." Lord Ragon crossed to the fireplace and

added a log, then stirred the embers until flames caught. "You have been in here for three days, Leah. Even Zeus has left to stretch his legs a few times."

The dog wagged his tail at the mention of his name, then jumped up onto the leather chair by the fire and curled into a ball.

"I'm almost done," Leah said.

"You said that yesterday."

"I mean it this time."

Lord Ragon studied her with those red eyes, the ones that saw too much. "You are not reading anymore. You are hiding."

Leah's jaw tightened. She looked back at the book, at the faded margin note about manipulation. "I'm researching."

"You have read that one book's appendix more times than I have, and I have owned this book for one hundred and sixty years." He moved closer, his prosthetic leg tapping softly against the wood floor. "What are you hiding from?"

"I'm not hiding."

"Then why have you not left this room? Marcel has been asking about you. Bedivere is concerned you are not eating enough. And Paige—"

"I don't want to talk about Paige."

The words came out sharper than she'd intended. Lord Ragon raised an eyebrow but said nothing. He just stood there, waiting, giving her space to either fill the silence or let it stretch.

Leah hated that he was right. Hated that after three days of avoiding everyone, of burying herself in this book and pretending she was learning something useful, he could walk in and see through her in less than a minute.

"She hates me. I almost paralyzed her, and she almost

killed my shadow," Leah said finally. The words tasted bitter. "If those claws had gone deeper, I'd be—" She gestured at the book. "Permanently damaged. Shorter lifespan. Possible long-term consequences. I healed her, but I don't think she even cares that she almost ended me."

"Have you asked her?"

"No."

"Why not?"

Because I'm afraid of the answer. Because if Paige did know, if she went for the kill on purpose, then everything between them was broken beyond repair. And if she didn't know, if she'd just been caught up with her werewolf family and the full moon, then Leah had to forgive her. Had to let it go and move forward.

Both options felt impossible.

"I paralyzed her," Leah said instead. "I slammed the back of her head into the ground so hard her neck broke. She couldn't feel her legs. And I was ready to use *Chesed* on her, to heal her, but you..." She stopped, the anger from that night flaring up again. "You told me I'd have to leave if I used Tree of Life wells. You made me choose between healing her and staying here."

Lord Ragon's expression didn't change. "I gave you a boundary. You still healed her."

"She was paralyzed."

"And you healed her." He crossed his arms. "You were tasked with using the Tree of Death. Testing your limits. You are not a child. Hiding in my studio for three days will not change what happened. It will only make the next time you see her more difficult."

Leah bit the inside of her cheek. She knew he was right. Knew that every day she stayed in here, the confrontation grew more impossible. But the alternative was walking out that door and facing Paige. Looking her in the eyes and trying to figure out if their friendship, tenuous as it was, had survived.

If Paige even wanted it to survive.

"What if she hates me?" The question slipped out before Leah could stop it.

Lord Ragon tilted his head slightly. "Then she hates you. From what I understand, you two weren't friends before. But you will not know unless you speak with her."

"That's not helpful."

"No, but it is honest." He moved toward the door, Zeus hopping down from the chair to follow. "You cannot avoid difficult conversations forever. Not with Paige. Not with yourself. And especially not if you intend to face Helen."

He paused at the doorway and looked back. "Get some rest. We resume training tomorrow, and I will not go easy on you because you spent three days feeling sorry for yourself."

The door closed behind him with a soft click, leaving Leah alone with the book and the dying fire.

She looked down at the appendix and glanced at all the warnings and consequences she'd memorized over the past three days. At the permanent damage from losing a shadow. At the black flames that killed indiscriminately. At the cryptic margin note about manipulation that she still didn't understand.

All this knowledge, and none of it told her how to fix things with Paige. How to move forward when every well she used could destroy her. How to face Helen when even the Ancient One wouldn't.

Leah closed the book and pushed it away. Lord Ragon was right; she couldn't hide anymore.

The green tome had given her what she needed. An understanding of the costs. Proof that every shadow she created put her life on the line. Confirmation that *Golohab* could kill her if she ever lost control again.

But it couldn't tell her what to do next. Leah had to figure that out on her own.

She stood, her muscles stiff from sitting too long. Zeus had left with Lord Ragon, probably hoping for dinner and attention from someone who wasn't wallowing in guilt. The studio felt colder without the dog's warmth, emptier without his quiet company.

She needed to eat and sleep. She needed to stop thinking about Paige's yellow eyes and the way her shadow had bled across Lord Ragon's field.

Leah picked up the green tome and placed it back on the shelf. Her fingers lingered on the spine for a moment, then she turned and left the studio, pulling the door shut behind her.

CHAPTER 24
EXCALIBUR

On her way up to her room, Leah found Bedivere sitting at the top step of the stairs, a large sword resting across his legs. He cleaned it with slow, careful strokes, the cloth moving over the blade with quiet reverence.

The butler looked up. "Evening, Miss. Heading to bed?"

"Yes. Lord Ragon forced me to take a break."

"I did warn you."

"Yeah, yeah." Leah stopped and took a closer look at the sword. It was simpler than she'd expected. Basic hilt, no intricate designs or gemstones. She glanced at the shield still mounted on the wall above the central stairs and looked back. "Is that Excalibur?"

Bedivere froze for a couple of seconds. "He did tell you, then."

"We spoke about it a couple of days ago, yes."

"I'm surprised. Lord Ragon doesn't really speak to anyone. And yet, if he told you about this, he probably told you everything else."

Leah scratched the back of her head, unsure of Bedivere's feelings. It was hard to read him. "I guess so? We had a heart-to-heart while I was recovering."

Bedivere finally looked up at Leah, a deep smile on his face. "That makes me happy. My king has always been a very closed-off person."

Leah smiled back and shrugged. "I mean, if he kills half of the guests he gets, I can see how it can be hard for him to make friends."

Bedivere chuckled and continued to clean the sword. "I've always told him that loneliness is an even stronger poison than the Holy Grail he drank so long ago."

The words landed heavier than Leah expected. She thought of the last few months, trapped in that hotel room with only Asmodeus for company. "Oh, trust me, I know."

Bedivere stood back up and raised the sword. It was enormous, but he maneuvered it with ease in one hand. His eyes darted toward Leah. "Would you like to hold it?"

"Ah, yeah!" Leah said excitedly.

"Just be careful," Bedivere said, lowering it and giving the handle to Leah.

Leah curled her fingers around it and raised it up. The large sword was surprisingly light for its size. She gave it a couple of clumsy swings and almost lost her balance.

"I mean, clearly I need practice, but wow, this is awesome."

"It is a remarkable sword."

Leah lowered it and handed it back to Bedivere. "Could I ask you a personal question?"

Bedivere inserted the sword back in its sheath and turned to the wall where the shield was located. "Sure."

"How are you still alive? You're not a vampire, but you don't seem like you've aged a day."

The butler placed the sword behind the shield on the wall and said, "I'm not sure myself, to be honest. After I stopped Lord Ragon in his bloodlust frenzy, he spent a few days healing. Most of the knights who swore an oath to him deserted. Only a few of us stayed. Once he got better, he wanted to reward me for what I'd done and for staying. He asked his maidens to turn his daughter's red blanket into a cape and gifted it to me. Said that it was imbued with the Holy Grail's water, and that as long as I wore it, it would keep death at bay. I thought it was a touching gesture, but I never expected it to actually work."

Leah frowned. "But you aren't wearing it now?"

Bedivere chuckled, unbuttoned his black jacket, and showed her the inside. There was a bright red cloth embroidered inside. "Capes ran out of fashion in the late 1800's, so we needed something more inconspicuous."

"Wow," Leah murmured, getting closer. "So, if you take this off, you'll die?"

Bedivere smiled and closed his jacket. "Not quite. I can take it off, but after a few days without it, I'd begin to age rapidly and soon meet my maker." He moved his hand to his chest. Leah noticed a cross necklace beneath his white shirt.

"I see. Watching those you cared for age and die while you remained... that's a painful kind of torture."

Bedivere took a deep breath. "It was."

Leah tilted her head. "How did you do it? How did you pull it off?"

Bedivere looked back at Leah, a look of confusion on his face. "What do you mean?"

"How did you manage to stay sane? To not give it to someone you love who was on the brink of death or something like that?"

Bedivere pushed his chest up and stood a little taller. "I'm a knight of the Round Table. I swore an oath to my king to protect him at all times. Personal struggles don't matter when you swear an oath. I'm going to be with my king until his last breath. Helping him, defending him, and following his rule. That's what it means to be a Knight of the Round Table. That is what it means to sacrifice yourself for what you believe in."

Leah admired him. A mere mortal—if not for that cloth in his jacket. Yet his sense of duty remained intact.

"I respect that," Leah finally said.

To her surprise, Bedivere smiled. "I appreciate that. Now, off to bed, Miss. You have a long day tomorrow."

Leah stopped at her door, her hand hovering over the doorknob, when she looked left. Paige's door was closed. She had chosen to give her some space after their sparring match. That said, part of her had hoped they would have solved things by now. With sparring resuming tomorrow, it might be a good idea to talk to her.

Go to her, Asmodeus whispered.

"What if she isn't ready to talk?"

You will not know until you try.

Leah smirked. "Look at you, slowly becoming my therapist."

Asmodeus grunted and rolled his eyes. *This is just in the back of your head all the time. Guess who lives in the back of your head? Me. Your worrying thoughts are annoying neighbors, so it is best to deal with them.*

Leah took a deep breath and walked over. She knocked on the door and waited as she bit her lip anxiously. After a few seconds, the door opened. Paige looked a lot better than she had when Leah last saw her. Her hair was neat and combed, and her slender body looked good, even in the old pajamas Bedivere had given them. Paige eyed her up and down, exhaled, and rolled her eyes before stepping aside.

"Come in, let's get this over with."

Leah entered the room, which was a mirror copy of

Leah's, except this one had different art on the wall. A small desk lamp next to Paige's bed illuminated the room. Paige closed the door behind Leah and leaned on it, her arms crossed.

"I know we aren't on the best of terms," Leah began. "But we're going to be here, training, for a while. I was hoping we could just talk things out."

"How can you be okay with having the demon who killed Alma and so many others inside you? I mean, he almost killed you that night, too!"

Leah took a deep breath. "I spent a long time questioning that. It's not like I suddenly began to trust him. He gained my trust over time."

"See, but that's already a red flag for me. Demons are evil. Period. You might not know much about the first great war against him, but that creature killed a lot of Mystics, my uncle included. He was the Legion of that time."

"I understand that, but he's not the same demon anymore. He—"

Paige interrupted her. "Do you? Because I don't think you heard what I just said. He killed hundreds of us. Even more humans."

"Yes, but he's changed."

"Demons lie, Leah. They do it all the time. They lie, and they manipulate."

Leah's nostrils flared. She stopped the urge to stomp on the floor. "I came here to talk, not to be lectured. Trust me, I've dealt with enough demons to know what they're capable of. I know what he's done. I'll remind you that he was the one who possessed my father and killed my mother." Leah stepped closer. "Do you think I'm stupid enough to trust a monster like that?"

"Well, you haven't exorcised him, so I'm not sure what else to think."

"No, because the demon that lives within me now is not the same one who possessed my father. He is not the same one who got Alma killed. The demon within me helped me save Isaac's life, even when it meant putting ourselves at risk. We fought together on multiple occasions. Him being with me means I can wield the Tree of Death without suffering significant corruption. He was set on destroying Legion as much as you or me. And we did it. Together."

Paige also stepped closer. "Have you wondered why? Demons don't just do selfless things. If you believe that, then you're as naive as you were back at the Outpost."

Leah felt a soft, warm pull, as green flames clouded her thoughts. Within seconds, a shadow stood next to her, with his arms crossed.

"I'm over this. Time to talk, you and I."

Paige stepped back, her eyes glowing in the darker corner of the room, as fangs formed. "You."

Leah turned to Asmodeus, intending to protest, but the shadow just raised a hand in her direction and said, "No. This one is on me." Asmodeus lowered his hand and continued. "Paige, you understand how *Yesod* works, yes?"

The Chimera just stared back before nodding once.

"You did not make it that far, but you do know that young people get bonded. Do you know who Leah was bonded to?"

"Eric."

"Eric. Do you know what happened to him?"

Paige remained silent, her jaw tightening.

"Eric sacrificed himself to save her. You know what that means for a young Mystic, don't you?" Asmodeus shifted his weight. "Yet here she is. Wielding both Trees like it's second nature."

Paige shook her head, standing a little taller. "Why does that matter? Most Mystics bond with the Tree eventually."

"Most *older* Mystics, yes. You remember the bonding trial, don't you? Even if you didn't make it that far." His voice stayed level. "Bonding to the tree is much worse, and yet Leah bonded in months. With my help, yes—but she still had to survive it. Sarah and Isaac barely made it through with her guidance." He paused. "Gabe didn't make it at all, which cost him his life later."

Paige went pale, and Leah realized this was the first time she'd heard of Gabe's death. She spoke with a trembling voice. "What does that have to do with you?"

"Everything." Asmodeus stepped closer. "Leah and I faced that trial together. Unimaginable pain. Trauma that would have broken most people. We even saw Alma herself." His starry eyes locked onto Paige's. "At the end, Leah had a choice. The Tree or me."

The room went quiet.

"She chose me." His voice dropped. "And you know what the Tree of Life did? It blessed us. Alma blessed us. Gave us a direct connection to both Trees."

Paige diverted her gaze and murmured, "That's impossible."

"Is it?" Asmodeus tilted his head. "You're standing there with werewolf traits in a Chimera body. You really want to lecture me about what's possible?" He let that hang for a moment. "You've changed over the past few years, Paige. So have we. Maybe instead of judging, try to understand that."

Paige looked back up, and they stared at one another defiantly. Leah sensed the tension in the room reach its peak and wanted to call Asmodeus's shadow back to give Paige space to process. But then, she remembered the fight they had at the motel, and the promise she had made to him, to never pull him back in without his consent.

Paige's jaw worked. She looked at the floor, then back at

Asmodeus. "You don't understand. I've lost so much because of your kind."

"Your kind?" Asmodeus's voice went quiet. "You mean demons who worked with Legion. The ones who were capturing Chimeras and using them in rituals."

Paige's entire body went rigid.

Marcel had mentioned the warehouse, but seeing Paige's face made it real in a way secondhand knowledge never could.

"Yes, I know about that. Leah and I hunted down those ritual sites. We stopped them from sacrificing more of your people. Tell me, Paige, where were you during all of that? Do you remember?"

Paige's breathing became shallow. Her hands clenched into fists at her sides.

"You were captured, were you not?" Asmodeus continued, his tone softer now. "Held somewhere. Waiting to be the next one chained to a tree and burned alive. And who saved you?"

"Maria," Paige whispered.

"Maria. A werewolf who took pity on a Chimera and brought you into her pack. While Leah and I were fighting to end those rituals, you were being rescued by someone who saw past what you were and gave you a chance." Asmodeus tilted his head. "Sound familiar?"

Paige's eyes glistened. She blinked rapidly and looked away.

"I am not asking you to trust me," Asmodeus said. "And I am not asking you to like me. But I am asking you to recognize that I am not the same demon who killed your uncle. I am not the demon who captured you. And maybe, just maybe, consider that Leah choosing me was not naivety. It was survival. It was a necessity. And it became something more." The shadow paused. "Do you consider yourself wiser than the Tree of Life, Paige Jones?"

Paige closed her mouth, her lips tight. Leah could sense the inner struggle within and stepped in between the two, holding her shadow's arms. "I think we can give Paige some space and time to think, Asmodeus."

Paige and Asmodeus stared at one another for a few more seconds before the demon's eyes turned to Leah and nodded. The shadow dissipated in a cloud of smoke. Leah felt some vertigo, but given the short time, she didn't have any seizures, thankfully.

She looked back and added, "Thanks for listening to us," before stepping out of the room and closing the door behind her, leaving a conflicted Paige behind.

CHAPTER 25
AN EXPECTED VISITOR

Marcel's fist came at Leah's face. She ducked, pulled from *Nehemoth*, and yanked him forward. The vampire twisted mid-pull and drove his elbow into her ribs.

Leah hit the ground hard. Stars bloomed across her vision. She rolled and came up in a crouch, but Marcel was already moving.

Three days since Paige left. Three days of sparring with Marcel while Lord Ragon watched from the field's edge. The vampire grew stronger each night as the moon waned toward new, and without *Netzach* to protect her, every mistake could be fatal.

Marcel circled left. Leah mirrored him, keeping her weight on the balls of her feet. Somewhere in the distance, Zeus barked at something. Lord Ragon said nothing, arms crossed over his chest.

At one point during yesterday's session, Leah could have sworn she saw a large silhouette far into the field. Two shiny dots stared at them from the tree line. But Marcel had taken advantage of her distraction and swept her legs out from under her. By the time she looked back, the silhouette was gone.

The training helped. Not just with the Tree of Death wells, though Lord Ragon's instruction had sharpened her control of *Gamaliel* and *Samael*. But the fighting released something inside her. That tension between her and Marcel bled away during their sessions, leaving only the challenge, the movement, the split-second decisions that kept her alive.

She fought him like each strike might be her last. The thought should have terrified her. Instead, it made her feel sharp.

Yesterday, he had stabbed her in the arm. Blood poured down her sleeve while Marcel froze, shock spreading across his face. Leah used the pain to trigger a *Satariel* shadow that materialized behind him and knocked him flat with a strong *Nehemoth* pull. Lord Ragon took her deep into the fields afterward, away from the animals, and sealed the wound with *Agshekeloh*.

The exercises afterward were brutal. Lord Ragon made her whisper *Gamaliel* commands to the animals around the farm, testing how softly she could invoke the well while maintaining control. Or practice short, labored breathing while using *Samael* on him. Those sessions felt like sucking air through a straw, but the Ancient One insisted they were building her "lung capacity."

But it was the small moments. Zeus lying across her lap while she read in the studio. Quiet breakfasts with the vampires after long nights of training. Even with her friends kidnapped somewhere, even with the Librarian's eye still appearing on random surfaces, Leah finally felt like she was moving in the right direction.

It was during one of these breakfasts, right before

dawn, that Bedivere came into the dining hall. The butler was usually asleep by now.

Leah watched him approach while Marcel launched into another lecture about *Satariel*.

"There has to be a way to distribute the energy so you could create a shadow without giving it fifty percent of everything."

Leah rolled her eyes. "I've told you a billion times that's not possible. Splitting happens in seconds. There's no way to avoid it. Besides, none of the books here says anything about that."

"Yes, but if we could somehow practice it, maybe there is a way. Imagine creating fifty shadows, each one with just a tiny bit of energy. It would reduce your risk while giving you more ground to cover when gathering intel. You could overwhelm an opponent."

Leah twitched at the idea of reabsorbing fifty clones. "I don't think you understand how this works."

Marcel shrugged. "I think it is worth a try."

Bedivere whispered something in Lord Ragon's ear. The Ancient One raised his hand, silencing them. Leah looked back at Marcel. The color drained from his face.

"What's happening?" Leah whispered.

Lord Ragon gave them a grave look and stood. "King Helen is coming. Marcel, follow our plan. Work with Bedivere to ensure my staff uses the safe passages. They all know what to do. Meet at the safe house in Iowa, like we discussed. You have three days to get there."

Leah jumped to her feet. Her heart slammed against her ribs. Helen? Here? How could that be? This location was secret unless she...

"She killed Father and Mother," Marcel said. "That's the only way she could find this location."

Leah's hands curled into fists. "We need to fight her."

"We need to leave." Marcel stood and grabbed her arm.

Leah pulled away and gave the vampire a death stare. "No. If the three of us can take her on together, we can beat her."

"No." Lord Ragon's voice cut through the room. "You only have a few minutes. Do as you are told."

"Why not? This is what we've been training for!" Leah shouted.

Zeus, who had been lying next to her feet at the table, curled into the corner of the kitchen.

"Leah, don't be stubborn. If the Ancient One says we go, then we go." Marcel's voice carried an edge she hadn't heard before.

Lord Ragon clearly knows things we do not. It is best if we take off, Leah. We do not want to fight the King prematurely. Asmodeus whispered in her mind.

Leah hesitated, then met Lord Ragon's red eyes. "If I'm not ready now, then I'll never be. If we all fight together, there's a chance."

The Ancient One's expression softened. He understood; of course he did. Leah's logic wasn't outlandish. After a few seconds of silent meditation, he shook his head.

"There is no time for an explanation. Your connection to both Trees is unheard of, but I'm afraid it will not be enough. You need to escape and find your true potential, Leah. The Trees have been guiding you there with your dreams. Follow them. Trust them."

At that moment, Bedivere opened the door and walked in with Excalibur in his hands. He took a knee and handed the sword to his king.

Lord Ragon took it and secured the sheath around his waist. "Thank you, Bedivere. Follow the plan, like we discussed."

The knight got to his feet. Lord Ragon placed a hand on his shoulder. "Thank you."

Bedivere pursed his lips and nodded once, then turned and picked up Zeus. Lord Ragon approached the dog and gave it a long kiss on the head. Zeus licked back, tail wagging.

"Be a good boy, okay? I'll be back."

Lord Ragon headed to the door. Marcel tried to pull Leah's arm once more, but she didn't move.

Leah stood frozen. "But what's going to happen to you? No, I'm staying. I want to fight."

Lord Ragon turned. Pride shone in his eyes, but when he spoke, his voice was low and grave. "You are to escape now, Leah Ackerman—"

"No!" Leah yelled and covered her ears, but it was futile.

"Follow Marcel's instructions until you are out of harm's reach. Do not try to come back."

Her body began acting on its own and turned. Her mind slowly grew cloudy and disoriented. Leah forced her head to look back at Lord Ragon one last time.

The Ancient One gave her a solemn smile and said, "Perhaps it is time to see my daughter again."

CHAPTER 26
CLASH OF KINGS

L eah's mind slipped away every time she strained to regain control. Her muscles tensed. Her feet dragged against the floor. She needed to stop.

Lord Ragon's curse pulled her under.

She surfaced again in a long hallway. Marcel walked ahead of her. Bedivere was gone. Zeus trotted beside her, his tail wagging. When had that happened? She tried to stop, to turn around, to do anything. Her body kept moving forward. The void wrapped around her thoughts like cotton, muffling everything.

Another blink. She stood in the basement dungeon where she had trained. The cold stone pressed against her back through her shirt. Marcel opened a secret door in one of the cells. Yellow light spilled from the tunnel beyond.

"I need to go and get the rest and make sure everyone evacuates safely. Keep going down this tunnel until the end. Don't stop."

Something in Marcel's red eyes made Leah's stomach drop. He looked scared. She hadn't seen that before.

Her body nodded. Marcel guided her into the tunnel,

and then he was gone. The stone walls closed in on either side. Her feet took another step forward.

Green flames exploded across her vision. The void shattered. Leah gasped and stumbled, catching herself against the tunnel wall. Her shadow stood in front of her, arms crossed.

"What are you doing?" Leah asked.

"For the past months, we have only heard rumors about Helen. This is our chance to see it firsthand."

She understood, and that realization made her sick. "You want to see the fight."

Her shadow nodded. "Lord Ragon cursed you, not me."

"No, Asmodeus, you can't—" Leah's body started moving again. She dug her heels in, but the curse dragged her forward anyway.

Her shadow began to disappear as Asmodeus stepped backward. "This is our only chance, Leah. We can finally learn Helen's true power. We will know what we are dealing with."

Leah took another step. The blissful nothingness pulled back under.

"I will be careful. Trust me."

The pristine mansion looked wrong under the sickly yellow light of the Astral Realm's first layers. Decay crept through the walls, spreading like frost across glass. Asmodeus took advantage of the deterioration and slipped through a hole in the structure to reach the entrance faster.

He froze at the threshold.

Helen Nielsen stood at the door wearing a long white trench coat over a white uniform. Lord Ragon faced her from the center of the lobby, one hand resting on his longsword.

"It was wise of you to show up alone." Lord Ragon's voice boomed.

"I wasn't going to put anyone else at risk. I wouldn't underestimate the power of the Ancient One like that."

"And yet, you are here."

"The Family is dead. Your reign of terror is over."

"I have been retired for the better part of three decades now. And if memory serves me well, we had an agreement with the Infinity Board. I signed it myself." Lord Ragon shifted his weight slightly. The prosthetic leg creaked.

"That agreement still allowed your kind to convert humans and spread misery. The Infinity Board has a new King now, and I will not let that happen under my watch."

"Right. You are not the first Mystic to do this, you know. Try to take control."

Helen slid her hands down her trench coat, opening it, and placed them on the katanas on either side. "I succeeded. It's now time for a new world order of peace and prosperity without the likes of you who hurt humans."

Cold spread through the space. Energy rolled off Helen in waves. Asmodeus felt his knees shake. Lord Ragon did not even blink.

"What do you want, Helen?"

"Your vampires left Leah Ackerman here. What did you do to her?" Her voice dropped several degrees as she glared at Lord Ragon with her ice-blue eyes.

Lord Ragon studied Helen for a long moment, then chuckled. "You actually came here to rescue her. How ironic. She came here on her own accord."

"Why?"

"Well, that is not really your business, is it?"

Helen clenched her jaw. The words came out through gritted teeth. "Where is she?"

Lord Ragon drew Excalibur with practiced ease and aimed it at Helen. "This conversation is over. Get off my land or face the consequences."

Helen lowered herself into a crouch. A predator preparing to strike. "The legendary King Arthur, reduced to a one-legged vampire. How pitiful."

"Helen Nielsen. The one who calls herself King after stealing someone else's power." He laughed, bitter and sharp. "You are not a King. You are simply a fraud."

The two stared at each other.

Lord Ragon's eyes narrowed. The air pressure changed. Something coiled tight in the room, building and building until Asmodeus felt it pressing against his essence. He recognized that sensation. *Gamaliel*. Cursed speech.

"Leave." The command carried impossible weight. Black threads erupted from Lord Ragon's mouth, writhing through the air toward Helen like snakes made of shadow.

Helen's body jerked. Her foot shifted backward.

Then she stopped.

The threads against her skin dissipated like smoke. Helen tilted her head, smiling. "Is that all you've got?"

Lord Ragon's jaw tightened. He drew a deeper breath. When he spoke again, his voice thundered through the lobby with enough force to make the chandelier shake.

"Leave my land!"

More threads poured from him, thicker and darker than before. They wrapped around Helen's arms, her legs, her throat. She stumbled several steps backward.

Golden symbols flared to life across Helen's exposed skin. The threads burned away in an instant.

Helen looked at Lord Ragon with what might have been

respect. "It won't work, Arthur. My body does not answer to anyone's commands but mine."

Asmodeus stared at the vampire in shock. Even attempting to command Helen was costing him. Lord Ragon possessed more power than almost any being on this continent. He had lived for over fifteen hundred years.

How strong was she?

"Then we do this the old way." Lord Ragon's words were raspy.

In the blink of an eye, both bodies vanished. The strike of metal rang through the space. Asmodeus tracked them only by sound. Lord Ragon's prosthetic leg struck the marble floor with a metallic clank, then the wall with a heavy thud, then the ceiling with an impossible crack. The impacts came so fast they blurred together into a percussive rhythm.

Sparks exploded where their blades met. The force of each collision sent ripples through the Astral Realm that Asmodeus could see as bursts of distorted light. Helen kept teleporting from one spot to the next, but Lord Ragon's enhanced senses tracked her perfectly. He predicted her attacks and met each one with Excalibur.

But he was on defense. Helen never stopped attacking.

Helen materialized on the second-floor balcony. Lord Ragon stood near the entrance below. Across the open space, they faced each other.

Asmodeus felt something change. He called on *Tiferet* and watched the energy shift. Not from the environment but from within Helen herself. Golden symbols blazed to life across her skin, glowing with the same light he had seen at the warehouse when she absorbed the scroll with those golden chains. He had encountered countless Mystics over the centuries. None of them had ever done this.

Mystics pulled energy from the wells of the Tree. They drew power from an external source.

Helen's essence simply grew. As if she contained her own well.

Lord Ragon must have sensed it, too. One moment, he stood at the entrance. Next, he was swinging Excalibur at Helen's neck with enough speed to create a sonic boom. The blade crashed into the wall where she had been. Stone exploded outward. Helen appeared behind him.

The vampire's kick caught her square in the chest. The impact sent her flying backward down the stairs. She twisted mid-air and landed on her feet like a cat. They collided again.

This time, every swing from Helen sent out a shockwave. The reverberation sliced through the air with enough force to carve furrows in the marble floor. The walls cracked. A priceless painting fell and shattered. Lord Ragon's defense started to fail. No block he attempted could fully stop Helen's blades. Dark blood splattered across the white marble as the two bodies moved too fast to follow properly.

Then Asmodeus saw it. A void of energy opened exactly where Helen teleported. Right on her leg. The crack echoed through the lobby like a gunshot. Lord Ragon spun and drove Excalibur through Helen's inner arm in the same motion. The blade punched through cleanly and emerged on the other side.

Asmodeus pumped his fist. Helen's eyes went wide with surprise. She dropped the katana from her injured arm and jumped back on her good leg, putting distance between them.

"Your *Netzach* was going to run out eventually," Lord Ragon said, breathing hard now.

Helen stared at the wound in her arm. Bright red blood

spurted out at an alarming rate. "Your body doesn't seem to be holding up well either."

Asmodeus noticed the pool of dark blood spreading beneath Lord Ragon's feet. The vampire had taken more damage than he let on.

Lord Ragon chuckled. The sound came out wet. "Who will bleed out first?"

Helen pulled energy from within again. Her presence in the Astral Realm grew impossibly bright. The stab wound in her arm began to close. Flesh knitted together. The broken leg straightened with a series of cracks as the bone reset itself. Within seconds, both injuries had healed completely.

"The bitch used *Chesed* on herself," Asmodeus whispered. His voice shook.

But it was more than that. She kept drawing power from within, with no apparent limit. Asmodeus was certain Helen pulled energy from the Core, but in a completely different way than Legion. With Legion, multiple entities seemed to live within the same body, fighting for control. With Helen, everything was unified. Singular.

That was terrifying.

"Two can play that game."

The air around Lord Ragon turned hot. The room began to spin. Pressure built in Asmodeus's head like someone was squeezing his skull. His knees gave out. He dropped to the floor as the material layer crashed into his senses. Colors became too bright. Sounds too loud. Everything hurt.

Lord Ragon's *Agshekeloh* could only pull energy from living entities. There were only two in the vicinity.

King Helen and Lord Ragon turned toward him at the same time, shock written across both faces. Helen vanished and reappeared next to him in the same instant. She cradled Leah's shadow.

"Leah, are you okay? Leah!"

Cold sweat formed on his brow. The person they had been training to fight and kill looked genuinely worried about him. The irony would have been funny if his head was not splitting apart.

"I told you to get away, goddammit!" Lord Ragon stumbled to the floor, breathing heavy as his wounds closed.

Helen pressed her fingers against the shadow's wrist, checking for a pulse. "You're stable. Just rest here, I'll take you to safety and then..." She trailed off. Her eyes met his, and she paused.

Helen placed both hands on either side of the shadow's face. Her eyes turned golden as she called on *Tiferet*. Searching for something.

"No." Helen's voice dropped to whisper. "This is not..." Her eyes went wide, then a hatred settled across her face. "Where is she?" The question came out like a growl. "Where is Leah?"

Asmodeus tried to speak, but Helen squeezed his face hard. "Her body is here, but she is..." Helen pulled back slightly. "Gone. Her soul is gone."

Her voice rose. "What did you want with Leah?"

In one motion, she went from cradling the shadow to pinning it against the wall by the neck. She lifted Leah's body off the ground. Helen's face was inches away, and those cold blue eyes that had held concern moments ago now spilled murderous intent.

Asmodeus gasped for air. Nothing came. Her grip on his throat squeezed.

"She trusted you!" Helen shook the shadow violently. "I felt her bond with you. I saw her defend you. And you did what? Consumed her? Replaced her?" Helen's other hand grabbed the shadow's face, fingers digging in hard enough to hurt. "You're wearing her like a suit. You do not deserve her body. You do not deserve to wear her face."

Pressure built in Asmodeus's head. His vision started to gray at the edges. This was it. This was how he died.

"Where is she?" Helen's voice cracked. "Tell me where Leah is, demon!"

Helen disappeared. A sword swung through the space where she had stood. Asmodeus dropped to the floor and gasped for air. His throat burned. His whole body shook.

"Your fight is with me." Lord Ragon turned toward the lobby where Helen had teleported. "Do not disrespect me like that."

Helen picked up her second katana from where it had fallen and sheathed them both. "It has been interesting to test my abilities with you, Arthur. But now I have more pressing issues. Out of respect for who you once were, I will give you a merciful death."

Asmodeus managed to pull himself back to a wall just in time to see King Helen and Lord Ragon charge at one another. This time, the two bodies collided only once. Excalibur penetrated Helen square in the chest.

At the same moment, Helen's free hand touched Lord Ragon's forehead.

Brilliant light flared up from her palm. Not the golden chains. Something else. Something that made Asmodeus's essence recoil. The light was warm and inviting and impossibly bright. It poured into Lord Ragon through the point of contact, flooding behind his eyes.

Lord Ragon's body went limp. Excalibur remained lodged in Helen's chest as golden chains began wrapping around the blade, slowly absorbing it into her skin. But Lord Ragon didn't seem to notice. His face transformed. The hardness melted away. The ancient weight that always pressed down on him lifted.

His eyes blazed with golden light.

"Ursulet?" The word came out broken. Fifteen hundred years of grief compressed into a single breath. "My little Ursulet?"

Helen's expression changed. The cold calculation faded. Her eyes softened in a way Asmodeus had never seen before. When she spoke, her voice carried a gentleness that seemed impossible from the woman. "I am here, Papa."

"I tried." Lord Ragon's hand reached up, trembling, to cup Helen's face. Tears streamed down his cheeks and into his beard. "I tried so hard to save you. To find the Grail in time. To make you well. And I failed. I failed you."

"I know." Helen smiled sadly. "I know you did, Papa. You did everything you could."

"All these centuries." He pulled her close, wrapping his arms around her in a desperate embrace. His whole body shook with sobs that seemed to tear themselves up from somewhere deeper than bone. "I never stopped thinking about you. Never stopped missing you. Every dog I saved, I thought of you. Every sunrise I watched from the windows, I remembered your laugh."

Asmodeus felt his throat tighten watching the burden of ages pour out of the legendary King Arthur. How much pain could one being carry? How long could someone endure before they broke?

"It is okay," Helen whispered, holding him. "You did not fail me. You loved me. That is what matters."

Lord Ragon pulled back slightly, looking at her face with wonder and disbelief and absolute peace all at once. "You are really here?"

"I am really here."

"Then I am not alone anymore." A smile broke across his face.

Helen slowly pulled the wooden stake from her coat. Lord Ragon looked down at it, and he didn't even flinch at the sight. The smile never left his face.

"Will you stay with me?" he asked softly.

"Until the end."

Helen drove the stake into his heart with one smooth motion. Lord Ragon gasped once, but the smile never left his face. The golden light in his eyes began to fade.

Helen held him as his body went still. For a long moment, she didn't move. Then, carefully, gently, she began to lower him to the ground.

Asmodeus managed to pull himself back against the wall, his chest heaving. He tried to invoke *Thagirion* to disappear into the Astral layers, but his energy was gone. Lord Ragon's *Agshekeloh* had drained him completely.

From across the lobby, he watched Lord Ragon's lips move. Whatever he said made Helen freeze mid-motion. Her whole body went rigid.

She tried to pull away.

Lord Ragon's hand shot out and locked around her wrist.

Even from this distance, Asmodeus could see the change in Helen's posture. The way her shoulders tensed. The way she wrenched backward, trying to break free.

Lord Ragon spoke again. His voice carried across the lobby, weak but clear enough to make out: "You must have read about my vision somewhere." He coughed, dark blood on his lips. "Smart. Research how to kill your enemies. Find their weaknesses."

Helen yanked harder, but his grip held.

"But there was one thing I always left out of every

account," Lord Ragon said. "One detail I never wrote down, never told anyone. A trap, if you will."

"Let go!" Helen's voice cut sharp across the space.

Even dying, Lord Ragon's smile widened. "*Fire.*"

CHAPTER 27
A NOBLE SACRIFICE

Blue flames erupted from Lord Ragon's free hand.

Asmodeus's essence recoiled at the sight. *Golohab*. The all-consuming fire. The flames that fed on Tree of Life energy. The flames that had a mind of their own.

For the first time that night, Asmodeus saw real fear flash across Helen's face.

The flames spread up Lord Ragon's arm, across his chest, consuming him from the inside out. The wooden stake in his heart caught fire and disintegrated. His fingers began to crumble to ash, and his grip on Helen's wrist finally loosened.

She yanked her arm free and staggered backward, putting distance between them.

The blue flames spread outward in hungry waves. They devoured the furniture, the walls, the priceless artifacts. Everything turned to ash in seconds. The fire moved with terrible intelligence, reaching out toward anything that could burn.

Helen's head snapped toward Asmodeus. Those cold

blue eyes locked onto him across the burning room. She took a step in his direction.

The flames surged between them, cutting off her path. They moved faster than they should have, spreading across the floor like water. Chasing her. Hunting her.

She vanished and reappeared on Asmodeus's other side.

The fire was already there. It knew where she would go. Blue flames climbed the walls and spread across the ceiling. The heat became unbearable.

Helen tried again, teleporting near the entrance. The fire followed. A tongue of blue flame licked across her uniform, leaving another singe. She looked back at Asmodeus one more time. Her eyes narrowed, calculating.

The *Golohab* roared between them, a wall of consuming fire that wanted her Tree of Life energy more than anything else in the room.

Helen vanished.

The flames continued to spread, relentless and alive. Lord Ragon's body collapsed into ash where he'd stood, the last of the Ancient One scattering across the burning floor. But the *Golohab* didn't die with him. It fed. It grew.

Asmodeus pressed himself harder against the wall. The heat seared his skin—*Leah's* skin. The smoke filled his lungs—*her* lungs.

No way out. No energy left to escape.

The ceiling groaned. A beam crashed down three feet away, erupting in blue fire. The flames spread across the floor toward him.

This is how I die.

They flew past him, devouring a bookshelf nearby.

Cold hands grabbed his shoulders.

"Move!" Marcel's voice was strained with effort.

Asmodeus felt himself being dragged backward. His heels scraped across the marble as Marcel hauled him toward the entrance. The *Golohab* spread across the floor, ignoring them as it jumped from shelves to table to curtains, as if gleefully destroying everything.

"The tunnel," Marcel said through gritted teeth. "We need to reach the tunnel."

They burst through a side door. The smoke was thicker here. Marcel coughed but kept moving, navigating hallways that Asmodeus barely registered. Behind them, the fire roared. Glass shattered. Wood splintered and burned.

A massive shape appeared ahead through the smoke. Paige, already in wolf form. Her yellow eyes found them through the haze.

"Follow her!" Marcel shouted.

Paige turned and bolted down the corridor. Marcel dragged Asmodeus after her, moving as fast as he could while supporting the demon's weight. Asmodeus's legs barely worked. Lord Ragon's *Agshekeloh* had drained everything.

I almost died. The thought kept repeating. *I almost ruined every chance we had to take out Helen.*

Paige led them through twisting passages. She could see through the smoke and smell the safe path. When burning debris fell from the ceiling, she darted around it. When a hallway collapsed ahead, she pivoted and found another route.

Stupid. So stupid. Asmodeus's thoughts spiraled. *Had to watch. Had to know. Almost cost Leah everything.*

They reached the basement—the dungeon where Leah had trained. Paige shifted back to human form at one of the cells and yanked open a secret door. Yellow light spilled from the tunnel beyond.

"In. Now." Her voice was rough from the smoke.

Asmodeus stumbled forward into the tunnel. Marcel and Paige followed, slamming the door shut behind them.

The temperature dropped immediately. Stone walls pressed in on either side, but the smoke was gone. The roar of fire muffled to a distant rumble.

They didn't slow down. Paige took the lead again, moving fast through the narrow passage. Marcel kept one hand locked around Asmodeus's arm, pulling him forward.

"How?" Asmodeus managed to gasp out. "How did you know?"

"Lord Ragon told us to wait," Marcel said. His jaw was tight. "He said you'd break his command. That the demon would come watch. When *Golohab* started, we were supposed to get you out."

Need to reach Leah. Asmodeus could barely think past the panic. *Need to rejoin. Make sure she's okay.*

They rounded a corner. The tunnel opened into a wider space. Stone gave way to packed dirt. Roots hung from the ceiling. Fresh air hit Asmodeus's face.

Behind them, an explosion shook the tunnel. Dust rained down from the ceiling.

"Faster!" Paige said.

The tunnel sloped upward. The air grew colder. Asmodeus could see light ahead. Electric light.

They burst out into an underground garage. The space was small, with concrete walls on three sides and a metal door leading to the surface on the fourth. Two vehicles sat waiting. A black van and a small Toyota sedan.

Bedivere stood beside them, Zeus in his arms. Next to him stood Leah.

Her eyes were distant, unfocused. She swayed slightly, as if standing took effort.

The butler's expression was grim when he looked at Marcel. "Is he dead?"

Marcel nodded once. "It's done."

Bedivere closed his eyes and exhaled slowly. "Then he finally found peace."

Behind them, blue light flickered at the tunnel entrance, throwing dancing shadows across the concrete.

"Will it follow us?" Paige asked.

"No," Bedivere said. "It'll feed until there's nothing left, then burn itself out. By the time Helen searches the grounds, she'll only find a collapsed cellar. No one knows about these tunnels."

Asmodeus slumped against the Toyota. His vision blurred at the edges. He was losing his grip on the shadow.

Leah. Need to rejoin with Leah.

He closed his eyes and reached for *Satariel*. As he vanished, he could feel something against Leah's mind. It was like a tight tether, pulling at her thoughts. But it was weak and fraying.

Green flames wrapped around his essence, and he pulled on the tether, snapping it as he dissolved.

The world swayed. Everything blurred together. Then he was falling into Leah's mind.

Leah gasped. Her knees buckled.

Strong hands caught her before she hit the ground. Bedivere lowered her carefully, supporting her weight until she found her balance.

The memories slammed through her. The tunnel. The fight. Helen's face inches from hers, full of rage and grief. Lord Ragon dying with a smile. The *Golohab* consuming everything.

"He's dead," Leah whispered.

I'm sorry, Leah. Asmodeus's voice was quiet. *I know you cared for him.*

The Ancient One. The vampire who'd trained her, challenged her, and treated her like an equal. Gone. Turned to ash by his own hand.

And Helen had killed him. Absorbed Excalibur. Healed from mortal wounds like they were nothing.

"Leah." Marcel's voice cut through the thoughts. "We need to move. The fire's spreading."

She looked up. They were in an underground garage. Paige stood by a van, her clothes torn and singed. Marcel was covered in soot. Bedivere held Zeus near the sedan.

Heat pressed against her back. She turned and saw a blue light flickering at the tunnel entrance.

"What's happening?"

"Lord Ragon's mansion is burning," Bedivere said. "The *Golohab* consumed it. We need to evacuate immediately."

Leah pushed herself to her feet. Her head spun, but she forced herself to focus. "Where are we going?"

"Paige and I are going to Chicago," Marcel said. "The Family will be in chaos. News of the Ancient One's death will spread fast. Elders will fight for territory, for power. We need to be there to find anyone who survived. Protect who we can."

"And me?"

Bedivere stepped forward and pulled an envelope from his coat. The wax seal bore Lord Ragon's crest. "This is for you. Read it. Follow his instructions. Do not tell us what it says."

He also held out a set of keys. "The Toyota. It's clean. No way to trace it back to Lord Ragon."

Leah took both with shaking hands.

Behind them, another explosion shook the garage. The van's windows rattled.

"Open it now," Paige said. "We need to leave."

Leah broke the seal and unfolded the letter. Lord Ragon's handwriting was precise and familiar.

Dear Leah,

I'm sorry this is the way our story ends. In the short time we had together, I have learned not only to admire you but also to care for you. If you are reading this, it means my last efforts to stop Helen were in vain, and that the responsibility now falls on your shoulders. You must finish this.

You now know exactly what you are facing. I believe you can reach your true potential in Corpus Christi, Texas. The lavender fields are lovely this time of year.

Please give Zeus one last hug for me.

All the best, King Arthur

Leah read it twice. Corpus Christi. Texas. Alone.

She looked up at the others. Bedivere watched her with sadness in his eyes. Marcel stood impassive, but his jaw was tight. Paige had her arms crossed.

"He wants me to go alone," Leah said.

"Yes," Bedivere confirmed. "He believed you would be safer that way. Harder to track. And we would only slow you down."

"This is bullshit," Paige said. "We should stay together."

"We can't," Marcel said. "Helen's hunting all of us, but she's fixated on Leah. If we stay together, we all die. Separately, we have a chance."

"What about you?" Leah looked at Bedivere.

"I will take Zeus north," the butler said. "Lord Ragon maintained a safe house. A place for our kind. I shall prepare it, send word to what's left to the Families. Somewhere they can go to ground until this is over."

Another explosion.

"We're out of time," Marcel said. "Move. Now."

Leah walked to where Zeus sat in Bedivere's arms. The

dog's tail wagged weakly. She picked him up and hugged him close, burying her face in his soft fur. He licked her cheek.

"This is from Lord Ragon," she whispered. "Be a good boy, okay?"

She set him down and turned to the others before she could change her mind.

Paige stepped forward first. Her blue eyes met Leah's.

"I still hate your demon," Paige said. "But don't die. That's an order."

Leah offered a faint smile. "I'll do my best."

They hugged quickly. Paige squeezed hard enough to hurt, then let go and stepped back.

Marcel approached next. He held out his hand. Leah shook it, and he pulled her into a brief embrace.

"Stay smart," he said quietly. "You've got the potential to be something extraordinary. Don't waste it."

"You, too. Don't let Chicago tear itself apart."

"We'll try."

Bedivere was last. He shook her hand formally, his grip firm. "It has been an honor, Miss Ackerman. I hope we meet again under more fortunate circumstances."

"Thank you for everything."

He nodded once, then turned to the others. "Everyone in. We leave in thirty seconds."

Leah got in the car. The keys shook in her hand as she started the engine. Through the windshield, she watched Marcel, Paige, and Bedivere climb into the van with Zeus.

The metal garage door began to rise, revealing the night beyond. In the distance, Lord Ragon's mansion was an inferno. Blue flames reached toward the sky, consuming everything the Ancient One had built over fifteen hundred years.

The van pulled out first, heading east toward the main

road. Leah waited until it disappeared into the darkness, then put the car in gear.

She drove out into the night, leaving the burning mansion behind. In the rearview mirror, she watched the flames grow smaller until they were just a distant glow on the horizon.

Corpus Christi. Her only hope now was to embrace her true potential. To become what Lord Ragon believed she could be.

An Immortal Witch.

Because, based on what Asmodeus witnessed tonight, that was the only way she'd ever stand a chance against Helen.

CHAPTER 28
TO LAVENDAR FIELDS

Rain hammered the windshield. Leah blinked, her eyes burning from staring at the endless gray highway for hours.

The GPS displayed southern Iowa—still six hundred miles to Corpus Christi. Flat fields stretched on both sides, filled with corn stalks. She'd left northern Minnesota behind somewhere around hour eight. Or was it nine?

She was unstoppable. Like a force of nature.

Asmodeus's voice filtered through again, not directed at her but bleeding into their shared space. Those cold blue eyes flashed in her memory. Helen was standing over Lord Ragon. The wooden stake. The smile that never left his face even as he died.

Leah's jaw tightened. Her hands ached from gripping the wheel.

Her stomach grumbled. When had she last eaten? She opened the glove compartment, hoping to find something, anything.

Instead, she found cash. A thick stack of bills, rubber-banded together.

Something appeared beside it. The blue eye formed, watching her.

Leah grabbed the money and slammed the compartment shut.

She took the next exit and stopped at a small chain cafe. Inside, the fluorescent lights were too bright overhead. She ordered a large coffee, egg-and-cheese sandwich, and blueberry muffin. The woman at the register stared at her a beat too long. So did the man behind her in line.

Were they Mystics? She didn't know, and she wasn't about to wait around and find out.

Leah grabbed her order and hurried back outside to her car, stepping into the damp air.

Back in the car, she tore into the sandwich as she got back onto the highway. The bread stuck in her throat, but she forced it down anyway. The coffee only helped a little before burning her tongue.

A semi-truck roared past her, spraying water.

Lord Ragon's last words lingered in her memory. *Maybe it's time to see my daughter again.* Then the blue flames consumed everything. She saw Helen's face when she realized what he'd done.

Leah's throat burned. She swallowed hard and focused on the road.

"Can you come out?" she said. "I need some company."

Green fire erupted in the passenger seat. When it cleared, her shadow sat buckled in, staring out at the rain.

A hush fell between them. A mile passed. Then another.

"We should talk about the fight," Leah said finally.

Asmodeus glanced at her. "We remember the same things. What is there to discuss?"

"Humor me."

Her shadow leaned back against the seat. "Fine."

"At first, Helen fought like she always does. Testing

Lord Ragon's speed, finding weaknesses. Then she paused on that second floor, and you saw it. Her energy grew."

"She pulled from the Core."

"Right. She had to stop fighting to do it. "That means it takes time. She can't just use it freely."

"Not much time," Asmodeus said. "Who is to say she cannot pull while fighting?"

"But she didn't. She put distance between them first. What if that's the opening? If we can get her somewhere she can't access the Tree of Life easily, maybe force her to keep pulling from the Core."

Asmodeus was quiet for a moment. Outside, the rain started to let up. "You are thinking of the Astral Realm."

"Coral pulled me there once. And in the Astral, Mystics can't use their wells without their essence breaking down." The idea crystallized as she spoke. "If I become an Immortal Witch, maybe I could bring Helen there. Cut her off from the Tree."

"Assuming you *can* become one. Assuming you survive long enough to do it."

Leah clenched her jaw. "Lord Ragon sent us for a reason. He thought I could do this."

"He also thought he could kill Helen." Asmodeus looked out the window. "And remember what the Shifter said? How she struck, again and again, like an army in one body."

The memory surfaced. That terrified creature in the van, talking about Helen's unstoppable assault. *If you can't be directed, you'll be exterminated.* Then later, dying in front of them all. Its last shocked words.

Leah's hands went white on the wheel. "She took out the Shifters. All of them, and with their last breath, she saw me."

"She consumes, just like Legion." Asmodeus's fingers drummed against the passenger door. "The Core is always hungry. Always devouring. She has to keep feeding it, or it will consume her instead."

"She has to be careful when pulling energy. The more she uses, the harder it gets to control."

"Maybe. But we're guessing a lot. We do not know if the Witches will help or if you can bring Helen to the Astral. Or what happens if we destabilize the Core."

"It's something," Leah said quietly.

"It is."

They fell silent again. The rain had stopped completely, leaving only wet roads and a gray sky. A green road sign appeared ahead. Next exit: 10 miles.

Leah's vision blurred. She blinked hard, then again. The white lines on the road started to blend together.

"You need to stop," Asmodeus said.

"I'm fine."

"You have been driving for twelve hours straight. You are going to kill us both."

Leah glanced at the GPS. Six hours left to Corpus Christi. They could make it by morning if she just pushed through. Find the Immortal Witches. Get answers. Figure out how to save Sarah and Isaac.

Her eyes drooped. The car drifted right.

Leah jerked the wheel back, pulse spiking. "Shit."

"We're stopping at the next exit and getting a motel."

"We don't have time."

"Helen won't find you. We're already far enough. If you crash this car and kill us both, then what's the point?"

The exit sign grew larger. 5 miles.

Leah's whole body ached. Her neck. Her shoulders. Her hands cramped from gripping the wheel. When was the last time she'd actually had a full night's sleep? She'd been studying and worrying so much that she'd been tossing and turning for weeks.

She couldn't remember.

"Fine," she said. "But just a few hours. We leave before sunrise."

"Good. Finally, you have some sense."

Asmodeus dissolved into smoke and merged with Leah again.

As Leah continued down the highway, she focused on staying awake for the next five miles. The sky was darkening now, the gray clouds turning to deep purple. Headlights from oncoming traffic cut through the dusk.

She thought about Lord Ragon's letter in the passenger seat, still tucked in its envelope. His handwriting. His final instructions sent her to Texas. To Frank. To the Immortal Witches who might be able to help her become what she needed to be.

If they would help. *If* she could convince them. *If* any of this would actually work.

So many ifs.

The exit finally appeared. Leah took it, following the signs off the highway toward a cluster of gas stations and chain motels visible in the falling dark. One had a vacancy sign glowing in the twilight.

She pulled into the parking lot and killed the engine.

CHAPTER 29
A LUCKY ACCIDENT

Leah woke before sunrise to rain splattering against the motel window. Her back ached from the lumpy bed, and her neck was stiff. She checked her phone. Five thirty. Good enough.

After a quick, lukewarm shower, she grabbed bitter coffee from the lobby machine. The burned flavor fit her mood. She was back on the highway by six, dawn breaking over the horizon before clouds devoured it.

According to the GPS, Corpus Christi was six hours away.

Have you thought of how we are going to find these witches? Corpus Christi is quite big, you know, Asmodeus said.

"I figured we'd hit one of the no-man's-land bars. Gather intel."

She sensed his disapproval but ignored it. There was only so much she could plan for.

The rain vanished an hour later, and sunlight flashed off the wet roads. Even as she squinted against the glare, something across the highway caught her eye.

A battered black Dodge sat on the shoulder, hood up and smoke billowing from the engine. Two people stood beside it. As Leah got closer, she could make out details. A tall, lanky man in a long, tattered coat. A Black woman with blond locs falling past her shoulders.

The woman's head turned as Leah's car approached.

For just a second, the woman's eyes flashed violet.

Leah's foot hit the brake before she'd fully processed what she'd seen, her heart beating fast with a sudden jolt of adrenaline and confusion.

You have got to be kidding me.

She slowed and turned the wheel toward the grass median separating the roads. The highway was empty this far from any city. She crossed over, flipped on her blinkers, and pulled onto the shoulder about twenty feet behind the smoking Dodge.

Leah killed the engine and stepped out.

The woman watched Leah, arms crossed, her expression blending of amusement and relief. The man leaned against the dead car, head on his arm, incredulous smile spreading across his pale face.

"Bloody hell, my fucking luck!" His voice carried a sharp Irish lilt. He raked a hand through his cropped ginger hair and pushed off the car. "See, Mo? I told you. My dice never lie."

He shoved up the sleeve of his tattered trench coat and held out his forearm. A tattoo of two dice marked his skin, the pips made of spirals instead of dots.

Snake eyes.

Frank grinned at the tattoo. "Breakdown on the road, but here you are." He looked up at Leah, his smile widening. "Luck always delivers."

The woman rolled her eyes. "Oh shut up, Frank."

Frank. The only surviving Immortal Witch from the old coven. Leah had met him once, briefly, at the Witches' Parlor when she'd gone with Helen years ago. Before everything fell apart. He was the one Cora had tried to contact from inside Legion.

And Mo. She was new.

They were real. Standing here on a Texas highway with a smoking car and duffel bags.

Mo walked over and extended her hand. Up close, Leah could see the intricate tattoos covering her bare arms. Snakes coiling around skulls. Ravens in flight. Symbols Leah didn't recognize, all rendered in deep black ink. Her dark skin gleamed with a light sheen of sweat from the Texas heat, and her brown eyes held Leah's gaze with an intensity that made Leah's breath catch.

"I've seen you a few times. Name's Mo," Mo said. Her grip was warm and firm. "Good to finally meet you face to face."

"Yeah," Leah managed. "Likewise."

Mo glanced back at the smoking Dodge. "We need a ride. That piece of junk finally gave out." She turned back to Leah. "We'll take you to the parlor."

Frank grabbed two duffel bags from the back of the dead car and strode over, hand extended. "Good to see you made it, Leah!" He barked a laugh and shook her hand with enough enthusiasm to rattle her arm. "We were just about to hunt you down, but Luck brought you right to us. As soon as Mo started losing faith in me, too." He swung the bags up. "Pop the trunk?"

Leah hesitated for just a second, then hit the button. Frank tossed the bags in and slammed the trunk closed.

Mo held out her hand, palm up. "Keys. I'll drive."

"Wait, what?" Leah pulled the keys back. "It's my car."

"Oy!" Frank walked back around. "I'm your senior, so I'm driving."

"The last car you drove is up in smoke." Mo gestured at

the Dodge, then turned back to Leah. "And this girl looks like she hasn't slept in days. I'm taking over driver duties."

Leah opened her mouth to argue, then stopped. She was exhausted. Her back ached and she'd been driving for hours already. These people were taking her exactly where she needed to go.

"Fine." Leah dropped the keys into Mo's palm. "But I'm riding shotgun."

Mo's lips curved into a slight smile as she slid into the driver's seat. "Fair enough."

Frank threw his arms up. "Really. No respect for the elders." But he was already moving toward the back door, still grinning.

Leah almost smiled. Even Immortal Witches bickered like siblings.

"Wait." Leah turned to look at them both. "How are you even here? Am I just supposed to be okay with randomly finding you?"

Mo opened the driver's side door. "That's how Frank's luck works." She slid into the seat and started adjusting the mirrors. "We'll explain on the way. Come on."

Leah stood there for another moment, looking at the smoking Dodge, then at Frank cramming his long frame into her backseat. Lord Ragon's letter still sat in the passenger seat. The letter that had sent her here. To find these people. To get help with saving her friends.

And here they were.

She walked around and got in the passenger seat.

For immortals, these people do not waste time, Asmodeus said.

Leah had to agree.

Mo merged onto the highway, the charred Dodge vanishing behind them.

CHAPTER 30
REBUILDING

"The dreams," Leah said, looking out toward the Texas desert. "That's how you found me?"

Mo kept her eyes on the highway. "Yeah. Frank's luck brought us to that stretch of road, but I'm the one who saw you coming."

"Saw me how?"

Mo lifted her left arm off the wheel and rolled up her sleeve. A tattoo marked her forearm—a woman's face, her eyes replaced with spirals that looked like tiny galaxies.

Leah frowned. Spirals again. Like the ones she saw on Frank's dice moments ago, or the design Cora had shown her when they met in the parlor, or the spiral walk she had to make to get to the Tree.

"Clairvoyance," Mo said, letting her sleeve fall back. "I can see things before they happen. Sometimes days in advance."

From the backseat, Frank leaned forward. "Useful when you're trying to avoid the Infinity Board." He glanced at Mo. "Though maybe save the full tour for after we know why they're hunting her."

Leah's stomach twisted. How much should she say?

These were Cora's people. Or what was left of them after Legion. But Cora was dead, and Leah had turned her down when it mattered.

"I met Cora a few years back," Leah said. The words came out quieter than she intended. "Before Legion killed her. She said I had Immortal Witch potential."

Frank's expression changed. Something like grief flickered across his face before he buried it. "And you turned her down."

It wasn't a question.

"I did." Leah met his gaze in the rearview mirror. "I chose to stay with the Infinity Board instead."

"Why the change of heart?" Frank pulled a silver flask from inside his coat and took a drink.

"Dude, it's barely ten in the morning," Mo muttered.

"It's five o'clock somewhere, dear." Frank pocketed the flask and waited.

Leah's hands curled into fists against her legs. "Because the woman I trusted most just became a tyrant. She's consumed half the magical world, caused my friends to be captured, and now she's hunting me across three states." Her throat burned. "So yeah. Desperate times."

"What did you—"

Red and blue lights flashed in the side mirror.

"You gotta be fucking kidding me." Mo checked the rearview. "I wasn't even speeding!"

Leah twisted around. A patrol car followed fifty feet back, lights blazing against the late afternoon sun. "Shit. Do you think it's them?"

"Relax," Frank caught her eye. "They're probably bored and gonna say we have a busted taillight or crossed the lines."

"I didn't cross anything," Mo gripped the wheel, easing off the gas.

"I know," Frank said, "but these are out of state plates. I bet they're just nosy."

Leah shook her head. "Or it's Helen."

"She has no idea where you are. Can you imagine how many resources that would take?" Frank checked his dice tattoo. "We've got a four. Not the best odds."

Mo guided the car onto the shoulder. Gravel crunched under the tires. "Everyone stay calm. Let me do the talking."

The patrol car stopped behind them.

Leah pulled on *Tiferet*. Warmth spread through her chest, and her senses sharpened. She twisted in her seat to watch through the back window.

The driver's door opened. A man stepped out. Thick mustache, cowboy hat, Ray-Bans. Stereotypical Texas cop. He moved to the front of his vehicle, hand resting on his holstered gun.

"See?" Frank settled back. "Just a speeding ticket. We'll be fine."

The passenger door opened.

A woman stepped out. Short hair, dark sunglasses. She walked around the front of the patrol car.

Something about the way she moved was off. And she definitely didn't look like a cop.

Sunlight hit the woman's face.

Yellow eyes glowed behind her sunglasses.

They found us! Asmodeus said.

Leah's chest tightened. "Mo. Drive."

"What?"

"Drive! Now!" Leah's voice cracked. "She's Board!"

"Wait, what?" Frank sat up. "How do you—"

"Yellow eyes! Go!"

Mo slammed the gas pedal.

The engine roared. The tires spun against gravel.

The woman's hands came together with a sharp clap.

A wave of energy rippled through the air.

Everything stopped.

The car froze mid-acceleration, wheels spinning uselessly against gravel. Leah's muscles locked. Her lungs seized mid-breath. The world turned thick and sluggish.

Hod.

Do not panic, Asmodeus said. *Conserve your energy. Wait for an opening.*

Her eyes still worked. Mo sat rigid behind the wheel, only her eyes moving, darting frantically toward Leah. In the rearview mirror, Frank had gone statue-still.

Footsteps crunched on gravel.

Leah tried to pull on *Malchut*. Nothing happened.

A third officer climbed out of the patrol car's back seat. Tall, dark skin, cold eyes. He walked past Leah's window without looking at her.

The woman appeared beside the driver's window. Hands still pressed together. "Smart move trying to run. Unfortunately, you were too slow."

The male driver came around to Leah's side. He peered through the window at her, then back at Frank.

"Here's how this works," the woman said. "You three sit here nice and quiet while we wait for transport. We can hold you like this for hours." She smiled. "So don't bother struggling."

The woman moved toward the back of the car to examine Frank. Her back turned to Leah.

In the rearview mirror, Leah watched Frank. His eyes tracked the woman.

His fingers twitched.

His hand jerked against the binding. Sweat beaded on his forehead. He kept pushing, forcing his hand toward his forearm millimeter by millimeter.

The dice tattoo began to glow.

The spiral pips shifted beneath his skin. Rolled.

Snake eyes.

Something sour touched the back of Leah's tongue.

His luck is turning, Asmodeus said. *Get ready.*

Frank's eyes locked onto the woman.

The woman stumbled. Her hands broke apart.

The binding vanished.

Leah sucked in a breath and pulled hard on *Satariel*. Her shadow peeled away as she opened the door. It materialized outside the car and sprinted toward the scrub brush.

"Stop her!" the male officer shouted.

The woman spun and slammed her hands back together. Energy hit the shadow, and it froze mid-stride.

Leah pulled on *Thagirion*. Cold washed over her and sounds muffled. The Texas sun turned sickly yellow as the astral layer slipped over reality. She stepped out of the car.

The male officer drew his gun. The third officer invoked *Gevurah*. Red fire gathered in his palms.

Get the woman first, Asmodeus said. *She can bind us again.*

Leah gathered *Malchut* in her chest. Pressure built until her ribs ached. She aimed at the woman and released it.

The blast caught her side. She flew sideways, hit the ground hard, and rolled three times before coming to a stop. The shadow clone dissipated in green smoke.

The male officer fired where the clone had been. Dirt kicked up.

The third officer hurled fire at the car.

Leah lunged between them and the car, calling on *Netzach*. The flames licked against her skin, warm but harmless. She gathered more *Malchut* and sent it like a fist into his chest.

He went down hard.

The male officer scrambled backward, trying to create distance. Leah sent two *Malchut* blasts at the patrol car's tires. They burst with sharp cracks.

"Mo, drive!" Leah shouted and jumped back into the car.

Mo floored it. Gravel sprayed as they peeled onto the highway.

Leah dropped *Thagirion*. Color and sound crashed back. She twisted in her seat. The patrol car shrank behind them, two figures kneeling beside the third on the ground.

Nobody spoke. The highway stretched ahead, heat shimmering off the asphalt.

Leah's hands shook. Sweat soaked into her shirt.

Well done, Asmodeus murmured.

"What the hell just happened?" Mo's knuckles were white on the steering wheel.

"Board." Leah checked the mirrors again. Empty highway behind them. "They must have tracked the car somehow. Maybe the plates, or—" She stopped. Lord Ragon's letter sat in the cup holder. Had he given her a car they could trace? "Doesn't matter. They found us."

Frank examined his dice tattoo. The snake eyes had shifted back to something higher. "Our luck's improving, but it won't last long. We need to get off this highway before they send more."

Mo's eyes flashed violet. When they cleared, she nodded. "There's a turnoff about three miles up. Rougher road, but it'll get us to the parlor without passing through any towns."

"How far?" Leah asked.

"A few hours if we push it." Mo glanced at her. "And when we get there, you're explaining everything. Start to finish."

Leah nodded. Her throat felt raw.

Mo took the turnoff when it came. Smooth highway gave way to cracked asphalt that rattled the car. They drove for hours, only stopping at isolated gas stations for fuel and restroom breaks. Scrub brush and cactus pressed close on either side. Eventually, the sun settled low and orange on the horizon.

Buildings appeared ahead. Small at first, then growing. A convenience store. A church with peeling white paint. Houses with cars in gravel driveways.

Mo slowed as they entered what passed for a town. A few people walked the sidewalk. Violet lavender bloomed in small gardens. The place felt old, like it had been here long before highways cut through Texas and would be here long after.

They drove through a roundabout that circled a massive oak tree, its branches spreading wide enough to shade half the street. Mo took the last exit onto Main Street.

Neon lights flickered to life as the sun slipped lower. Purple and red tubes spelling out words in cursive script. As they got closer, Leah could make out the full sign: *Witch's Ink*.

Frank leaned forward and tapped Leah's shoulder. He nodded toward the old brick building beneath the neon.

"Subtle, right?" he asked. "Welcome to the parlor. Let's get inside. You've got a lot of explaining to do."

CHAPTER 31
WITCH PRIORITY

Leah's eyes watered as a wall of smell slammed into her nose the second they went through the door. Herbs and smoke mixed together so thick she coughed.

Mo groaned, went straight to a window, and threw it open. "Jesus, Frank. How much did you burn?"

Frank dropped the bags by the counter and stretched with a grunt. His shoulders popped. "Just a bit of luck, love. Can't be too careful."

"A bit?" Mo grabbed a fan and turned it on high. "It smells like a Bath & Body Works fire in here. Bergamot, rose hips, and rosemary? You calling luck or making stew?"

Frank grinned. "Worked, didn't it? She found us. Let's talk out back where we can breathe."

The tattoo shop was small. Flash designs covered the walls in neat rows, everything from skulls to flowers to geometric patterns. A padded chair sat in the center under a bright lamp, next to a rolling cart of ink bottles and wrapped needles. The smell of antiseptic cut through the herbs.

Frank crossed to a door marked *Staff Only* and pushed it

open. A dim hallway stretched beyond, lit by a single bulb. Two doors on either side, both closed. He flipped a switch, and fluorescent bulbs hummed to life at the far end, revealing a cramped break room.

Leah followed them inside. A round wooden table dominated the space, scarred and worn, surrounded by mismatched chairs. A kitchenette huddled in the corner with a small sink piled with coffee mugs. The whole place smelled like stale cigarettes and a cheap air freshener trying to mask them.

Frank pulled out a chair and dropped into it. "Sit."

Leah took the chair. Mo grabbed beers from the fridge, handed one to Frank, and offered one to Leah.

Leah shook her head. "I'm good."

Mo raised an eyebrow but didn't push. She put one of the beers back and cracked hers open, then sat between them. For a moment, nobody spoke. Just the drone of the fridge and the distant sound of traffic outside.

"Are we safe here?" Leah asked.

Mo twisted the cap off her beer and took a long drink. "This whole town is warded six ways to Sunday. Took us two years to layer the protections after Legion tore through. Anyone looking for Immortal Witch energy hits a dead end at the city limits." She leaned back in her chair. "We're good. Now, mind catching us up on what the hell is happening?"

Leah took a breath. Where to start? Helen's betrayal. The fight with Lord Ragon. Leaving Sarah and Isaac. The Core inside Helen is growing stronger.

She started talking and found she couldn't stop. Mo and Frank didn't interrupt. They just listened, Frank working his way through his beer while Mo's eyes flashed violet every so often, like she was seeing more than just Leah's words.

Heat built in Leah's throat as she described the fight. How Helen had just absorbed Excalibur like it was nothing. How Lord Ragon had ordered her to run. The Ancient One's last words. *Maybe it's time to see my daughter again.*

Leah's voice cracked. She cleared her throat and kept going. The escape through the tunnels with Marcel. The two-day drive to Texas. Finding them on the highway.

When she finished, her hands shook. She pressed them flat against the table.

Mo set her beer down slowly. Her voice came out thin. "So, the same thing that consumed Cora and the rest is inside the leader of the Infinity Board?"

"Looks like it." Frank's expression had gone hard. "I did hear about the Board cleaning house lately. Shifters, vampires, werewolves, Chimeras, oni, banshees. Whole species are on the brink of extinction, if not wiped out completely. Which honestly sounds like a good thing."

Leah's jaw tightened. "She can't be trusted. That hunger doesn't just go away. Legion consumed everything in his path, and now Helen has that same Core inside her. She'll lose control eventually. And not all creatures deserve to die. Some are just trying to survive."

Frank held up a hand. "I'm not arguing, doll. That Core killed my Coven. Might be purified of its demon essence, but the hunger's still there." He leaned forward, elbows on the table. "It needs to be destroyed before it spills over into the Astral Realm and gets to the Well."

Mo's voice dropped to a whisper. "Do you think this is related to Leo?"

Frank's face went grim. He stared at his beer for a long moment. "Could be. I had my suspicions about that creature the moment it showed up, right when we retrieved the coordinates."

The name clicked in Leah's head. She sat up straighter.

"Leo. That's the guy you left behind, right? I heard you talking about him in one of my dreams. Something about the... what was it... Phovias finishing him off."

Both witches turned to stare at her.

"The Phovias layer," Frank said slowly. "How the hell do you know about that?"

"I've been dreaming about you two for a while now." Leah looked from Frank to Mo. "At first, it was distant, like watching through fog. But it got clearer over time. I started hearing your conversations. Then I saw you." She pointed at Mo.

Mo glanced at Frank. "Is that normal? I thought I saw her because of my clairvoyance."

Frank exhaled and rubbed his face. "Someone with high potential gets drawn to other Immortal Witches. Especially in dreams." He looked at Leah, studying her. "I met you once before, actually. Years ago, when you were wandering the Astral. You probably don't remember."

But Leah did remember. The image surfaced in her mind, sharp and clear. A man in a tattered trench coat on a foggy street, surrounded by abandoned homes. She'd been terrified, thought he was connected to Asmodeus, back when he was trying to kill her. She'd run from him. "You were on that street. In my dream. I ran from you."

"Yeah. That was me." Frank paused and frowned. "It's curious you heard that exact conversation about Leo. Almost like the Well wanted you to hear us."

"Leo might be an Ethereal, too," Mo said. "Like the Core."

"Maybe." Frank took another drink. "If we're going to initiate Leah, and I'm still not convinced we should, we'll have to go through the Phovias layer. That's where Leo is."

"Why not?" Leah and Mo said at the same time.

Frank set his beer down. "You came for power, Leah.

That's noble, but not the right reason to become an Immortal Witch." He met her eyes. "Too much anger. Too much resentment. The Well might reject you, kill you—or worse, turn you into something like Lord Ragon. Worse, you becoming a witch could lead Helen and that Core to the Well. Doom us all."

"That's happening anyway!" Leah slammed her hand on the table. "Legion's hunger didn't die with the demon. Helen is feeding it."

Mo shivered. "I remember seeing that hunger. It was..." She trailed off, staring at nothing. Then she shook her head. "We're a part of this, Frank. We have to help her."

"We don't have to do anything." Frank's voice went quiet. "I'm trying to live. For two years, I ran. Avoided my fate. Left reality's survival to chance." His voice cracked. "I watched my Coven get devoured. Every single one of them. Cora. Omari. All of them."

He looked away, jaw working and cheeks tight. When he turned back, his eyes were red and glossy.

Leah reached across the table and grabbed his hand. Her throat felt thick. "I know what it's like—losing people you care about. I'm sorry."

"It's not your fault," Mo said.

Frank pulled his hand back and wiped roughly at his eyes. "The point is, I made a mistake. If it weren't for Mo here, I never would have recovered the Coordinates. They're the map we use to reach the Well and initiate new Immortal Witches. The only map."

Leah crossed her arms on the table and leaned forward. "So, the only way to initiate me is by following the coordinates. But those lead straight through the Phovias layer, where you trapped Leo. And there's a good chance Leo is an Ethereal, same as the Core."

Mo nodded slowly. "Double risk. Leo on one end. And if

your plan is to kill Helen and destroy the Core, you might end up leading them both straight to the Well."

Silence settled over the table. The refrigerator hummed. Somewhere outside, a car drove past.

Frank rubbed his face. "The Well is the source of everything. You Mystics call it the Seed, right? Where both Trees grow from." He waved vaguely upward. "It's all the energy that falls into our world. Creates reality. Everything flows from there." He leaned forward, elbows on the table. "One wrong move and that ends up in the wrong hands. Game over."

Leah's stomach twisted. Lord Ragon had mentioned the Well, but he'd never explained what it actually was. Just that it existed. "If Helen reaches it—"

"She becomes God," Frank said flatly. "Or whatever passes for God in this reality. Unlimited power. No more hunger because she'd be the source itself."

He paused, studying Leah's face. "I know you need power to face Helen. But our magic is different from Mystic abilities. If we initiate you, there's no guarantee you'll survive it. Especially with Asmodeus in you." He leaned forward again. "If you do become an Immortal Witch, you'll lose him, but your power will be amplified in the Astral Realm and limited in the material realm..."

Leah shook her head. "Cora told me. Years ago. But Lord Ragon said something different. He said if Asmodeus is part of my essence now—if our souls have blended—then maybe the Well wouldn't see anything to burn away."

"Maybe," Frank said flatly.

"That's what he said, too." Leah's voice hardened. "But he also drank from that Well. He knows what it does."

Frank and Mo exchanged a look.

"Lord Ragon was rejected by the Tree of Life," Frank said. "His experience isn't—"

"He's also bonded to the Tree of Death and survived," Leah cut in. "Just like what Asmodeus did when we bonded to the tree."

Mo's eyes flickered violet for just a second, then back to brown. She tilted her head, studying Leah. "You really believe you two are that merged?"

"I do."

"I could look," Mo said quietly.

Frank's head snapped toward her. "Mo. Looking could make it worse."

"Not if I'm careful." Mo turned to face him. "We need her, right? If there's even a chance the demon burns away during initiation, we need to know before we start anything."

Leah's heart hammered. "You can see if he survives?"

"Maybe." Mo's expression was serious. "If I look ahead, it could set us off course. But I could try and see as many outcomes as possible and get a sense of what's likely." She paused. "Do you want me to look?"

Yes, Asmodeus said immediately in Leah's mind.

"Yes," Leah echoed aloud. "Please."

Frank nodded. "Fine, just be quick. Look for one answer and don't focus on anything else."

Mo nodded and her eyes glowed violet, the color swallowing her pupils entirely. She trembled in her chair, head looking up to the ceiling.

Seconds passed. Then a minute. Then two.

Finally, Mo blinked. The violet faded, and her normal brown eyes returned. She looked at Frank first, then at Leah.

"Well?" Frank's voice came out rough.

"There are so many possible futures," Mo said slowly. "Different paths, different choices, different outcomes." She focused on Leah. "But in every single one I could reach, the demon's still there with you."

Frank took a long drink from his beer, then set it down with a *thunk*. "Well. That's one complication dealt with." His eyes narrowed. "Doesn't solve the rest of our problems. If you do become an Immortal Witch, your power will be amplified in the Astral Realm and limited in the material realm. My fear is that you won't have enough power to face Helen on this side and you'll bring her into the Astral Realm to use your full strength. And if you do that, you put the Well at risk."

Leah bit her lip and shifted in her seat. That was exactly the plan forming in her mind. Should she tell them, or keep quiet? If she confessed, they might throw her out. But silence might give her a chance to pull it off.

Tell them, Asmodeus said in her head.

Why? Leah thought back.

Last time we tried to hide our intentions, the Librarian kidnapped Sarah and Isaac. The stakes are even higher now. We need them on our side when we face Helen.

What if they decide I'm not worthy?

It is a risk we will have to take, Leah. We cannot hide this forever.

Leah wiped her palms on her jeans. They felt clammy. "That is my plan."

Mo's eyes went wide. Frank's expression didn't change. He just kept staring at her, reading every detail of her face.

"Leah, you can't." Mo shook her head. "Bringing the Core into the Astral willingly is too dangerous."

"Leaving it in the material realm is just as dangerous." Leah's voice came out harder than she meant. "Legion traveled through the Astral Realm when he brought his demon army over. He had access for years through Chimera sacrifice rituals. And what's the point of protecting the Astral Realm if the material realm gets consumed?"

"Life finds a way." Frank's tone had gone cold. "The Immortal Witches' loyalty is to the Astral Realm and the Well, not the physical one. Bringing that thing over puts everything at risk. We don't gamble with reality's survival."

"And what did that loyalty do for the last Coven?" Leah stood up, and her chair scraped against the floor. "They're all dead because they ignored Legion's threat. Are you really going to make the same mistake?"

Frank stood, too—fast enough to knock his chair backward. It banged against the wall. He stared at her, nostrils flared, but didn't say anything.

Leah pressed on. "Legion attacked through the Astral Realm and into our reality. He had access for a long time. But you know all this. Cora knew it too, and at least she was brave enough to admit she'd made a mistake."

Mo jumped to her feet and held up both hands. "Okay, that's enough. Both of you. Step back and calm down."

Frank glared at Leah, but she held her ground.

"Hear me out," Leah said. "Please. I saw Helen fight Lord Ragon—the oldest vampire alive. The second she felt like her normal energy wouldn't be enough, she pulled from the Core. Consciously." Her words came faster now. "Mystics aren't supposed to use their energies in the Astral Realm. If I bring her there and fight her, her Mystic powers will drain faster. She'll have to draw more from the Core to stay strong. We can destabilize them. Just like we had to destabilize Legion with the mandrake potion before we could hurt him." She took a breath. "I saw Helen get stabbed in the chest with Excalibur. The legendary sword. She didn't even flinch. Just absorbed it like it was nothing. No wound left behind. Right now, she's invincible. This is the only way to weaken her and fight on equal footing."

"And then what?" Frank's voice came out rough. "Do you know what happens to an Ethereal Core when it destabilizes? Because I sure as hell don't."

Leah opened her mouth, but no answer came.

"We could ask Leo." Mo's voice cut through the tension, as they both turned to look at her. "He's an Ethereal. Or at least, there's a good chance he is. We can ask him the best way to kill his kind."

Frank laughed, dry and bitter. "And he'll just hand over that information? Assuming he's not dead already? Assuming he doesn't kill us first?" His voice rose. "Our magic didn't work on him, Mo. You remember that?"

Leah's mind raced, putting pieces together. When she spoke, Asmodeus' deeper voice layered underneath hers. "I can use the energies from both Trees on him. Force him to talk. This could be the key to defeating Helen. Maybe we don't even need to bring her to the Astral Realm."

"You'll be in the Astral Realm," Frank yelled. "You said it yourself. The Tree energies drain fast there. Once you're out, you're dead."

Leah's hands curled into fists, but Mo stepped between them.

"Look." Mo faced Frank, her back to Leah. "We wanted to initiate another witch and expand the Coven. That was always going to be risky. And if you ask me, Leah's plan is worth exploring. It's dangerous, yeah. Getting information out of Leo won't be easy. But if the alternative is leaving Helen and the Core here to do whatever they want, never initiating another witch again?" She shook her head. "I choose Leah's plan."

Frank stared at Mo, then past her shoulder at Leah. His jaw worked like he was chewing on words he didn't want to spit out. Finally, he looked down.

He pulled a pack of cigarettes from his coat pocket and stuck one between his lips. "I'm going out for a smoke."

The door slammed behind him hard enough to rattle the frame.

Mo and Leah stood in the sudden quiet.

"He'll come around," Mo said softly. She picked up the fallen chair and set it upright. "Frank always does. He just needs time to process."

Leah sank back into her seat. Her legs felt weak. "What if he doesn't?"

"Then we figure something else out." Mo sat down and took another swig of her beer. "But between you and me? I think you're right. About all of it. Helen with that Core is a threat to everything. The material realm, the Astral Realm, the Well—all of it." She met Leah's eyes. "We can't just hide and hope the problem goes away."

"No," Leah said quietly. "We can't."

CHAPTER 32
THE OLDEST WITCH

Mo pushed through the back door, and Leah followed. They walked down an alley, brick buildings on either side. The scent of food wafted from somewhere, and Leah's stomach growled. When had she last eaten? That egg sandwich at the gas station yesterday?

"You sure this is safe?" she whispered.

Mo laughed. "Yes. Trust me."

Voices and laughter grew louder as they walked. Music spilled from somewhere up ahead, maybe jazz. The sky had turned deep purple, spring chill biting through Leah's jacket. She shoved her hands in her pockets and kept her head down.

They emerged onto a street packed with people. Restaurants spilled onto sidewalks, their tables crowded with diners drinking and laughing under string lights. A bar down the block had a crowd gathered outside, music thumping into the street. Mo waved at a couple walking past. The blue eye of the Librarian flickered in Leah's peripheral vision, then vanished.

The taqueria sat tucked between a coffee shop and a

closed boutique. Its neon sign read *Melting Taste* in looping cursive, pink and green against the darkening sky. Grilled meat hit Leah's nose, and her mouth watered.

Mo walked straight to the entrance and waved at a woman in the kitchen. Round face, bright smile, commanding the chaos of cooking with practiced ease. The woman spotted Mo and lit up. She rushed out, wiping her hands on her apron.

"My dear Mo! It's good to have you back. Where have you been the last couple of weeks?"

"Hola, Mariana. Been busy, but we're finally back in town." Mo gestured at Leah. "Got a spot for two? In the back, if possible."

Mariana's eyes found Leah. Her smile widened. "Claro! Of course, please follow me."

The restaurant overwhelmed Leah with noise and smells and color all at once. Paintings of mariachis and women dancing covered the walls. Papel picado hung from the ceiling in loops, cut into flowers, birds, and skulls. The kitchen sizzled and clanged. People laughed and talked over each other at tables crammed together. Leah followed Mariana through the narrow space between chairs, trying not to bump into anyone.

Mariana led them through a door and then a second door into a small patio. Three tables, all empty, with a wooden canopy overhead, with warm lights strung across it. The noise from inside muffled when the door closed.

Mo took a seat, and Leah sat across from her. Mariana handed them two menus and stepped back. Before Leah could even read it, a waiter came in with two cups of water, a basket of chips, and guacamole.

"I recommend the tacos al pastor," Mo said. "They are to die for."

"I don't eat pork, but thanks." Leah grabbed a chip and

dipped it in the guacamole. Avocado, lime, cilantro. Her stomach growled, demanding more. "What about the grilled fish tacos?"

Mo ate a chip of her own. "Really good. Honestly, you can't go wrong here."

The waiter returned. Leah ordered three grilled fish tacos, and Mo got carnitas. They both ordered sparkling water with lime.

As the door closed behind the waiter, Leah turned to Mo. "You seemed pretty popular around here."

Mo laughed and waved her off. "Nah, not really. I know some of the older folks who were here before things got better. This town was pretty much run by narcos before. But Frank and I pushed them away a couple of months ago. Ever since, the town's been flourishing."

"Do they know you're a witch?"

Mo shook her head. "Nope. But we don't hide it. I think they just don't care to question it. Frank and I really wanted to form a community around us. Protection, you know? Something to come back to." She ate another chip. "The old coven was sparse around the world. They'd meet for initiations or special meetings, but that was rare. We're changing that."

Leah grabbed another chip. "Okay, I've been meaning to ask. How did you become an Immortal Witch? What's the process?"

The waiter came in and placed two sparkling waters on the table. Bubbles rose through the clear liquid, lime wedges floating at the top. Mo thanked him and took a sip. As the waiter went back inside, she cleared her throat.

"Frank showed up at my doorstep asking me to retouch his tattoo."

"The one on his arm? With spirals instead of pips?" Leah took a sip of her water. The bubbles fizzed against her tongue, lime cutting through the richness of the guacamole.

Mo nodded. "That's the one. I was about to close, but he offered double the money. Seemed desperate. As I worked on it, I saw a flash of violet light." She chuckled. "I still remember his shock when he realized I had potential. I tried to convince him to help us get rid of the narcos. I'd just seen light coming from his arm, so I hoped he could do something. But he wasn't interested." She paused, eating another chip. "Then Raul showed up—the narco who collected protection money. I was late on my payment. But that wasn't Raul anymore. Something else was possessing him."

Leah's eyes went wide. "Something like a—"

She stopped as the waiter came in and placed tacos on the table. Leah's mouth watered. The smell of grilled tilapia, charred lime, and fresh cilantro filled the small patio. As he walked out, Leah leaned forward and lowered her voice. "Like a demon possession?"

Mo shook her head and took a bite from her taco. Leah did the same. The tortilla was warm and soft, and the grilled fish flaked apart on her tongue. Lime crema cooled the heat from the salsa verde. Sharp cilantro and onion cut through it all. She barely stopped herself from groaning.

"No, something weirder. An Ethereal. Frank said he'd encountered one before and believed it was the same one. He thinks it could be Leo, the one we trapped."

Leah swallowed and took another large bite. She spoke with her mouth half full. "Why does he think that? This is delicious, by the way."

Mo smiled. "I'm glad you like it. He thinks it's too much of a coincidence. Two encounters with possessed people, then an Ethereal, all in a short time. Plus, the encounters stopped once we left Leo trapped."

"Hold on." Leah set down her taco. "Back up. How'd you get from fighting a possessed narco to trapping Leo?"

"After we dealt with Raul, Frank offered to initiate me. But we had to retrieve special ink from their old tattoo shop first."

"Magic ink?"

"Mixed with water from the Well, I think. We fought some interdimensional worms and recovered the ink. That's when Frank gave me this tattoo." Mo showed her the lady with spiral eyes again. "But the initiation wasn't done. We needed the coordinates."

Leah frowned and ate more chips. "Coordinates? You said that before. What are they?"

"Think of it as a map. Goes from our dimension to the one where the Well is. It was lost during Legion's last attack. We had to astral project to the parlor shop and follow the dimensional crack to where the old Immortal Witch was attacked."

"Hold on, why don't you just astral project there directly?"

Mo frowned. "Doesn't work like that. The first layer is decay, where the past of a space breaks down. That we can all access, even non-Immortal Witches. That's where you go when you're dreamwalking."

Leah nodded. She knew that place all too well.

"Right, well, after that, you can go into other layers, too. But if you don't know where you're going, it's like walking in a city you've never been to. The alleyways to get to a different street are hidden and miles apart."

Leah frowned. She was certain she'd been in other layers before. She thought back to the time she'd gone inside Tom, the corrupted spirit she'd met at the academy. His soul had been consumed by a book, and she'd been the one to help him recover his consciousness by going inside his essence.

"You following?" Mo asked.

Leah blinked and nodded, taking the last bite of her second taco. "Yeah, sorry. Keep going."

"I have clairvoyance, which made it easier. My grandma had it, too. But once Frank gave me the tattoo, it turned real. Before, it was passive. I'd look at a door seconds before someone walked in, or I'd find lost things really quickly. But after the tattoo, I could tap into it. Amplify that perception."

Leah ate another chip and considered that. "So, you used your clairvoyance to find the coordinates?"

"That's right. We astral projected to the parlor, went through the crack, followed it to the black desert layer where Omari died. I could see the past there, see the fight between Legion and the witches. With my clairvoyance amplified in the Astral, I was able to retrieve the coordinates from Omari's memory."

"Wait, you retrieved something from the past?"

"Not an object. Knowledge. It's hard to explain." Mo drank more water. "That's when Leo appeared. First, he was this massive burning wheel with six wings and eyes all over it. Different shapes, different colors. Then he shifted into human form."

Leah wondered what that looked like. "Did he attack you?"

"No. He wanted to escort us to the Well. Said these were dangerous times to be traveling alone. He gave us bad vibes from the start, but Frank said we probably couldn't take him on. His luck powers, my clairvoyance, neither one helps much in combat. And we didn't know how strong Leo actually was. So, we accepted."

Mo paused to eat more of her taco. Leah did the same,

savoring the grilled fish and the tang of lime. She grabbed her third taco and bit into it.

"When we reached the next layer, everything went dark," Mo said. "Dim red light, shallow cold water up to our toes. You couldn't see anything, but you could hear things high above us. Crawling and scratching."

"Sounds creepy."

"The Phovias. That's what Frank calls them. Monsters that take the shape of your worst fears. I wanted to get out of there fast. Thanks to Frank's luck, we found a fire stick and used it to locate the next crack. As we got close, Frank rolled the dice again. That's when he grabbed my hand and yelled at me to run."

Leah leaned forward. "What happened to Leo?"

"Don't know. Either he tripped, or something stopped him. We heard a lot of commotion behind us. Water splashing, creatures growling with this high-pitched scream, Leo yelling. But we crossed into the next layer and never went back."

"Holy shit. Then what?"

Mo finished her second taco. "Went through a couple other layers. All of them have different defense mechanisms. Eventually, we reached the Well. I drank from its waters and completed the ritual. Officially became an Immortal Witch."

"Wow." Leah sat back in her chair. "How did it feel?"

Mo scratched her nose. "Strange, but comforting. Frank said what I felt was completely different from what anyone else would experience. It does change you, though."

"In what sense?"

Mo paused, looking up at the dark sky. "It's really hard to put into words. It just is." She met Leah's eyes again. "I'll say that using my powers afterwards felt natural. Like breathing. I thought it was easier with the tattoo, but once I drank from the Well, it was like another sense."

Leah thought about that. Ever since her parents died, she'd spent so much time learning about the wells of the Tree of Life and later the Tree of Death. Practicing, strengthening her connection to the Trees. The idea of drinking some liquid and suddenly having everything click seemed too good to be true. But maybe she was closer to reaching Helen's level than she'd ever been before. Closer to getting revenge.

And justice.

"Have you tried to look back into the layer with Leo?" Asmodeus asked through her mouth. His voice layered underneath hers, deeper and more resonant.

Mo raised an eyebrow. "Your demon speaks."

"Our objective matches yours, Watcher."

"The last person who called me Watcher was Leo. Watch your tone."

Asmodeus looked down through Leah's eyes. "My apologies."

Mo eyed them, and Leah felt an odd warm sensation that made the hairs on the back of her neck stand. Like Mo was seeing through her, into her.

"I see." Mo cleared her throat and gestured to a passing waiter for the check. "We've tried. But everything's too dark to really make out anything."

The waiter came and handed her the bill. Leah tried to pull out the cash she had, but Mo waved her hand. "I got you. Both of you." She pulled two twenties and left them on the table.

Leah felt Asmodeus' amusement pass through her. She wondered if this was the first time anyone had shown him kindness.

"That's a good sign, right?" Leah asked.

Mo sighed. "Unclear. It's unnervingly quiet. The only way to be certain is to cross over and look for ourselves."

They stepped back onto the street. Music thumped into the night from the bar down the block. Mo told her more about the town as they walked, the renovations underway, how things had changed since they'd driven out the narcos. Leah tried to listen, but her mind kept wandering.

Helen and the coven. Leo trapped in the Phovias layer. The coordinates to the Well. The Infinity Board hunting her.

When they arrived back at the tattoo shop, Mo guided Leah up the tight stairs to the second level. The floorboards creaked under her steps. She glanced down the short hallway and paused when she heard pacing behind one of the doors.

"Don't worry about him. He'll come around." Mo opened the door to her left and showed Leah a small but cozy room. Single bed, dresser, window looking out over the alley. She handed Leah a towel and some toiletries. "Bathroom is this way down the hall."

Leah took the towel. "Wait. When did Legion attack the coven? When did Omari die?"

Mo paused in the doorway. "According to what I saw in the vision, it was around early September. Why?"

Leah's thoughts started to come into focus. *No.* "What day in September?"

"I don't know the exact date. But Frank said it was right before they went into hiding. They'd been planning Christina's initiation for weeks. Why?"

Leah sat on the bed. The springs creaked. "Helen brought me to meet Cora that same month. Early September. She said she wanted Cora to see my potential, help me understand my connection to both Trees. But Cora was supposed to be initiating Christina that day."

Mo's eyes narrowed. "You think Helen pulled Cora away on purpose?"

"The strongest witch in the coven, away from the initiation when Legion attacked?" Leah's jaw clenched. "That's not a coincidence."

Mo leaned against the doorframe. "Helen was working with Legion."

"Or using him. I don't know." Leah's hands curled into fists. The sheets bunched under her fingers. "But she knew. She had to know. She brought me as bait. Made sure Cora would be interested enough to leave."

"That's awful."

"That's Helen." Leah looked up at Mo. "So many people died."

Mo crossed her arms. "And Helen helped make it happen."

Leah's jaw ached from clenching. All those witches. Christina. Omari. Dead because Helen needed Cora distracted.

"More reason for us to get you initiated," Mo said quietly. "Channel it. You'll need that fire tomorrow."

Leah nodded. "Helen needs to be stopped, one way or another."

Mo stepped into the hallway. "Get some rest. Tomorrow's gonna be a busy day."

The door closed, and Leah listened to Mo's footsteps fade down the hall.

CHAPTER 33
SURVIVOR

Leah stood surrounded by rotting buildings that looked like they'd been pulled straight from a post-apocalyptic New York. Crumbling brick facades stretched up toward a sickly yellow sky. Rusted fire escapes clung to walls.

Frank stood about twenty feet away, his back to her. He pressed his hand against what looked like a shimmer in the air.

"Frank?"

He spun around, and his jaw went tight. "How the hell did you get here?"

"I don't know. I fell asleep and just appeared here." Leah took a step closer.

"Of course you did. It had to be you," he mumbled.

"What is that?"

"Nothing." He turned back to the shimmer, shoulders tense.

Leah bit her lip. She should leave. Give him space.

"I wanted to apologize," she said. "I shouldn't have yelled at you like that."

Frank took a drink from his flask. "You were honest. That's not the same as rude."

"Still. You're trying to help me, and I threw it back in your face."

He laughed. "Help you, right." Another drink. "The problem with being the last? You start thinking you have authority over others."

Leah waited.

Frank stared at the shimmer. "Want to know why I care about your motivation?"

"Yes."

"Come on." He pressed his hand to the shimmer, peeling it back like a curtain.

Leah followed, and the change hit her immediately. Her feet touched worn floorboards. Music drifted from somewhere inside the building. Jazz. The scent of cigarette smoke and bourbon mixed with something sweet. Perfume maybe.

They stood in what looked like the entrance to an old bar. Dark wood paneling lined the walls. Red velvet curtains hung in doorways. Through one of them, Leah could see tables and chairs, a small stage in the corner.

Frank walked through the main room without stopping. He pushed open a back door and stepped outside.

Leah followed him onto a small wooden deck. A river stretched out before them, its surface reflecting a sunset that shouldn't exist in the Astral realm. Orange, pink, and deep purple painted the sky.

Frank sat down on a bench near the railing. He looked different here. Younger. Less worn down.

Leah approached slowly and sat beside him. "How did you make this?"

"I didn't. Cora made it for me, back when I first joined

the coven." He pulled a cigarette from his coat pocket and lit it. "It's a preserved space. As long as I come here and maintain it, it won't fade. If I stop visiting, it'll decay like everything else in the Astral."

Gray smoke curled around his fingertips. He gestured at the river. "This place is from before I became a witch. Before I forgot what it felt like to have something worth saving."

"What is it?"

"A speakeasy. One of the few places in New York where men like me could breathe and let loose." Frank took a drag. "It's where I met William."

"William?" Leah asked, then paused. "I'm sorry. You don't have to tell me."

"I know." Frank stared at the water. "But maybe I do."

He offered her the flask. Leah hesitated, then took a small sip. Bourbon burned down her throat, smoky and warm. She handed it back.

"I grew up in Ireland. Small town outside Dublin. Irish Catholic family." Frank's voice went flat. "My father was a baker. Good man by most standards. Went to mass every Sunday. Provided for his family. But he had very specific ideas about how the world worked. How men were supposed to be."

A breeze came off the river.

"I knew I was different by the time I was twelve. Knew I had to hide it."

Leah hugged her knees, waiting.

"When I was sixteen, there was another kid. Patrick. We were friends. Good friends." Frank flicked ash into the river. "One night, we were drinking behind the church, and I kissed him. His father caught us. Beat me until I couldn't stand. Beat Patrick worse."

"Frank, I..."

"The next day, Patrick was gone. His family sent him

away. I never found out where." He stubbed out the cigarette. "My father found out later that week. He didn't beat me—that would've been easier. He just looked at me like I was diseased. Like I'd brought shame on the family name."

Leah watched his jaw work as he spoke.

"I left. Lied on my paperwork, claimed I was eighteen, and got on a ship to New York. I was barely seventeen."

"What did you do when you got here?"

"Got work on the docks. Loading ships. Breaking my back twelve hours a day for pennies." Frank stood and walked to the railing. He leaned against it, staring out at the sunset. "Didn't have a trade. Didn't have connections. But I was tall and Irish, so that was enough."

Leah thought she saw flashes of a younger Frank in front of them. Working the docks, sweaty and desperate. She stood and joined him at the railing.

"The speakeasies were where people like me could finally breathe," he continued. "Underground places where the normal rules didn't apply. You just had to know which ones were safe. Which ones welcomed us instead of just tolerating us."

"How did you find them?"

"Word of mouth. Careful questions. You learned to recognize the signs." Frank's voice softened. "I met William at this place about six months after I got to New York. He was older. Twenty-one. Worked in construction. Had the same look in his eyes. Like he was running from something, too."

The river flowed below them. Leah could hear the soft echo of music drifting from inside the speakeasy.

"We started meeting up every week. He made me laugh. Made me feel like maybe I wasn't broken after all."

Leah glanced back at the building. "Was it always this place?"

"Yeah. Our spot." Frank touched his trench coat. "William wore this coat everywhere. He looked good in it. Really good. We'd been seeing each other for about a year. Started making plans. We'd heard stories about Berlin. About how things were different there. How men like us could live openly. We were going to save up money and go."

"What happened?"

Frank's hands gripped the railing. "Someone must've tipped off the cops. They raided the place. The raid turned into a brawl, and someone knocked over a lantern. The whole place went up."

Leah looked back at the speakeasy. It stood pristine and whole in the golden light. Preserved exactly as it had been.

"The smoke was so thick I couldn't see. Couldn't breathe." Frank's voice cracked. "William threw his coat over me. Soaked it with water from a pitcher. Told me to keep my head down and run for the back exit. He said he'd be right behind me."

A lump formed in Leah's throat.

"I ran. Got outside and waited. Watched people streaming out, coughing and burned. Waited for William to come through." Frank closed his eyes. "He never did. They found his body three days later."

Leah didn't know what to say. This was the kind of pain that didn't care for sympathy.

"I had his coat. That's all I had left of him." Frank ran his fingers over the worn fabric. "I've kept it for over a hundred years. Maintained it. Made sure it didn't fall apart. Same as I maintain this place."

A trumpet from inside hit a long, mournful note.

"You asked me once if I had the spark for magic before I became an Immortal Witch. I did. Nothing like what I can do now, but I could always change my luck. Pull probability in my favor."

"But the fire..." Leah started.

"My luck was my own back then. I couldn't share it." Frank turned to face her. "I lost myself after that. Drank too much. Took up fighting. When I pulled on that thread inside me, strange things happened. My opponents slipped. I'd miss a hit to the jaw that would have knocked me out. That's how Cora found me. She saw me win a fight I had no business winning."

Leah leaned back against the railing beside him. "She offered you immortality."

"She did. Said I had the potential. Said she could teach me magic." He pulled out the flask again. "I jumped at it. Thought if I could just become something different, the pain would stop."

"But she warned you."

"She said I was trying to outrun something I wasn't ready to face. That immortality wouldn't fix what was broken. She wanted me to wait. Said I wasn't ready." Frank finally took a drink. "But I insisted. Thought I knew better. She agreed, and we did the ritual."

"Do you regret it?"

Frank stared at the water for a long time. "I've made peace with it. But she was right; immortality didn't make the pain stop. It just gave me forever to carry it around."

His eyes were red when he turned back to her. "The coven became my family. The real one I'd never had. Cora, Omari, the others. They were spread across the world most of the time, but when we came together for rituals, it felt like coming home."

"Then Legion killed them all," Leah said softly.

"Yeah." Frank sat heavily on the bench. "When I found

Mo, something changed. She made me want to protect someone again."

Leah followed and sat beside him again. The bench creaked softly.

"You're so much like I was," Frank said. "Angry and desperate and ready to burn yourself up if it means saving the people you love."

"That's different. I'm not running. I have to save Sarah and Isaac."

"Are you? Or are you running toward power because you can't stand feeling helpless?" Frank's gaze pinned her. "Because every time you close your eyes, you see Helen taking everything from you, and you need to hurt her back?"

Leah's hands curled into fists.

"I'm not saying your reasons are wrong," Frank said. "I'm saying they're complicated. You want to save your friends—I believe that. But you also want revenge. You want to make Helen pay. And you're willing to become immortal to do it."

"So what? Helen deserves it."

"Maybe she does. But what happens after?" Frank leaned forward, elbows on his knees. "After you've saved your friends. After you've stopped Helen. After the war is over and you're still here, still immortal, still carrying everything you did to get there. What then?"

Leah shook her head. "I don't know."

"That's what worries me." He looked at her. "Cora always said the coven only worked because we had a purpose. It wasn't an escape or a grab for power. We serve something bigger. I think immortality only amplifies your purpose. Or... that's what it did to me. If you're running from something, you don't ever really stop. And power just keeps asking for more."

He met her eyes. "And if you're fueled by rage, that rage will burn you hollow."

"But you just said you joined to escape." Leah sat up straighter. "You were running from William's death. So why are you lecturing me about having the right reasons when you didn't?"

Frank was quiet for a moment. "Because I'm living proof it doesn't work. The coven gave me purpose for decades. Gave me a family. But it didn't fix what was broken inside me. That's why when Legion killed them all, I fell apart. Why I've been running ever since." He looked at her. "I can't lead the way Cora did. Something in me was already cracked. I just didn't want to admit it. But maybe I can help build something better. With Mo. Maybe with you. If you go in with your eyes open."

Leah swallowed. Her throat felt tight.

"If you choose immortality because you genuinely want to protect people, because you want to serve a purpose bigger than your pain, then maybe you have a chance." Frank's expression softened. "Maybe we both do."

The music from inside the speakeasy changed. Something slower. Sadder.

"Mo thinks we should help you," Frank said. "She believes in second chances. And maybe she's right. Maybe building a new coven means giving people like you and me another shot at getting it right."

"What now?"

"Now I need to think." He stood. "I won't let you make the same mistake I did. If we initiate you, it'll be because you've proven you understand what it means. Not just the power. Not just the sacrifice. But the responsibility."

Leah stood, too. "What do I need to do?"

"Show me you're not just chasing revenge. Show me you can put your friends' safety above your need to hurt

Helen." Frank walked to the edge of the deck. "Show me you understand that some victories aren't worth the cost."

"And if I can't?"

Frank's smile was sad. "Then I'd rather watch you burn yourself up than give you an eternity to render everything else to ash."

CHAPTER 34
ASTRAL PATH

The next day, Leah waited. Frank kept to himself, sitting for hours with distant eyes, lost somewhere she couldn't reach.

Part of her wanted to yell at him. Couldn't he understand every second mattered? But another part feared her honesty the night before had cost her everything. If they didn't initiate her, she was done. There was no other path left to reach Helen's level.

After a restless night, Frank woke her early the following morning.

"We're doing it. Get ready. No breakfast."

Leah sat in one of the leather chairs, flanked by Mo and Frank. Her stomach grumbled. She eyed Mo's tattoo gun on the table, shifting to find a comfortable position.

Frank walked to a small fridge in the back and pulled out two beers. He handed one to Mo, who took a long gulp before setting it aside and pulling on black gloves.

"Dude, it's like nine in the morning," Leah said.

"Oh, this is not for you, doll." Frank opened his bottle and raised it. "Part of the tradition."

Leah thought back to walking in on the Witches initiating that girl. Everyone there had been drinking, the mood celebratory until Helen showed up.

Frank took a drink and met her eyes. His eyes were still bloodshot, still tired. "I thought about what you said last night." He paused. "You're as ready as you're going to be."

Her shoulders dropped, and she smiled. "Thank you."

"Here it is." Frank set down a small jar of ink next to Mo.

There was nothing special about it, or not at first glance. Just black ink in a glass container.

"What design am I getting?" Leah asked.

"We don't know." Frank leaned against the wall. "Whatever Mo sees, she'll draw on you. Once the process begins, it's like tracing over an image."

"Great. I'm glad my mom's not alive to see this. She would have killed me."

Mo chuckled. "Parents are usually not big fans of tattoos. Imagine becoming a tattoo artist. My momma wasn't a fan either."

Leah shook her head. "Yeah, my parents are Jewish. That was a big no-no for them."

Frank snorted. "Have they been to Israel? Everyone and their mothers have tattoos."

Leah shrugged. Mo turned on the needle, and coldness spread around Leah's face and neck. Her hair stood on end.

"Does it hurt?"

"Yes," they both said.

Mo rushed to add, "But it depends on the location."

"Can I decide the location?"

"Nope. It's all inspired by the Well." Frank gestured to the table. "Sit back and relax."

Mo's eyes began to glow violet as she scanned Leah's body. After a moment, she smiled. "You got lucky. Left forearm, please."

Frank raised his beer. "Cheers! Good luck, Leah."

Leah swallowed. Her mouth felt dry. She extended her arm toward Mo, who grabbed it with gentle hands.

"This one is really cool." Mo bent forward, studying the invisible design. "Let me show you what it feels like first."

She ran the needle across Leah's skin without ink. Sharp. Like dragging nails over sunburned skin.

Leah sucked in a breath.

"That's as bad as it gets," Mo said. "Maybe a bit worse over bone. Ready?"

"Yeah."

Mo dipped the needle in ink and started.

The vibration scratched at her skin. Not unbearable, but Leah tried to keep her arm relaxed. Then violet light flashed from the needle's tip, illuminating the room. With each line Mo drew, warmth flooded through Leah's spine. Light and strange, like nothing she had felt before. Her mind reached toward it, tapping into something vast.

Another flash of violet. The warmth grew stronger.

Mo's smile widened. "It's looking good so far."

Leah glanced at Frank. He kept his eyes on her arm, hugging his drink close. When he noticed her watching, his expression softened. He raised his bottle and took another sip.

The scratching vibration continued. A slow burn began building beneath it. Leah blinked. Her father's hand on her arm. That night. The demon mark searing into her skin.

But this was different.

We have come far, Asmodeus said quietly.

Leah watched the violet light pulse with each stroke. *Yeah.*

She thought of Helen. Of how their friendship had twisted into something toxic. How Helen had used her, manipulated her, killed Eric, and so many others.

Could she change?

"No." Both Leah and Asmodeus said it together.

"Okay, we're good to go." Mo leaned back and wiped sweat from her forehead with a small towel.

"Oh, that's edgy. Badass, I like it!" Frank said. He finished his beer and set the bottle down.

Leah sat up and looked at her tattoo for the first time. A black demon-like claw wrapped around her forearm, gripping a human hand. The fingers intertwined, holding onto each other like they were refusing to let go. At each fingertip, both demon and human, twin spirals curved inward. They rotated in opposite directions.

Well, I did not expect that.

"Me neither."

"What was that?" Mo asked.

Leah raised her arm, opening and closing her hand. "This looks like my demon mark, but different."

"Oh yeah. At first, I thought I was tracing over the mark, but before I could begin, it morphed." Mo studied the design. "It was strange. Felt like I was tattooing for two people."

Frank stepped closer, squinting at the tattoo. "Interesting. Mine was straightforward. Dice for luck, obvious enough." He glanced at Mo. "Hers, too. Eyes for seeing."

Mo tilted her head. "But yours... a demon claw and a human hand gripping each other with spirals? I'm not sure what that means."

"Me neither," Frank admitted. "Guess we'll find out when you use it." He gestured toward the back. "Come on. The most challenging part is about to begin."

Mo removed her gloves and followed Frank to a door on the left, then to the kitchen. As soon as he opened it, incense hit Leah's nostrils, making her slightly dizzy. The small room had no windows. Multiple candles throughout the space provided the only light, casting enough brightness to reveal a large white circle in the center with odd symbols. Both Mo and Frank began speaking in whispers as they entered.

"Here, Leah. Let's sit." Frank gestured to the center of the circle.

The three of them sat down. Mo and Frank held hands and extended their other hands to Leah. She took them. Whatever magic filled this room intensified the flow of energy through her spine.

"I have the coordinates and will be your guide," Mo said. "Just close your eyes and relax."

Leah nodded and did as instructed.

Frank whispered, "We step outside the bonds with time to protect the place between. We break free from mortal lives beyond to ensure this world's safety. Eternal Watchers of the veils beyond, be safe in your passage to the Well."

Leah felt like she was falling. Not fast, but gently. When she landed, light pressed against her closed eyelids. She opened them slowly.

A black desert stretched around them under an extremely dark sky. Yet there was a strange ambient light that was enough to see her surroundings. When she tried to stand, her hand hit hard glass. She and the other two witches were inside a glass disk, as if the sand around them had melted.

"Come on." Frank was already on his feet, waving them forward. "We need to get moving before any Astral parasites show up."

Mo shivered as she stood. "Yeah, let's go. I hate those things."

Leah frowned but hurried after them. She had no desire to find out what that meant. Mo moved ahead, eyes glowing violet as she followed the invisible path only she could see. Frank walked beside Leah, his gaze sweeping their surroundings.

"Your tattoo is the source of your energy," Frank said. "Your connection to the Well. It can be used in the Material realm, but not to its full potential. Here in the Astral Realm is where we Immortal Witches truly shine." He glanced at her arm. "Still, yours is limited until you drink from the Well and we complete the ritual. We won't know what it does until then, but be ready. You might need to use it before we're done."

Leah nodded. Ahead of them, Mo paused and turned back.

"I see two Anthrogis approaching," Mo said, her eyes still glowing bright violet as she looked past them.

"What are those?" Leah squinted, trying to make out two dark figures running through the black dunes toward them.

Frank waved dismissively. "Lost souls that get stuck in this layer. We're almost to the next crack. No point in fighting them." He checked his tattoo, watching the dice pips shift. "Let's save our strength for the Phovias layer and Leo."

They kept walking, Mo leading the way as she followed the coordinates. Leah glanced at the creatures every few steps. Their frenzied run made her nervous.

Do not worry, Asmodeus said. *Frank has been through these layers many times. He knows what threats to avoid.*

I know. Just wish I knew what we were walking into.

The unknown is always frightening. But we are not alone.

"Here we are." Mo stopped and raised her left hand. Her hand drifted down, as if piercing an invisible wall. Just a couple of feet ahead of them, a linear crack appeared in midair. It opened, and Leah raised her hand to shield herself from the blinding light that spilled through.

They stepped in. A warm wave wrapped around Leah. She blinked multiple times to adjust to the bright sunlight. The heat was considerable, and the humidity so thick she could see fish swimming around strange-looking trees. They ranged from green to red to yellow, with odd shapes. They grew far enough apart to let sunlight through.

"Oh, careful there." Frank hovered his arm in front of Leah, who paused mid-step. "See those mushrooms below? Try to avoid stepping on them. Their spores are toxic. For you, at least." He added the last part with a grin.

They walked through the eerie jungle. Fish swam away quickly with every step they took. Mo stayed at the front, her eyes occasionally flashing violet as she followed the mental path. Leah rushed to catch up to Frank.

"These are the coordinates?" Leah asked. "They guide you through the layers, like a map?"

"That, and they also serve as a sort of key to go between layers," Frank said. "Usually, we can only go through a specific number of layers in specific spots. As an Immortal Witch matures and gains more years, they get more access to more layers, but it's not straightforward. Cora, being our High Priestess, moved almost freely between layers. But to reach the Well, there's only one path, and that's through using the coordinates."

"I see." Leah thought back to her training with Eli at HQ. "You know, the sage of *Yesod*, Eli Abrams, had that ability to travel through layers with ease."

Frank's eyes diverted from watching Mo for a moment. "Yeah, but remember Mystics belong to the Material layer. They have a strong connection to the Tree of Life through *Yesod*, and that can sometimes grant them an advantage in the Astral layer. But their reach and abilities are still limited. We, on the other hand, might be limited in the Material Realms, but here..." He gestured around them.

"Well, this is our playground. And the more time that passes, the larger it gets."

Ahead of them, Mo stopped and turned back. "Found it. The entrance to the Phovias layer."

Leah looked where Mo pointed, but could only see the odd trees here and there. Fish swam away from them while others watched from a distance.

"This is the Phovias layer?" Leah asked.

Frank moved up beside Mo. "Yes. It'll be very dark, so stay close to Mo. She can see better than either of us in there. We also don't know where Leo is or if he's waiting to ambush us, so be on your guard." He checked his tattoo again, watching the dice pips shift and change. "How's the path looking?"

"Clear so far," Mo said, her eyes glowing brighter. "I can see the way through."

Frank nodded. "I'll keep rolling the dice until we're inside." He looked at Leah and shrugged. "Superstition, I guess. Maybe luck will be on our side. Stay close, Leah. This is by far the most dangerous layer."

Leah nodded. Her stomach churned.

"Okay then, ready?" Mo asked, her hand already rising to create the crack.

"Let's go," Leah answered.

Mo opened the passage, and the three of them walked through the Astral crack and into darkness.

CHAPTER 35
ORDER AND CHAOS

Leah stepped into warm water. The splash echoed in the silence, followed by quiet. Just her breathing, along with Frank and Mo's.

The fissure behind them sealed with a sound like stone grinding on stone. Darkness swallowed everything.

She froze and waited for her eyes to adjust. Still nothing. Just a faint red glow somewhere ahead, too dim to show where it ended. The water reached her ankles and didn't move. Stagnant. She caught the smell then, like something sweet and rotting.

Frank moved in front of them. He reached under his shirt and pulled out a silver cross on a chain. He held it in his left hand, his right hand resting on his dice tattoo. His lips moved, whispering words too quiet to hear at first.

"Stay between us," Mo said. Her eyes flashed violet.

Leah called on *Tiferet* without thinking. Her eyes flashed yellow, and the space in front of her became more defined.

"Careful with that, doll," Frank whispered, glancing back at her. His voice grew clearer as he prayed: "Saint Michael the Archangel, defend us in battle. Be our protection..." He didn't avert his gaze from the darkness. "Tree magic drains fast here. Use it sparingly."

The red light grew brighter with her enhanced vision, pushing back the dark but still not reaching an end. Like standing inside a dome surrounded by nothing.

Her gaze drifted up.

Giant red eyes stared back.

Leah stumbled backward and fell in the water, soaking her jeans.

The creature hung above them. No, dozens—maybe more—eyes flashing like rubies. Their segmented, chitinous bodies stretched upward. Spider legs and two massive, serrated claws at each head.

One extended toward her, claws opening.

Frank and Mo moved to her sides fast, Frank still gripping his cross with white knuckles. The creature snapped its fangs and jerked back. Its eyes stayed locked on Leah, but it kept its distance from the two witches.

"They won't attack us," Mo said, her violet eyes still glowing as she looked past the creatures. "But they're tracking her. All of them."

"The prayer is keeping them back," Frank said. "But we need to move. Now."

Frank extended his arm, the cross still in his grip. "Told you to stay close, doll."

Leah took it and got to her feet, careful to keep herself between the two witches this time. She walked forward and noted that the creatures above tracked her movement. Their red eyes had small dark spots that followed her like pupils. Behind the larger ones, smaller versions clung to their legs and bodies. Dozens of them. Maybe hundreds. All watching.

A violet flash lit the space for a second. Leah turned and saw two glowing dice falling from Frank's arm into the water. He looked back and gave them a nod, then returned to his prayer, the words flowing steady and low.

Good roll then.

"I see something ahead," Mo said suddenly, her glowing eyes fixed on a point in the darkness. "It's large. Could be him."

Leah squinted through her *Tiferet*-enhanced vision. Something large broke through the red haze. A cocoon. Six feet tall, maybe more, with the top extending past the creatures and into the darkness above.

"That's him?" Leah asked.

Mo nodded, her eyes still violet and focused. "And I see our exit, too. It's close—maybe twenty feet past the cocoon on the left. We get what we need, and we go."

Frank's jaw tightened. His prayer continued under his breath, words steady, but his voice showed strain.

They got closer. Leah could make out someone inside the cocoon. A man, hunched over with his right arm dangling free. The rest of him was wrapped in sticky webbing. Small creatures latched onto his neck, shoulders, and chest, like fat ticks feeding. What was left of his curly hair stuck to his forehead in greasy clumps. His skin looked gray and clammy.

Leah's *Tiferet*-enhanced vision caught something else. A faint pulse of energy, barely there. The creatures were trying to drain it, but no matter how much they tried, it remained.

Still alive then. Barely.

Could that be Leo?

The man's eyes snapped open. Deep green. Alert.

His head tilted, and a smile spread across his face, too wide. "Well, Watchers. Leo knew you would return. Why did you trap me here?"

"You know why. You're after the well. We aren't stupid," Frank said firmly, then resumed muttering his spell.

Leo let out a dry laugh and rolled his head around his neck, leaning into the creatures still latched to him. "Leo was just trying to protect you."

"Stop lying. We know about Legion and the Core. It's time for answers, Leo."

Leo turned quickly and bit down on one of the creatures near his shoulder. It shrieked and tried to pull away, but he shook his head like a dog until the body ripped in half. He spat out the upper portion. It hit the water and kept moving, legs scrambling like a roach that had just been sprayed.

"Why would Leo do that?" His eyes moved around, unfocused.

It was like talking to a madman. How long had he been trapped in this layer? Time moved differently in the Astral depending on where you were.

Leah took a step forward. "You'll answer whether you want to or not."

Leo laughed again, the sound bouncing off the space and echoing back. Another small creature crawled down the cocoon and latched onto his shoulder in the same spot as the one he had bitten. He didn't seem to notice.

"Leah, wait," Frank said, his hand catching her arm. His prayer faltered.

"I need answers."

"If he gets a hold of you, I don't know if Mo or I will be able to save you."

"I don't have a choice. We need to know how to kill Helen."

Frank's eyes dropped to her arm. His expression changed.

Leah looked down. A faint purple glow emanated from the demon claw on her wrist, pulsing softly under her skin.

Frank's gaze met hers. "Whatever you two are planning, do it now." He returned to muttering his prayer, and the creatures backed away.

Leah walked closer. Both she and Asmodeus could feel the Trees at the edge of their consciousness. Thinner here than in the physical world. Like trying to breathe through a straw. Every pull would cost more.

We need information, Asmodeus said. *But if we pull from the Trees here—*

I know. It'll drain us faster.

But they needed answers. About how to kill Helen. If she burned through her Tree connection now, she might not have enough left if things went wrong. If Leo somehow broke free. If the creatures turned on them...

Still, Leo looked weak, barely clinging to whatever energy he had left. And if she really needed it, Leah had *Netzach*. One pull and she could protect herself long enough to get out.

She got within arm's reach of Leo and stared up at him. The smell hit her harder from this close. Rot and decay.

"Your Watcher magic doesn't work on me. Want to prove me wrong?" he challenged, straining against the cocoon.

"I'm no Watcher."

Leo's fist shot out.

It connected with her jaw before she could move. Before she could even think about calling on *Netzach*.

The crack echoed through the cavern.

Leah stood there and blinked. She hadn't felt anything. No pain. No impact. Just the sound.

Leo's fist was still pressed against her face, frozen mid-punch. His expression shifted from feral to shock.

Something drained from him. She could see it with her enhanced vision. His energy, what little remained, was bleeding away from that one strike.

Leah raised her hand slowly and touched her jaw. Cool. Smooth. Hard as carved stone.

She looked down at her hands. Obsidian scales covered her skin, black and glassy, fitted so perfectly they looked like they had grown there. The demon claw on her wrist pulsed brighter now, violet light spreading up her arm as the scales formed.

"Holy shit," Mo breathed.

Leah pushed Leo's arm away with two fingers. "Seems to me like you're weaker than you originally thought. A couple more of those and you'll burn through the little energy you have left."

"That blow should have taken your head off, human!" Leo spat the words.

Leah leaned in until her face was inches from his. For the first time, his expression changed. Fear flickered in those green eyes. "Are you going to answer my questions, or do I have to force you?"

Leo leaned back into his cocoon as much as he could. His yellowed eyes filled with hate. "Fuck you."

Anger rose hot in Leah's throat. Asmodeus caught it and redirected the emotion, channeling it toward *Gamaliel*.

But using cursed speech here would cost her. Just like pulling from any of the Trees in the Astral drained faster than it should. She could feel the well waiting, coiled and ready. One command, and she would burn through energy she might need later.

She didn't have a choice.

"What are you?"

Her voice blended with Asmodeus's, echoing loudly in the cavern.

Leo tensed up and looked away. His jaw clenched, and he held back the words, fighting the command. The longer he resisted, the more it hurt. Pain bloomed sharp in Leah's throat, like swallowing glass. The creatures latched to his skin all wriggled.

She grabbed his face and forced him to look at her. "Answer me! What are you?"

Leo screamed. The sound bounced through the cavern and came back distorted.

Leah held on. The pain in her throat intensified, twisting deeper. But she didn't let go. She needed this. They needed to know how to kill Helen.

Leo's eyes lost focus. His expression went slack and neutral.

"I'm an Ethereal Avatar."

"What is an Ethereal?"

"Order."

Sounds erupted above them. Wriggling, stepping, crawling. Leah looked up and froze. A large creature's face hovered inches from hers, its red eyes locked on her with predatory focus. Behind it, smaller ones began crawling down the cocoon.

One of them wrapped around her wrist. Leah jerked her hand away so fast she tore the claw loose, and it splashed into the water. The creature screamed and scurried back up into the darkness.

A hand landed on her shoulder. "The creatures are sensing Leo's lack of fight. They're moving to finish him off. Hurry." Frank's voice stayed calm, but his prayer had grown strained, words coming faster.

The large creature above her retreated a few feet but kept watching.

Leah looked back at Leo. More small creatures latched

onto his neck, shoulders, and right arm. His energy was fading. She was running out of time.

"What is an Ethereal's Avatar?"

Leo's mouth moved, and the words came out flat. "A physical representation of an Ethereal force in a different domain."

"What is your Avatar doing here?"

"I came here to ensure the Core's birth."

"What's the Core?"

Leo tried to resist. His body tensed, and his jaw clenched. Pain shot through Leah's throat, sharper now. She could taste copper spreading across her tongue.

But she pulled harder on *Gamaliel, feeling* herself grow weaker. The well was draining her faster than it should.

"The Core is the seed from which an Ethereal is born."

Behind her, Frank's voice grew strained. "Leah..."

Mo's voice came tense. "The rupture is still there. But if these things swarm us, we won't make it."

Leah's vision blurred at the edges. She blinked it away and kept going. "How is an Ethereal born?"

"The Core must consume enough energy to go over the singularity and become self-aware."

"How much energy does the Core need?"

"Enough to power multiple dimensions."

"The Well," Frank mumbled behind her, his prayer a hushed sound now.

Leah's throat throbbed. She could feel herself getting weaker with every second she held *Gamaliel*. But she needed one more answer. The most important one.

Frank's prayer wavered. "Leah, we're out of time. The protection is failing."

"Just one more question," Leah said through gritted teeth. "How do you kill your kind? How do you kill an Ethereal or destroy a Core?"

Leo's eyes snapped back into focus. Rage poured from him. More creatures crawled down from the top of the cocoon and latched onto his head and neck. His energy was almost gone.

"Tell me!" Leah yelled.

Black threads sprang from her chest and wrapped around his head. They slithered down past his lips and into his throat.

No, Leah, that's too much! Asmodeus shouted in her mind.

She needed this answer. Helen had to be stopped.

Leo tried to move his head away, but the cursed speech and black threads kept him in place. He wriggled his whole body, trying to fight off the command. The threads just tightened in response. Pain exploded in Leah's throat. Tears formed in Leo's eyes, and saliva dripped from his mouth. The creatures crawled around his head and face now, sensing the end.

Leah's throat felt like it was tearing apart from the inside. Her vision went gray at the edges. She could barely stay standing. But she was close. She could feel it.

A guttural sound ripped from Leo's mouth. His head twisted back, and his body trembled.

"Chaos."

Leah let go of *Gamaliel* and fell backward. Frank's arms caught her before she hit the water. Her *Tiferet* gave out, too, and darkness swallowed everything. She tried to breathe, but her throat wouldn't work right. Each breath scraped. She coughed and tasted blood, the iron spreading through her mouth and reaching her nose.

Frank started speaking, but the words came muffled and distant. Her head was spinning. Everything felt wrong. Too light. Too far away.

Mo grabbed her other arm and helped Frank pull her

through the water. Leah tried to walk, but her legs wouldn't cooperate. She kept coughing.

"Let's go, the rupture is right here!" Mo shouted, her violet eyes burning brightly as she guided them forward.

Frank still had the cross in one hand, his other arm supporting Leah. His lips moved in prayer, words slurred with exhaustion.

A bright light appeared a few feet ahead.

The two witches carried her toward it. Leah looked back once through the darkness. Leo's form was barely visible, the creatures swarming over him completely now.

They stepped through the light and left the layer behind.

CHAPTER 36
A LIGHT STROLL

They stepped through the light into a forest thick with the smell of dry leaves. The moon loomed overhead, silver and massive, three times larger than any moon Leah had ever seen. Wind moved through the trees, cold enough to make her shiver.

Leah stumbled and caught herself against a fallen trunk. She sat down hard on the rough bark and looked at her hands.

They were translucent.

She could see straight through her palms. The texture of the wood beneath them was visible, as if she were made of colored glass. Her fingers trembled as she turned them over, trying to understand what she was seeing.

Mo dropped to a crouch in front of her. "Frank."

He crouched next to them. "You used too much."

Leah opened her mouth. The coughing hit before she could stop it, violent and wet. Blood splattered across her translucent hands, black in the moonlight. She pressed her fist against her lips, shoulders shaking.

"Don't." Mo's hand hovered near Leah's arm like she was afraid to touch. "Please, don't try."

The coughing finally stopped. Leah wiped her mouth and looked down at herself. She could see the tree trunk through her chest now. Through her ribs. Parts of her were barely there at all.

Frank stood and turned his back to them. His hands clenched at his sides.

"The Well will bring her back, right?" Mo's voice dropped to almost nothing. "There has to be enough of her to bring back."

You overdid it, Asmodeus said. Not angry. Just tired. *I warned you.*

The information was worth it. We know now.

Do we?

"Can you walk?" Frank asked.

Leah pushed herself up. Her legs seemed disconnected, like they belonged to someone else. She nodded.

"Then we need to move. The longer we wait, the worse this gets." He started into the forest.

Mo stayed close as Leah followed. Close enough to catch her if she fell. They walked without talking. Just wind through branches and the crunch of leaves beneath their feet.

The silence gave her too much room to think. About Leo's final word. About her throat. About how little of her was left.

She reached for that familiar space—the room with the round table where she and Asmodeus always talked.

Pain lanced through her chest. Not her throat this time. Deeper. Like something was tearing.

Frank spun and grabbed her shoulder. "Stop. Right now."

The forest snapped back into focus. Leah blinked at him.

"Your essence is scattering." His dice tattoo flared

bright. "Whatever you were trying to do, stop, or you'll end up who knows where."

He let go and kept walking.

Leah stood there for a moment, pulse racing in her translucent throat. That had never happened before. She'd gone to that mental space hundreds of times.

Something is different, Asmodeus said in her mind. *We should not push it.*

Leah hurried to catch up. *Fine. We'll just talk like this.*

Your vocal cords might be permanently damaged.

She kept her eyes on Frank's back ahead. *I know.*

You might never speak again.

I know.

Then why—

Because we needed to know. She thought it hard enough that he'd feel the edge in it. *We needed to know how to stop Helen, and now we do.*

Asmodeus was quiet for a long moment. *Chaos. That is what we have. One word.*

That's all we need. Golohab. Chaotic fire.

That would be certain death.

Then maybe the Immortal Witches know of a layer. Something like Phovias but worse. We leave the Core there.

They have not exactly been helpful.

Leah sensed his doubt but also something else. Consideration. After what Frank and Mo saw with Leo, they might listen. They know what the Core is now. What it can do.

Perhaps.

They walked in silence again. The wind picked up, cutting straight through Leah's translucent body like she wasn't even there.

That obsidian armor, she thought. *The one that appeared when Leo hit me. It looked like your demonic form. The one I saw in Eli's trap.*

I did not summon it consciously, Asmodeus said. *This magic. Witch's magic is old. Passive. I can feel it there, waiting, but it moves on its own. Like breathing.*

If that's what we have here, it'll help when we face Helen. I wonder if it'll work the same in the Material Plane.

I do not—

Leah's attention snapped back to the forest. A silhouette stood between the trees ahead. Human-shaped but frozen.

She tapped Mo's shoulder and pointed.

Mo's expression softened. "That's Merlin. Cora's former master."

Everything in Leah went cold. Lord Ragon's story. Merlin taking him to the Well. As they got closer, the details sharpened. An old man, skinny and bent, beard down to his chest. He was stone with a book in one hand, the other stretched out like he'd been trying to push something away.

His face stopped her. Mouth open. Eyes wide. Every line in his stone features pulled tight with terror.

"He broke our most sacred law." Frank's voice was flat. "Took a Mystic to the Well. Let him drink."

The realization hit Leah. Just like they were doing with her.

"Cora turned him to stone." Mo looked away. "The Mystic who drank got worse."

Lord Ragon. They were talking about Lord Ragon.

She forced herself to keep walking. Merlin's frozen scream faded behind them.

Frank stopped and turned. They all faced the same direction as the statue, looking out over the forest.

"The witches who created this layer made it as a last defense." Frank raised his arm. "We have complete control here. We can shape reality as we need it."

He twisted his wrist.

Sound exploded through the forest. Shattering. Grinding. The ground shook beneath Leah's feet, hard enough to make her stumble. The air in front of them rippled and tore. Giant black stones appeared, floating, forming stairs that reached up toward the massive moon above.

Leah's mouth fell open.

Frank turned back to her with a slight smile. "Almost there. You afraid of heights?"

He climbed the first few steps without waiting for an answer.

Mo gestured toward the stairs. "After you."

Leah stepped onto the first stone. It was solid beneath her feet despite floating in empty air. She started climbing. Each step took her higher. The gusts whipped around her, colder and stronger the farther she went. Her pulse quickened. She could feel it in her damaged throat, taste it in the blood still coating her mouth.

I hate this, Asmodeus said.

Me too.

She kept her eyes up, focused on the moon growing larger above. Don't look down. Just don't look down.

She looked down.

The forest spread below her, treetops tiny as scattered leaves. Her stomach lurched. The stone beneath her feet suddenly felt too narrow. One wrong step and she'd fall. Just fall and keep falling, and there was barely enough of her left to survive it.

Her knees started shaking. Her breath came short and quick.

Mo's hands pressed against her shoulders, firm and steady, pushing them up until Leah was staring at the moon again. "Eyes up. Just keep looking up."

Leah focused on the silver surface ahead. On Frank

waiting at the top. On putting one foot in front of the other. Her legs trembled with each step, but she kept moving.

Frank stood on the last stone, waiting. Then he stepped onto the moon and flipped upside down. He looked down at her. Or up at her. Leah's brain couldn't make sense of the space.

"This part is strange." His voice drifted down from above. Below. Wherever he was. "Just step. The physics here will do the rest."

Leah reached the final stone. She stood at the edge, looking up at the moon's surface, at Frank standing on it as if it were the ground, and she was the one upside down. Her translucent foot hovered over the threshold.

She stepped.

One moment, the forest was below her, the next it stretched above like a ceiling of trees. She stood on the moon's surface, gray dust beneath her feet, staring up at the forest that was now her sky.

Her stomach twisted.

She opened her mouth. Tried to say something. Anything. Her throat seized. The cough tore through her, so violent she dropped to her knees. Blood hit the moon dust in dark drops. She kept coughing, each one sending glass shards of pain through her ruined throat, until finally she spat the last of it out.

Mo helped her up. "Just a little farther."

They walked across the moon's surface. The dust was fine and soft, different from sand. After a few minutes, Frank stopped at the edge of an enormous crater and slid down. Leah looked over the rim. A cave entrance sat at the bottom, small and dark against the pale surface.

They slid down after him. The descent was steep, but the moon dust made it smooth, almost like floating. They reached the bottom in seconds.

Frank moved to the cave entrance. He raised his arm and began speaking in a language Leah had never heard. The words were beautiful and old, lulling her into a better time, with her parents, before all this.

She blinked, and light appeared in the cave, deep in the darkness. Two spirals formed, rotating in opposite directions, weaving together into a single glowing circle. The glowing circle dimmed, leaving in its place a door of light.

CHAPTER 37
IMMORTALITY

Frank placed his hands on the door and swung it open. Leah stepped through behind him, and warmth enveloped her. It cascaded down her scalp, her neck, her shoulders. The constant ache in her muscles dissolved. The fog pressing against her thoughts lifted. She drew a breath, and for the first time since confronting Leo, it didn't hurt as much. Her throat still burned, but the rawness had dulled to a low throb.

Leah looked down at her hands. Solid. Her fingers had color, substance, weight. The ghostly translucence from overusing *Gamaliel* was gone.

She blinked and focused on Frank walking ahead. His back was completely bare, pale skin catching the dim light. Her gaze trailed lower, and she realized he was entirely naked. Frank turned slightly, and Leah jerked her eyes away, warmth flooding her face.

A glance to her right showed Mo, also naked. Intricate tattoos covered her arms and torso, the ink standing out against her dark skin. Mo's body seemed to glow faintly, as if lit from within.

Leah looked down, realizing she was naked, too.

The embarrassment that should have consumed her faded as quickly as it came. Something about this place, about the warmth still spreading through her limbs, made the nudity feel natural. Expected, even. Like shedding clothes was the same as shedding everything else she'd carried with her.

But then Leah noticed something else. Frank's skin was smooth. No scars. No marks. Centuries of life, and his body showed none of it. Mo looked the same. Her tattooed skin was flawless, unblemished by time or violence.

Leah glanced down at herself again. The blackened scar from Lord Ragon's spread across her chest like fractured glass, purple at the center. Smaller scars marked her arms. A burn on her forearm. A cut across her thigh. She was a map of every battle, every wound, every moment she'd barely survived.

Her new tattoo began to glow brighter than the rest of her body. Leah stared at her hands as violet, green, and blue light pulsed beneath her skin. She looked around, trying to make sense of what was happening.

Frank's dice were no longer inked on his forearm. Two small cubes floated next to him, spiraling pips glowing as they tumbled through the air. They darted around his shoulder before settling near his head.

To her right, a ghostly figure hovered beside Mo. It looked like an older woman, her eyes replaced by bright spirals that turned in opposite directions and glowed violet. The figure rested a hand on Mo's shoulder. They exchanged a look, and Leah recognized the expression. Familiar love. The kind that didn't need words.

"I cannot believe this."

The voice came from beside her, not inside her head. Leah's breath caught. She turned.

A large obsidian statue stood next to her, at least seven

feet tall. Asmodeus stared at his hands, opening and closing them slowly. His starry eyes glowed in his stony face. He looked as shocked as she felt.

They stared at each other. Leah raised her arm and touched him. The surface was smooth, cold, like polished glass. Asmodeus reached for her hand and squeezed gently. His grip was solid. It was like seeing a close friend after years apart.

His glowing eyes shifted to her hands. He held them between his, and that was when she noticed the light pouring from her palms. Violet, green, and blue swirled together like an aurora, the colors bleeding into each other and separating again.

Leah opened her mouth to speak. She braced for the pain, for the tearing sensation in her ruined throat. Nothing came. Her mouth hadn't moved at all. The words had come from somewhere deeper, from the center of her chest.

"This is incredible." She paused, touching her throat. Still sore, but the words hadn't hurt. "What is this?"

"You are pure essence here," Frank said. His voice seemed to come from everywhere at once.

Leah looked over. Frank watched her with a small smile, his eyes fixed on her glowing hands even though a seven-foot obsidian statue stood right next to her.

"What?"

"Cora was right about your high potential. She always had a keen eye for it. But I don't think even she could have predicted this."

Mo and the ghostly woman stared at Leah's hands, too, both of them grinning.

"She mentioned that once," Leah said, the words flowing from her center without her throat moving. "But I never understood what it meant. Does it make me stronger?"

Frank shook his head. The dice floating beside him also shook. "In a nutshell, potential translates to your relationship with energy. Someone with low potential will have a more active or alive energy like Mo's."

"This is Grams!" Mo aimed her thumb at the ghostly figure. The ghostly woman nodded at Leah.

"Yes," Frank continued, his omnipresent voice filling the space. He extended his arms, and the dice rolled, floating inches from his palm. "Someone with medium potential, like me, will have a tattoo that is more solid and material. It is an easier way of channeling the energy from the Well. Someone with high potential just connects. The connection is far more abstract. But you seem to be something else entirely. It is almost as if your two essences are both reacting to the Well's energy. Two essences, two tattoos, two powers."

Leah glanced at the obsidian statue. It mirrored her movements, turning its head when she did.

Frank rubbed his hands together. "We shouldn't linger. Come."

He led them through the dark cave toward polished marble steps. The stairs climbed to a small platform lit by a single beam of light that poured down from somewhere impossibly far above. They reached the top and found a circular well in the center. The water was crystalline and still except for two spiral vortexes that turned in opposite directions. They looked like twin drains, the water flowing into both, though one spiral was almost twice the size of the other.

Something about it felt wrong. Frank's expression confirmed it.

"Hasn't really stabilized itself yet," Mo whispered.

"What's going on?" Leah asked, the words emanating from her essence.

"We don't know." Frank stared down at the spirals. "I think it happened when all the Immortal Witches were slaughtered. I thought bringing Mo and others and growing the coven might stabilize the Well. But it seems to be getting worse."

"Maybe it's because of Helen and the Core?"

"Maybe." Frank sighed and looked up into the distance. He reached out, and a crystal goblet materialized around his fingers. He pulled it from thin air, submerged it into the water without touching the surface with his skin, and filled it with the translucent liquid. The beam of light bent as it reached the water, and a prism of colors shone through and around them. Frank smiled and handed Leah the cup.

She held it with both hands. The crystal was cool and smooth. She stared down at the water, watching it catch the light. This was it. The moment Cora had seen in her. The potential she'd turned down years ago, only to crawl back to now.

Asmodeus's obsidian form stood beside her, his starry eyes locked on the goblet. Across the platform, Frank and Mo watched, their faces equal parts anticipation and encouragement.

Leah raised the goblet to her lips and drank.

The first sip hit her tongue like spring water after crossing a desert. Cool. Clear. It slid down her throat, and she realized how thirsty she was. Not just her throat. Something deeper. The water spread through her chest.

She drank again. The liquid traced through her body, following her veins like it knew the map better than she did. It found the dark places. The damaged places. The blackened scar on her chest began to tingle. Leah gasped between swallows as the dead tissue lightened. The purple center faded to pink. The black veins threading outward receded like frost melting under the sun.

A burn on her forearm vanished. The raised tissue smoothed until her skin looked as if it had never been touched. A scabbed-over cut across her thigh sealed, the edges knitting together and disappearing. Every wound she'd accumulated, every mark left behind, the water found them all and erased them.

But it was more than healing. With each swallow, something built in Leah's spine. Energy, but not like *Malchut* or *Nehemoth* or any well she'd learned to pull from. This felt different.

The goblet emptied, but the sensation grew stronger. The energy in her spine expanded, reaching up through her neck and down through her legs. It connected her to something vast, something that stretched beyond this cave, beyond the Astral Realm, beyond anything she could name. A river of energy flowing through every living thing. Through every witch who had drunk from this well. Through every soul that had crossed over.

Through her parents.

Leah felt them before she heard them. Her mother's essence wrapped around her. The scent of vanilla and old books filled her senses. Her father's presence settled beside her, steady as bedrock.

"Mom?"

"We're so proud of you, sweetheart." Her mother's voice was exactly as Leah remembered it. Soft but certain. "We've always been so proud."

"Go," her father added. She could hear the smile in his voice. "You don't need us anymore."

"No, wait." Leah reached for them, trying to hold on. "Please don't go. Not yet."

Their essences slipped through her grasp. The warmth faded. The voices grew distant. She tried to call out again, but they were already gone.

The connection to the vast river of energy began to soften. The heartbeat of the universe grew quieter. Leah became aware of her body again, of the platform beneath her feet, of the light pouring down from above. She realized her head was tilted back, her eyes closed. The beam of light that had illuminated the well slowly retracted, pulling back into the infinite dark above them.

The two uneven spirals in the water continued their endless turn.

Something squeezed her hand. Leah turned.

The obsidian statue was gone. In its place stood a man, naked like the rest of them. His black hair was combed back from his face, revealing features she'd only glimpsed in fragments before. Strong jawline. Broad shoulders tapering to a lean, muscular frame. He looked solid, real, human in a way he never had when manifesting in the Material Realm. His starry eyes shone brighter than she'd ever seen them, and a small smile appeared on his face.

An expression she'd never seen him wear before.

Joy.

"We did it," Asmodeus said. His voice came from his mouth, not her mind. Solid and real and human. "It appears we are both Immortal Witches now."

CHAPTER 38
ASTRAL THREADS

The Well chamber's glow lit up the path heading out of the cave. The Well's power continued to surge through Leah's veins, making everything sharper. She could see each layer of rock in the walls, hear every sound echoing off the cavern, and she felt Asmodeus beside her, sensing his awe as it mingled with her own.

Frank led the way, his dice floating beside him instead of tattooed on his forearm. Mo followed, her grandmother's ghostly shape walking beside her, looking back at Leah and whispering in Mo's ear.

"Our coven is growing," Frank said, glancing back at them. "Welcome to the family. And a two-for-one, that's what I call a deal!"

Asmodeus stared down at his hands, flexing his fingers. "I didn't think it would." His voice was full of wonder. "After everything I've done. Everything I was."

"The Well doesn't judge like that." Frank gestured ahead, where pale light filtered through the cave entrance. "It sees what you are now, not what you were. Though I'm guessing you won't remain in physical form once we leave this cave."

"We should head back," Mo said.

They stepped out onto the dusty surface of the moon, leaving the glowing cave behind.

As Frank had predicted, Asmodeus's physical form dissolved into smoke. The sensation of him flooded back into Leah's mind, settling in that familiar space behind her thoughts. Beside her, Frank's dice spun once in the air before flowing back into the tattoo on his forearm. Mo's grandmother faded, her essence returning to the tattoo on Mo's shoulder.

Well, that was interesting while it lasted, Asmodeus said.

"At least you got to try having your own body again," Leah said aloud, her throat healed, but a little lower and raspier than she remembered.

The moon crater stretched around them, dust clinging to Leah's feet. Stars burned overhead, closer and brighter than they'd ever been on Earth.

Frank cracked his knuckles. The dice tattoo on his forearm shifted, pips changing in patterns Leah couldn't follow. "Ready to head home, ladies?"

Mo nodded, but Leah frowned. Her left hand tingled. She flexed her fingers, trying to shake off the sensation. It persisted, a warmth flowing between her fingers like water.

The tingling in Leah's hand intensified. She looked down. Her palm glowed faint gold. The glow pulsed, matching a rhythm she could almost hear. As if her heartbeat and this glow had synced with something beyond her.

"How do we get back?" she asked. "Through the coordinates?"

"Same way we came," Frank said. He paused, frowning at her hand. "Though we'll need to move fast through the Phovias layer. Don't want those spider bastards thinking we're a meal if they've already killed Leo." His frown deepened. "Leah, what's happening to your hand?"

She held it up. The glow was brighter now. "I don't know. It just started tingling after we left the cave."

Mo stepped closer, her eyes flashing violet. "Let me see."

The moment Mo touched her hand, light exploded from Leah's fingertips. Thin threads unfurled like spider webs, stretching in different directions across the crater. Some pointed toward the horizon. Others angled up toward the stars. One reached straight ahead, pulsing brighter than the rest.

"Holy shit," Leah whispered.

Frank moved beside them, staring. "Well, I'll be damned."

Leah could feel them. Each thread hummed with a different frequency. Some felt warm against her skin. Others were cold enough to make her joints ache if she thought about them for too long. One smelled like bergamot and rose hips.

"What is this?" Her voice came out shaky.

Mo released her hand, but the threads remained. "They're paths. Connections between layers." She looked at Frank. "She's threading."

"Threading?" Leah touched one of the threads. It vibrated under her fingertip like a plucked guitar string.

Frank circled around her, examining the threads from different angles. "It's an ability some Immortal Witches have. Cora had it. She could sense the connections between the Astral layers and move through them without needing coordinates." He stopped directly in front of Leah. "But I've never seen so many of them visible before."

"Well, will any of these get us home?" Leah asked.

The thread that bergamot and rose hips pulsed brighter. Leah's fingers wrapped around it instinctively. It solidified in her grip.

"This one," she said. "This one goes home."

Frank's eyebrows shot up. "You can feel which layer it leads to?"

"I think so." Leah pulled gently on the thread. Where it touched the air, reality cracked. Harsh fluorescent white spilled through.

"What the hell," Frank breathed.

Through the opening, Leah could see the tattoo parlor's break room. The round table. Three bodies slumped in chairs.

"You opened straight to the Material Realm," Mo said, stunned.

"Is that bad?" Leah asked.

Frank whistled low. "Bad? Doll, Cora spent decades learning to do that. *Decades*." He stared at the opening. "You just did it on instinct."

"We need to go," Mo said. "Now. Before she accidentally closes it or something."

Frank stepped through first, his form vanishing into the fluorescent light. Mo followed.

Leah moved toward the opening, but the moment she crossed the threshold, the world lurched. The thread yanked her forward. Reality compressed, folded, twisted.

Everything went dark.

Then the universe slammed back into place.

Leah gasped. Her body convulsed. She felt pain, everywhere. Her lungs strained to work. Her heart stuttered.

Close it, Asmodeus said urgently. *Close the opening before it destabilizes.*

Leah forced her eyes open. Reality swam back into focus, and she found herself inside the break room. Frank and Mo stood beside the table. Nearby, the crack in reality still hung open.

She reached up with a shaking hand. Found the thread. Pulled it closed.

The opening zipped shut. The thread vanished.

Leah collapsed forward onto the table, gasping.

"Easy," Frank said. His hands steadied her shoulders. "You're okay. We're back in the Material Realm. Your body isn't used to the disconnect yet."

"How long?" Her voice came out hoarse. Different.

"Until what?"

"Until I stop feeling hollow?"

Mo moved to her other side. "A few days. Your spirit needs time to adjust."

They helped her stand. Leah's legs shook, but she stayed upright. The fluorescent lights hummed overhead. The smell of stale cigarettes and cheap air freshener filled her nose.

"That was incredible," Frank said, studying her. "Threading straight to the Material Realm on your first try. I've never seen anything like it."

"Your voice is different, too," Mo added.

Frank moved to a drawer and pulled out a small mirror. "You'll want to see this, too."

Leah took the mirror and stared. The woman looking back was her, but not. Her honeycomb eyes were somehow brighter and more striking. Her skin was flawless. Even the burn scar from Helen's chain had faded to a faint discoloration.

And her hair was a vibrant auburn. All her black dye was stripped clean.

"The Well strips you clean, and purifies you," Mo said quietly.

Leah couldn't stop staring. She looked beautiful. Not normally beautiful. Something beyond that. The kind of beauty that made people stare. The kind Helen had.

Will Sarah and Isaac even recognize me?

They will, Asmodeus said. *You are still you.*

She set the mirror down and flexed her fingers.

Like Cora, she could thread. If she could master it, she could pull Helen into the Astral Realm, where the Core would drain. Where the King would be vulnerable.

"I need to control this," Leah said, looking at Frank and Mo.

Frank nodded slowly. "It's a powerful gift."

"Can you teach me?"

"We can try," Mo said, eyeing Frank. "But it'll take time. Practice."

"Then let's start, as soon as possible," she said. "Helen won't wait, and neither can I."

CHAPTER 39
TIMING

Leah flexed her fingers and reached for the threads.

Nothing.

She stood in the backyard behind Mo's tattoo shop, morning sun already baking the scrub brush and cracked earth. Sweat rolled down her back.

It'd been three days since she'd found the threads and got them out of the Astral Realm. And three days since she'd been trying to open a door from the Material to the Astral, with nothing to show for it.

She closed her eyes and tried again. Pulled on the memory of that tingling warmth, the way the threads had exploded from her fingertips when Mo touched her hand. The feelings and scents each thread had.

Her palm stayed empty.

"Dammit."

The back door creaked. Mo leaned against the frame, coffee mug in hand. "You know, standing out here cursing isn't helping, right?"

"It's helping me feel better."

"Fair enough." Mo took a sip. "But Frank's done making breakfast. You should eat."

Leah's stomach growled at the mention of food. She hadn't eaten since yesterday afternoon, too focused on making this work. "Five more minutes."

"You said that an hour ago."

"This time I mean it."

Mo snorted and went back inside. The door clicked shut.

Leah spread her fingers wide. "Come on," she muttered. She'd drunk from the Well. Became an Immortal Witch. Cora was able to bring her into the Astral just by sitting there in her office. She could do it too. She just had to try harder.

Her eyes burned from lack of sleep and the bright Texas sun. She'd been pushing herself every day since the transformation, testing the limits of her new body. Learning what changed.

Some things worked. Frank and Mo were encouraging her to test her other abilities and give this one a rest. She'd discovered she could use the wells of both Trees in the Astral realm now without her essence fading. That gave her an even greater advantage against Helen if she could pull her there.

But this? The threading? Nothing.

You are exhausting yourself, Asmodeus said. *Perhaps rest would serve you better.*

"I don't have time to rest."

You collapsing from fatigue won't make facing Helen any easier.

"I know." Leah lowered her hand. Her arm ached from holding it up. "But I need this. If I can't thread, how am I supposed to pull Helen into the Astral realm? How do I get her away from using the Trees?"

If it is meant to be, we will find a way.

"This is the answer. I have to figure it out."

Leah felt Asmodeus retreat deeper into their shared mental space, that familiar presence settling behind her thoughts without another word.

She tried one more time. Closed her eyes. Reached.

Nothing.

The back door opened again. "Leah, seriously. Come eat, or Frank and I will bewitch you, too."

"Can you really do that?"

"Wanna find out?"

Leah turned and trudged inside.

The tattoo shop's break room smelled like bacon and coffee. Frank stood at the stove, spatula in hand, flipping eggs in a cast-iron pan. Mo sat at the round wooden table with her coffee, scrolling through her phone.

"Sit," Frank said without turning around. "You look awful."

"Thanks."

He scraped eggs onto three plates already loaded with toast and some kind of fried potatoes with peppers. "You're running yourself thin. You might be immortal, but you still need food and sleep."

Leah grabbed her fork and ate without responding.

Frank joined them with his own plate. "I take it the threading still isn't working?"

"No."

"Might be a Material Realm thing." Mo set her phone down. "Maybe you need to master it in the Astral before getting it to work in the Material."

"That doesn't help me."

"Have you tried from the decaying layer?" Frank asked.

Leah paused mid-bite. "What?"

"The first Astral layer—the one that brushes right up against the Material world." Frank gestured with his fork. "Maybe if you listened to us and actually practiced in the Astral..."

Mo leaned back. "You'd at least get comfortable with how it feels. Then work on translating that skill back here."

"I don't have time to—"

"And standing outside for three days is helping you how?" Frank asked.

Leah took another bite. "Fine. I'll try it your way."

"*After* you sleep," Mo said firmly.

"I slept last night."

"You projected and practiced using the Trees last night."

"You spied on me?"

Mo's eyes flashed violet. "Obviously. And if you keep this up, you'll be useless against Helen."

Leah prodded her toast with a butter knife.

"Fine," she said quietly. "I'll rest. But after that, I'm practicing."

"Deal." Frank refilled his mug. "And once you're rested, I've got something else to show you. A few spells that might help when you go up against Helen."

Leah's head jerked up. "What kind of spells?"

"We have a few rituals. Old ways of manipulating energy." Frank sat back down. "Most take years to learn. But there are a couple of quick ones I can teach you. Protection charms. Binding rituals. Nothing fancy, but they might help."

Leah sat up. "How long will that take me to learn?"

"A day or two for the basics," Frank said. He waved his finger. "But not until you rest."

They stood in an abandoned building. Broken windows lined the walls, gray sky beyond. Vines crawled up the concrete, black and withered.

Leah peered out. She could see the street where Mo's shop stood, but the buildings sagged. Doors hung crooked. Paint peeled in long strips.

"Now thread," Frank said.

Leah raised her hand, closed her eyes, and reached.

The tingling started immediately.

Her palm warmed. That familiar sensation spread between her fingers like invisible water. She opened her eyes and saw thin threads of gold light spreading from her fingertips.

"Finally," she whispered.

Dozens of them. Maybe hundreds. They extended in every direction like a spider web made of light. Some thick as rope. Others thin as hair. Each one buzzing with energy.

"Don't try to grab anything yet," Frank said, moving beside her. "Just feel them. Get a sense of what's out there."

Leah focused on the closest thread. The moment her attention landed on it, sensations flooded through her. It was warm and left a honeyed taste in her mouth.

"What is that?" she asked. "It feels warm."

Frank squinted at it. "Hard to say without pulling it. Could be a peaceful layer. Somewhere with light and growth." He gestured to another thread, this one darker. "What about that one?"

Leah shifted her focus. A jolt traveled through her knuckles. The metallic taste of old pennies filled her mouth. She heard screaming in the distance, though whether it was real or just an impression from the thread itself, she couldn't tell.

"That one's bad," she said.

"Yeah. Trust those instincts." Frank pointed to a thin green thread that wavered in and out of existence. "That one looks strange. Never seen anything like it."

Leah reached toward it carefully. The moment her consciousness touched it, nausea rolled through her stomach. "It feels... wrong. Not like anything in the Astral I've been to."

"Hmm," Frank muttered. "Cora suggested there were places beyond, but she never found them..." He trailed off, studying her hand. "You're stronger than she was, from what I can tell."

Leah pulled her attention back. The nausea faded. "How do I know which ones are safe?"

"You don't. Not really. That's why you practice." Frank gestured at the web of threads. "Feel as many as you can. Learn the differences. Some will feel inviting. Others will feel dangerous. And some will feel like nothing—just empty space between layers."

Leah started working through them methodically. One thread felt like heavy rain, and she immediately knew it was the jungle layer. Another was dark, leaving a feeling of sand in her mouth.

Following what seemed like an eternity, her head started to ache. Too many sensations. Too much information flooding in at once.

"Take a break," Frank said.

Leah lowered her hand, and the threads vanished. She rubbed her eyes. "There's so many."

"Who knows what places you might find." Frank leaned against the wall. "Cora was the strongest witch with the threading. Before her, there were only a few who mastered navigating a few dozen doors in their lifetime—the ones close by."

Leah thought about that. "When I was on the moon, I found a thread that led straight back to Mo's shop. It smelled like bergamot and rose hips."

"Right. You pulled it and opened a crack home."

"Can I find that same thread from here?"

Frank frowned. "It won't be the same. The threads you have here link this layer to wherever you are looking to go. But it would be smart to sense the one that links here to the Material Realm if you can."

Leah raised her hand again. The threads reappeared. She searched through them, looking for anything that felt like the Material world.

There, a faint hint of bergamot.

A thread so thin she almost missed it. She focused on it, but the thread pulled tight against her mind, like it was on the verge of snapping.

"I think I found it," Leah said. "But it feels weird."

"Weird how?"

"Like it's too thin." She wrapped her fingers around the thread. It solidified, but barely. "The one on the moon was like a thick rope."

"That might be because you were traveling far," Frank said. "The Material Realm is a thought away, maybe that means the thread is so thin because it doesn't take much to unravel."

Leah pulled gently on the thread. Pain shot through her palm and into her elbow. She gasped and let go.

"Careful now," Frank said. "Take your time, be gentle."

She pulled slowly, and a tiny tear formed in the air in front of her.

"There it is," Frank said. "You found it on this side. Get a feel for it, maybe that will help you find it on the other side."

Leah focused on the thin strand connecting to the Material Realm again. She didn't pull this time. Just felt it. Memorized the sensation. The resistance. The way it strained.

"This is the thread that takes me from here to Mo's shop, but if I..."

She focused on the way the thread felt, holding it between her thumb and forefinger as other threads passed by her other fingers. She paused, finding another thin strand, and another. They all left a different taste in her mouth. Wildflowers that would take her to a field in the Dakotas. Cigarette smoke that led to a bar in a small town that spoke a foreign language she didn't know. But they all felt the same, and she knew they would lead back to the Material Realm.

"I can feel where these go," she whispered. "There are threads everywhere."

"There are," Frank said. "The Material and Astral are always connected."

"All right. Let's go back, I think I know what I'm looking for now."

The next five days blurred together.

Mornings in the Material Realm, reaching for threads. Afternoons in the Astral, opening cracks to different layers. She found tons of new layers, from peaceful ones to a place filled with mirrors. And once, by accident, a back door to the Phovias layer where they'd left Leo trapped. She'd slammed that crack shut faster than she thought possible.

In the evenings, Frank taught her spells. A protection ward drawn in salt with whispered words in a language she didn't recognize. A way to hide her energy signature using smoke from specific herbs. Each one required precision, repetition, and focus until her fingers cramped from drawing symbols.

Leah practiced until her voice went hoarse from incantations.

On the sixth day, Leah was practicing in the backyard, frustration building after another failed threading attempt. The anger sat hot and sharp in her gut. She was about to give up when she felt Asmodeus stir.

Wait, he said. *Let me try something.*

Black smoke poured from her skin without warning. Obsidian scales formed along her arms, her chest, her legs. The armor clicked into place, solid and strong.

Leah stared down at herself. The blue eye among the scales on her left arm blinked slowly.

I can manifest in the Material Realm now, Asmodeus said, satisfaction in his voice. *It took some adjustment, but I understand how to do it.*

"Great. At least you figured your power out," Leah whispered.

We figured it out. And now we have even more advantage.

That evening at dinner, Frank raised his beer. "To progress."

"To progress," Mo echoed.

Leah clinked her water glass against their bottles and allowed herself a small smile.

She still couldn't thread from the Material Realm. But she could do it from the decaying layer. She could invoke the armor. She knew two protective spells. And her body felt stronger than it ever had.

It wasn't perfect. But it might be enough.

"Alright," Frank said, setting his bottle down. "Ready to contact Jan Xie?"

Leah took a breath. "Yeah. I'm ready."

"Good." Frank pulled out his phone. "I'll call her tomorrow. Set up a meeting."

"Where do you think they are?" Mo asked.

"No idea. But knowing Jan Xie, somewhere secure." Frank scrolled through his contacts. "She's paranoid. Has been since Helen took over."

"Do we tell her about me?" Leah looked across the table. "Or do I stay hidden?"

"Stay hidden at first," Mo said. "Let us meet with them. You come invisible with *Thagirion*. Listen. Then decide if you trust them."

"Smart," Frank said.

"And hopefully all this practice doesn't go to waste," Leah muttered as she downed the last of her water.

CHAPTER 40
OLD FRIENDS AND FOES

Leah opened her eyes. Rain drummed against the car roof, droplets sliding down the window where her head had been resting. She sat up, her spine popping as she stretched. Her neck ached.

Mo's eyes found hers in the rearview mirror.

"We're here, Leah. Get ready."

Leah rubbed her face and nodded. Asmodeus reached for *Thagirion*, and coldness washed through her body. Sounds muffled. The gray afternoon light turned sickly yellow. She existed between layers now, in that decaying space where the living world looked wrong.

The car stopped in a narrow alley. Buildings pressed close on either side, brick and concrete darkened by rain. Mo killed the engine and opened her door. Frank climbed out of the passenger side, pulling his tattered coat tight.

Leah slipped out behind them. Her feet touched wet pavement, but *Thagirion* dulled the sensation.

They stood before a single-story post office that looked abandoned. Low-slung brick with aluminum lettering that had lost most of its letters. Faded and boarded up. Plywood covered the windows. Graffiti marked the walls.

"What do you see?" Frank asked.

Mo's eyes flashed violet. She stared at the building for several seconds. "There's at least ten people inside. And they know we're here. How's our luck?"

Frank pushed up his sleeve and checked the dice tattoo on his forearm. The spiral pips had settled into a pattern. "Got a pretty decent roll, but hopefully we won't need to use it. We know the plan, so let's see what they're up to, then we reassess."

A side door opened. Light spilled into the dark alley. A silhouette waved them forward.

"Come in, come in. Follow me." The man rushed them inside and closed the door behind them.

Leah slipped in before the door shut. The man didn't notice. He was tall, Asian, with silver hair and glasses. He led Frank and Mo down a hallway lit by blinking fluorescent tubes. The air smelled stale, like old paper and dust.

They turned a corner. Two people stood guard in front of double doors. Both tall, copper-skinned, attractive. Light eyes that tracked Frank and Mo's approach.

Leah stopped walking.

Buck and Serena Bacchus. The twins who had been with her from the start, back in Mystic Outpost.

Buck had changed. The class clown was gone. A scar cut across the bridge of his nose. Muscles corded his arms and shoulders. He stood like a soldier now, feet planted, hands ready. His face had hardened into something Leah barely recognized.

Serena matched him. Beautiful still, but with edges that hadn't existed at the Academy. Life had carved away her softness.

The last time Leah had seen Buck, he'd been hauled off for Shadow Board training. The last time she'd seen Serena, the girl had been crying in the Academy halls after failing her final trial. Serena had chosen to leave, to find her brother.

And she'd found him. They were together now.

Leah wanted to talk to them. Ask if it had been worth it. Ask what they'd been through. Ask if they remembered the old days before everything fell apart.

But she had a job to do.

The twins stepped aside. Frank and Mo walked through the doors. Leah hurried after them, keeping her footsteps light.

The conference room was simple with a long table, a whiteboard on one wall, and a corkboard covering another wall, packed with newspaper clippings, printouts, and photos.

A woman stood behind the table. Dark suit. Black blouse. She approached Frank and Mo.

Jan Xie.

The former Queen looked older. Wrinkles creased the corners of her mouth and eyes. Dark bags shadowed beneath her one good eye. Her black hair, now streaked with gray and white, was pulled into a tight bun. The eyepatch over her missing eye gave her the look of a war veteran who'd seen too much.

It was odd seeing her smile; Leah had only ever seen Jan Xie angry or calculating.

She extended her hand. Jan Xie formally introduced herself, then returned to her seat across the table from them.

"My colleague should join us so we can begin."

A knock sounded. The door opened.

Leah's breath caught.

Jaime McMillan walked in and bowed. The four-square insignia of the Infinity Board decorated his white uniform, but his Rook symbol had changed. White instead of black.

And most jarring of all, his neck was bare.

The iron chains were gone. The spidery black veins that had marked where the Shifter virus lived under his skin had vanished. His ginger hair and beard had grayed, and exhaustion lined his face, but his smile remained. That good-natured warmth that made people trust him.

He'd been healed.

"Apologies for my delay, I hope I didn't miss too much." The Scottish accent was exactly as Leah remembered.

"Not at all." Jan said. "The Immortal Witches just got here. Frank and Mo, this is Jaime McMillan. Sage of *Hod* of the Infinity Board."

They shook hands. Jaime took the seat beside Jan Xie.

"Don't you mean the former Sage of *Hod*?" Frank asked.

"No, I serve as a double spy."

Leah's alertness spiked. Why would Jaime turn against the Infinity Board? He and Jan Xie had never liked Helen; that much was true. But the rest of the Sages had stayed loyal when Helen took Legion's Core. Yuki, Desmond, Zafirah. All of them had fallen in line.

So why was Jaime different?

I do not trust this, Asmodeus said.

Neither do I. But we need to hear them out.

Frank crossed his arms. "I don't trust double spies. They have no loyalty."

"Good, you shouldn't trust them." Jaime's smile didn't waver. "Or to be more frank, you shouldn't trust *anyone* these days. But you're here, so I'm guessing you are at least mildly interested in what we have to say."

Frank said nothing.

Jan Xie cleared her throat and placed her hands on the table, fingers intertwined. "As you well know, the Infinity Board has a King now—King Helen. Well, we believe that the King cannot be trusted, and that her concentration of power is worrisome."

"Okay, so what does that have to do with us? You know we don't interfere with matters in the Physical realm."

"I know, but I have information that might be interesting for you. Information related to the being that killed your coven."

Frank and Mo exchanged looks.

"Go on," Frank said.

"Around two years ago, there was a fight between the Infinity Board and Legion. We were barely able to defeat him, but then the Queen took over his Core. The same Core that killed your Coven."

They are using the same argument we used. But to what end?

Mo spoke carefully. "We know about that."

Leah caught Frank's sharp look at Mo. A warning, maybe.

Jaime raised an eyebrow. Jan Xie's expression didn't change. "Then you must know that the Core is dangerous and that the King should be stopped at all costs."

Frank leaned forward, one finger raised. "And you want our help to stop her. Let me stop you right there. You see, we are everything that's left of the Immortal Witches. We're in charge of protecting all the layers in the Astral Realm, while you all play your games here in the Material one. We don't have the power to join you in a fight. We can't risk dying for your cause."

"If the Material realm dies, the Astral realm will be next. We are not asking you to fight with us. We are asking for your support. You both have direct access to the Astral Realm. From our reports, King Helen's reach there is limited. Even with Legion, he needed over a dozen different Chimera sacrifices to break through the Astral realm. The only thing we are asking is for logistical support. If we could do an ambush through the Astral Realm that the King won't see coming, then maybe we have a chance."

The idea took shape in Leah's mind. Working with Jaime and Jan Xie. Using their resources, their manpower. Suddenly, killing Helen seemed less impossible.

But was it real? Or was this a trap?

Leah's eyes drifted to the corkboard. Photos pinned between maps and news clippings. She recognized faces.

Images of Yuki, Desmond, and Zafirah stared back at her.

Leah's stomach twisted. The last time she'd seen them, they'd attacked the Family. Desmond had fought Father over Yuki's dying body. Zafirah had been ready to burn them all. And Leah had nearly killed both Desmond and Maria trying to save Yuki, pulling so hard on *Chesed* and *Nehemoth* that she'd drained everyone around her.

Their photos were on Jan Xie's board like targets, with notes on their last known whereabouts.

Frank chuckled. "Let me get this straight. You want to use us to guide you and your army through the Astral to do a surprise attack on the King, is that right?"

"Yes." Jan Xie's voice was firm.

Part of Leah wanted to believe them. They seemed to be mounting a real rebellion. But something bothered her. For the past months, Leah had watched Mystics fall in line under Helen's rule. None of them had fought back the way she'd expected. The Sages all seemed complacent, accepting the new normal.

This rebellion should have happened on day one. Why had it taken them over two years?

Calm down and listen, Leah.

"Do you know what would happen if you fail? Which, no offense, but based on the recent accomplishments by the

King, you probably will. Helen isn't stupid, and she will know we helped you. What if she decides to go after us next? If she gets rid of us, the Immortal Witches will disappear, and the Well that sheds the water of our realities will be at risk. So, you might understand why we're respectfully declining your offer."

Jan Xie opened her mouth to respond.

Jaime leaned forward first, cutting her off. "Okay, I'm going to stop this conversation right here and ask you both to cut the bullshit." His eyes sharpened. "We received reports that Leah Ackerman was spotted with you down in Texas. There were only a handful of us who survived the fight with Legion and saw Helen absorb the Core. The fact that you both know about that is only further proof that you've been in contact with her." He paused. "Are those reports true? Where is she now?"

Jan Xie pressed her lips together. She didn't look pleased at being interrupted, but she didn't argue.

"Why do you want to know?" Mo asked.

"I've been looking for that lass for over two years. Ever since our fight with Legion, she disappeared without a trace."

"Why are you looking for her?"

"Because I care about her." Jaime's voice dropped. "And if you both were spotted with her only a few weeks ago and then suddenly agree to see us, knowing full well you were going to reject our request, I get even more suspicious." His gaze moved around the room, searching. "Is she here?"

Leah froze.

How could Jaime read her so well, even when she wasn't visible? She watched him scan the empty spaces of the room. His eyes passed over her once, then twice.

Isaac and Sarah were still trapped. The Librarian held them in his library, waiting for Leah to return. Every day she delayed was another moment they suffered. She couldn't wait around, hiding in the corner, invisible.

This was the moment. Trust Jaime and Jan Xie and work together, or do this alone.

She was an Immortal Witch now. She could technically navigate the Astral Realm on her own. But where was Helen? How protected was the King? What was her schedule? When was the best time to strike? How do you surprise the most powerful Mystic alive, someone who could teleport anywhere?

One wrong move and her element of surprise would be over.

If she had support from Mystics like Jaime and Jan Xie, her odds might improve. They might actually win.

But if this was a trap, she was walking into it with her eyes open.

What do you think? Leah asked Asmodeus.

I think we have little choice. The Librarian will not wait forever. And we cannot face Helen alone.

Leah studied Jaime's face. The exhaustion there. The hope. It had to mean something.

She took a breath and let *Thagirion* drop.

The world rushed back. Sounds sharpened. Light returned to normal. The air smelled like stale coffee and old wood.

"Yes, I'm here."

CHAPTER 41
REBELLION

Jaime jumped out of his chair, which rolled back and bumped into the wall. "Leah!"

He rushed around the table and engulfed her in a tight hug. "I told Jan you were still out there, lass."

Leah hesitated for a moment before returning the hug. The wool of his coat scratched against her cheek. "It's good to see you, too, my friend."

Jaime let go and held her at arm's length, his eyes going up and down. "But look at you. You're radiant."

Leah chuckled, rubbing her neck as her face warmed. "Yeah, that's new."

By the door, Buck's mouth hung open. His eyes were wide, darting between Leah and the two witches. Serena stood frozen beside him, one hand gripping the doorframe.

Jan Xie turned to Frank and Mo, who had also gotten to their feet. "I see she is part of your coven now."

Jaime looked from Leah to Frank and Mo a couple of times until his eyes widened. Understanding settled across his face.

"Yes, and apologies for the deception. We still won't be

joining your cause, but she is. Leah wanted to make sure you were still trustworthy."

"Guards." Jan Xie's voice cut through the room. Buck and Serena both straightened. "This conversation is classified. You will speak of nothing you hear today."

"Yes, my Queen," they said in unison.

Leah caught Buck's gaze. He gave her a small nod, something like pride flashing in his eyes before his expression went neutral again.

Jan Xie gestured to an empty chair next to Mo and Frank. "A cautious approach. Like your uncle." She returned to her seat, fingers interlaced on the table. "I respect that. But I can assure you, Leah, that every member of the rebellion wants to see King Helen gone."

They all sat. Leah cleared her throat. "How can you be so sure? Helen defeated every enemy the Infinity Board was facing. Even the Shifters are gone, and with them the curse that was killing you, Jaime. Why go against the King?"

"She took the Core." The Sage's voice was flat. No hesitation. "Right under our noses, she used us and took the power into her own hands. Someone who acts like that is no King of mine."

Jan Xie leaned forward. "Helen restructured everything. Dissolved the Outer Council. New laws, new rules."

"All to consolidate power," Jaime finished.

"And the Outer Council let that happen?" Leah's hands gripped the armrests of her chair.

Jaime chuckled. "They basically proclaimed her King. You see, before she took the Core, we were losing on every front. To her credit, she turned things around rather quickly."

"What about the Inner Council? Jaime, you must be there if you're a Sage."

He exhaled through his nose. "The Inner Council is still

there, but only for show. Having the Sages' support gives her credibility. 'These are the strongest Mystics alive, and they all see me as King.' That's the message she wants people to hear."

Leah thought about Zafirah and Desmond. How they'd fought without question. How they'd defended Helen even after everything she'd done. "I fought Zafirah and Desmond. They both seemed almost blindly loyal to Helen."

"Different people have different interpretations of her actions." Jan Xie's fingers tapped once against the table. "It's easy to see all the good she has done and trust that she knows what she is doing. That this is what was supposed to happen. That a King will one day come and defeat humanity's enemies."

Leah leaned back in her chair. Asmodeus' memories surfaced. Helen absorbed the sword that had gone straight through her chest. "So then, what are we thinking? How do we want to get her?"

The former Queen and Jaime exchanged looks.

"Our idea is to ambush her," Jan Xie said. "Helen is always on the move, but she will return to HQ for appearances from time to time. That is why Jaime is, right now, our most important asset. If we could somehow put together a ritual or spell to use the Astral Realm to ambush her, then maybe we might have a chance. We assemble a special force, train it, and then attack. With Jaime's mastery of *Hod*, we can hold her in place and kill her before she can react."

Leah recalled how Helen had moved during the fight. The way she'd healed. "I don't think that's going to work. I saw firsthand how a sword went right through her chest, and she just absorbed it. Similar to what Legion used to do."

Jan Xie and Jaime exchanged grave looks.

"We tried researching the site where the fight with Legion happened," Jan Xie said slowly. "But it was a wreck, so using the same spell your mother and Helen used is out of the question."

Jaime pursed his lips. "Do you have a better idea?"

Leah had a plan, albeit not a great one, but she had one. Bringing Helen into the Astral and forcing her through the chaotic layers, so she would use enough energy and become destabilized. Then strike the killing blow and detach her from the Core. That said, one problem was how to get to the Queen and bring her into one of her layers in the Astral. Maybe that's where Jan Xie, Jaime, and the Rebellion come into play? Maybe they could help her reach Helen. Perhaps take care of the high-level Mystics and Sages around her.

Frank cleared his throat. Everyone in the room turned to him. "Jan Xie, you mentioned you had a whole infrastructure behind this rebellion. Why don't you take a look at what resources you have and make a better plan of action then?"

"Are you sure you won't join us?" Jan Xie's one good eye studied Frank's face.

"We can't." Frank's voice came out rough. "Our responsibility is with the Astral. We did our part to help Leah, but this goes beyond our reach now."

Mo's jaw clenched. She looked at her hands.

Jan Xie leaned forward. "We need every advantage. If you have access to the Astral Realm, if you have powers that could help us get close to Helen, then you could be the difference between success and failure."

"You don't understand." Frank stood. His chair scraped against the floor. "We're the last Immortal Witches. The last ones. If Helen destroys everything, if the Core consumes the Material Realm, someone has to survive to keep the Well hidden and protect the Astral."

"So, we're just meant to let her win then, are we?" Jaime's voice rose slightly.

"We're making sure something survives," Frank said. "And we're giving you a powerful witch. One that has more potential than both of us combined."

Leah's throat went dry. She knew their cause, but a part of her had hoped coming here would change their minds.

Mo finally spoke. "If Leah fails, if the worst happens, then we can't let Helen get to the Well. If she does, then we'll lose everything. The whole of existence will be taken by this wannabe god."

Jan Xie sat back. Her expression was unreadable. "I understand your position. I don't agree with it, but I understand."

"I'm sorry, Jan." Frank stood. Mo rose beside him.

Something sharp lodged itself behind Leah's ribs. Her hands felt cold. She got to her feet.

Before she could say anything, Frank engulfed her in a hug. His coat smelled like sage and smoke. She felt his heartbeat against her shoulder. Mo joined in, wrapping her arms around both of them, and the three of them stood there for a long moment.

"Come back to us, you hear me?" Mo's voice was steady but soft. "Kick this Mystic with a God complex's ass, and come back."

"Yeah." Frank's voice came out gruff. "We trust you. You're family now."

Leah held on tighter. Her eyes stung. She blinked hard and buried her face in Frank's shoulder. Six months ago, she'd been alone. Hunted. Dying. Now she had people who called her family. People who believed in her.

And she was about to lose them again.

No. Not lose. They'd be there. Waiting. Protecting the Astral while she dealt with Helen.

"I will." The words came out rough. "Thank you for your trust."

They let go. Frank stepped back first. He shook hands with Jan Xie, then Jaime. Mo did the same.

Frank gave them both a small bow. "Good luck with everything."

"Likewise." Jan Xie inclined her head.

The old witch turned and walked toward the door. Buck pulled it open, his eyes tracking Frank as he passed. Mo squeezed Leah's hand one last time. Her smile was small but real. Then she let go and followed Frank out into the hallway.

CHAPTER 42
THE SHADOW BOARD

Buck and Serena flanked Frank and Mo as they left, closing the door behind them. Leah felt a lump form in her throat. They hadn't been together long, but she already missed them.

They'd be back at the tattoo shop, with Mo using her clairvoyance to see what future was most likely to happen and Frank preparing spells to help guard the Well. All while she walked straight into the heart of Helen's empire.

"Come, Leah. It's time to show you what the Shadow Board is." Jan Xie turned toward a different door on the other side of the conference room. Jaime followed.

Leah took one last look at the empty hallway, then followed them into a corridor lit by flickering lights above. Some of the bulbs buzzed and sputtered. Others had gone completely dark. The single-story building had looked small from the outside, so when they stopped at an elevator, she frowned.

Jan Xie pressed the button. The doors slid open with a metallic groan. Inside, the carpet smelled damp and old. They stepped in, and Jan Xie spoke as the elevator began its slow descent.

"We have multiple locations like this one throughout the world. The Shadow Board was created as a safety mechanism to oversee the Infinity Board and ensure its leaders adhere to the rules. Mystics are still human, and humans corrupt when exposed to power. Look at every politician out there. When you have Mystics with raw and political power, corruption becomes inevitable. That's where we come in. To keep them in check."

The elevator stopped. The doors slid open.

Leah's jaw dropped.

The parking garage had been completely transformed. Training installations lined one wall, and squads marched past her. Someone had built an entire office suite in the center with glass walls and computers. Young Mystics studied in makeshift classrooms, bent over textbooks and laptops. At the far end, past all the training and equipment, people had erected cabins and tents like a small village.

"Holy shit," Leah whispered.

Jaime leaned close. "Yeah, I had the same reaction."

Two men in black military uniforms approached and snapped to attention. "My Queen. You have a call."

"It can wait. I'm busy." Jan Xie's voice carried absolute authority.

The man straightened further. "I understand, my Queen, but it's from the informant."

Jan Xie raised an eyebrow, then turned to Leah and Jaime. "I need to take this. Jaime, can you carry on? I'll join you once I'm done."

"Of course." Jaime bowed.

The Queen gave Leah a quick nod before leaving with the two men.

"This is insane," Leah said, watching a group run an obstacle course.

"And this is just one of many bases. I think Jan Xie has been planning this for a while."

They moved farther into the facility. Jaime pointed toward a shooting range where uniformed figures fired handguns fitted with silencers. The pops were muffled, almost gentle, compared to the chaos around them. A squad of men and women marched past, all of them glancing at Leah with open curiosity. Heat crept up her neck. She dropped her gaze and noticed their insignias. Four checkered squares like the Infinity Board, but the piece was different. A copper lance on a pawn base.

She leaned toward Jaime. "What's that chess piece?"

"Not technically chess. That's a Shogi piece. Japanese chess. Those are Lances."

"And what do they do?"

"First responders. They get to locations fast with everything the Shadow Board can provide. Diplomatic passports, private jets, and helicopters. Remember when we moved from headquarters to Sekrè Fami after Legion's attack? The infrastructure was already in place. Lances built it."

"Oh." Leah nodded slowly. She'd never thought about that until now. "They don't wear their Board insignias, correct?"

"Correct. The Shadow Board works in the shadows of the Infinity Board. Logistical labor, influence, and espionage. They're the reason the Infinity Board stays effective while remaining under the radar."

Jaime paused, eyeing the entrance to a cafeteria. The smell of cooked food drifted out.

"Are you hungry?"

Leah's stomach turned over. She wanted to keep learning, to get down to business. "I'm fine for now."

Jaime slapped her back and pushed her forward. "Come on, lass. I think they have salmon tonight."

They entered the cafeteria. It was nearly empty except for a group of Mystics sitting on the far side. Smaller than the one at Sekrè Fami, but it could still hold fifty people easily.

"It's pretty empty."

"People usually eat around six. It's almost ten now. Lucky for you, this place stays open late for the night shift." Jaime nodded toward the serving line. "Grab a plate. I'll get us a table."

Leah walked to the counter, ignoring the obvious glares from the servers. She kept her eyes on the thick salmon fillet and roasted potatoes, the Caesar salad on the side. She turned toward Jaime's table when a familiar voice stopped her cold.

"Leah?"

She froze. Goosebumps raced down her arms. It had been almost three years since she'd heard that voice.

She turned.

Jenna stood behind the counter, light-brown hair pulled into a tight ponytail. She was older and much taller. The last time Leah had seen her, the girl had been unconscious in a bed at Sekrè Fami, skin pale as death, dying from rootworker poison.

"It's really you!" Jenna's face broke into a wide smile.

She ran around the counter. Leah barely had time to grip her tray with both hands before arms wrapped around her shoulders. The rebellious girl who used to sneak into Voodoo Town had grown into a lean, muscular young woman.

Leah hugged back with one arm, relief spreading through her chest like warmth.

"What happened to you? When I woke up, you were just gone."

"It's a long story." Leah shifted the tray. "I was taken

somewhere for two years, but it felt much shorter than that. Then I was hiding for a while. It's really hard to explain, but I'm finally here." She looked Jenna up and down. "But look at you."

Jenna grinned. "And you? You look gorgeous, Leah. Did you do something to your hair?"

They both laughed.

"You could say I had a bit of a change," Leah said. "But what happened to you? The last time I saw you—"

"I was half dead in bed? Yeah, I don't know. Apparently, King Helen healed us all from that Voodoo curse or whatever we had. Shortly after, we resumed training as Black Pawns, but I didn't make the cut. Shocking, right?" Jenna smiled, but bitterness edged her voice.

Leah knew what Jenna had seen when her Outpost was attacked. It haunted the girl back then and probably still did, though she seemed better at hiding it now. That's why she'd struggled keeping *Nehemoth's* corruption at bay.

"That's how you ended up in the Shadow Board?"

Jenna shrugged. "Pretty much. Shortly after, King Helen moved to disintegrate the Shadow Board and reassign us, and that's when a lot of us went rogue under Queen Jan Xie. She's a badass. Do you know her?"

Leah chuckled. "Yeah, I've run into her a few times."

"Well, hello there, Jenna." Jaime's voice boomed behind them.

"Hi, Jaime. Good to see you."

"Good to see you, lass." He glanced at Leah's tray. "Why don't we grab a seat?"

Jenna beamed. "I'll bring you both some dessert. Be right back."

They hugged again before Jenna rushed behind the counter and into the kitchen. Jaime tilted his head toward an empty table.

"You knew she would be here, didn't you?"

Jaime chuckled. "Figured you'd want to see her."

"Thanks." Something loosened in Leah's shoulders. A soothing warmth filled her. "Really."

They sat at the table Jaime had chosen. Leah ate her salmon, hunger hitting her now that the food was in front of her.

Jenna appeared a few minutes later with two small cups of chocolate ice cream. "Here you go. Let me know if you want more, okay?"

"Thank you, lass."

Jenna smiled at Leah. "It's really good to see you again. I'll let you two catch up." She headed back toward the kitchen.

"She's grown a lot," Leah said, watching her go.

"That's what happens to teenagers. She's a good girl. I'm glad she ended up on our side."

Jaime's usual jovial tone shifted to something more serious. "So where were you all this time? After our fight with Legion and Helen stole the Core, you, Sarah, and Isaac just disappeared."

Leah knew there was no way around discussing it. She kept it short while finishing her meal. The Librarian, Lord Ragon's death, and the Immortal Witches' training. The important parts. She left out the rest. After months of hiding, she'd learned to be cautious about what she shared.

By the time she finished, her plate was empty. She pushed it aside and grabbed the chocolate ice cream Jenna had brought. The sweet chocolate flavor spread across her tongue, waking her up.

She drank some water and noticed Jaime staring at her, his expression unreadable. He hadn't touched his ice cream.

Leah frowned. "What happened to my other Squares? Do you know? Ricky, Callum, Ashley, Zoe?"

Jaime pursed his lips. "Most passed the initiation phase. Jenna was the only one who didn't. I lost track of them shortly after."

After another long moment of silence, she said, "I know it's a lot."

Jaime pulled out his flask and took a long sip before speaking. "Not at all, lass." His voice came out quieter than usual. "I'm just embarrassed."

Leah frowned. "Why?"

"When Helen took the Core, and you three disappeared, I looked for you everywhere. I kept a suspicious eye on Helen's ascent and actions, but I couldn't do anything to stop her. If I'd found you sooner, maybe I..." He looked down.

That's when Leah saw it. The exhaustion carved into his face. His smile, pink skin, and beard hid it well, but now she could see the hollowness in his eyes. *Hod's* insomnia was taking its toll on the old Mystic.

Leah grabbed Jaime's hand and squeezed. "You couldn't have known. The only one who knew was Helen, and that conniving bitch clearly didn't say or do anything. Besides, I didn't want to be found. When I came back, the landscape had changed so dramatically. I wasn't sure who I could trust. so I trusted no one."

Jaime looked at her with sorrowful eyes and squeezed her hand back. "You could have trusted me, Leah. I understand why you made that decision, but know that you can trust me."

Leah smiled. "I know." She paused. "Care to tell me what happened on your end? How are you healed? I haven't really spoken to anyone who was there that night. Well, unless you consider my fight with Zafirah a friendly conversation."

They both chuckled. Leah took another spoonful of ice cream.

Jaime took a long sip from his flask before placing it on the table and drawing a deep breath. "You've probably heard most of it already. Helen's skyrocketing support after our battle with Legion and her unnatural increase in power."

"How could the other Sages let that happen? When I faced them, they all seemed blindly loyal to Helen. Even when I questioned Zafirah, she seemed more stubborn than usual. I could swear I saw some logic in her, but she immediately turned and went back to blind loyalty."

Jaime exhaled. "Actions speak louder than words. Take the Shifters, for example. We were at war with them for over seven years, and we were losing badly. Then out of nowhere, our Queen comes in and destroys them in less than a month. It's thanks to that my infection is gone." He tapped his neck. "When a Mystic shows such a display of strength, and all they do is help achieve the Infinity Board's goals, it becomes increasingly difficult to question them."

"Yes, but she did it through lies and deception! So many died because of her!" Leah's voice rose. A few heads turned at nearby tables.

Jaime raised an index finger to his lips. "It's best to be discreet while we talk about this, Leah. Besides, look where you are. Not everyone bought Helen's performance."

"Sorry." Leah said.

"Try to understand them. Your average Knight or Bishop has seen many of their fellow Mystics die in battle. Suddenly, your leader seems to have achieved a new level of strength, and she begins to obliterate your enemies. Makes everyone's job considerably easier and safer, all while putting herself in danger. Her level of power seems godlike at this point. At the same time, we've always left the King position open to the Mystic who achieves *Keter*. Never in history have we seen something like what Helen has achieved. Which means I can understand why many throw their unwavering support at her."

A chill ran through Leah. "Do you really believe she achieved *Keter*?"

Jaime thought for a moment. "No, I don't think so. I think she's using the Core to increase her powers, her connection to the Wells. But then again, you never know with Helen. She has achieved some pretty remarkable things."

"Why are you here then? Helen killed the Shifters, who had been your main focus for a very long time. You're fully healed thanks to her." Leah tried to keep her tone neutral, not accusatory.

Jaime chuckled and shrugged. "I guess I don't like being lied to and used for the greater good. You know me, lass; I've always been against the concentration of power into a single person. Power corrupts, no matter how good your intentions are. They will always get twisted by the greater good."

Leah finished the last of her ice cream and set it aside. "Then why do the other Sages who saw what Helen did still support her?"

"I don't know. When I'm there, I try to keep a low profile. Asking questions about the Queen's intentions could attract some undesired attention. That said, you can see with Jan Xie that not everyone sees her as our new savior. When she moved to try and disintegrate the Shadow Board, Jan quit and went into hiding with most of the Shadow Board's assets."

Leah leaned forward. "Right, but how do you know everyone here can be trusted?"

"Most of the members from the Shadow Board were

rejected from the Infinity Board one way or another. They've been preparing for this moment their whole formation here. The objective of the Shadow Board was to keep the Infinity Board in check and prevent the power they wielded from corrupting them. That said, Jan Xie and a close group of allies have scrutinized every single person involved in this operation. The former Queen can see a lot more through that patch of hers than you might think. So, I can confidently say everyone here is trustworthy."

His gaze shifted over Leah's shoulder. "Speak of the devil; she's here calling for us. Time to get going."

Leah turned. Jan Xie stood near the cafeteria entrance, flanked by the two uniformed men. Her expression was grave, and she looked even more exhausted.

Leah nodded and got to her feet, but Jaime reached out and placed his hand over hers. "Leah. Now that I've finally found you, I want you to know that I'm always here for you."

Leah smiled and placed her other hand over his. "I know. Thank you, Jaime."

CHAPTER 43
THE INFORMANT

Leah waved goodbye to Jenna before stepping into the hallway with Jaime and joining Jan Xie.

"What happened?"

"It's our informant. They know when Helen plans to attach next. They've managed to find a copy of their plans, but we have little time. They've managed to find a copy of her plans, but I told them to bring them to me right away. Luckily, they weren't too far away."

"The informant is coming *here*?" Jaime asked, surprised.

"Yes, the information was too sensitive and detailed to be provided over the phone. You never know who else might be listening. They should be arriving shortly, and I want you in the meeting with me." Jan Xie turned to Leah. "Could you join us as well?"

Leah's stomach twisted. Walking into a Shadow Board meeting meant more eyes on her and more chances for someone to recognize her. At this point, if things went sideways, she could use her Immortal Witch powers to get out.

And Jan Xie and Jaime both trusted this person. That had to count for something. The whole point of coming here was to plan an attack on Helen. She didn't have to do this alone.

"Yes, count me in."

Gratitude flickered across Jan Xie's face before she turned and started back toward the elevator. Leah followed, catching the stares and whispers from Shadow Board members as they passed. A few even pointed. It reminded her of walking through camp in Sekrè Fami.

The three of them stepped into the elevator, the two guards staying behind. Within minutes, they were back in the conference room where they'd originally met.

Jan Xie sat at the center of the table. Jaime and Leah took seats on either side. Jaime closed the door and asked, "Any information the informant shared that we should know before we meet?"

"They mentioned something about the Oni encampment that Helen just took out on her own. It was in the deep Colorado Mountains. Apparently, it took a toll on her, so she is back at headquarters getting checked."

Leah sat up straighter. She remembered the Oni she'd killed for intruding into Family territory. Mostly large, dumb creatures, but their brute force and heavy constitution made them formidable opponents. "Helen did that?"

Jan Xie smoothed her jacket. "Seems that way. The informant should have more details. The important thing is that the King ended up more injured than in previous encounters, so she is nursing her wounds in secrecy back at headquarters."

Leah rubbed her hands together, her brain spinning through possibilities. If the King was hurt, then now was the time to strike.

I saw how she healed herself during her fight with the Ancient One, Asmodeus said. *I find it hard to believe that a group of Oni could have truly hurt her.*

"That's all they could tell you?" Leah frowned. "Just that she's injured?" She'd watched Helen absorb a sword straight through her chest. A few Oni shouldn't have been able to touch her.

Jaime leaned back in his chair. "The informant works close to the King, but information is scarce. Helen keeps her cards close. We're lucky to get this much."

Something nagged at Leah, but she pushed it aside. Any intelligence was better than none.

"Who is this informant?" Leah asked.

Jaime turned to look at her across the table. "Black Rook Abercromby. Do you remember him from the Academy?"

The name rang a bell, but Leah couldn't place a face. She shook her head.

He was a Black Knight who recruited some of the newly appointed White Pawns back at the Academy.

Leah snapped her fingers. "Wait, I remember now. Stocky guy, bald, with that massive red beard? Picked Omer and Deepak during the bonding ceremony?"

Jaime chuckled. "Aye, that's the one. Though his beard's gone mostly gray now."

"How'd he get promoted to Rook?"

"Earned it fighting Legion's forces. His family's been Mystics for generations, but he's one of the few questioning Helen openly. When she took the Core and proclaimed herself King, Abercromby didn't bend the knee like the others."

A knock sounded at the door. Jan Xie stood, and Leah and Jaime followed suit.

"Come in."

The door opened, and Buck Baccus stepped inside. His eyes met Leah's briefly before he returned to attention.

"The informant has arrived. Should I send them in?"

"Yes, Baccus, we are ready for them."

Buck nodded and stepped back to open the door wider. He paused, glancing at Jan Xie. "My Queen, if time permits after the briefing, Serena and I would like to request a moment to catch up with Knight Ackerman."

Jan Xie gave a curt nod. "We'll see."

A tall figure walked in, wearing a long black cloak with the hood drawn up, obscuring their face.

Leah frowned. The person in front of them was far from stocky or broad shouldered.

The door closed behind them with a soft click.

"Thank you for coming to us," Jan Xie said. "This was not something we wanted to risk getting intercepted."

The informant reached up and pulled down their hood. Pale hair spilled across black fabric. "Of course. I came here as soon as I could."

No.

Ice flooded Leah's veins. Every muscle in her body locked up as she stared at the woman in front of her.

Helen Nielsen.

CHAPTER 44
KETER

King Helen's cold blue eyes locked onto hers.

Ice flooded Leah's veins, and every muscle in her body seized up. Her thoughts crashed into each other, refusing to form into anything coherent.

"Please, have a seat." Jan Xie gestured to the empty chair beside her.

Leah's mouth opened, but nothing came out.

"That won't be necessary, Jan." Helen's voice cut through the silence. "This meeting is over. You have information on my condition and will leave this room with Jaime to begin planning an assault on HQ. I'll stay here coordinating with Leah on the best day and time to strike. Assemble a squad and prepare to act."

Something invisible passed through the room. A pressure against Leah's skin that vanished as quickly as it had come. Different from *Gamaliel*. Different from anything on the Tree of Death.

"What..." Leah's voice cracked.

Both Jaime and Jan Xie stood without another word and walked toward the door.

She is controlling them.

The door closed behind them, leaving the two of them alone.

"Now that we finally have some privacy, I want us to talk."

The blue eye of the Librarian materialized over Helen's shoulder on the door behind her. That was enough to bring Leah to her senses. Pressure built in Leah's chest as she pulled on *Malchut* and started to stand.

Her body locked in place.

"I said talk, not fight." Helen raised her left hand, and Leah watched her index and middle fingers intertwine.

Hod.

An invisible force slammed into Leah and pushed her back into the chair without hurting her. The binding held her completely still from the neck down.

"Are you going to behave, or do I need to keep you locked in like this?"

The two glared at one another. Leah's jaw worked, but she couldn't move anything below her neck. Couldn't reach for *Malchut*. Couldn't summon her shadow. The invisible restraints held her fast.

Helen's expression changed, and something like regret crossed her face. "Please, at least listen to me." She waited, watching Leah's face. When Leah didn't respond, Helen's fingers relaxed slightly. The binding loosened just enough for Leah to breathe easier, but not enough to move.

Helen pulled out the chair across from Leah and sat down slowly, never breaking eye contact. "My dear Leah, how much you've changed. I'm sorry that things turned out this way."

"Sorry?" Leah spat the word. "You're going to be a lot more than just sorry after I'm done with you."

Helen chuckled and shook her head. "You still don't get it, do you?" She paused, and her lips pursed as if choosing her next words carefully. "There is no fight to have, Leah. Humanity has already won."

Leah strained against the invisible bonds, but they held firm.

"This rebellion?" Helen gestured toward the door. "The others I've cultivated? Hoaxes. I show them what they want to see, and they bring my enemies to me. That's when I show them the truth, and they join the system." She folded her hands in her lap. "Control both sides, and you're never blindsided. Never at risk."

'Show them what they want to see.' She already speaks differently. Speaks almost as if she is above this.

Leah frowned, still testing the hold Helen had on her, and forced herself to focus. "How are you controlling them?"

Helen leaned back in her chair. "I'm not. I'm shaping their view of reality. I make them see what they need to see in order to protect humanity. This is what reaching *Keter* looks like, Leah."

She had to wait for the right moment. She had to keep Helen talking. Leah had never released a shadow while under *Hod*. Testing it now could give everything away, and unleashing it too early would leave that shadow and part of her essence exposed. Still, her rage burned hot and dark inside her. That part of her wanted to release a hundred shadows and have them all hit Helen as hard as possible.

"You've lied, manipulated, and killed so many people to gain this power." Leah's voice shook. "All just to achieve *Keter* and reach the top."

Helen shook her head slowly. "You still don't get it, Leah, I—"

"There's nothing to get!" Leah yelled. "What were you going to say? Did you do it for the greater good? That you somehow have humanity's interest in mind? You don't achieve that by betraying your friends. You brought in a corrupted Ethereal that killed thousands. You manipulated so many in your little games. You don't just—"

Another invisible force pushed Leah back, and her chair slid until it hit the wall. The words died in her throat.

"Enough" Helen stood and crossed the distance between them in three quick strides. She looked down at Leah. "Do you think this ends with Legion? He was an infant compared to the other Ethereals out there in the universe." Helen moved to the window and stared out at the parking lot below. "Whoever sent the Core, whatever sent it, they expected this world to be consumed by now." Her jaw tightened. "When we stopped that, when we killed Legion, we declared war on something we can't even comprehend." She turned back to face Leah. "They will come. And I'm the only one strong enough to face them."

Leah stared at Helen but held her tongue.

"You can stand next to me, Leah. Can't you see? The enemies the Infinity Board has faced in the past are nothing compared to what is out there. But you are special, whether by chance or something greater. You both are able to wield the energies of the Trees, and now you've also become an Immortal Witch. Your power sets you apart from the rest." Helen's expression softened. "Look at all the good I've done. If we join forces, then we will become unstoppable."

More silence as Leah glared.

Then Leah began to laugh. It was an angry cackle, and she strained with everything she had to push out of Helen's grip. "After all you've done? All the death and pain you've caused. You want me to join you? Over my dead body."

Helen moved both arms and displayed the katanas on either side of her waist. "I could kill you with one swing if you desire to die. It would make the most sense, seeing as you are my strongest foe right now, and you cannot see the truth. But killing you would be a waste." She stepped forward. "We are facing grave dangers both in our world and beyond. And I need the strongest to stand beside me."

Helen's eyes began to glow white, and she crossed the remaining distance between them. Leah tried to move away, but the King still kept her under the *Hod* grip, which now extended to Leah's head.

Asmodeus! Now!

"You are Elizabeth's daughter, through and through. But I forced her away all those years ago. I won't make the same mistake again." Helen's voice dropped to a whisper. "It's time for you to see the Truth, Leah Ackerman."

The light grew more intense, and Helen extended her arm, placing two fingers on Leah's forehead.

White light exploded behind Leah's eyes. Her thoughts scattered like dropped chess pieces. Memories peeled away one by one. She felt herself unraveling.

Asmodeus!

Everything went dark.

CHAPTER 45
LUCK

Green flames engulfed Leah's body, and in an instant, Asmodeus formed on the table, staring down at Helen, who still placed two fingers on the original Leah's forehead. Both of their eyes glowed white.

Asmodeus pulled on *Malchut* and aimed a kick toward Helen's head. The King's reflexes were quick, and she lifted her other hand, attempting to block it, but the force still sent her flying through the conference room. She collided with the wall, leaving behind a massive crack.

Asmodeus stepped back and caught Leah as her eyes returned to normal.

"Leah, are you okay? Talk to me."

Leah blinked a couple of times, and her gaze wandered unfocused.

Asmodeus let go of *Satariel*, and his shadow disintegrated into a cloud of green smoke. Back in Leah's mind, he could sense her jammed thoughts and beliefs. As if Helen had stopped halfway through rewiring her brain. *Asmodeus* let his own thoughts and beliefs flow through.

You are Leah Ackerman. A warrior and a witch. And Helen is not your friend.

Leah snapped awake and sucked in a breath. She scrambled to her feet.

Helen stood across the room, and her hand hovered over a bruised jaw as it healed.

The door on the other side of the conference room burst open.

"What the hell is going on here!" Buck screamed and looked from Leah to Helen.

"Leah?" Serena asked as Buck pulled out his walkie-talkie.

This was bad. If they sounded the alarm, they would be surrounded. Leah leaped forward using *Malchut* and tackled Helen through the wall. Glass shattered around them, and they tumbled outside. Helen stayed on her feet as they slid through the gravel and came to a stop a couple of feet away.

"You seem to be improvising now." Helen released a *Malchut* push in all directions, sending Leah rolling away.

Leah had activated *Netzach* just in time. The invulnerability absorbed most of the impact, and she got to her feet. Helen walked calmly toward her and unsheathed her katanas. An alarm sounded in the building, and floodlights turned on, bathing the road they stood on in harsh white light.

"You could still join me, Leah. It does not have to be this way."

Leah got to her feet, and heat built in her fists as she pulled on *Gevurah*. But just then, Mystics began to rush out of the building. Some of them had their weapons drawn, and others simply looked confused.

"Seems like you are out of luck." Helen raised a sword at her.

An engine roared somewhere behind Helen.

Leah's eyes flashed yellow with *Tiferet,* and she spotted Frank and Mo speeding toward them.

Her luck hadn't run out.

Mystics turned their guns to the car, but each gun clicked as they pulled the trigger. Every gun had jammed.

The car was fast approaching, and Leah needed to do something to help. Anything.

She extinguished the *Gevurah* flames and reached out, imagining hundreds of threads passing through her hands.

Come on. Come on.

The car barreled toward Helen.

Leah reached with her mind. A thread, thin and fragile, solidified in her mental grip.

The car hit Helen, and she stumbled forward.

Leah yanked on the thread.

Reality ripped.

The crack opened with a sound like tearing fabric, and sickly yellow light spilled through. Helen tumbled toward it, and the car plunged after her. Leah didn't think. She pulled on *Malchut,* pushed herself through the crack, twisted mid-air, grabbed the edges of the tear, and pulled it shut.

She hit the ground hard, rolled, and came up on her feet.

The decaying Astral layer stretched around them. Yellow light shone down from an unseen source above, and moss crept through the broken pavement. The car's brakes screamed as it skidded to a stop, sending Helen sliding down the broken road.

Leah ran toward the car as Frank and Mo got out.

"What are you two doing here?"

Frank scoffed. "Don't look at me. Ask Mrs. Clairvoyant there."

"Had a vision of Helen coming in." Mo's eyes shone a deep violet. "Had to leave you in the dark. It was the only way this might work."

"But the Well?" Leah asked, feeling both concerned and deeply grateful.

Frank turned to her. "We said we would leave you in good hands, not hand you over to Helen."

Helen got to her feet and spoke through gritted teeth. "Why can't any of you understand? I don't want to fight you! We are the good ones! We have the power to fight the Ethereals. We are the ones who can protect humanity."

"Oh yeah? Then why do you have the Core that killed my Coven?" Frank said.

"Because I'm the only one who can use it."

Helen's body vanished, and before Leah could yell a warning, she appeared right in front of Mo and swung her sword down.

CHAPTER 46
IRONIES

Leah's shadow formed between them and pushed Mo back, receiving the blow of the cut, which was followed by a *Malchut* blade that hit her square in the chest. But the shadow held her ground as the rest of the obsidian armor formed around Leah.

Black scales clicked into place across her arms, her chest, and her face. The transformation made her taller. Her hands darkened into demonic claws, fingers elongating with razor-sharp tips.

Helen's eyes widened. She took a half step back, studying the armor. "What have you become?"

The shadow lunged forward and tried to punch the King, but Helen vanished and reappeared a few feet back. Her gaze remained fixed on Leah's transformed state, calculating.

"Your fight is with us," Asmodeus panted through Leah's armored form.

Leah pulled on *Nehemoth* and yanked both Mo and Frank off their feet. She focused on the threads, pulled, and tore open a different crack that both Frank and Mo fell through. Sunlight spilled from what looked to be a rocky beach.

"Leah!" Mo yelled from the other side as they both tried to get up and rush back.

She looked back at them and smiled. "I got this."

Leah pulled the crack closed, and the two Immortal Witches disappeared along with the beach.

Asmodeus's shadow dissipated into a cloud of smoke, and Leah felt his essence as well as part of hers flowing back. They couldn't afford to let the shadows out for too long, or the reabsorption process would leave them vulnerable.

"So, you know *Satariel*," Helen whispered and then stared down at Leah and began to cackle. "You think you are some big hero, and then you invoke one of the upper three wells of the Tree of Death? The irony here is baffling."

Leah let the obsidian armor form around her skin like scales while she reached out with her mind and found the threads of the different Astral layers.

"The irony here is that you sacrificed so many for your so-called 'greater good' and you still have the audacity to lecture me." Leah's hands curled into fists. "Have you stopped to think that maybe you're wrong? You think you're strong enough to control the Core. Helen, that Core has been manipulating you since the very first day you conjured it with my mother."

Helen's expression hardened.

"I've met an Ethereal," Leah continued. "One the witches trapped. He said that Core will consume everything and birth another of his kind. You're literally feeding this thing until it consumes you and the rest of humanity, including the Trees."

"The scroll allows me to keep the Core under control. I don't consume anything or anyone unless they pose a threat to humanity. I can live with the hunger if that is what it takes to keep everyone safe."

Leah shook her head. "Even now, you deny the truth. You're too blinded by your own ego. This thing will consume everything unless you let it go."

For a moment, the two just stared at one another.

Helen dropped her gaze and spoke softly. "Your mother was as shortsighted as you are. But unlike her, you have been able to see this new world order. No one else has died under my watch. Thanks to me, we are protected by the Core. We are standing together against evil. We are one."

"You sound like an Ethereal, and you don't even realize it. That just shows how blind you are to your own doing."

Helen pursed her lips, but her eyes showed sadness and regret. "I'm sorry that it has to come down to this."

For a moment, the only sound was the wind moving through the fractured street. The sickly yellow light dimly illuminated the deteriorated old buildings, and moss emerged from the cracks and extended to the road where the two stood. Then Helen raised her gaze, and her cold blue eyes fixed on Leah before her body vanished.

Leah used a *Malchut* push to dash out of the way and pulled on *Thagirion*. Cold swept through her body, making her invisible. She landed and sent a *Malchut* push where she had stood just a second ago. The force hit Helen square in the chest as she appeared. But the King stood her ground and pulled on *Netzach* to protect herself. The impact ripped off her black robe, revealing a pristine, white, military-style uniform. Helen jerked her head and sent out a *Malchut* blade.

Leah barely dodged it, then used a combination of *Malchut* dashes and jumps to circle around the King while shooting *Gevurah* fireballs. Helen tried to avoid them, but after a couple of hits, she was set part of her uniform ablaze. She yelled in frustration and sent out a powerful *Malchut* push in all directions, looking like a bright, expanding wave. Leah was landing from a jump when it hit her, knocking her off balance and sending her rolling. Her own *Netzach* and obsidian armor protected her.

She got to her feet just in time to see Helen's familiar symbols around her skin glowing brighter.

Careful, Leah. She is replenishing her wells.

Helen turned toward Leah, and her eyes shone brightly with *Tiferet* energy.

"Do you think she can see me?" Leah asked *Asmodeus* in her mind.

Before the demon could answer, Helen sent a huge line of *Gevurah* fire in Leah's direction. *Asmodeus* reacted and jumped out of the way, but part of the fire hit Leah's leg. The obsidian protected her just enough to avoid a serious burn. Still, as she landed and got back to her feet, she could feel the warm glass around her leg.

Unlike Leah's fire, which was a yellowish orange, Helen's was a bright yellowish white and burned much hotter.

We must avoid fire at all costs.

Another ray of flames came her way, but Leah was ready this time. She leaped forward, and the bright light of *Malchut* formed around her feet, and she dashed just low enough to avoid them. She reached Helen and sent a bright *Malchut* punch her way. The King blocked, and her *Netzach* absorbed most of the damage.

As Helen slid a few feet back, Leah pulled on the thread, and a crack formed behind her former mentor. The King crossed the Astral crack, and Leah leaped forward and crossed as well, and closed the opening behind them.

CHAPTER 47
UGLY TRUTHS

The stench hit Leah the moment they crossed through. Thick, humid air forced its way into her lungs. She coughed once, tasting copper and rot beneath the obsidian scales that covered her face.

The poison. This layer was full of poison.

But the armor filtered it. Barely breathable, but she could manage.

The cave stretched wide around them, walls gleaming with bioluminescent organisms that pulsed like diseased hearts. Green light cast everything in sickly shadows. Water dripped somewhere in the dark.

A heavy cough echoed through the cave.

Leah spun. Helen was on one knee, skin blistering across her face and hands. The King looked up, eyes watering, and spotted Leah in her full armor. Something like recognition crossed her features, then hardened into determination.

Leah pulled on *Malchut*. Pressure built in her chest as energy gathered in her demonic claws. She released it in a concentrated punch that slammed into Helen's face, knocking her backward. Before the King could recover, Leah followed with *Gevurah* fire. The line of flame struck Helen's body, setting her jacket ablaze.

"Was that really your plan?" a voice whispered behind her.

Leah started to turn. A blunt force cracked against the side of her head. Obsidian scales shattered and scattered across the cave floor. She stumbled sideways and grabbed the rocky wall to keep from falling. The ringing in her ears made it hard to focus.

When she turned back, Helen stood upright. Unaffected. Golden scroll symbols glowed softly across her exposed skin, and the burnt flesh healed itself in seconds. Her jacket lay in a smoking heap on the ground.

For a moment, Helen's outline flickered. Translucent at the edges. The symbols blazed brighter, and she drew power from deep within. Solid again. Steady.

"If your plan is to trap me in the Astral Realm, you're in for a disappointment." Helen brushed ash from her shoulder. "I can teleport myself back. Might take me a couple of tries, but I've done it in the past."

"Eat shit, Helen," Leah spat and tried to ignore the ringing.

If it weren't for the armor, that blow would have cracked her skull open. Leah could feel where scales had broken off, leaving patches of exposed skin on the side of her head that already started to burn.

She is not holding back. She is reading your moves, measuring your strength. Remember, she wants to borrow just enough power from the Core to beat us, just like she did with Lord Ragon.

Asmodeus's memories of that fight flashed through her mind. Leah clenched her jaw.

"Why does it have to be this way, Leah?" Helen's voice

carried no fear. "Why can't you be better than your mother and see the truth?"

Helen vanished. She reappeared directly in front of Leah and started throwing punches. Leah dodged the first few, but Helen was faster than anything Leah had faced. One punch broke through her guard. Leah barely blocked it with her forearm. The *Malchut* force hit so hard, it shattered more obsidian scales and sent pain through her muscles and bones.

Leah stumbled back. Another punch passed inches from her jaw. A third and fourth slammed into her stomach, breaking through armor and bruising the skin underneath.

Helen's speed was impossible.

Leah sent a *Malchut* push at the ground between them and let herself fly backward. She needed distance. When she landed, she pulled on *Nehemoth*. Frost spread from her feet. Cold swept through her, and the whispers quieted the ringing in her ears.

Helen teleported. Leah unleashed a gravitational pull from all directions. When Helen appeared on her left, she lost her balance for half a second.

Helen frowned as she regained her footing. "You're not fading." Her voice held genuine surprise. "Even pulling from *Nehemoth*, you stay solid. How?"

Leah didn't answer. Her shadows materialized on either side of the King and launched *Malchut* punches. Helen's reflexes let her block them both, but she couldn't block Leah's own strike. Leah gathered every bit of energy she could and punched Helen as hard as possible in the face.

The King fell back.

Leah grabbed one of the threads she'd been holding ready and ripped open a crack beneath them. They both dropped through.

Leah pooled *Malchut* and *Gevurah* fire in her fist. The

energy burned hot enough to melt the obsidian on her knuckles. But Helen's glowing eyes saw the attack coming. She vanished right before they hit the water below. Leah's punch connected with nothing but shallow liquid.

Helen reappeared several feet away. The scroll symbols glowed bright across her skin, healing the damage to her face.

They stood in ankle-deep water that stretched in every direction. Four silvery moons hung in a blue sky overhead. Nothing else. Just water and sky.

Helen's form wavered for a moment. Ghost-like. The symbols pulsed, and she pulled more power. Color returned.

"It's pointless, Leah. You cannot beat me." Helen held her hands loosely at her sides. "I'm going to give you one more chance to come to your senses. I know you're angry with me, but it must not blind you from the truth."

Something moved in the water near Helen's feet. Just the tip of a tentacle sliding out for a second before disappearing again.

Leah held her aching arm. Some of her skin showed through where the armor had broken. Her stomach hurt where Helen's punches had left holes and bruises. But the pain sharpened her anger instead of dulling it.

She needed time. She just had to keep Helen talking.

"I'm the only one who can keep everyone safe." Helen's voice took on a lecturing tone. "All the sacrifices we've made happened so I could be in a position to protect everyone else. Ever since I took power, there has been no death in the Infinity Board. None. I've reinstated order in the world, and soon we'll all be united with the same objective. No one would ever have to go through what we've been through."

Another tentacle. Closer this time. It broke the surface for just a moment near Helen's left side.

"How fucking dare you lecture me like this?" Leah's voice rose. "You think you just built this great utopia by sacrificing and betraying the ones most loyal to you, and want me to just look the other way?

"You keep justifying all the things you did, like you didn't have a choice, when you were working with Legion all along." Leah took a step forward. Her demonic claws curled into fists. "But because you can manipulate people with *Keter* or whatever, no one ever tells you the truth."

Helen's nostrils flared. Her jaw tightened.

Good. Leah had struck something.

"Well, here it is." Leah pushed through. "Every crime Legion committed, you committed as well. You sent Asmodeus to kill my mom and dad. You were an accomplice with William and Ian when they were kidnapping young Mystics. You led the Queen's Gambit astray, then sacrificed them all for your little power grab at HQ."

Leah eyed the water for a second. Nothing had broken over the surface. *Come on, take the bait.*

"You knew Legion's plan to possess the whole Infinity Board and went along with it because you thought you could still get control afterwards." Leah's eyes burned. "And you lied to me! After I trusted you all these years. After I told you about the terrible deal I was forced to make with the Librarian. You still lied to me and used me to perform the ritual you and my mother had done, so you could steal the Core.

"There's blood on your hands, Helen Nielsen." Leah's voice came out raw. "No matter how many good deeds you try to do, it won't wash that blood off."

Helen raised her chin. Her chest rose as she took a deep breath.

"You are just as stubborn as your mother." Helen paused. Something dark crossed her face. "That's why I cursed her out of the Infinity Board."

"No, you didn't." Leah stepped back. Her foot splashed in the shallow water.

Helen smirked and pressed on.

"Oh, I figure you knew about that too, since you seem so good at keeping score." Helen's voice stayed level. Almost gentle. That made it worse. "Your mother never left the Infinity Board willingly. No, she didn't trust that I could control the Core. Like I am now."

Helen gestured to the symbols covering her skin.

"After we defeated Asmodeus, she wanted to come clean. Tell the Infinity Board about our Ethereal ritual. Even return the scroll bag to the Librarian and beg for forgiveness." Helen shook her head. "Elizabeth was a lot of great things. But trusting was not one of them."

A tentacle broke the surface near Helen's ankle. Several more wavered in the waters behind her.

"Just as we were reaching new heights, making a real difference and protecting humanity, she wanted to throw it all away." Helen's jaw set. "But I was not going to let her. No."

"You took away her choice," Leah spat.

"For the greater good. I cursed her with *Gamaliel*." Helen placed a hand on her chest. "Commanded her to forget about what we'd done and leave the Infinity Board. Commanded her to have a happy life away from all of this."

Leah's hands trembled.

"It killed me to do that." Helen's voice cracked. "My voice took time to heal. But to reach our full potential, we must make sacrifices. Even if it is the ones we love."

She stepped forward, crossing her arms and letting a tear fall onto her cheek. "I truly wanted her to have a normal family and be happy. I would protect her from afar." Helen met Leah's eyes. "But Legion had other plans. And although I hoped Asmodeus would be weak and disoriented, and that I could slow him enough to save your mother, you had other plans." Helen paused. "Or do you forget your little Ouija board game night?"

Leah's hands curled into fists. She didn't respond. Couldn't respond.

Helen smiled. "Ah, you see, I can also talk about truths and mistakes you made, Leah Ackerman. Or should we ignore the fact that your parents' killer lives right under your skin?"

You bitch! Asmodeus yelled.

But Leah could feel his shame pouring through their bond.

"What is he to you now?" Helen tilted her head. "A friend? You call me a murderer when the demon that lives within you killed my mentor. Killed so many of the people I love and cherish. Fred, Ana, Bobby, Steph." Helen listed the names slowly. "Do those names mean nothing to you or that demon of yours? They meant the world to me, and Asmodeus killed them without a second thought. Like they were ants he could simply crush."

The water around Helen's feet churned. Tentacles writhed just beneath the surface.

"And if memory serves me well, you disobeyed orders and saved that Chimera, did you not?" Helen continued. "The same Chimera Legion's little minion used to bring him into the academy. What would have happened if you followed orders, Leah? Would your uncle be dead?"

Leah's ears beat heavy with blood as she clenched her hands into fists.

"You were the one who made the deal with the Librarian, not me." Helen took a step forward. "And I'm guessing the Librarian is the one who has Isaac and Sarah kidnapped. Am I correct?"

Leah clenched her jaw. "Shut up."

"No." Helen unsheathed her katanas. The blades caught the light from the four moons overhead. "It is time for you to grow up and face the truth, Leah. The only difference between you and me is that I have the bigger picture in mind. I want to protect humanity. I want people to stop dying. You, on the other hand, are a selfish little brat who only wants to save her friends and fix her own mistake." Helen's voice hardened. "And you are willing to sacrifice the whole world to do so. But I won't let you."

The King vanished. She reappeared in a crouch directly in front of Leah and unleashed a *Malchut* push that hit like a freight train. Leah flew backward through the air.

Helen appeared in Leah's path mid-flight and slashed with both katanas. The blades cut through Leah's unprotected arm. But Leah had pulled on *Netzach* just in time. The well cushioned some of the damage. She twisted and sent a *Malchut* blade at Helen's head.

Helen vanished. She reappeared directly below Leah as gravity pulled her down. The King gathered her swords together. The symbols on her skin blazed brighter than ever before, and the water around her feet began to move. It coiled upward in a spiral tower that shot up and engulfed Leah mid-fall.

"Shit, shit, sh..." Leah and Asmodeus yelled together as warm water wrapped around her body.

Leah tried to focus on *Malchut* as water rushed into her lungs. Panic spread through her chest. Her heart hammered too hard. Too fast.

She gathered energy and released a wave. The water around her burst outward. Leah gasped for air, but the liquid rushed back in before she could get a full breath.

Helen stood in the center of the spiral, one katana drawn as she walked closer through the churning water.

A shadow appeared behind the King. Helen spun fast and slashed the shadow in half. It dissipated into green smoke. As the shadow rejoined her, Leah felt the ghostly blade cut through her own body. She tried to scream, but the water drowned the sound.

"You won't do that to me again." Helen's voice came through the water that engulfed Leah.

Leah's body froze. The water around her dropped back to ankle depth. She tried to gasp for air, but an invisible force locked her in place. Her lungs burned.

Helen stepped closer. Her hand raised in front of her face with two fingers intertwined. The King's cold blue eyes blazed with something that looked like regret mixed with certainty. With one swift motion, she drove her katana forward and stabbed Leah in the stomach.

CHAPTER 48
PARASITE

The katana slid free.

Pain ripped through Leah's stomach. White hot and spreading. Her knees gave out, and she dropped into the shallow water. Blood ran warm down her legs, mixing with the liquid around her feet.

Fuck.

Her hands pressed against the wound. More blood seeped between her fingers. The obsidian scales around her midsection had shattered, leaving jagged holes where Helen's blade had punched through.

Can't breathe. Can't think.

Leah tried to pull air into her lungs, but her body wouldn't cooperate. Each attempt brought in only tiny gasps that did nothing.

Helen stood over her. Water dripped from the King's katana blade. "For what it's worth, Leah, I take no pleasure in this."

Something wrapped around Helen's left ankle.

The King's eyes went wide. She looked down, and her face twisted with pain. A second set of tentacles wrapped above the first. Then a squid-like creature leaped from the water and latched onto Helen's waist. Its translucent skin began to glow as it fed.

"What the hell are these things?" Helen blew apart the creature on her hip with a burst of *Malchut*. The energy scattered into the air.

More came. Two jumped onto Helen's sides. A third landed on her back. As she spun to shake it off, four more swarmed in. Within seconds, dozens of the creatures clustered around her.

Leah lifted her head through the haze of pain. She could see them now, swimming through the shallow water toward Helen.

"Lolios," Leah gasped. "Astral parasites."

"Parasites?" Helen ripped one off her arm and crushed it. "Where have you taken us?"

"Their feeding grounds." Leah's vision blurred at the edges. The blood loss was catching up with her.

Hundreds of Lolios converged on the King. They swarmed over her like flies on carrion, stabbing and draining. Through *Tiferet*, Leah watched golden energy flow from Helen into the translucent bodies. The creatures swelled larger with each moment.

Helen fought hysterically to shake them off. She burned them with *Gevurah*. Blew them apart with focused strikes. But for each one she destroyed, three more took their place.

"Took them long enough," Leah whispered. Nausea rolled through her gut.

This is not over.

Asmodeus surged forward and took control. Energy flooded through Leah's body. He forced her to stand despite the pain screaming from her stomach. Her vision cleared slightly.

Asmodeus moved her hands into position. Knuckles pressed together, one set of fingers aimed at Leah's chest, the other at Helen and the writhing mass of parasites covering her.

Helen's face was barely visible beneath the tentacles of a Lolios that had attached to her head. She struggled to free herself, but the creatures kept coming.

Rage built in Leah's chest. Not *her* rage, but Asmodeus's. It mixed with her own anger at Helen until she couldn't tell where one ended and the other began.

Asmodeus pulled on *Samael*. He breathed in.

Helen froze mid-struggle. Her body went rigid. Through the gaps in the swarming Lolios, Leah saw Helen's eyes go wide with recognition. Then pain crossed her features.

Warmth flooded Leah's stomach, but it *wasn't her* warmth. Helen's life force pulled across the distance between them. The sharp agony in her gut dulled with each breath. Asmodeus kept inhaling, drawing increasingly more energy from the King.

Flesh knit itself back together beneath the broken scales. Muscle reformed. The bleeding stopped.

Asmodeus didn't let go. He kept breathing, kept pulling, until the wound was completely sealed. Only then did he release the well. Leah hunched forward, hands planted on her knees as she tried to catch her breath.

A splash of water made her look up.

A massive ball of Lolios squirmed in front of her. The creatures crawled over each other, hundreds of them fighting to reach Helen at the center. Some had doubled in size, their bodies full of swirling golden energy. Through gaps in the mass, Leah caught glimpses of an arm. A leg. Helen's blond hair matted with water.

"Is it over?" Leah asked.

Light exploded from the center of the swarm.

Asmodeus invoked his Immortal Witch power. The

broken obsidian scales reformed across her stomach and sides.

You had to ask?

Beams shot out in every direction, so bright Leah had to shield her eyes with her arm. Through her fingers, she watched the Lolios swell. Four times their normal size. Five times. Their translucent skin stretched thin, glowing like lanterns about to burst.

Then they did.

The parasites exploded. Sharp bursts of energy rippled outward in waves. More Lolios burst. Then more. The light intensified until Leah couldn't see anything at all.

A shockwave slammed into her, sending the shallow water rushing in all directions. Leah dug her claws into the ground beneath the water to keep from being knocked over.

The light faded.

Leah lowered her arm and looked up.

Six golden wings spread wide above the water. They barely moved, holding a brightly glowing Helen covered in scroll symbols.

King Helen looked down at her.

There was no anger in those eyes. No triumph. Just calm certainty, like she was looking at a child who had finally exhausted their tantrum.

CHAPTER 49
THE GOD KING

Leah's knees threatened to buckle, and the nausea from her mostly healed stab wound crawled up her throat. She was prey—small and cornered by something vast and unstoppable.

Stay focused. We can do this, Asmodeus said.

He was still confident, and that gave her enough to breathe. Leah reached for the invisible threads, searching for something dangerous, somewhere to trap Helen with no escape. A pit into an endless void. Anything that might give them an edge, or an escape.

The strands slipped through her fingers. There were too many to choose from.

Then Asmodeus's presence surged. He grabbed hold of something, and Leah felt it through their connection. A thread that felt dry and warm.

It cannot be, Asmodeus said.

Before she could ask, he gripped the thread and squeezed tight.

Her nostrils flared. Panic turned to something sharper, something that burned. She stood straighter and met Helen's gaze. "I've made mistakes. I know that." Her voice steadied. "But I never manipulated people. Never used them like pawns. Unlike you, we recognize when we're wrong. We try to improve." She took a step forward. "You're blinded by power. You think your way is the only way, and you don't even see what's growing inside you. That Ethereal is using you, just like it used Legion to consume The Valley. The whole demon world." Leah's hands curled into fists. "Just look at yourself, Helen. You're being controlled, and you're too proud to admit it."

Helen blurred forward. One moment, she stood twenty feet away; the next, her shoulder slammed into Leah's chest. The impact drove Leah backward, her feet skidding through shallow water before she stumbled and fell. Helen's hand locked around her throat before she could rise. Cold eyes stared down at her, impassive, calculating. The shallow water covered Leah's mouth and nose as she struggled. Her obsidian scales held against the crushing grip, but water rushed into her lungs as she gasped. She shoved upward, breaking the surface for half a breath before Helen's weight forced her down again.

Lolios launched at Helen's arm, latching on, but the King didn't even flinch. Those cold blue eyes never left Leah's face.

Asmodeus took control and yanked on the thread he held. The ground beneath them gave way, but this wasn't like threading to an Astral layer. The tear opened, and instead of falling through, they were pulled. Fast. Impossibly fast.

Helen's hand stayed locked on Leah's throat as the water disappeared. Darkness swallowed them, but Leah felt movement. They hurtled through something that wasn't quite space. The sensation pressed against her skin like she was being squeezed through a tunnel that shouldn't exist. Lights streaked past. Her stomach lurched. Her ears popped. The pressure built until her bones ached.

Then they hit.

Hard earth gave way under the impact. The momentum sent them rolling, tumbling down a steep incline. Sand filled Leah's mouth and nose. Helen finally let go, and they separated, rolling down what felt like a massive dune.

Leah stopped first, gasping and spitting out grit. Helen rose a few feet into the air, hovering and scanning their surroundings.

"How curious. How fitting." Helen's lips curved into something that might have been a smile. "To end you both in The Valley, where it all began."

Leah pushed herself up and looked around. The desert spread out infinitely in every direction. Red sand covered everything, dunes rising and falling like frozen waves. A reddish sun settled low on the horizon, its dying light turning her obsidian scales copper. The air felt dead. Empty. Like nothing lived here and nothing had for a very long time.

Memories swept through her. Not only her memories, but Asmodeus's as well, tangled together. Moving statues. Oceans of luminous gas-like energy that glowed and flowed. Demons emerging from those bright seas, taking form from pure power. All of it gone now. Just sand and ruins and silence.

Why are we here? Leah asked. *This wasn't the layer we planned.*

Trust me, Asmodeus said.

The thread had felt different when she'd pulled it. Heavier somehow. The tearing sensation when they'd crossed through had been sharper, more wrenching than any Astral transition. Something about this place felt solid in a way the Astral layers never did. Like the weight of it pressed down on her bones.

She squared her stance and called on all the energy from both Trees, feeling them rush to her command. After *Samael*, after Lord Ragon's training, the wells felt sharper. Her wounds had healed. The energy sat ready in her chest, in her hands, behind her eyes. But none of it changed the fact that Helen floated there, unbeatable, with that Core burning inside her.

Helen looked down at her and spoke quietly. "I've been searching for you since the moment I learned you survived. I sent the entire Infinity Board to find you. I tried to convince you. To show you the path forward. I tried to share the truth with you through *Keter*, but you and your demon rejected my touch." She shook her head slowly. "I've done everything I could for you, Leah. But you've made your choice. This ends here. For the sake of humanity."

Leah pulled *Malchut* down into her legs. The serpent uncoiled through her muscles, pressure building until it ached. "You're right. For the sake of humanity," she said. "This ends here."

She leaped. Helen flew toward her. Their fists met, and Leah's punch connected with Helen's jaw, *Malchut* exploding from her knuckles in a wave of force. At the same time, Helen's fist slammed into Leah's left arm. The obsidian scales held, and her replenished *Netzach* absorbed most of the impact.

Helen's head didn't move. Not even a fraction of an inch. But Leah flew backward, hitting the sand hard enough to knock the air from her lungs. She rolled to her feet just as Helen appeared inches from her face and threw another punch. This one caught Leah's ribs and sent her tumbling down to the bottom of the sand dune.

Leah scrambled to her feet. Helen teleported again, closing the distance. Leah thrust both hands forward and let two cones of *Gevurah* fire shoot out, spinning until the flames caught Helen's body. The fire burned through skin and muscle, exposing bone, but the golden symbols carved into Helen's flesh blazed brighter and healed the damage almost instantly. Leah put both hands together and screamed, pouring the rest of her *Gevurah* well into the attack. A massive tunnel of orange-red flame engulfed Helen completely.

The King walked through the fire. Her hands wrapped around Leah's wrists and stopped the flames at the source. The smells of burned hair and charred flesh filled the air with a sickening sweetness, but Helen's body healed as fast as the flames consumed it.

Helen turned, yanking Leah over her shoulder and slamming her into the sand. The obsidian scales and *Netzach* protected her, but the impact drove every bit of air from her lungs. She gasped, struggling to breathe.

"Now you understand," Helen said, voice emotionless. "You cannot beat me."

She kicked Leah in the ribs. Leah rolled across the sand, came up on all fours, and pulled on *Thagirion*. The reddish sky turned purple. The sun behind her and the sand beneath shifted to deep blue, mesmerizing and hypnotic. She forced herself up and dodged sideways just as a *Malchut* blade sliced through where she'd been standing, cutting through sand like it was water.

"Hiding again?" Helen's eyes flashed yellow. "Come face me, coward!"

Lord Ragon's training kicked in. Leah, flanked on the right, called on *Nehemoth*. The void pulled at the King, dragging her sideways. In the same motion, Leah invoked three

Shadows and leaped over Helen, bringing *Malchut* blades down as she passed. Two of Helen's wings fell to the sand, severed clean. The King lost control and dropped toward the ground. Leah switched from *Nehemoth* to *Malchut* right before Helen would have collided with her and punched as hard as she could. She felt ribs crack beneath her fist. Helen stumbled backward, pain flashing across her face for the first time.

Leah clasped her hands together and invoked *Hod*. Helen froze mid-step. Leah's Shadows moved in and hammered the King with *Malchut* punches and blades. Each strike connected, cutting and opening flesh. The golden symbols glowed, healing every wound, but the healing slowed. Just slightly. Just enough to see.

Leah sent two more shadows forward and poured more energy into her *Hod*.

Helen's eyes snapped open. Bright light poured from them, and a sinister smile spread across her lips. "There you are."

Golden chains erupted from her chest. They moved like snakes striking prey and wrapped around Leah before she could react. The chains yanked her and all her Shadows out of the *Thagirion*, slamming them into the sand. Searing heat radiated from the chains, burning through her defenses, trying to melt the obsidian scales.

Leah's *Netzach* energy drained fast. Too fast. She pulled the Shadows back, and they dissipated into green smoke. Her split essence rushed back into her, and she used the returned energy to push outward with *Malchut*. The chains loosened just enough for her to break free. She sent another wave into the ground and launched herself backward, putting distance between them.

How could Helen use those chains while paralyzed by

Hod? The well was supposed to stop all energy from the target.

"I don't mind burning you again, Leah." Three golden chains lashed through the air toward her.

She is not holding back anymore. We need to push harder!

Leah dodged the first chain. It cracked like a whip where her head had been. She rolled under the second. The third she blocked with a *Malchut* barrier, but the force still knocked her sideways. Meanwhile, Helen's body healed completely, and new wings sprouted where the shadows had cut the old ones away.

Helen sent *Malchut* bullets while Leah dodged the chains. Most of the energy missed or ricocheted off her armor, but one bullet punched through her scales and slashed across her leg. She lost her balance. Two chains whipped at her head and side simultaneously. The impact sent lightning down her spine and through her arm. She hit the sand hard, blood dripping from her leg and torso where the chains had torn chunks from her obsidian armor. Pain throbbed through her body, dulled by *Netzach*'s aftereffect, but growing sharper with each passing second.

"Fuck." She gritted her teeth and curled her hands into fists.

This was impossible. She'd run out of *Netzach* soon, and then she'd be torn apart in seconds. Meanwhile, Helen didn't bother dodging. Nothing Leah threw at her mattered. The healing was too fast, the Core's power too absolute.

A chain wrapped around her feet and jerked her upward. The world spun as Helen slammed her into the sand, driving the air from her lungs. The chain lifted her again, and every nerve screamed. This time, Helen threw her into a dune. Leah hit hard, and something inside her cracked. Each breath felt like knives sliding between her ribs.

Helen hovered closer. Three chains arched behind her like scorpion tails, their golden tips morphing into long spikes. She wore a cold, determined expression. No pleasure in this. No anger. Just the grim certainty of someone doing what they believed must be done.

Leah tried to move, but her body refused. Even the thought of shifting an inch sent waves of pain through her bones.

Desperation made her pull on cursed speech. Dark energy set her throat on fire. "Sto—" The word twisted, and *Gamaliel* tore at her vocal cords. The pain was too much. She couldn't invoke it again.

"It's over, Leah." Helen raised her arm. "Time to rest."

The chains hung in the air for one suspended moment. Then they came down.

Hold her, Leah! Asmodeus shouted.

Eric's face flashed through her mind. Her uncle, stopping Legion's chains with *Hod*. She clasped her hands together, calling on everything she had left. The golden chains slowed. Slower. They stopped inches from her face, trembling against her hold.

Asmodeus exhaled in her mind.

Thank you, Leah. For everything we have shared. For giving this old demon a chance at redemption. Hold her steady.

Something left her. The presence that had lived beneath her ribs for years, the weight she'd grown so used to, she'd forgotten it was there. It ripped away, and the space it left behind went cold and hollow.

Any remaining bits of obsidian armor dissolved as a shadow appeared next to her and leaped forward, *Malchut* energy crackling around its fist. Asmodeus attacked Helen head-on.

Three more chains burst from Helen's chest and pierced the Shadow's torso.

"No!" The word tore from Leah's throat. She tried calling it back, pulling on the connection that had always been there, but her mind hit empty air. The space where Asmodeus had been was just... gone.

Asmodeus turned to her and smiled. Blood poured from his mouth, dark and viscous. He turned back to Helen and grabbed the chains with both hands. Black flames formed where his fingers touched the gold.

For the first time, genuine fear crossed Helen's face.

Before she could move, the fire spread. It raced along the chains like oil igniting, hungry, chaotic, and alive. Helen tried to teleport, but Leah's *Hod* held her, and her chains locked in place. Helen conjured new chains and drove them through Asmodeus's chest, but that only ignited the shadow's entire body. Black flames spread from him to Helen's new chains, then into her body itself.

Helen screamed.

The sound cut through the desert, echoing repeatedly. The chaotic black fire of *Golohab* consumed everything it touched with ravenous, mindless hunger. It ate through her shoulder, exposing bone. The golden symbols flared brighter, trying to heal, but the flames moved faster than the Core could regenerate.

"You fool!" Helen shrieked at Asmodeus. Her voice cracked, turned raw. "You've killed us both! Leah, call it off! Call it off!"

Leah held her *Hod*. Her hands shook, but she didn't let go. Couldn't let go.

"Please!" Helen's voice broke. Not the King anymore. Just Helen—the woman who'd taught her, guided her, who'd been her mother's friend. "We could've saved them, Leah. God, it hurts so much. Please make it stop!"

Asmodeus's Shadow burned down to ash, his form crumbling away. But Helen's body kept fighting. Burning and healing, burning and healing. The golden marks carved into her skin began to dim as the black flames consumed them. They flickered and faded. Then, they started to peel away.

Golden letters lifted from Helen's flesh like leaves caught in the wind. Symbols and strange script floated upward, drifting toward the sand. Helen reached out with a charred hand, desperate.

"No!" Her voice was hoarse. "Don't leave me! Please, I can still—" She clawed at the air, trying to grab the symbols as they scattered. "Come back! I need you! I can control it! I can—"

But the letters kept rising, kept fleeing.

The black flames burned deeper. The Core became visible through bits of charred flesh and melting muscle.

Helen stopped screaming. Her eyes found Leah's through the flames. For just a moment, they weren't the King's cold blue anymore. Just Helen's. Eyes that were scared and sad and sorry.

Then, she was gone.

The small silver sphere within Helen's charred body shook violently. A crack formed across its surface. The fire rushed inside, burning everything within the Core itself.

More cracks spread like spider webs. Light burst through them, blinding and pure. Then the Core exploded.

The wave of energy rushed outward. Leah felt heat on her face, saw the light expanding. Then something burned in her palm. The eye of the Librarian shone from her skin, its pupil dilating.

Vertigo slammed into her. Reality twisted and warped.

A voice resonated from everywhere and nowhere. "Even

dimensional boundaries cannot shield you from our agreement."

The red dunes and dying sun disappeared. The burning bodies vanished. The exploding Core faded away.

The last thing she saw was the charred remains of Asmodeus.

CHAPTER 50
LONG OVERDUE

"Are you there?" Leah's voice cracked around the words.

She tried to call on the obsidian scales, but nothing formed as it fell onto the grass that couldn't decide what season it belonged to. Cherry blossoms drifted past on a warm breeze while snow dusted the ground twenty feet away. She lay in an impossible garden, spring bleeding into summer bleeding into fall bleeding into winter.

Leah closed her eyes and reached for their shared space, hoping to find him waiting at the table like he always was. The gray room materialized around her. The wooden table. Two chairs.

Both were empty.

She walked to the table where a single teacup sat, steam still rising from the surface. That was it. Just the cup. No Asmodeus sitting across from it. No note. No goodbye. Nothing.

He was gone.

The room disappeared around her, and she opened her eyes to the garden.

"Asmodeus." Her voice came out strained. "I...I'm sorry."

A lump formed in her throat as she sat up and turned toward the Library entrance. The massive doors towered ahead, their impossible angles stretching up into a star-filled void. Symbols carved in the marble shifted and changed, showing different moments from history she didn't recognize.

She limped forward. Every step sent pain shooting through her ribs where Helen had struck her. Her shoulder screamed where fingers had dug in.

The doors swung open before she reached them. The sound resounded like thunder.

Inside, the Library stretched forever. Marble staircases spiraled into darkness. Small candles floated in the air. Books lined every surface, stacked in tall towers.

In the distance, the Librarian glided between shelves. A mass of tattered robes and too many arms, its pale face covered in eyes of every color. Some human. Some animal. Others glowed with their own light.

"Leah Ackerman." The voice came from everywhere at once, reverberating through the infinite space. "You've done it. You killed Helen Nielsen, thief of the Library of Alexandria."

Leah tried to straighten despite the pain lancing through her side. "I have. Now it's time for you to uphold your end of the bargain."

The Librarian's many eyes fixed on her, unblinking. "You were to recover what was stolen and return it to me. The scroll that your mother and Helen Nielsen took. Yet you did not do so."

"Because it burned." Leah's hands clenched into fists. "The only way to kill Helen was *Golohab*. The chaotic fire consumed everything. Her. The scroll. My..." She couldn't finish.

Multiple hands raised from beneath the creature's robes, stopping her protest. "However. Given that the only method to destroy an Ethereal is through chaos, and that Helen Nielsen could not be defeated by any other means, perhaps I can fulfill the final step of your bargain. But first..."

The Librarian glided closer. Dozens of arms extended from its robes, hovering over Leah's injuries. Warmth radiated from its palms, seeping into her skin. The pain in her ribs faded. The burns on her arms cooled. Her shoulder stopped screaming.

"A small token of appreciation for your efforts." The Librarian's mouth stretched into something that might have been a smile. "Now, let us move on to the matter at hand."

The warmth concentrated, pulling inward until it pooled in Leah's palm. She looked down and watched the creature's eyes appear on her skin, dozens of them shrinking and closing until they vanished completely. She opened and closed her hand. The weight she'd been carrying for six months lifted.

Free. She was free.

"One moment." The Librarian's many hands disappeared beneath its robes and emerged holding a blank scroll. The creature held it aloft, speaking words in a language that almost sounded like Hebrew but older, stranger, the syllables catching in ways that made Leah's ears ache.

Symbols materialized on the parchment. First faint, then growing darker. Words peeled from the air itself, flowing onto the scroll.

"Knowledge unbound always returns." The Librarian

rolled the scroll and placed it within their robes. "These words were stolen, then bound to flesh. Now that their prison has been destroyed, they answer my call." Every eye blinked in unison. "All knowledge comes back eventually."

Two of the Librarian's arms clapped twice. The sound cracked through the infinite space like breaking stone. Footsteps echoed from somewhere above, growing louder.

Leah's breath caught.

Two figures appeared at the top of a spiraling staircase, waving and moving fast. Sarah's hair flew behind her as she took the steps two at a time. Isaac kept pace beside her, one hand on the railing.

"Leah!" They shouted in unison, their voices overlapping.

Something in Leah's chest cracked open. She'd been fighting for so long. Saw so many people die. Everything she'd done for this moment. And they were still here. Still alive.

Her legs moved before she could think. She ran toward them, ignoring the protest from her recently healed ribs, ignoring everything except closing the distance between them.

They collided in the middle. Arms wrapped around her from both sides, squeezing tight. Sarah's shoulder dug into her collarbone. Isaac's chin pressed against the top of her head. They both smelled like old books and dust.

"I'm sorry." Leah's voice came out muffled against Sarah's shoulder. "I'm so sorry I took so long."

"Damn right." Sarah laughed. Her fingers dug into Leah's back. "Three weeks. Do you know what three weeks in this place feels like?"

Isaac pulled back first, keeping one hand on Leah's arm. His hair was tied back in a small bun. Dark circles shadowed his eyes. His shirt hung loose on a frame that had lost too much weight.

"Three weeks here, but for you..." Isaac looked her over. "It had to be so long for you."

Leah looked between them. Sarah's cheekbones stood out too sharply. Isaac's wrists looked thin enough to snap. They'd both lost weight they didn't have to lose.

"Six months."

"You look different." Sarah stepped back, studying Leah's face with narrowed eyes. "I mean, you look like you, but there's something..." She waved a hand vaguely. "Did you get taller?"

"I...uh. I'm an Immortal Witch now." The words felt strange in Leah's mouth. "Long story."

"Holy shit." Sarah's eyes widened. "Are you serious?"

"We have a lot to catch up on." Isaac pushed his hair out of his face. "But first." He leaned in. "How did you do it? How did you kill Helen?"

The question hit harder than Leah expected.

"I met another Ethereal. He said chaos was the only thing that could destroy them." Leah's throat tightened. "Asmodeus figured it out. He knew what needed to happen."

"What did he do?" Sarah asked quietly.

"*Golohab*." Leah forced herself to meet their eyes. "The chaotic fire from the Tree of Death. He told me to hold her still while he... he..."

Isaac sucked in a sharp breath. Sarah's hand found Leah's shoulder and squeezed.

"He didn't tell me." Leah's voice came out rougher than she meant. "Just did it. One second he was there, the next..." She couldn't finish.

"I'm sorry." Isaac's voice was soft.

"Yeah." Leah wiped at her eyes with the back of her hand. "He died so I could live. So we *all* could live."

They stood in silence for a moment. Sarah pulled Leah and Isaac into another hug. When they separated, Isaac frowned.

"What?" Leah asked.

"You said you met another Ethereal." Isaac crossed his arms. "That means they're already here?"

"One. Yes." Leah's stomach dropped. "But the coven, my coven, captured his avatar. Helen said more would come."

Sarah's expression darkened as she looked at Isaac. "Great. That means what we read was real."

Isaac nodded. "I think so." He turned to Leah. "We learned some things while we were here. Things about the Trees. About how they work. And there are prophecies. A war with things beyond this realm. Ethereals, I bet."

Leah shook her head. "We wouldn't last a war. Helen was so powerful. One person able to wield *Keter* was hard enough."

"Not exactly," A voice boomed behind them.

The Librarian slowly crawled toward them, eying the three.

"What do you mean?" Leah asked.

"Helen Neilsen didn't use *Keter*. She never could. She used its twin, *Thaumiel*, to twist the perceptions of reality." The Librarian's focus turned to Isaac and Sarah. "These two mortals, however, have proven infuriatingly resilient." The Librarian's mouth stretched into something that wasn't quite a smile. "I fear the knowledge they have gained here will not simply vanish once they leave."

"Meaning what?" Leah asked carefully.

"Meaning they are now permanent repositories of knowledge that should not exist in your realm." Every eye on the Librarian's face focused on Sarah and Isaac. "Knowledge about the Trees' origins. About the true nature of *Keter* and its opposite. About how to win a war, you all didn't stand a chance of winning."

"Good." Sarah lifted her chin. "Maybe that advantage will keep more people from dying."

The Librarian stared at her for a long moment, then made a sound that might have been a laugh. "Foolish. You do not understand what you carry. But you will. In time, you will wish I had been able to take it from you."

Leah looked at her friends and saw the determination in their eyes. They knew the weight they carried. They'd chosen it anyway.

That's why they're my friends. Stupid, probably, but brave nonetheless.

"The freedom of your friends is sealed." The Librarian gestured broadly with multiple arms. "The bargain, struck in desperate need and fulfilled in blood and fire, has reached its conclusion. What was bound is now released. You may leave when you wish."

A blue line began to trace a circle around the three of them, glowing brightly against the dark marble floor.

"Wait." Leah looked up at the Librarian's many eyes. "Will the people Helen manipulated with *Thaumiel* snap out of it? Or will they stay under her influence?"

The Librarian paused, considering. "With her death, the false realities remain but are no longer fueled." The creature bent forward. "Their perceptions are brittle, but their faith in Helen may need some persuading."

The blue circle glowed brighter. Leah felt the pull of it, the magic preparing to transport them out of this place.

"The entire Infinity Board thinks Helen was a hero." Leah's voice came out quiet. "How am I supposed to convince them otherwise?"

Sarah's arm wrapped around Leah's shoulders. "We'll figure it out. You're not alone anymore."

Isaac moved to her other side, his hand finding hers and squeezing. "Yeah. You've always got us."

The light of the circle intensified, washing out the Library around them. Leah tightened her grip on her friends and looked at the Librarian one last time.

"Thank you."

The creature's many eyes blinked in unison. "May our paths never cross again, Leah Ackerman."

CHAPTER 51
FAREWELL TO THE FALLEN

Gravel crunched under Leah's shoes as she walked between Sarah and Isaac. The cemetery stretched out in front of them, rows of headstones baking in the summer heat. Sweat beaded on the back of her neck.

Sarah looked healthier than she had in months. Her face had filled out, the gaunt look finally gone. Isaac walked steadier, too, shoulders relaxed instead of hunched forward like they'd been when they first got back from the Library.

Leah's throat tightened. She'd gotten them kidnapped. She'd caused them to lose three years.

"Hey, you two, I know we've talked about this, but I wanted to say it again while it's just us. I'm sorry. I still feel responsible for you getting kidnapped like that."

Sarah rolled her eyes. "Here we go again. Leah, we told you we don't blame you. The Librarian was an all-powerful psycho. Of course, he manipulated you."

She glanced at Isaac. "You know, it's okay if you feel differently, Isaac. I wouldn't blame you."

Isaac smiled. "Listen, we learned a lot while we were there. It's thanks to that we got these." He pointed at his new Black Rook insignia. "The youngest Mystics ever to reach Black Rook status. Now that we're part of the Outer Council, I think we can push real change within the Infinity Board."

Leah smiled back. Something hollow opened inside her. "I think you two will do an amazing job there."

They walked in silence for a bit. Birds sang from the trees lining the cemetery. A car passed on the street behind them.

"You know you can still join us," Sarah said. "No one's kicking you out, and I'm sure Jan Xie will welcome you with open arms."

"I think the White Queen already has a lot on her plate. Bringing in the person who killed Helen might make her life more complicated."

Isaac snorted. "Since when do we not make life more complicated for the higher-ups?"

The three of them laughed. But they shared a look—the kind that said words weren't needed. Sarah and Isaac now knew about the Trees. More than any Mystic. And they were able to use that to help snap people out of Helen's manipulation.

Leah's smile faded. She wished this could still be her life. The trio working together on the Infinity Board. But she'd made a promise to Frank and Mo. To protect the Astral Realm. To rebuild the coven.

"How does immortality feel?" Sarah asked after a while.

Leah scratched the back of her head. "Physically? I've never felt better. Peak condition." She looked at her two friends walking beside her. Sarah's face had filled out again. Isaac walked with that familiar, thoughtful stride.

They'll get old. Gray hair, wrinkles, aching joints. And I'll still look like this.

Her throat ached.

"But?" Isaac prompted.

"It's just..." Leah struggled to find the words. "I have you both back. After everything. And now I'm realizing that someday..." Her voice caught. "Someday you'll both be gone, and I'll still be here."

Sarah's expression softened. "Hey." She wrapped an arm around Leah's shoulders. "We're not planning on dying any time soon. We have a lifetime together ahead. Even if we're not roommates anymore, we'll still see each other. That's a fact. At least once every few months, dinner. To make up for all the meals we missed while we were at the Library. Deal?"

Leah forced a smile. "Deal."

The hollow feeling stayed.

After a few seconds of silence, Isaac spoke again. "Oh, by the way, I almost forgot. We looked into the alliance you mentioned. Paige and Marcel are in New Orleans, recruiting existing vampires and werewolves into a new Family."

Leah's eyebrows rose. "They are?"

"Yeah." Isaac smiled slightly. "They're cooperating with the Infinity Board now. Jan Xie's been working with them directly. Apparently, your introduction helped broker that."

Sarah grinned. "Who knew you'd end up playing supernatural diplomat?"

"Interesting," Leah smirked. "Thanks for letting me know."

They kept walking. The breeze brushed through the grass. Birds sang in the early morning. They reached the row they were looking for and walked among the gravestones until they stopped in front of four of them.

David Ackerman. Elizabeth Mizrahi. Leah Ackerman. Eric Mizrahi.

Leah stared at her own name carved in marble. Like looking at herself from the outside. That version of her had died the moment she blew up the house. Leah Ackerman, age sixteen. Gone.

After a few moments of silence, Isaac asked, "Are you ready?"

Leah nodded. She reached for the threads of reality and found the layer of decay. She pulled, opening a small crack in front of her. Sickly yellow light spilled from it into the Material realm. She stepped inside and found the same four gravestones, covered in moss and grime.

Leah took a second to clean them off. She brushed the moss away with a soft *Malchut* push. The pressure built in her palms and released gently. The stones cleared.

She approached her own gravestone and kneeled. She focused her *Gevurah* fire into her index finger. Heat gathered at the tip. She began to write.

Here Lies Asmodeus
Kyjak of the Valley
Savior to Humanity
Unexpected Friend

She reached for his obsidian scales again, wishing for even an ounce of his essence to still be there somewhere inside her. Nothing came. Nothing had come since he'd left her.

She stepped back. The inscription looked right.

The layer of decay was quiet except for distant wind. Leah stayed there a moment longer. Then she pulled herself back to the Material realm.

"Looks great," Sarah said while Isaac nodded in agreement, their eyes flashing yellow.

"Really? You think it does him justice?"

"I think it's perfect," Isaac said. He patted her back softly.

Leah looked at the four gravestones and sighed. She took out four smooth stones from her pocket. These stones marked remembrance. Something permanent and enduring. A bond that didn't break.

On her father's, she placed a blue one she'd found in an Astral layer full of beautiful blue oceans. Blue like his eyes.

On her mother's, she placed a red one. To remember her fiery, lively presence.

On her uncle's, Leah placed a jade stone. To keep Eric's former apprentice close to him.

On Asmodeus, Leah placed an obsidian carving in the shape of a scale.

They stood there quietly, paying their respects. Leah's mind drifted to the fun memories. Cooking with her dad, David, in the kitchen. Gossiping with her mom, Elizabeth, about school drama. Uncle Eric's lessons and jokes kept her in good spirits through the most tumultuous time of her life. And Asmodeus. From mortal enemies to something like family. She wouldn't have made it here if it weren't for him.

Leah took a deep breath and hugged her two friends tightly. "Thank you for coming."

They stood there hugging for a long time. Finally, Leah broke off. "Okay, ready to head back?"

Both of them nodded. Sarah brushed away a single tear that slid down her cheek.

They walked back in silence. Simply enjoying each other's company and the beautiful summer day around them. They finally reached the entrance, and Leah saw Jaime McMillan leaning against a black car. He beamed as they approached and stood up.

"I didn't expect to see you here," Leah said, smiling.

Jaime shrugged. "I wanted to pay my respects. Plus, I'm a Black Queen now, so I get to do whatever I want."

Leah snorted. "Oh no, that sounds kind of dangerous."

Jaime laughed and opened his arms. They embraced in a lasting hug.

"You know you're always welcome to visit us down in HQ, right?"

"I know." Leah stepped back and looked across the street where Frank and Mo's car was parked.

"We'll work closely together!" Sarah rushed to say.

"Yeah, rebuilding the Infinity Board isn't going to be easy, so having good communication and cooperation with the Immortal Witches is key," Isaac added.

Leah laughed. "Yes, of course."

"The other Sages, as well as the White Queen Jan Xie, send their regards. They wanted to come, but they have their hands full with everything going on. However, we all agreed on giving you this." Jaime handed Leah a small red box.

Leah opened it and saw a gold Rook insignia inside.

"We know you're no longer part of the Infinity Board, but we're still honoring you with a Gold Rook decoration for your services to humanity. We're indebted to you, Leah Ackerman."

Leah closed the box and nodded. "Thank you for this. It means a lot."

Jaime clasped his hands together. "Well, I'm terrible with goodbyes, so we'd better get moving. Lassy, I'll see you around." He winked and gave Leah one last hug before walking around the car and getting in the driver's seat.

Leah turned to her two friends. She smiled, trying to hold back tears.

They rushed in and hugged one more time.

"You know where to find us." Sarah's voice broke. "And now you have our number because now, as higher-ups, we get actual phones like normal people."

"Plus, dinner!" Isaac said between sniffs. "You owe us dinner for life. Don't forget!"

Leah's vision blurred. "I would never forget. I love you both very much."

"We love you too, Leah," Isaac said.

"Yeah, you're alright," Sarah added, sniffing. They all burst out laughing.

They stood there as cars passed by. Finally, Sarah pulled back and wiped her nose. Isaac turned away, one hand covering his mouth, shoulders rigid.

None of them moved.

Leah forced herself to step back. Then another step. Something inside her felt like it was tearing.

"I'll see you soon," she said.

"Next month," Sarah said firmly. Tears streamed down her face.

"Next month," Leah repeated.

They walked to their cars. Jaime's black sedan was next to Frank's beat-up station wagon. Leah climbed into the back seat. Frank started the engine. For a moment, the two cars sat side by side.

Through the window, Leah could see Sarah crying. Isaac, with one hand over his eyes. She raised her hand and waved.

They waved back.

Jaime's car pulled away first, turning left. Leah watched until it disappeared around the corner.

Frank, who was in the driver's seat, turned on the car and glanced back at Leah. "Where are we off to now?"

Leah brushed away the tears and took a deep breath. She needed to remember she would see them again. Their paths were no longer intertwined as before, but their friendship would endure.

After a few seconds to compose herself, Leah said,

"Portland. Mo, you said there was a potential witch there, right?"

Mo nodded. "I did. Thought I saw the spark form last night."

"Portland it is." Frank accelerated and began driving down the street.

Mo looked back at Leah. "I know goodbyes are never easy. But you'll see them again!"

"I know," Leah said. But the ache stayed.

Mo didn't seem convinced by Leah's answer. "Is there anywhere we could go for some comfort food? A good meal always lifts my spirits."

Leah thought for a moment, then she smiled. "I know of a spot down the highway. It has the best blueberry donuts."

"Perfect," Mo said.

The car pulled onto the highway. Through the window, Chicago's skyline shrank behind them. Somewhere back there, Sarah and Isaac were starting their work on the Outer Council. Jaime and Jan Xie were rebuilding what Helen had broken. The Infinity Board would heal.

And Leah would be in the Astral Realm. Protecting the layers. Growing the coven. It wasn't the path she'd expected when she first pulled on *Malchut* at fifteen. But it was her path. Her choice.

A Small Request From Us, The Authors

Thank you for finishing Leah's journey. It means a lot to us that you sticked with her until the end.

As independent authors, reviews are so important to spread the word and reach new readers.

If you have a few seconds to spare, would you please consider leaving an honest review on the website you bought this book?

Your support helps so much in promoting Leah's story and the many others we plan to write in this world.

All the best,

A.B. Cohen & JP Rindfleisch IX

LUCKY WITCH
SHORT STORY

Go beyond Leah Ackerman

Delve into the broken world of Frank, an unlucky Witch, who is trying to find his way after a demon slaughtered his coven. From the shared universe of the Leah Ackerman series, check out this short story now!

https://dl.bookfunnel.com/5d4xcg9hov

THE ASTRAL LAYERS
SHORT STORY

Go beyond Leah Ackerman

Delve into the secret world of the Immortal Witches, their impending alliance, and a common enemy. From the shared universe of the Leah Ackerman series, check out this short story now!

https://BookHip.com/QQTLNDW

CURSED JADE
AN ERIC MIZRAHI NOVELETTE

Eric was once a rising Black Knight with a bright future ahead.

Together with his mentee, Jade, a promising White Pawn, they made a formidable duo.

But everything changed after that mission at the mysterious "Elsa's Rehabilitation Institute for Young Women."

A place with strict rules, odd characters, and an eerie presence.

This is the story behind the flask.

Are you ready?

https://abcohenwrites.com/cursed-jade

Acknowledgments

In January 2020, before the world ended, two authors took a train from Los Angeles to Oakland and stayed in a haunted mansion with other writers for the weekend. That weekend we brainstormed a horror short story, then spent hours mapping out the entire Leah Ackerman universe. Much of that story has stayed true all the way to the end. We knew our big villain since before the very first chapter was written, and it has been such a blast slowly peeling back the layers of this world.

None of this would exist without our mentors, J. Thorn and Zach Bohannon. On that fateful train ride, we clicked instantly, and you both believed in us when we were just two strangers with a wild idea. Six years, six books, and four short stories later—we made it. Thank you for everything.

A special shout-out to our amazing editor Zach Bohannon; our beta readers Chris, Claudia, and Nissim, who have been with us since the beginning; and our cover designers at Getcovers.com. This has been a team effort from day one, and we couldn't have brought Leah's story to life without you.

A.B. Cohen here: In the time it took to write this series, I got married to my incredible wife, Raquel, we adopted our amazing dog, Snoopy, and moved across the country to start a new chapter of our lives together. You've been my anchor through every draft, every Sunday writing session, and every moment of doubt. Thank you for believing in me and in Leah's story.

JP here: Josh, we've celebrated fifteen years together in the same house while I chased this dream. You've stuck with me through early morning writing sessions, Sunday writing marathons, and every strange twist this journey has taken. Thank you for being my constant.

And finally, to you—our wonderful and weird readers—thank you. Like all great things in life, this too must come to an end. It is this finality that gives meaning to the story we wrote. We hope you've enjoyed reading Leah's journey as much as we enjoyed writing it. To us, getting your most precious possession—your time—means everything.

Thank you for being here.

We love you all,

A.B. Cohen & JP Rindfleisch IX

About the Authors

A.B. Cohen is an author of freaky stories for weird people. He focus mainly on thrillers, horror and urban fantasy tales. Originally from Caracas, Venezuela, today he lives in Miami, Florida. Along with his passion for writing, he also loves dancing, soccer, and traveling. You can find out more about A.B. Cohen's upcoming writing projects using the link below:

www.abcohenwrites.com

JP Rindfleisch IX is the author of speculative fiction with a focus on urban fantasy and queer fantasy. They live in Rockford, Illinois, with their partner of fifteen years, a judgmental Siberian husky, and a sassy African grey parrot.

JP is represented by Elaine Spencer at The Knight Agency.

www.9thBooks.com

www.ingramcontent.com/pod-product-compliance
Lightning Source LLC
LaVergne TN
LVHW040036080526
838202LV00045B/3359